A QUIVER OF COBRAS
-BROKEN-

By
Christopher Merlino

To Cecilia
My Wakie-Doo
Always

Acknowledgements

No matter where I am in my career, I am profoundly encouraged that my passion for this series never seems to fade, and the characters within the pages grow more and more real in my heart and mind with each scene and chapter.

To my amazing wife, Charmine, words fail me when I try to express what your love and support mean to me. Your willingness to read, reread, edit, and discuss is invaluable to me as a writer, but even more so as a husband. Without you, I think very little writing would ever get accomplished. Thank you, and I love you.

My daughters, Alexis, Cecilia, and Isabella, you are my precious loves and my constant joy. Lexi, I'm still working on the big house…maybe someday.

Mom, who threatened me with a barbecue utensil to hurry up and give her the next book in the series, after reading the ending to HEAT…that was actually the nicest compliment anyone has ever given me. Thank you for your encouragement and advice on "how a mother would respond/act."

To my cousin, Amy, who might be my biggest fan, thank you for your encouraging words, for finishing one book and demanding the next one. Lizzy, my niece, who *finally* read Beginnings, then blew through HEAT, and then joined the chorus demanding the third installment…thanks for being such an encouragement. Between you and my mom, I just about pulled my hair out trying to finish this one.

To my best friend and confidant, Duane Eaves. After the first two books, there isn't much left to say because nothing has changed. You're still my best friend. You still devote your time, thoughts, energy, and passion into getting these books right. Thank you.

Finally, to those who read these books…thank you for your support as well. I appreciate your investment of time and money in these stories. I don't take that investment lightly and I promise to continue to work hard to make each story worthy of you, the reader. We are just beginning this journey.

Preface

All great stories involve conflict.

If conflict is absent, there is no story. Why? Why is the presence of conflict necessary to pique our interest? Why does conflict draw us with such intensity? Why do we revel in conflict, creating more as we resolve others? Why is it so necessary for conflict to consume our lives to the point that we even enjoy reading about it?

The answer is simple. Humans can only relate to conflict. A story without conflict offends the human psyche. The notion of peace is foreign, even contrary, to the human condition. People are hardwired to require conflict and angst to make sense of the world. It is sick and twisted, but without those negatives, there would be no joy, no happiness.

Without conflict, without misery, without suffering, the human mind would go insane. Who wants a life with no turmoil? Who wants a life lived in complete and utter peace? That we even ask such questions should tell us just how awry the human race has gone.

It is not because the world was created this way. Scripture tells us the world was a perfect creation, and there was indeed peace and tranquility in the universe. Do we really believe that? How can we? We are bound by what we see, are we not? Reason tells us we would never intentionally bring misery upon ourselves. If misery was not present at the beginning, why do we suffer from it so much now?

The answer is simple. We strive for the peace and joy that was long ago lost. We can never replace it on our own, but we crave it…always. God offers it, but we tend to reject it. Even when we believe in Him and accept Him into our hearts we still reject the peace and joy he offers. Why?

Because we're broken, just like the world.

Chapter 1

The best always prepare for the worst. It is the job of a coach to consider every possible scenario and prepare his team to respond. But sometimes, when everything goes wrong, it comes down to heart…what's inside…that can't be taught. That is what counts most. There is no substitute for heart.

It would take place on the grandest stage the state had to offer, the Dobe Arena, located just off the Turnpike in East Wayford. The professional football stadium sat eighty-two thousand, including ten thousand luxury seats and four club lounges. The stadium was sold out for the matchup between the Central City Lions and the Kendall Cobras. The region was in the throes of a Christmas blizzard. It had been snowing since morning and by game time the field was covered in eight inches of powdery accumulation and still counting. The stadium was still packed with thousands more partying in the parking lot.

Quarter 1

Kendall set to receive the opening kickoff. Delaney Walker had done a great job all season returning both punts and kickoffs. He was also the Cobras' number three receiver. Kevin Sinclaire's incredible talent at the wide receiver position had pushed him to the side for his senior year; he went from being the number two receiver to number three. In the Cobra offense it meant he would usually be a slot receiver, catching balls in traffic and taking hits from the bigger defenders, but he had a great attitude and figured it was better to win as a kick returner and slot receiver than to lose as a number two.

The disaster began on the opening kickoff of the State High School Football Championship. Delaney took it at the goal line and sprinted forward, doing his best on an impossible surface. The grounds crew cleared the field two hours prior, but snow continued to fall. The best they could do by game-time was to clear the boundaries and major yardage lines every five yards across the field. Just to keep up with it, they were going to have to come out during timeouts and between quarters with snow blowers. As Delaney crossed the ten-yard line, his blocking broke down. Delaney shifted direction and saw a sliver of daylight between two approaching Central Lions. The gap closed quickly as he struggled to maintain his footing. They hit him hard, one high, the other low, sending him spinning to the ground as the ball flew from his arms. The Lions picked it up and ran it in for an easy score.

Scott Webber was a quick strike master, but he was not impatient. He was not the kind of quarterback to get riled by a mistake or mishap. Delaney's fumble was unfortunate, but it didn't change Scott's approach. With the weather, the passing game would have to be executed with caution. He felt like he could grip the ball okay, but the guys still had to be able to get open and catch it. Also the line had to be able to hold their blocks in the icy conditions against a bigger defensive front. Scott would to have to rely on the running game and hope the Cobras could power their way down the field against the Central City Lions' defense.

Anquan pounded inside for two runs and managed to get a total of three yards. The Cobra line was unable to push the Central City defensemen back. The Lions swallowed Anquan up and forced Scott into a passing situation. He called a play and brought the Cobras to the line. Kevin shifted into the left slot with Matt Kildare to the outside.

"Twelve! Thirty-four! Twenty-two!" Scott called the signals. As the players motioned into their set, Scott called his cadence, taking the shotgun snap and drifting back to throw. His feet shuffled through several inches of powder. He found the look he wanted and drilled a perfect pass into the arms of Pete Sobolewski…and then the ball flew *out* of Pete's hands and into the arms of a Lion defender, who took the gift and darted past the stunned Cobra players and into the end zone for another turnover and touchdown.

***

A hush fell over an already disconcerted Kendall Cobra fan base. The VE-NOM chants that had begun with such enthusiasm were replaced with stunned silence. It was the second turnover resulting in a score that would have to be overcome. With the weather so extreme, it would be difficult enough to overcome even *one* mistake like that against a championship caliber team, but two in a row to start the game could prove catastrophic.

Lindsey and Emily exchanged nervous glances. It wasn't the way anyone imagined the Cobras would start. They had been flawless throughout the state tournament, raising expectations so high that the Kendall fans had no concept of their boys failing to bring the championship trophy home. As the girls sat amidst a disconcerted Kendall fan base, they both sensed a new feeling beginning to emerge…fear.

***

The Cobras tried to settle down, but the universe would have none of it. Scott took another snap and quickly rolled right, looking for Kevin downfield. As he threw the ball, he was hit from behind. The pass had nothing on it and it fell short, right into the arms of a Lion linebacker who returned it to the Cobra nine-yard line. Three plays later, the Lions were celebrating their third touchdown of the game. It was 21-0.

The Kendall bench was stunned. It was becoming ridiculous and there was still a long way to go in freezing, wet conditions. The Central City Lions were not about to give up anything deep, so they sacrificed a man from their defensive front and began playing a two-deep formation to ensure that anyone who tried to go long would be easily covered. Scott had little choice but to take what the defense gave him. He ran Anquan and threw short passes. Considering the weather, it was probably the best plan, anyway. After three quick first downs, he noticed the Central City defensive backs begin to creep forward, anticipating another run.

Scott took the snap and immediately set up to throw to Kevin. His pump fake was so perfect, the defenders all bit and charged Kevin. When Scott pulled the ball down and started to run, they all converged. Kevin took off down the field. At the last moment, Scott pulled up and lofted a perfect spiral through the falling snow. Kevin took it seventy yards, and the Cobras were on the scoreboard. The Kendall bench and their fans finally had something to cheer about.

It didn't last long.

The Lions took the kickoff and drove straight down the field, cutting through the Cobra defense like butter. Their offensive line was blowing the Cobra defensemen off the ball, leaving gaping holes for the Lion running attack, eating up yardage in chunks. Kevin and Tony were stuck making most of the tackles, which is a bad thing for any defense. The safeties were the last line of defense against the running game. If they were the ones making all the tackles, it usually meant that the offensive line and the linebackers were getting beat. The Lions drove right down the field and scored.

Quarter 2

If the first quarter was a study in ineptness for the Kendall Cobras, the second quarter was a lesson in futility. Nothing worked. The Lions were too fast, too strong, and too big. The Cobras were deflated, and out of fight. With only time for one play left in the half, the score was 42-7. The Lions had the ball at the Cobra thirty-yard line and were set to kneel it down, running out the clock and ending the half. But the quarterback, Colby Jenner, faked the kneel-down and faded back for one more shot at the end zone. His receiver, a monster named Oscar Quigley, who was a lot faster than his two-hundred-pound frame let on, streaked across the field on a post route. Kevin, caught by surprise, saw the play develop and took off on a dead run, playing an angle to meet Quigley in the end zone. Just as the ball got to the big receiver, Kevin dove, and with his body fully extended, managed to knock it away with his fingertips.

He landed, and slid across the snow-covered end zone, his momentum carrying him right under the big receiver, taking Quigley's legs out. Quigley slammed down, hip first, all two hundred pounds landing on Kevin's left shoulder. The searing pain shot through Kevin's body as he felt the joint crackle and pop. His arm twisted under the weight of the big Lion receiver. When they finally skidded to a halt, Quigley tumbled off Kevin's back and immediately began jumping up and down, waving feverishly to the Kendall bench.

Kevin knew it was bad. His whole left side felt…wrong. While he could feel the excruciating pain of the injuries to his shoulder and elbow, he felt nothing in his hand or lower arm. The trainers skidded to his side as he propped himself up on his knees and right arm. His left arm hung low. The head trainer, Doctor Frederick Carter, called for a cart as his assistants immobilized the arm, and then got Kevin to his feet and onto the back of the cart. They drove off slowly with Kevin sitting on the back, and three trainers sitting with him to keep his arm immobile.

***

The scene in the Cobra locker room was dismal and depressing. They were getting thoroughly pummeled and now their star player was hurt. Matt had been in locker rooms when the Cobras were losing and struggling. There had always been a level of machismo. There had always been yelling, pushing, shoving, trying to pump each other up. There was none of that. There was no yelling, no tough talk, no inspirational smack-talk. The coaching staff was as shell-shocked as the players. Coach Shultz came in after conferring with Dr. Carter.

"Guys," he said. "Sinclaire's out. I'm not gonna pretend it's no big deal, but we still have one more half to play." He looked at every guy in the room silently. "Let's go out there this second half and give it everything we've got. Sinclaire made that last play out there because he thought it was worth it to keep playing hard. Play this half for the warrior hurting down the hall. Play it for the guys sitting next to you. Go out there and play for pride."

***

The trainers cut the sleeve under Kevin's left arm and removed his shoulder pads and jersey. They cut off the t-shirt he wore underneath and removed that as well. The entire upper left quadrant of his torso was black, blue, and purple. His shoulder and arm were swollen and out of alignment.

"We're gonna have to get this shoulder and elbow set, Kevin," Dr. Carter said, pulling a needle out of his bag. I'm gonna give you a quick shot to numb it up a little."

"Just do it," Kevin said, his head drooping and his breathing labored. "No drugs."

"Kid," one of the trainers said. "This is gonna hurt. Take the shot."

"No shot," Kevin replied firmly. "Just do it."

The doctor shrugged and shook his head. "You know; everyone thinks you're crazy."

Kevin nodded, closed his eyes, and took a deep breath. He slowly exhaled through his mouth, focusing his mind on his shoulder and elbow, searching. The key, he knew, was not to fight the pain, but rather to find it and focus on it. As the doctor and the trainers got Kevin's arm into the correct position, he began breathing very slowly and steadily, completely relaxing every muscle in his body and letting his mind focus only on his shoulder. He felt a massive jolt as the doctor rotated his arm and the joint popped into place. He let out a dull groan and a long exhale as the pain subsided. The astonished trainers looked at his ashen face as he opened his eyes.

"Tell me that did it," he said as he slumped over.

***

Karen and Jeff Timmons made their way to the training rooms, escorted by security and a Kendall High trainer. As they approached the room, they heard a heated discussion.

"You can't do it, son. That shoulder might need surgery. I can't let you go back out there."

"I'm not interested in your permission. What I am interested in right now is getting my shoulder taped, wrapped, or whatever it is you do to protect it, and then I'm going back out there and finishing this game."

Jeff and Karen entered at that point. "Kevin," Karen said anxiously. "How are you?"

"I'm fine." Kevin gathered his pads and jersey. "Right now I have to get back out there. The second half is getting ready to start."

"Are you nuts?" Jeff asked. "Your shoulder's hurt and you guys are getting blown out. Sit this one out and get better for next year."

Kevin looked right through him and shook his head, continuing to search around for his helmet. "Look, I need someone to tape me up. Now are any of you going to help me or do I need to get someone else to do it?"

Karen looked at the doctor. "Can he play like this?"

Doctor Carter shook his head emphatically. "Absolutely not. This kind of injury can get worse. He needs to get to a hospital for x-rays and MRIs to assess the full extent of the damage. Going back out and playing football tonight is insane."

Karen held up a hand before Kevin could respond. "If he goes back out there, will he risk permanent damage?"

"Definitely," Dr. Carter said. "He might already *have* permanent damage as it is. Taking another pounding for an hour will only make things worse."

"Kevin," Karen said. "Sit down and stop being ridiculous. You're not playing."

"Yes, I am, Mom. This is the State Championship game. I'm not going to lose the game from in here. We're either gonna win this game or I'm gonna *kill* myself trying."

Karen shook her head. "Sorry if I'm coddling you, Sweetie, but you're not playing."

Kevin laughed. "Tell you what, Mom. Let's pretend we spent a half-hour arguing and just skip to the end of the conversation where you finally give in. The sooner you do that, the better chance we have of winning the game."

She shook her head and laughed. "Kevin, this is crazy. This injury could affect your future. And for what? Do you even think you *can* win at this point?"

He nodded. "Absolutely…*if* I get back out there *now.*"

Quarter 3

The Kendall Cobras emerged from the locker room for second half warm-ups depressed, defeated, and demoralized. Kevin was more than a great player. He was a tone setter, and the heart and soul of the team. When he was on the field, the Cobras had swagger, an attitude. Without him, no one felt it. Tony tried to pump everyone up, but his usually infectious energy fell flat. He wasn't really feeling it himself.

The Cobras went out on defense and played hard. Since the game was all but out of reach, the Central City Lions chose to run time off the clock and get the game over with. The Cobras got after the running game and shut it down, allowing only three yards on two plays. As the third down pass fell incomplete, a rumble started in the stands. At first, Tony thought it was just cheering for the defensive stand, but as he looked up, he saw all eyes focused on the end zone. He heard the VE-NOM chant begin. Delaney Walker took the punt, brought it back to the Cobra thirty-nine-yard line, and the Kendall offense ran out onto the field.

Then Tony saw what all the fuss was about. Kevin emerged from the cluster of security personnel and jogged toward the Cobra bench. He was in his game uniform and his helmet was on.

The coaches and players watched as he approached, and without even looking at the coach, Kevin sprinted out onto the field and motioned Devon Mays back to the bench. Coach Shultz realized what had happened and began gesturing from the sidelines and screaming at Kevin.

"Sinclaire! Get back here! You're *out*! You think I'm joking around here, son?" To whoever was listening, he said, "Is he crazy?"

Kevin ignored him as he strode to the huddle where the team was waiting for him in stunned silence. "Let's go, guys. We have two quarters. It's not over and we're *not* losing."

The looks from the other guys in the huddle were a mixture of astonishment and awe, except for Tony, who beamed from ear to ear. He started bouncing from one toe to the other.

"Okay, boys!" he shouted. "Let hit it and get it!"

Scott called his plays and they quickly got to the line. Kevin lined up outside to the right and awaited Scott's cadence. He ignored Coach Shultz's furious stare from less than twenty yards away.

"Sixteen-eighty!" Scott shouted. "Huuut! Hut!"

Kevin broke from the line on an inside slant, quickly pivoted, then spun to the outside as the defender came up to make a play. Before his opponent knew what was happening, Kevin ran by him and took off on a dead sprint up field and Scott's pass hit him perfectly. He grunted as the ball hit his hands and the pain seared through his shoulder, but he hung on and coasted across the goal line for an easy score.

***

One the sideline, Kevin took deep breaths while Tony stayed close to ensure no one bumped his shoulder. Coach Shultz stared in Kevin's direction. For a quick second their eyes met and Kevin gave him a slight shake of the head. *Don't even think about taking me out of this game.* Shultz shook his head and turned away. The Cobra defense went out looking for a quick turnover. They knew the Lions were running the ball to keep the clock moving, but they also had the weapons to strike quickly, and the Cobras could ill afford to give up any more points, so Kevin and the other defensive backs refrained from cheating to the inside. When the ball was snapped, everyone in the stadium gasped as Colby Jenner dropped back to pass. Kevin read it in an instant. Mason Posner was cutting to the inside on a slant right in front of him. Kevin sprinted to the spot where the ball and Posner would meet.

This is really gonna hurt.

He used his right shoulder and obliterated the play. He took Posner high on his right side and his feet went flying out from under him as he spun and slammed to the ground. Kevin immediately dropped to his knees as the pain pulsed through his injured left shoulder. He quickly got back up as Posner lay dazed in six inches of snow.

"You okay?" Kevin heard someone ask. He shook his head as he tried to regain focus. The pain was threatening to overtake him. Darkness clouded his vision, but he took some deep breaths and blinked several times, pushing it back. Posner was helped to his feet and off the field. Kevin and the rest of the Cobra defense huddled up and prepared for the next play.

A couple of hard hits later, and the Cobras got the ball back on a fumble. Kevin somehow managed to stay conscious and recover the loose ball. He trotted off the field as the offense ran on.

On the sidelines, Coach Garret Sommers said, "You know, you're one crazy son of a gun, kid."

Kevin took a breather and the Cobras moved the ball into scoring position before they bogged down. Kevin hustled to the huddle. Scott nodded to him.

"Think you can handle one over the middle?"

Kevin nodded. They broke the huddle. The ball was snapped on the first sound and Scott immediately stood up as if to throw a quick outside fade pass to Matt Kildare. He pump-faked and everyone bit. Then he fired a bullet over the middle to Kevin, who caught it and got leveled in the end zone by the Lions' middle linebacker, Andre Parker. The fans in the stadium reacted to the brutal hit and everyone held their breath to see if Kevin held onto the ball. After a second, he held it up and the refs signaled that it was a touchdown. It took Kevin several seconds before he was able to get himself off the ground.

42–21

Lindsey was nearly hysterical in the stands and Emily was doing everything she could think of to keep her calm. She kept one arm around Lindsey's shoulders, sometimes needing it just to keep her upright. At this point, Emily wasn't sure who would collapse first, Lindsey or the maniac on the field with the broken shoulder.

"Why is he *doing* this?" Lindsey cried over and over again. With each hit Kevin took, Lindsey's body jerked violently as if *she* was taking the hit herself.

Emily shook her head. "I don't know what *anyone* down there is thinking."

Chapter 2

The Cobra defense stood tall and got mean. They didn't give an inch, and before the third quarter was over, got the ball back for the offense. Scott took advantage of the opportunity and wasted no time threading passes downfield. With seconds left on the clock, the Cobras punched it into the end zone on a quick toss to Anquan after Kevin and Matt combined for two long receptions to get them in position.

42-28

On defense, Kevin and Tony began a systematic dismantling of the Lions' offense, like they had done to their opponents all year. The Lions were thrown into turmoil and didn't know how to respond. One thing they did on every play was hit Kevin. They knew he was in a lot of pain. His shoulder didn't sideline him, but they figured if he was on the field, he was fair game.

The Cobra defense used their speed, swarming to the ball, relentlessly pursuing any running play. They wrought havoc in the offensive backfield, making it difficult for the Lions to set up their passing schemes. Kevin and Tony roamed the defensive secondary and dished out punishment on anyone who got near the football.

Quarter 4

The Cobras got a bit of luck to start the fourth quarter and recovered another Lion fumble as the snow got the better of Colby Jenner. The ball slipped from his hands on the snap and Guillermo "Tink" Enzo fell on it. He curled up and held on as players from both teams piled on. The Cobras turned it into another quick touchdown pass to Matt to bring them to within one score. The once-silent Kendall crowd was on its feet and screaming at the tops of their lungs.

42-35

On the next drive, with the snow still falling in thick, heavy chunks, the Lions woke up, got their act together and drove down the field. Most of their yardage was gained on the ground because Kevin and the rest of the Cobra secondary were all over the Lions' receivers, bumping them and disrupting their routes. Kevin was alternately blitzing and dropping into pass coverage, which threw off Jenner's timing and kept him skittish in the pocket.

But the Lions' monster offensive line stepped up on running plays. They pounded the ball right down the field, taking precious time off the clock, until Oscar Quigley made good from six yards out and gave the Lions back their fourteen-point lead. The Kendall fans groaned as the Central City faithful roared back to life. Oscar Quigley stood tall in eight inches of snow in the end zone.

"It's *our* house now, y'all!"

49-35

Tony slapped everyone's helmet in the huddle. "We can't score two touchdowns without scoring the first, so let's just get one, okay?"

Kevin nodded, his face ashen, but his eyes glowering with steely resolve. "Got that, Websy? One score…*then* the next. Let's get one, baby. *Come on!*"

They broke the huddle and Scott took them down the field like a surgeon, cutting up the Lions' defense. His throws were precise and he continued to use the running game as a battering ram. The Lions' defensive line began to wear down. Just as they made the decision to play the run, Scott made the decision to take them over the top. It was perfect. He faked the handoff to Anquan and immediately looked to Kevin running an underneath route. Everyone converged on the center of the field and Scott let it fly deep to Matt Kildare. It wasn't a perfect pass. How could it be in such heavy snowfall? But it didn't have to be because Matt was all alone, ten yards behind the nearest defender. He gathered the pass in and bolted for the end zone, easily outrunning the defense for another Cobra score.

49-42

With the quarter almost half over, the Lions should have sought to run the clock down and get one more score. When the Cobras set up to stop the run, Jenner faked a handoff and found Landry Smith loose in the Cobra secondary. He took the ball all the way up to the forty-seven-yard line. The Lions' fans sensed impending victory. The Cobras dropped into a more conventional defense, but when the Lions tried to run on the next two plays, they couldn't move the ball. The Cobras ran a full-out blitz on both plays and stuffed the run each time. The Lions were faced with a third and long, and there was still plenty of time on the clock.

They have to throw it.

Kevin squinted through the snow at the Lions' set and something tingled at the base of his neck. The Cobras were set up to stop the pass and the Lions had to make a decision in the heavy snow. Though they came to the line in a three-receiver set, Kevin sensed deception.

"Yavs!" he shouted. "Run!"

Tony threw him a thumbs-up and at the snap they were both on the move. The Lions' halfback, Jamel Louis, hit the hole in the middle of the line, and for a brief second, he had daylight, but before he could make his cut into the secondary, Kevin and Tony pounced. The hit stung Kevin's shoulder, sending shockwaves of pain thundering deep into his core. He got up, and with Tony's help, managed to drag himself off the field as the Lions' punting unit came on. The defense had gotten the job done. The punt was high and long. Delaney Walker lost sight of it in the snow and had to scramble to get out of the way. The Lions downed it at the eight.

And there it was. The Cobras had ninety-two yards to go and about four minutes. The snow had not let up and continued to accumulate. There was well over eight inches in places where the action on the field hadn't crushed it down. Scott Webber brought his team to the huddle and looked every player in the eyes. He was just a freshman, but had absolute control in the huddle. It was *his* offense. The team looked to *him* to take them to the Promised Land.

"All right, boys," he said with a confident grin. "Let's get it."

When they broke the huddle, Scott took his time, doing his best to read the defense. He called his cadence, and the first play was a run by Anquan, which went for a loss of two. Ninety-four yards left. That was when Kevin went berserk. Scott hit him with one pass after the next, each one eating up a little yardage but steadily moving the chains. Eleven consecutive passes to Kevin, and the Cobras were across mid-field.

With less than a minute left, Scott found Kevin one more time. Kevin ran a crossing pattern for first down yardage, but instead of going down and protecting his shoulder, he lowered himself and plowed over the nearest defender, and then spinning out of the grasp of the next one. He broke free and raced toward the goal line. The deep defenders came up to stop him and he lowered his shoulder again and ran over them, everyone collapsing in a heap on the six-yard line with nineteen seconds left. With no time-outs, the Cobras ran to the line as the seconds ticked away. Scott hustled into position, and when they were all set, he took the snap and quickly threw the ball into the ground, stopping the clock with six seconds left. The Cobras had time for one more play.

Kevin was in blinding agony. He'd taken several hits to his shoulder and nausea was becoming unbearable. It had already happened twice on the sidelines. He was probably in danger of dehydrating, but he kept downing water and Gatorade and figured he'd get plenty of attention at the hospital later. He couldn't wait to pass out, and felt the comforting tug of unconsciousness even as he stood on the freezing field waiting for Scott, who trotted back in from the sidelines.

They had one play, one chance to send the game into overtime and keep their championship hopes alive. Scott called the cadence and took the snap, dropping back to throw. The Lions brought pressure, forcing Scott to roll to his right. There was no one open! He drifted backward and the pressure followed him. Kevin broke off his route and tried to get open where Scott could see him. Scott was now in full scramble mode, first faking to his left and then spinning and rolling back to his right. He had defenders all over him as he ran toward the sidelines. Then he saw his chance. Kevin sprinted across the back of the end zone, working toward the corner. Scott let it fly.

It was a surreal feeling, running along the back boundary, behind the other players and locking eyes with his quarterback. Kevin's eyes widened as he watched Scott rifle it his way. The ball came in hard and fast, somehow threading through the sea of hands and bodies in front of him. Kevin jumped and felt the ball drill into his gut. He had both hands on it and came down with both feet in the end zone for the touchdown.

It was mayhem on the Cobra sidelines. Coach Shultz could scarcely get his team to stand still and quiet down. There would be a ten-minute break before overtime. The trainers took Kevin back to the locker room underneath the stadium for IV fluids. He agreed to go only as long as it took for the game to resume. The doctor shook his head and promised him they'd have him back in time.

In the stands, Lindsey and Emily both sat in terrified disbelief. The scene on the sidelines sickened Emily. Seeing Kevin barely able to stand was not something she was prepared for. He was so strong and confident, his movements always graceful and power-ful. When he returned to the sideline, he looked a bit better. He was at least standing upright.

"Oh, God!" Lindsey cried, horrified that he was still in his uni-form. "What does he think he's doing?"

Emily laid her head on Lindsey's shoulder. "He's trying to win a championship."

Overtime

It was the first overtime state championship game in over three decades.

The Kendall Cobras won the coin toss, received the kickoff, and began their first overtime series on their own twenty-eight-yard line. Coach Shultz sent in the offense but held Kevin back. Kevin didn't push his way past the coach but did look at him as curiously as his pain-glazed brain would allow.

"Look, Sinclaire," Shultz said, his hand grasping Kevin's face-mask. "I want to make sure you're able to play every defensive series. That means we use you sparingly on offense, understand? I want to limit the hits you're taking. Scott knows the deal. We're gonna pound the ball with Anquan. We've been working their d-line all game and it's time for someone else to carry the load. You've done more than enough."

Kevin sighed, but nodded his acquiescence, and stood by the coach's side. He gritted his teeth against the urge to join his team-mates as they battled, but he understood the coach's point. The team was better served if he was fresh on defense. Limiting his offensive plays would protect his shoulder, but it could also limit the effectiveness of the Cobra offense. It was a strategy designed to keep the Cobras from losing rather than one that gave them the best chance to win. It wasn't his style, but at that point, Kevin was too weak to argue.

Scott and the Cobra offense pushed the ball to mid-field, where Anquan was stuffed for a loss on third and two. The Cobras punted and Kevin ran out onto the field with the defense. The Lions had the same idea. They tried running the ball, slamming Jamel Louis inside and then rushing him around the edge. They hadn't abandoned one specific part of their game plan. On every single play, Kevin took at least one hit. If they could hit him more often, they did so. They had no more success than the Cobra offense and had to punt as well.

The seesaw battle went on into the second overtime period. Kevin and the Cobra defense held firm, but so did the Lions. The Kendall defense almost gave up a long play when Oscar Quigley got loose in the Kendall secondary. He broke free and found himself one-on-one with Kevin Sinclaire. He lowered his shoulder and Kevin took him on at a dead sprint. Both players crashed to the ground and Quigley landed a yard shy of the first-down marker. Kevin saw stars for several seconds and was slow to get up.

Matt and Tony got to him and helped him to his feet. The play took a lot out of him. Kevin didn't have much left, but once he got up, he walked off the field under his own power and made it to the Cobra bench.

Coach Shultz watched him collapse near the Gatorade cooler and shook his head as the trainers gathered around him. He turned to Garrett Sommers and shook his head.

"If that kid dies on this field, we're gonna go to jail; you know that, right?"

Garrett nodded, his own eyes wide with disbelief. "I've never seen anything like it."

"Who has?"

The game teetered back and forth with neither team able to get close enough for even an attempt at a field goal. By the end of the third overtime quarter, it was beginning to look as though neither team would have the energy to get the ball across the goal line. As the fourth overtime dragged on, Kevin knew he wouldn't make it much longer. He felt himself slipping in and out. The Cobras needed to end this game quickly, but it was the Lions who would get the first opportunity. They drove the ball into Cobra territory and were set up on the Cobra twenty-five. Under normal conditions, it would be a reasonable distance to try for a long, game-winning field goal, but that night, there was no chance of making a kick like that. If they could get another first down, the Lions would have a reasonable shot at it.

With three minutes left in the fourth overtime period, the Cobras held firm. On third down, Jenner dropped back to pass and Kevin once again charged in on the Lions' quarterback. Jenner never saw him. Though the Lions recovered the fumble, they lost fourteen yards in the process. They were backed up to the Cobra forty-two and well out of range for a field goal. They punted and Delaney Walker called for a fair catch at the Cobra eleven-yard line.

The Cobras took the field on offense with Kevin in at his receiver position. With just under two minutes remaining in the quarter, the Cobras needed to get the ball out of the shadow of their own goal post. Scott ran Anquan for six yards on first down. On second down, he ran the same play, but in a freak occurrence, or perhaps out of pure exhaustion, Anquan simply felt his legs go out from under him. He lost two yards and got up shaking his head, looking helplessly at his teammates. No one said a word. The tired Cobras just slapped him on the shoulder pads in silent understanding. They huddled up with less than a minute remaining.

"Okay, guys," Scott said. "Let's go run routes with Sinclaire coming underneath. I'll hit him on a crossing route and we'll try to get at least something positive, if not a first down."

Kevin shook his head. "They're gonna be all over that. Let's line up for that, but instead of me coming underneath, I'll bounce outside on a go, and maybe we'll catch 'em cheating."

Matt nodded. "I like that. Do it out of the slot, though."

Scott nodded. "Okay, so here it is. Spread left, counter fake, stop, out, in-out, cross, on two."

They broke the huddle and Kevin took his place in the right slot. He was to fake an in-route, and then bounce it outside and deep while Delaney came underneath him on a crossing pattern. The first move was designed to pull the defense in to defend Kevin on a short route, but when he bounced it outside, they would either stay with him on the deep route, or play the crossing pattern Delaney would run. Scott had to read the defense and make the right throw.

As he faded back to pass, Scott looked left at Matt and Tony, but he saw Kevin start on his inside slant out of the corner of his eye. When Kevin bounced it to the outside, Scott set his feet to throw to the right. The defense reacted to Delaney's underneath route and the safety stepped up to make sure he would be in position to make a tackle short of the first down marker.

At the snap, Kevin surged off the line, putting everything he had into selling his fake. He took the defender to the inside, then bounced it back outside and took off up the sideline. When he cut up-field, he knew he had the defender beat. He hoped Scott saw it as well. Just as Kevin was about to separate, the defender slipped, and knowing he was beaten, grabbed hold of Kevin's left arm and held on, dragging Kevin down by his injured shoulder.

Scott cringed. He had already let the ball go, lofting a perfect spiral into the falling snow to a spot where Kevin would be able to make the easy catch in the open field.

"Aaarrgghhh!" Kevin screamed as he felt his shoulder wrenched once again from its socket. The pain seared deep into his bones as every nerve in his body seemed to scream in protest. Somehow, he saw the ball soar through the air, and with all the mental will he could summon in an instant, he pulled his arm free from the defender's grasp, and reaching out with his good hand, made a spectacular one-handed catch. For a split second, the pain almost made him black out, but he pushed it aside and took off down the sideline. He passed the first down marker and crossed the fifty-yard line, struggling to run fast and stay upright in the heavy snow.

Defenders chased him desperately, and under normal circumstances, Kevin would have outraced them to the goal line with ease, but with his useless left shoulder throbbing with every step, he realized he would have to take on at least one defender if he wanted to score and end the game. As the nearest defender approached, Kevin cut to the inside, trying to get the defender to go with him. As the Lion safety grabbed at his shoulder pads, Kevin spun out of his grasp, and quickly regained his momentum. The Lion defender finally got hold of Kevin at the ten-yard line and tried to drag him down, but Kevin, ignoring the pain, kept his legs churning. He kept his body as upright as possible and dragged the defender across the goal line just as the rest of the Lions' defense caught up and piled on in an agonizing tackle in the end zone.

The refs pulled the pile apart and found, at the bottom, a barely conscious Kevin Sinclaire, still holding the football. The ref signaled touchdown and the game was finally over. The Kendall Cobras were State Champions!

Chapter 3

Joy filled Tracey's heart. Absolute. Unfettered. Joy. Her secrets were out. The weight of deceit and despair lifted when the boy she loved, with all her heart, looked at her with his gorgeous blue eyes and perfect smile, and told her he wanted everything she wanted. At that moment, Tracey Overton was unburdened for the first time in her life.

She was having a baby. Okay, that wasn't ideal, but she was back with Matt Kildare, the love of her life, and that *was* ideal. Just days before, Tracey's world was a dismal mess. She was alone, heartbroken, and prepared to terminate her pregnancy. She offered Matt one chance, a sliver of hope to reenter her life, and he seized it. He took her in his arms, and told her he loved her and wanted to be with her. He also wanted to be a father to their baby.

As she lay in bed after a restful night's sleep, her smile remained. It was Saturday morning. The Cobras were State Champs courtesy of Kevin Sinclaire's maniacal heroism. Lindsey would probably be crowned queen of the city just for dating the guy. Tracey was proud of Matt. He stuck it out, even when Kevin Sinclaire took the spotlight away. Things hadn't gone as planned, but Matt found a way to recover and contribute throughout the season, and he would receive a state championship ring. It was something he would cherish forever. The Kendall Township Golden Boy would graduate high school a champion.

Tracey thought of his smile the night before. With snow pouring from the heavens, Matt cried tears of joy most of the evening as the Kendall Cobras and their fans celebrated on the field at Dobe Stadium. Tracey was thrilled to be a part of his emotional moment. He squeezed her to his chest and let his tears flow, his face buried in her thick, flame-red locks. A season's worth of emotions, frustrations, ups and downs, highs and lows, all rushed out at once, and Tracey wrapped her arms around him and shared his moment. She was so thankful they'd reconciled their relationship before that incredible tender moment. She would have hated to miss Matt's greatest high school triumph. It was particularly special because afterwards, he would have to consider life as a father and everything that would entail.

She showered and dried herself, blowing her hair out and pulling it back into a loose ponytail. As she tightened the hair band, she caught her image in the mirror. In years past, she would never have bothered to look. Having grown up as the slightly heavy, slightly taller than everyone else, carrot top with splotchy skin, Tracey compensated for her low self-image by ignoring her reflection in mirrors. It wasn't intentional, just a subconscious need to protect herself. But about a year prior, as a freshman, with more than eight years of dance experience behind her, she began to see herself for what she had become.

She wasn't skinny, but she had no fat on her. Her figure was perfect, a highly toned, athletic frame wrapped in splotch-free, fair skin, soft and smooth. She was beautiful. Her striking red hair fell in thick wavy locks midway down her back. She was no longer a Carrot Top. The boys in school now called her a Ginger…a Ginger *Goddess* to be exact.

Uggh!

Now, with her arms over her head, tying her hair back, she noticed something she hadn't before. Her belly looked a little different. Could she be…? No…not this soon. The doctor told her…Tracey peered into the mirror, squinting her eyes. She shook her head. Nah. She was imagining things. Turning away from the mirror, Tracey shook her arms, and tried to loosen all her muscles. She turned back to the mirror, standing with her shoulders back, in perfect posture. She'd spent years looking at herself in that position in the mirrored walls at onStage dance studios. If anything was out of the ordinary, she'd see it.

It was there, almost imperceptible. Anyone else would think she was crazy, just another teen girl afraid of getting fat, but Tracey wasn't fearful of weight gain. She expected it. The doctor told her she might be well into her fourth or even her fifth month before she started to show. It was her first pregnancy. She was in athletic shape, and her stomach muscles were toned and strong. Tracey's doctor had told her not to expect much growth early.

"But it'll come." He smiled, patting Tracey's knee. "That you can bet the house on."

Now, she thought she could see it, and her eyes glistened as she imagined the little guy. *Why did she think it would be a boy?* She giggled as thoughts of little overalls and tiny work boots floated across her mind. Matt would probably get a bunch of Kendall Cobra baby gear from the Brette Girls. *The poor kid'll be sleeping with a hundred footballs before he's three days old.* The thought made her smile like an idiot as she finished her hair.

"Hey, Lindz!" she called out, opening the bathroom door. When no answer came, Tracey went out into the hall and leaned over the railing. "Lindz! You down there? Come up. I want to show you something!"

Abby Overton came into view on the first floor and looked up at Tracey. "Lindsey went to Emily's. She'll probably sleep over."

Tracey nodded. "Oh, okay. No big deal." She'd show her mom later.

Emily and Lindsey. They became best friends so fast, around the same time Tracey had gotten close to Brittany. She shook her head, determined not to think about sad things. She returned her thoughts to the little baby boy and his overalls…

…or girl…*oh! What if it's a girl?*

Tracey thought of all the beautiful dresses she would buy. She thought of doing her hair every day, her ginger locks cascading down her back, just like mommy's. *They could be blonde, couldn't they?* Matt's hair was blond! *Would the baby's hair possibly be blonde?* Tracey's heart soared at the thought of having a baby girl with beautiful golden locks…*just like Aunt Brit…*

And again, her heart sank, her shoulders slumped, and her mood fell. Almost everything in her life was perfect. She had her man. She had a baby on the way, one that she was falling in love with more and more every second. Her family and friends supported her. Even with all that joy in her life, something was missing. Even though the fear and emotional turmoil had been drained from her heart, there was one relationship left unreconciled. Tracey hadn't called or spoken to Brittany. Word had long since gotten around that Matt and Tracey were back together and keeping the baby. Brittany hadn't called and hadn't tried to approach her in school or at cheer practice. She'd even kept her distance during the championship game and the ensuing celebration. Tracey was so focused on her relationship with Matt, Brittany had all but faded from her mind.

But when she was alone, in the quiet of the night…

As Tracey dressed, she lifted her shirt time and again to admire the nominal bump on her usually flat stomach. *Was it really there already or was she imagining it?* She thought about Lindsey and Emily, sprawled out on Emily's bed, on couches in front on the TV, or even on the floor, talking about boys, movies, food, sex, school, and everything else best friends talked about, and tears formed in her eyes.

She missed Brittany. Nothing seemed right without her in Tracey's life. They'd laughed and cried through so much, but due to a sharp disagreement over the idea of Tracey terminating her pregnancy, they parted ways on unpleasant terms. Tracey wasn't sure the relationship could be repaired, wasn't sure she wanted it to be. Her idea of friendship included support no matter what, even when your friend does something you disagree with.

But hadn't Brittany come around? Didn't she say just that?

It was true. Brittany told Tracey in their last conversation that she wanted to be there for Tracey even if she went through with the abortion. The last thing she said to Tracey was "I love you."

Tracey ran her hand over her bare stomach, thinking about what she would tell her child to do. That was easy. How many best friends will a person have in a lifetime?

"Mom!" Tracey ran back to the railing. "Can you give me a ride?"

***

"Can you *believe* that idiot? What was he thinking?"

Lindsey's fear and anxiety turned to anger. She cried all night worrying about Kevin. Now, she wanted to slap his face. Late the previous night, Lindsey and Emily finally piled into Abby Overton's car and made the long trip home. There was nothing left for them to do at the hospital since Kevin was going to be in and out of surgery for most of the next twenty-four hours. He would be in no condition to receive visitors.

Emily shook her head. "Boys are stupid. What can I say? And football players are worse than most. He'll be okay though."

"He didn't *look* okay," Lindsey mumbled as she pulled the covers over her head and let out a long sigh that was really part growl.

They lay on Lindsey's bed as the morning sun cast its rays across the room. The bright sun and blue skies almost made Lindsey forget it was freezing outside. She alternated between anger and admiration. The fans worshiped Kevin as a hero. What he did the night before was courageous and miraculous. And stupid…sooo incredibly stupid.

Lindsey wondered how crazy the town had gotten the previous night. She wasn't interested in participating in the celebration. Kevin's injuries put a damper on an otherwise glorious victory. Kendall Township must have gone berserk.

"The guys were so happy, I swear half of them cried," Emily said. "Even Matt's dad cried."

Lindsey rolled her head to the side to look at her. "Can you imagine your kid being a champion? It must be pretty cool."

Emily rolled her eyes. "I wouldn't know. I never knew my dad. I know my mom is proud whenever I bring home a straight A report card."

Lindsey chuckled. "Yeah…mine too. My dad is another story."

"He's not proud of you?"

"No idea," Lindsey replied with a wistful snort. "He's never around and never calls. He never returns calls or even emails. It's like he doesn't want to know what's going on with us."

Emily nodded. "I know the feeling. Though I can't even call or write him. At least you have a face and a name to remember."

Lindsey shrugged. "I don't know, Em. Sometimes I think you're lucky. If my dad was never going to stick around and care about us, I kinda wish he'd never been in my life at all."

***

Brittany opened her eyes to brilliant sunlight streaming through her windows. The bright white of her walls and furniture reflected the light, making it even brighter than it should have been. She shook her head to clear the cobwebs. Rather than waste her whole Saturday sleeping, Brittany dragged herself out of bed and staggered to the bathroom. She turned the shower on, stripped, and hopped in.

"Yeeeooww!" she shrieked, hopping right back out. The water was ice-cold. It always took a minute or two to warm up. "That's great, Brit. You've only lived here your whole life."

Oh well. I'm awake now!

After a short wait, the water warmed and Brittany washed off a night of state championship celebration and anxiety over Kevin's condition. While Kendall Township partied into the morning, Kevin spent the night at the hospital near the stadium. He chalked up a third-degree shoulder separation and God only knew how much ligament and tendon damage to his already impressive hospital record.

The maniac!

Somehow, Kevin managed to bring a defeated and beaten team back from a massive deficit and tied the game in the final seconds, sending the state championship game into overtime for the first time in over thirty years. In the longest game in state high school football history, Kevin Sinclaire simply would not let the Cobras lose. She remembered the sickening feeling in her stomach every time he trudged off the field and removed his helmet, revealing the agonized expression on his ghost-white face as the trainers crowded around him, trying to do what they could to keep him comfortable.

Brittany hadn't known whether to watch Kevin's performance in proud amazement or run over and smack some sense into him. When he stretched his hand out and made that final spectacular one-handed catch and run, she cheered right along with the rest of the Kendall Township faithful. And as he carried the Lions' defense across the goal line and disappeared beneath a mountain of Lion defenders in eight inches of snow, she realized no matter what happened from that point on, Kevin Sinclaire would forever be worshiped in Kendall Township.

She stepped out of the bathroom, wrapped in a towel. She wrapped a second towel on her head. With a refreshed sigh, she sat on the edge of her bed and pulled on her Kendall High sweatpants, black, with the silver cobra logo on the left thigh, and a Kendall High Cheer Squad T-shirt. She threw on her favorite black button up cardigan sweater, which she seldom buttoned and never wore out of the house. It was just comfortable and warm on a cold January Saturday after a big night. As she brushed her hair, she chuckled at her appearance in the mirror.

Oh, Lord! I look just like a regular Kendall Cobra fan!

Pink was her favorite color and she always wore it on the weekends when she was not in school spirit mode, but somewhere along the line she exchanged her bright colored weekend attire look for the black, silver, and white. She would fit in at any Kendall Township gathering. Now that she was dating a Kendall Cobra, a *state champion* Kendall Cobra, she found a new level of acceptance.

She smiled at the thought. Brittany felt the difference in her face. Something changed throughout her entire body when she thought of Tony. The reaction was even more pronounced when he came into the room. When he looked at her and touched her, it was almost more than she could take.

Brittany now understood what Tracey meant when she described how out of control she felt around Matt, how the closeness consumed her when she was in his arms. Brittany never thought herself likely to make the same mistakes as Tracey, but now she wasn't so sure of her ability to suppress her passions. Now she understood the draw of sex, the insistent tug of passion.

"Tracey," she mumbled, her eyes filling with tears. She slid to her knees in front of her bed, her shoulders slumped in sadness. "Please, God, bring her back to me. I need my best friend. I promise I'll love her and hold her and be there for her. Thank you for saving her from destroying her baby. Now *please* let me be with her during her pregnancy...*please*, God, *please*. I just want to be her friend again."

Her mother, Glenda, gently knocked and opened the door. How her mother managed to time moments like this, Brittany would never know, but she was grateful. Glenda knelt beside Brittany and wrapped her arms around her shoulders. Brittany sobbed as she rocked back and forth in her mother's arms.

"I just want my friend back, Mom," Brittany whimpered.

"I know," Glenda replied. She kissed the crown of Brittany's head, as she always did.

At that moment, the doorbell rang.

"Now, who could that be?" Glenda released her daughter and stood up. "I'll be back, sweetheart."

***

Glenda composed herself and strode through the hall. It wasn't unusual for the Morgans to have unannounced visitors. The congregation of Grace Gospel knew they were always welcome in Pastor Peter Morgan's home if they needed to see him. Glenda had gotten used to some strange reasons people gave for dropping by. These days, she was prepared for just about anything that could be waiting on the other side of her door...

...except for the beautiful redhead standing on her porch, rocking back and forth on her heels and wringing her hands in anxious anticipation. It had been months since she had been at their house and even Peter and Glenda had begun to miss her. Tracey Overton was not just their daughter's best friend; she was like a daughter to them. When Glenda saw her, she gasped.

"Tracey!" she whispered, her hand shot instinctively to her mouth. Her eyes filled with tears and she beckoned both Tracey and her mother, Abby, inside. "Come in. Come in."

Tracey was no sooner over the threshold than Glenda took her in her arms and squeezed. "Oh, my dear! I'm so glad you came!" Glenda wiped her eyes and greeted Abby.

"I'm sorry, Abby," she said. "I'm just surprised. But happy!"

Abby smiled. "I told her we should call first, but..."

Glenda waved her hand. "Never. Tracey is a part of this family. Just a sec." She called out, "Brittany!" Turning back to her visitors, Glenda put her arm around Tracey's shoulders and touched her head to Tracey's. "Tracey doesn't have to call. She doesn't even have to *knock*." Turning toward the hallway, she took several steps and called out again. "Brit, come out! You have a visitor, sweetie!"

Seconds later, a composed Brittany Morgan emerged from the hallway and stopped short as she entered the room. As her eyes met Tracey's they instantly filled with tears and she let out a small cry. She raced over, practically crashing into Tracey as she threw her arms around her neck and squeezed. Both girls cried and held the other up. Glenda reached over and took Abby's hand. With a smile, she nodded toward the kitchen and mouthed *coffee?* Abby smiled and nodded back and they quietly left the room.

***

Brittany was the first to speak though she didn't release her hold on Tracey's neck.

"I love you so much," she kept whispering in Tracey's ear.

Tracey's throat felt too swollen to respond. They cried and cried and cried, locked in an embrace that caused their hearts to swell with joy. They didn't need words, and Tracey was glad for that because she had none. She only wanted to hold her best friend, and cry with her, and just be back in her life. They'd handled things poorly and they both knew it. Now, standing in one another's embrace, all was forgiven and a friendship restored.

Brittany finally loosened her hold. She took a step back and smiled through her tears. She held Tracey's hands in hers. "I'm so happy right now, I can't even tell you."

At that point, Glenda poked her head in the room. "Is it safe to assume Tracey will be spending the night?"

"Yes!" Brittany shouted out before Tracey could answer. They both giggled. She turned to Tracey. "You're coming to church, right? I know it's been a little while, but we all miss you."

"Actually," Tracey said. "I kind of promised Matt I'd ride to church with him."

Brittany nodded and made a face. "Well then, you'd better make sure he knows my address, 'cause you're sleeping over. No excuses. Matt can pick you up here."

Tracey nodded. "Okay, I surrender." Everyone laughed. "I'll just have to run home and get some clothes together."

"I'll go with you," Brittany chirped. She scurried back to her room, put on a pair of black Uggs, and grabbed her heavy coat and scarf. When she picked up her phone and saw the missed text messages, an idea occurred to her.

"Trace!" she shouted. When Tracey came to the door, she said, "Feel like getting some lunch at the mall? The boys are all there!"

Chapter 4

"Dude," Scott said. "I can't say that to her."

Tony ran a hand through the brown stubble on the top of his head. The idiot barber went too short again and Tony felt like he was about to deploy for boot camp. He really needed to switch to a hair stylist with a brain. He led Scott across the sidewalk to the mall entrance.

"I'm telling you, Websey, it's the best way. She'll get pissed and do the deed *for* you. Voila!"

Tony grabbed the door handle and pulled hard. The door swung open faster than he anticipated and almost hit him in the face. He always forgot about that door. Scott Webber laughed and pushed his floppy blond locks out of his face. He elbowed Tony in the gut and hustled in before his teammate could retaliate. Tony shook his head and stared brown lasers at his quarterback…*state champion* quarterback, that is. It probably wouldn't be great for the team if he were to throw the little blond-haired, blue-eyed, girl-magnet through a wall the day after he won the state championship. He growled and followed Scott to Jocko's Tacos.

Located in an offshoot of the food court, Jocko's was situated between the Eat Burger and the Ice Cream Palace. The bright red and green neon "Jocko's Tacos" sign adorning the space above the outlet flickered in places. The scent of hamburgers wafted across Tony's nose and intermingled with the savory aroma of taco spices. His stomach rumbled. The owner, Jocko, was already taking Scott's order. Jocko always amused Tony, but that was only natural. An Egyptian who came to America and opened up a Mexican restaurant was even crazier than Mexicans opening up pizza parlors, but Jocko's was the real deal.

Minutes later, the boys carried orange trays loaded with burritos, tacos, and little packets of hot sauce to tables situated in front of the three food outlets. To Tony, it seemed like the whole school was at the mall food court that day, recovering from their victory celebrations the night before. Scott, as starting quarterback, or QB1, got most of the attention, but Tony nodded to everyone and bumped some fists before he sat down.

"Here's the problem with your idea," Scott said after he extracted himself from a crowd of Brette Girls and sat down across from Tony. He peeled the wrapper off a steaming soft-shell taco. He opened the shell and drizzled a packet of hot sauce all over the meat. He wrapped it back up and took a bite. He savored the succulent taste before he continued. "I end up looking like a jerk. The other chicks will hear all about it in no time."

"*Other* chicks?" Tony asked as he sifted through the stacks of burritos. "I thought you had the next one all picked out." He scrunched his forehead as he considered where to begin on his mountain of food.

"Yeah, but what if that doesn't work out?"

Tony opened one of the burritos from the top of the pile and emptied a packet of sauce on the end. He took a mammoth bite, chewed it three times, swallowed, and squirted another whole packet before his second bite. He downed the last of the burrito before Scott took his second bite. He didn't pause before he dove into another.

As he deluged the burrito with hot sauce, he nodded. "Good point." He took another huge bite…more hot sauce…another bite, and it was gone. He swallowed, gulped down half his soda, and grinned. "That's why you're team captain, Websey! You're always thinking long term. That's what I love about you!"

"But what do I do about Kami?"

Kamille Pellegrazo was a super cute sophomore cheerleader who was crazy about Scott. The problem was, Scott was tired of the constant chatter about nothing. Kami was very outgoing in a squealy kind of way and was more interested in making sure everyone knew she was with Scott than she was about actually *being* with him. Even with that, things were hot and heavy between them for about six weeks before Scott started to complain about her to Tony. Kami was too absorbed in New Year's Eve outfits and shoes to realize he was losing interest. Adding fuel to the potential fire, Scott had taken a liking to Hannah Trotter over the past few weeks and now needed a gentle way to break things off with Kami. So far, none of Tony's solutions were palatable.

Tony shrugged. "How 'bout you just rip the band aid off? 'Kami…it's over. We're through.' Then just leave it at that."

"That's real gentle," Scott said. "How 'bout I just punch her in the stomach while I'm at it?"

"She'd definitely get the hint then, for sure," Tony replied. He took a huge bite out of a Monster Taco Supreme.

Scott shook his head. "I gotta figure something out soon. Hannah is really cute. I think she digs me too."

"Plus, she's quiet," Tony pointed out.

"Exactly."

Matt Kildare walked by and clapped Scott on the shoulder. The star wide receiver was a senior, and until Scott Webber showed up with his miracle arm, was doomed to play in yet another losing season. Tony knew what the state title meant to all the Kendall Cobra seniors.

"Hey, boys," Matt said. His grin faded when he saw the look on Scott's face. His blue eyes dimmed and his forehead wrinkled. He pushed his shaggy blond hair back. "What's with the face?"

Scott shrugged. Tony answered for him. "He's got girl problems."

"*Girl* problems?"

Tony shook his head as the Kendall High School womanizer pulled out a chair, spun it around, and planted a foot on it. Matt leaned in Scott's direction with his elbows propped on his knee. He was serious…at least, as serious as Matt Kildare ever got.

"You have my undivided attention," Matt said. "What seems to be the problem?"

Scott opened his mouth to answer, but Tony got there first. "He's got this one chick, Kami, but he needs to break up with her so he can go out with this other chick, Hannah."

Matt raised his eyebrows. "I see."

"Never mind," Scott said. "I'll figure it out."

Matt laughed and patted Scott on the shoulder like he was patronizing a little child. "No, you won't, 'cause you're a nice guy. Problem is nice guys don't know how to break up with girls. They always try to soften the blow. By the time they're done, she feels worse than if they'da just broke it off clean."

Scott looked skeptical and Tony furrowed his brow. Tony didn't know Matt well enough, and what he did know about the guy, he didn't particularly like. But he *was* the Kendall Township Golden Boy, and his reputation with the ladies was legendary.

"Look," Matt said. "You're magic out there on the football field, but in the world of women, which is *my* domain, you're an amateur."

Scott glanced at Tony, who raised his eyebrows. Facts were facts, after all.

Matt leaned on the table. "If you want to break it off with this Kami chick, all you need to do is feed her a compliment sandwich."

"A compliment sandwich?" Tony and Scott repeated in unison.

"Yep," Matt replied. "See, first you start it off by saying something nice." He flashed his bedroom blues and his voice deepened as he fed them the line. "You're so beautiful, it takes my breath away." He grinned. "That's the first piece of bread. Then you go right into the meat. You say something like this: 'But we both know that the timing isn't right for us right now.' Then, before she has a chance to object, you hit her with the last piece of bread. 'And sweetheart, you deserve someone better than a scrub like me.' Boom!" Matt grinned, spread his arms, and raised his eyebrows. "You're home free."

Tony and Scott stared at him, speechless. Without taking his eyes off Matt, Tony held out his fist for Scott to bump. "Compliment sandwich," Tony said in a reverent tone. With a slow nod, he shrugged his shoulders, in awe of the simplicity.

Scott nodded with a lopsided grin. "Yes, it is."

"See that?" Matt said, standing up straight and spreading his arms. "The Kildare Solution. For all your relationship needs."

"Kildare *Solution*?"

Her voice came from behind and Tony watched Matt's eyes widen in recognition. A smile crept onto his face as he lowered his arms and turned around. Tony chuckled as Tracey Overton, the stunning redhead with a dancer's body, stood with her hands on her hips and a skeptical expression on her face. Her bright blue eyes danced from one boy to the next as she waited for someone to explain.

Tony was more interested in the little blonde standing next to her. Brittany Morgan was the love of his life, and it appeared she'd gotten her best friend back. He'd have to ask her how that happened. When her electric-blue eyes met his gaze, his heart skipped beats and he felt dizzy. He wondered if he would ever get used to it. He hoped not. He got up, threw an arm around her, and kissed the top of her head.

"So, what's the Kildare Solution?" Tracey asked. "Sounds like a carpet cleaning product."

Matt chuckled. "Yeah, that's it. We're thinking of starting a business, right, fellas?"

Tony and Scott cast skeptical glances at each other. The girls weren't stupid. Tony knew Matt wouldn't be able to wiggle out of it like he could with the ditzy girls he'd dated in the past. The question for Tony was which side to choose.

Tracey looked at Matt, a teasing smile on her face. "So, what's the Kildare Solution, Matt?"

He tried to brush it off one more time. "It's nothing. Just giving Websey a little advice, that's all."

"About what?" Tracey prodded. She and Brittany exchanged knowing glances.

"Guy stuff," Tony broke in. When push came to shove, he was a guy. He wasn't about to leave another guy to twist in the wind while a couple chicks picked on him. At some point, guys had to stick up for one another, otherwise chicks would take over everything. "It's just guy stuff, Trace. Nothing to worry about."

Brittany joined in. "Yeah Trace…guy stuff. Hmmm, what would *guys* be talking about that they don't want to share with their *girlfriends*? Now that's a mystery."

"Know what?" Tony shrugged with a defiant glare. "We don't have to tell you anything. Right, boys?"

Matt glanced back and forth between Tony and Tracey before he grinned and nodded. "Yeah, dude. You're absolutely right." He stretched over the table for a quick fist bump.

Tracey and Brittany exchanged mock-offended looks. They raised their eyebrows and shook their heads. Tracey grinned at Brittany and glanced at Scott, who sat still, out of the line of fire. Tony felt Brittany's wicked smile. He didn't have to see it. The deer-in-headlights look on Scott's face spoke volumes. *Uh oh.* Things were about to go south in a hurry.

Tracey pursed her lips and nodded. "Well, well, well, Brit. It looks like we'll *never* get the answer now."

Brittany nodded. She clucked her tongue and detached herself from Tony, sliding past him to Scott's side of the table. Tracey made a similar move on the opposite side. Now, Scott had a pretty girl on either side of him with their big, tough boyfriends watching the whole scene just five feet away.

"So…Scotty," Tracey said in a sweet, husky voice. "What were you guys talking about?"

She grazed her fingers over his shoulders. She leaned down and grabbed his chin, and tugged him so she could look into his eyes. Scott looked like he was about to throw up. He gulped, but before he could attempt to wiggle out of the situation, Brittany ran *her* fingers through his wavy blond hair and crouched down on his left side.

"N-nothing, really, I swear," Scott tried.

Tony shook his head again. They were so screwed. He glanced at Matt, who didn't look any more confident than Tony felt. The girls were going to eat their poor, inexperienced quarterback alive.

Tracey hung her head for a minute in disappointment. "Now, Scott," she said, tickling the back of his ear. "You and I both know that you're going to tell me everything I want to know. And you're going to tell me one way…or another."

"I-I t-th—" Scotts eyes lowered and he turned his head downward.

"Scott," Tracey said, like a mother scolding her wayward child. "Look at me, Scott." He met her eyes. "*What*…were you talking about?"

Scott slumped, defeated and broken. "They were just giving me advice on how to ask this girl out."

"What girl, Scott?"

"Hannah Perriman."

"Awww!" Brittany said. "I love Hannah!"

Tracey stood up and folded her arms across her chest. She gave him a disapproving stare. "And you went to *these* two clowns for advice?"

Scott shrugged. "They were here and they seem to know what they're doing. I mean, they got *you* two."

Brittany's hand went to her mouth, and she made an *aww* face as Tracey smiled.

"That's really sweet, Scotty," Brittany said.

Tracey turned to Matt and Tony. "See? Was that so hard? Come on, Brit. Let's get some tacos. Beating confessions out of boys makes me hungry."

Tony and Matt watched as the girls headed to the counter to order. They exchanged glances and burst into laughter. Scott shook his head and let out an amused chuckle. He took a deep breath and pushed a golden lock out of his eyes.

"Too easy," he said with a shake of his head. "Way too easy. What were they thinking?"

"Dude…" Tony said to Scott, his eyes wide as saucers. "You even had *me* going for a minute there."

Scott grinned. "Girls aren't difficult. All you gotta do is pretend they're in charge and they'll buy everything you tell 'em."

The girls returned and they all sat and talked, laughing and teasing as Tracey and Brittany ate their food. Scott got up and wandered over to the rest of the football team…and the cheerleaders. Two pretty girls made room for him right between them and Matt chuckled as he watched. Tony knew why. That was Matt, three years ago.

"Yo!" Tony waved a hand in front of his face. When Matt blinked, they all laughed. "Zone out there, dude?"

Matt grinned. "Guess so."

Tracey slid from her seat onto his lap. "So, what were you thinking about?" she asked as she ran her fingers over his ear, like she had done with Scott.

Matt shook his head. "Won't work with me, baby cakes. I'm way harder to crack than Websey."

"Oh, please," she said. "I could make you tell all in five seconds if I wanted to."

Matt held up a hand in surrender. "Let's not find out."

***

Emily couldn't escape Lindsey's words. Listening to Lindsey talk about her father and how she longed for a relationship with him caused an ache in Emily's heart. She hated to know her best friend hurt in a place no amount of friendship could reach. On top of that, Lindsey stirred up thoughts Emily had suppressed for years. She wondered about her own father.

Emily never knew him. Her mother refused to talk about him. Whenever Emily broached the subject as a young girl, her mother told her he was gone and would never be a part of their lives. Emily was curious and sad to know she would never meet her father, but she'd always been content with her mother. Camila Vasquez worked hard to provide comfort and security for her daughter, and Emily loved her without condition. She saw the sadness in her mother's eyes whenever the subject of her father came up. For that reason, Emily promised herself never to ask about him. Considering all the sacrifices her mother made raising Emily alone, it was the least Emily could do.

But it didn't silence the questions in Emily's mind or reduce the ache in her own heart whenever she imagined what it might be like having two parents to love her. Even divorced parents could still love their kids. At least the kids could know both parents. But *not* knowing…that was the worst. It had to be. The feeling of abandonment scarred Emily, just as it did Lindsey. She felt abandoned and unloved by a man who was supposed to love her unconditionally and without limit.

At least Lindsey *knew* the guy. At least she could call him, write him, or go see him and tell him how she felt. Emily had none of those options. She didn't even know her father's name. It didn't stop her from writing to him, though. Since she was eight years old, Emily had written letters to her father, folding them up and carefully saving them in the box of an old Colombian board game her grandmother had given her. As she got older, and the number of letters grew, she moved them all to a large envelope, and whenever she had the urge to write something new, she would sit down and pour out her heart on paper. She addressed each letter to the father she knew she'd never meet.

Emily's heart couldn't take much more, and she needed a little perspective. As she sat, thinking about her life, Emily was overcome, not just with a desire to know her father, but with an intense need to meet him, talk to him, and see if he had room in his life for his lonely daughter. The question was, how could she make that happen?

Emily had no intention of involving her mother. She didn't want to cause her any unnecessary pain, but Emily had no information about her father. She had no pictures, no correspondence, not even a name. She had no idea if the man was local or even if he was in the United States. For all Emily knew, her father could be anyone, from her mailman to the president of Colombia. She had no idea where to begin her search.

Birth certificate! The thought struck her as something so obvious she couldn't believe she'd never thought of it before. She bounded up the steps to her mother's room. All important papers were kept in a small fireproof box in her mother's closet. Emily opened the closet and pulled down the box. It had a combination lock on it, three dials with numbers from zero to nine. Emily had no idea what the combination could be, but she knew her math. Three dials with ten possible options for each dial meant one thousand possible combinations.

She sat down on her mother's bed with the box in her lap. She had all night, if necessary. Camila had been called in to work overtime. She hated to give up a Sunday, especially now that Emily was taking a break from her social life. It was rare for the two of them to have an entire day together, but the opportunity to make overtime dollars was compelling. Emily knew her mother was determined to be able to pay for whichever college accepted her daughter.

Emily hated to miss a free day with her mother, but this one time it would work in Emily's favor. She needed to open the box and begin the search for her father. She started at zero.

0-0-0, 0-0-1, 0-0-2…

It took a lot less time than she expected.

4-0-6, 4-0-7, 4-0-8…click!

Emily's eyes widened. "Four oh eight," she muttered. April 8th was her mother's birthday. "Why didn't I try that first?"

Emily found what she was looking for in an envelope conveniently labeled "*Emily.*" As she pulled out the various papers, including her social security card and past report cards, she looked for anything that might give her a clue as to the identity of her father. Her birth certificate was near the bottom of the pile, folded in half. She took a breath and felt her heart skip a beat, or ten. She felt a fleeting rush of guilt for rummaging through her mother's private papers, but told herself it was best for everyone. She would get her information and her mother was spared the grief of thinking about the past.

She opened the document and breathlessly scanned from top to bottom. It bore the name of the hospital where Emily was born, with all her vital statistics. Her eye was drawn to the two little footprints pressed onto the paper. She giggled and tried to imagine how small she must have been on the day of her birth, how her mother must have felt to hold her for the first time. She wondered if she would ever have that moment. Not that she was in a hurry, but she felt a tinge of jealousy as thoughts of Matt and Tracey came into her mind.

She quickly dismissed the thoughts and returned to the business at hand. She continued to examine the birth certificate and found the section titled "Family History." Her mother's information was complete, including her birthplace, Neiva, Colombia, located in the valley of the Magdalena River, a little less than two hundred miles south of the Colombian capital city of Bogotá. In the spaces provided for the father's information, nothing was filled in. Emily's heart sank. They didn't even put his *name* on her birth certificate? It was like the guy never existed.

Emily sat in stunned silence for several minutes, holding her birth certificate in her hands and shaking her head. She was *so* close. She felt wetness on her cheeks; she hadn't even noticed the tears.

"All right. This is ridiculous."

She snapped out of her funk, got up, and put everything back into the box just as it had been and tucked it back on the top shelf of her mother's closet. She trudged to her own room and stood in the center, trying to figure out what to do next. Finally, she pulled out the envelopes of all the letters she had written to her father over the years and sprawled out on her bed. She flipped through them. Her throat felt swollen and sore as she fought back the feelings of helplessness and despair. About twenty minutes later, Emily found a letter written almost six years ago.

Dear Daddy,

I wish you were here. Tomorrow is my birthday and all I want for my birthday is to see my daddy and give him a hug. I asked my Nana if you could come to my party, but she said you couldn't. Then she and my mommy got in an argument…I think about you.

I know you won't see this letter in time, but just in case I ever meet you, you can see this then you will know that I was thinking about you.

Your daughter,
Emily

She read it over a second time. Something nagged at her but she couldn't put her finger on it. Then she saw it, a glimmer of hope. It was just a single word, but it could be a possible avenue of information. *Nana.* Her grandmother. She could be the key. Sylvia Vasquez had to know the name of the guy who impregnated her daughter.

Emily knew there was a great deal more to the story than either her mother or her Nana ever let on, but Camila didn't want any discussion on the matter, and whether or not she agreed with that decision, Sylvia always respected it. That was where Emily thought she might have an opening. She'd always allowed her mother to stop the conversation whenever things became uncomfortable, but she always knew there were things about which her Nana and her mother disagreed. She had to make the call.

Emily put the letters away and held her phone, ready to push the SEND button and make the most important call of her life. She had a right to know who her father was, and she would try asking. If her Nana wouldn't give her answers, Emily would be forced to pull out the big guns. After all, she was her Nana's only granddaughter. There really was nothing her Nana wouldn't do for her…nothing at all.

Chapter 5

Tracey picked at her scrambled eggs. She hadn't been to church in weeks. When abortion was still an option, Tracey and Brittany's friendship disintegrated, followed by Tracey's faith. She stopped going to church, assuming God had written her off. Now, she wondered if it was okay to return. Brittany was quick to assure her that God always welcomes His people back.

"That's the great thing about God," Brittany told her. "We're unfaithful over and over again, but He *always* loves us."

It sounded good, but what about the rest of the kids in the youth group? People were still people, and religious people tended to judge. Would they accept her once her stomach began to grow and Tracey became a constant reminder of the dangers of teenage sex? Would they consider her child an abomination like in movies when an unwed mother gave birth? Would they consider her an embarrassment to their group? Would they even want her around? She asked those questions to Matt the night before and he silenced her fears with one sentence.

"Whatever happens," he told her, holding her face in his hands, "I'll be with you and I'll hold your hand the entire time."

The doorbell rang, and moments later, Matt and Tony stormed into the kitchen. Brittany jumped from her seat with a squeal. She leapt at Tony and threw her arms around him. Matt grinned, leaning down to kiss Tracey on the cheek. He kept his hands on her shoulders and gently massaged them. He nodded at Tony.

"I figured I'd grab this guy and we'd hit the café on the way over, if it's okay with your parents."

Brittany looked at her mother, who smiled at the sight of her daughter with her first boyfriend. She nodded. "Be on time."

"We will. Thanks, Mom," Brittany said.

"And drive safely, Matthew. You're traveling with precious cargo."

"Yes, Mrs. Morgan."

***

When they arrived at the church, they piled out of Matt's car and headed for the Youth Building. It was freezing and windy, so the boys did their best to shield the girls from the gusts. Matt held Tracey as they approached the door.

"Remember," he said. "I'm right here with you. Trust me, if they accepted me, they'll accept you. You're way prettier."

That broke the tension and made her laugh. The butterflies in her stomach calmed a little. Matt wasn't embarrassed to walk into church with her. He loved her and would be right there with her. She felt safe and secure with him and ready to face the kids in her youth group.

How does he do that?

She needn't have worried. They entered the building, and in an instant, Tracey was embraced by the girls who made up the core of the female youth group. Tracey knew none of them condoned her, or any unwed person, having sex, but they all seemed proud of her for taking responsibility, and they all expressed joy at seeing her back in church. They seemed to want to be there for her, to share in her struggle and encourage her. They had a million questions. What changed her heart? What brought her back to church? How did she feel, knowing the father of her child was also in church?

Tracey felt like she was at one of Fontaine's parties with all the attention. Not that she was complaining. She was stunned to tears at the reception. The leaders embraced her along with the girls. When they had a moment alone, Tracey laid her head on Brittany's shoulder.

"You planned all that, didn't you?"

Brittany shook her head. "Nope. That was the real thing. Give them a little credit, Trace. Christians aren't all judgmental and self-righteous. We have a pretty good group here. They all want to support and encourage you."

"Well," Tracey said. "I'm totally grateful. I feel so…I mean…I feel…*whole* again. Complete, you know?"

Brittany nodded and hugged her best friend. "I know. Me too."

***

Robert Armand.

Thanks to Nana, Emily had a name. She wrote the name on a Post-it and stared at it for days, having no idea what else to do with it. Somehow, just having it felt like a victory. Her father's name was Robert Armand. Her grandmother told her Robert had been preparing for law school when Camila got pregnant. She believed he was still local and had gotten married before graduating. That was all Emily knew about her father.

But she refused to be discouraged. It was progress. The information made her feel closer to him, like he was real and not just some image she'd conjured in her mind's eye. That he went into law made perfect sense to Emily, as she had similar aspirations. Maybe it was genetic. Wouldn't it be something if she got her law degree and they opened up a father/daughter law firm? Armand & Vasquez had a nice ring to it. Emily imagined a fulfilling career working side by side with her long-lost father, but none of that could happen unless she found him.

During her study hall period, Emily took her laptop to the library and accessed the Internet, searching the name Robert Armand. Her heart raced as the results appeared on the screen. There was indeed a Robert Armand in the County Prosecutor's office in Ravenwood, one town over from Kendall. Had he really been that close to her all this time? Emily was on the brink, but try as she might, she couldn't find Robert Armand's personal address or contact information.

When the bell sounded, she shut down the computer and headed for the lunch room, lost in thought. She could just walk into his office one day. He'd have to see her then, wouldn't he? What if he threw her out in front of everybody? There was a chance humiliation like that could happen. After all, the guy hadn't made any attempt to contact her in sixteen years. What if he really had no interest in knowing her? The thought was too depressing to contemplate. And what if this particular Robert Armand wasn't even the right guy? How awkward would *that* be?

"I need more info," she mumbled to herself, walking toward the cafeteria. Lindsey wasn't at school. She had sent a text about taking the day off to see Kevin. That was good. Hopefully a little time with her boy would make her feel a better.

As long as she doesn't try to have sex with him right there in the hospital bed.

Emily's thoughts were interrupted as she approached the stairwell. She saw Vivian Parker walking hand in hand with her boyfriend, Mike Doyer. Emily smiled and waved.

"Hi, Em!" Vivian said with a bright smile. "How are you?"

Emily responded with an anxiety-laced smile. "Good. Do you have a sec?"

Vivian exchanged glances with Mike, who nodded. "Go ahead," he said. "I'll catch up with you after class."

When he was gone, Emily and Vivian sat down on a bench across from the cafeteria.

"What's up?" asked Vivian. "Are you okay? I feel like we haven't talked in ages."

"Yeah, it's been awhile," Emily replied. She looked at the ground. "Viv, are we friends?"

"Friends?" Vivian asked, frowning. "*I* always thought so." She puckered her forehead and put her hand on Emily's arm. "What's going on?"

Emily nodded and took a breath. "I'm looking for my father."

Vivian's eyes widened. She whistled softly. "Okay. That's pretty big, right? How is it going?"

Emily shrugged. "I thought it was going okay. I mean, I have his name, and I have an idea that he works close by, but short of showing up at his office unannounced, I can't think of what to do with the info."

"You can't find his home address or phone number?"

"He's a lawyer," Emily said. "If the guy I'm looking into is really my dad, he's a county prosecutor."

"Whoa!" Vivian grinned, nudging Emily in the side. "Pretty big time. It'd be nice to have connections in the prosecutor's office, especially if you want to be a lawyer yourself, right?"

Emily smiled. Of course, Viv would remember. She was one of those people who made everyone feel important.

"So," Vivian continued. "What can I do?"

Emily shrugged. "I don't know, really. I can't just show up at his office, I don't think. And I don't want to call him, but I think that information isn't made public for county prosecutors."

Vivian nodded thoughtfully. "You're probably right about that." She took a breath. "So, we need someone who knows how to access information."

"And?" Emily shook her head, waiting for Vivian to explain.

Vivian pointed her finger. "That's who we need to talk to."

Emily followed her gaze. "Who? Calista? Why her?"

Vivian grinned. "Where do you think the Brettes go for all their tech needs? Who do you think designs all their t-shirts, web pages, and stuff?"

Vivian waved Calista over. The pretty brunette was a no-nonsense type who was on her way to the ivy league. She was president of the Brette Girls.

"Hey, Viv," she said. "Hi, Emily. What's up?"

Vivian protected Emily's privacy. "We need someone who knows how to access information online that is not available to the general public."

"And you think *I* know how to do that?"

Vivian smiled. "No, but you Brettes have Geekville wrapped around your fingers. We just want you to put us in touch with the guy who can either do what we want or tell us who can."

Calista blew out a breath and considered for a moment. She held up a finger and nodded. "Jarrick Nettles. Know who that is?"

Emily nodded. "I do. He's in my lunch." She looked at her watch. "Right now, actually."

Calista nodded. "He's your guy."

"Great," said Viv. She turned to Emily. "You can talk to him right now."

"Yeah, listen," Calista said. "These guys…they're not used to being approached by girls like you, Emily. Don't intimidate him with your looks and don't dangle sex in front of him unless you're planning to follow through. Just be nice to him and treat him like a real person, okay? It's the only way you'll get what you want."

Emily found Jarrick Nettles with a group of kids in deep discussion. To her, it sounded like they were talking about a sci-fi novel or movie. Whatever it was, Emily was certain none of them were expecting her to stop at their table and talk to them. When she did, their eyes widened, they stopped talking, and stared at her. Emily tried rein in her personality.

"Jarrick?" she asked, looking at the boy on the end closest to her. She put on her best non-seductive, non-intimidating, you-can-trust-me-I-don't-bite smile.

"Uh…yeah?" he said, his soft brown eyes focused on his hands. He tapped the table in front of him, his fingers moving at blinding speed. He looked like he'd rather be anywhere but this close to Emily. It wasn't the reaction she was used to getting from boys.

"Can I talk to you in private for a minute?" she asked.

"Um…I don't…I mean…" His friends more or less pushed him out of the booth. "I guess so," he said in anxious resignation.

Emily took him to a booth out of the way. They brought their book bags and left them at the booth while they got food at the counter. Emily paid for his lunch.

"This is on me," she said with a sweet smile. "For your time."

When they were seated, Emily took a few bites of her salad and watched Jarrick. He couldn't even bring himself to look at her. He tapped the table again in rhythmic pace, like he was typing. She tried to get him to look up.

"Hey," she said, reaching over and lifting his chin. She smiled when he looked at her. "I don't bite, Jarrick, okay? Just relax."

He gulped and kept tapping the table. "O-okay."

"Good." Emily nodded. "The reason I wanted to talk to you is I have a problem. I need to access information that isn't available to the general public."

Jarrick's whole demeanor changed. His eyes focused and his fingers stopped tapping. He licked his lips and brought a hand up to his chin, stroking it like he had a goatee. Emily knew a look of confidence when she saw it. She'd just stepped into *his* world, *his* domain.

"What kind of information?" he asked. He raised his eyebrows. "If it's nuclear launch codes, I get paid extra for that."

Emily stared at him. "Are you serious?"

He shrugged and picked at his food. Emily shook her head. Jarrick's expression never changed. Maybe he *could* get nuclear launch codes…

"Anyway," she said. "I don't want to blow anyone up. All I need is to find the home address of a county prosecutor."

Jarrick's eyebrows rose even higher. He nodded and licked his lips again. If it was possible, his fingers tapped faster than before, but it wasn't a nervous tic this time. Did that mean he was interested?

"Is that something you think you can handle?"

He smirked and looked at her for the first time. "Why do you want a prosecutor's home address?"

Emily sat back. "It's personal."

He nodded. "I bet."

She looked at him. "What's that supposed to mean?"

"Look," Jarrick said. "Tracking down the personal address of a government official is serious business. There are only one or two reasons I can think of for that. One, you or someone else wants to do something to him or his family. Two, you're sleeping with him and want to make trouble for him by letting him know you can tell his wife at any time and ruin his life." He looked Emily in the eye. "So, which one is it?"

Emily's mouth dropped open. *Whoa!* All she wanted to do was find her father. Now this computer geek called her a murderer or a home wrecking slut. She resisted the urge to reach across the table and slap his geek face.

"Look Jarrick, all I'm trying to do is track down my father. I think he's a county prosecutor, but I've never known him. I have his name and I know he's a lawyer. If he's the right guy, there ought to be information we can use to prove it. That's the reason I need you."

He cringed and looked down at his hands. "I didn't mean anything by it." He shook his head. "But it *is* risky hacking into government databases. They don't like it."

Emily relaxed. "But can you do it?"

"Of *course*, I can do it," Jarrick spat, his own indignation erupting for just a second. He quickly recovered. "But why would I? If we get caught, you get to claim you were just looking for your daddy, but I illegally accessed a government database. That's *years*…not months. It's also tens of thousands of dollars in fines."

Emily nodded. "So, what do you want?"

He bit his lip. She could see he had something in mind, but was afraid to come out and say it. Emily rolled her eyes and shook her head. "I'm not sleeping with you, Jarrick."

His eyes widened. "I…no…I didn't mean…I mean…I wasn't gonna ask…" He hung his head. "I'll get you whatever you want." Jarrick took another breath and shook his head.

Emily sighed. "Just tell me, Jarrick."

He looked right into her eyes for the first time. They were so close Emily could see every detail of his light brown eyes. They were a pleasant soft brown with flecks of gold and even a little hint of green around the edges.

"I need your help with a girl," he finally said, closing his eyes and lowering his head as his face turned beet red, all the way down to his neck.

Emily's face broke out into a grin. "A girl?"

Jarrick nodded, his head now buried in his arms. Emily reached over and grasped his hair, pulling his head out of his arms.

"Why don't we start with a name?"

He shook his head, but Emily gave him a look telling him the conversation would only be over when she said so.

"Her name's Kayla," he said with an embarrassed sigh. "Kayla Helmsley."

"Kayla," Emily repeated. "I don't think I know her. Is she in your grade?"

"Yeah, she's a junior like me." He gestured with his head to something behind Emily. "She's right over there."

Emily subtly turned her head and scanned the room.

"Jeans," Jarrick said. "White shirt and black boots. Hair dyed really light blonde."

Emily found her. She was sitting with a group of girls Emily didn't know. They were a clique that wasn't involved in the athletic programs and all the school spirit stuff. The group was an eclectic mix of goth, geek, and various other "outsider" styles. Kayla was a cute girl with a pretty smile. She would have looked terribly out of place were it not for her hairstyle. She wore it in little dreads, dyed to a frosty platinum shade. The tips were dyed turquoise.

"Cute." Emily turned back to Jarrick and smiled. "She looks nice."

"She *is* nice."

"So, what's the problem? Go ask her out."

Jarrick's eyes glazed over. "Uh…yeah…I don't think so."

Emily shook her head. "So, what are you gonna do? How can I help?"

He shrugged. His eyes told her the story. He was crushing hard. "I was hoping you might help me figure out how to do it. Is that stupid?"

Emily took pity on him. She couldn't help it. She had a soft spot for romance. She loved it when a guy really liked a girl. It was so sweet how petrified Jarrick was about the mere thought of talking to Kayla. She had to help him.

"All right," she said. "I'm going to help you, but if you refuse to talk to her, this ain't gonna work."

Chapter 6

Kevin groaned as his eyes fluttered open. His shoulder throbbed as he lifted his head to look at the clock. The past three weeks were little more than a painful blur. His first night at the hospital, he went through seven hours of surgery to repair his injured shoulder. He was in surgery again, just two hours later, when the doctors discovered internal bleeding. A piece of bone had splintered off his shoulder and pierced an artery, as though he needed the additional damage. Then they pumped him full of antibiotics and morphine. He hated the loopy feeling and tried to limit the amount they gave him.

Once he got home, he had far more control over what went into his body. He was supposed to take two of the gigantic opiate horse pills twice a day. Kevin decided to cut the dose to a quarter or half of a pill on an as needed basis and try to deal with the pain using breathing techniques and mental focus. So far, he managed to keep his medication to one pill per day total. But he paid the price, especially when he woke up.

He moved gingerly until he lay propped up in his bed with several pillows. He flicked the television on and watched in absent boredom. He preferred to read, but the pain made it hard to focus and he always ended up with a bad headache. Plus, it was hard to stay comfortable in one position.

"Kevin?" His mother, Karen, knocked before opening the door, then she entered with a tray, atop which sat a bowl of homemade cream of chicken soup, Kevin's favorite, and a mug of steaming Earl Grey tea, also Kevin's favorite. She brought the tray in and placed it on the dresser while she removed Kevin's laptop from his latest creation, a handcrafted rolling table that he usually used for his laptop when he was seated on his bed. Now, it would serve as his food stand.

Moving the laptop to Kevin's nightstand, Karen then placed the tray on the table and rolled it into position in front of her injured son. Kevin looked up at her with his most pathetic sad face, his emerald eyes pleading with his mother to take the pain away. She knew this game. Her son was a borderline psychotic when it came it pain. Two weeks ago, he played six quarters of football with a severely separated shoulder, in eight inches of falling snow. He'd undergone two surgeries, all the while fighting with the doctors over the amount of painkillers they gave him. He'd been cutting his pills into quarters and halves for two weeks and now wanted only over-the-counter medicine. All those decisions had been his alone, and now he was sitting there with those precious green eyes, silently conveying his pain to the only person in the world that might be able to make it all better. Her heart melted. Moments like this didn't happen anymore with Kevin.

"Scoot up," she said. Kevin slid forward, moving with deliberate ease. Karen climbed onto the bed behind him and began massaging his swollen shoulder. She felt the tension in his body melt away as her fingers kneaded his black and blue skin in soft, delicate strokes.

"Abby Overton called a few minutes ago," she said. "She told me Lindsey's been trying to call and text you but you don't respond."

Kevin nodded. "I know. I've been meaning to call her. I just don't want to be on the phone. It drains me and it's hard to keep my thoughts straight. Even texting is painful because it always turns into a conversation and then I'm stuck reading as well as typing."

Karen nodded, continuing to run her hands over Kevin's shoulder, grimacing every time she lowered her eyes to look at the swollen, black, blue, and purple mess. "It's just that she didn't get to see you much in the hospital and you were out of it almost the whole time."

"That's because those idiots wouldn't cut the morphine," he replied. "I felt like I couldn't access my brain. Do you have any idea what it's like to have such brilliant faculties and not be able to access them?"

"Oh," Karen snorted. "Well, God forbid you can't access your *faculties* for a few days while you recover from *multiple* surgeries. And how were those *faculties* working when you decided to exponentially increase the damage to your body by continuing to play the game after you were badly injured?" She shook her head as Kevin grinned and slurped his soup. She hated when he did that. "Eat like a human being. And, by the way—"

"*Exponentially?*" Kevin smirked. "Who said *that?*"

"The *doctor* said that," Karen retorted. "You know…the guy who had to *fix* the damage you did to yourself."

"Well," Kevin said. "The doctor doesn't know what the word "exponential" means then. And it doesn't mean "drastically," like you were using it."

"Oh? Then what does it mean?"

"To increase exponentially is to increase by doubling itself over and over again, depending on what the exponent is. For example, to increase the number 2 exponentially, you would multiply the number 2 by itself over and over again. So, 2, 4, 6, 8, 10 is not an exponential increase. 2, 4, 8, 16, 32 is exponential increase."

"Anyway," Karen shook her head. "I told Mrs. Overton she could bring Lindsey over after school and I would take her home after dinner so you two could spend some time together."

"Okay, cool." Kevin went back to his soup as his mom left the room.

As he ate, he contemplated the peace his mind had experienced over the past two weeks. Aside from all the pain, the one thing

Kevin enjoyed about the whole experience was the time he had to himself. Things with Lindsey hadn't been the best lately. They started high school as the perfect couple. That perfect façade soon crumbled under the pressures of popularity and sexuality. Lindsey dealt with those pressures by convincing herself she had to have sex in to save their relationship. Kevin knew, by instinct, she wasn't ready, and though he had to exercise enormous self-control around her, he was in no hurry to act on her sudden desire to take the plunge. In the end, Lindsey and Kevin did take their relationship "to the next level," as Lindsey put it. Kevin could not imagine a more beautiful night than the night he and Lindsey had spent together for their first time.

But then things went sideways. It wasn't uncomfortable or weird, but it was different, that much was certain. The floodgates of Lindsey's sexuality opened and she wanted to be with Kevin all the time. He didn't mind that. He loved being with Lindsey. He loved having his hands on her and her hands on him, but they never *talked* anymore. Before, they'd shared an intellectual and emotional connection. Now it felt purely physical. It was a lot of fun. Who doesn't like sex? But Kevin felt like they veered onto dangerous ground and he was having trouble seeing the road ahead.

The time apart gave him a chance to think about what went wrong and make some decisions about how to proceed. The problem was how to explain his feelings without driving her away and making her feel trashy. She didn't deserve that. Kevin loved Lindsey. Well…he loved the girl he was dating when the school year first started. The new Lindsey was incredibly sexy and confident, which was attractive, but not if the rest of her qualities suffered as a result. He wanted *his* Lindsey back.

He glanced out the window as Mrs. Overton's car pulled in. Kevin couldn't believe how quickly time had passed. His thoughts about Lindsey had taken up almost two hours. He heard a gentle tap on his door and Lindsey pushed it open. As soon as he saw her face, he realized how much he'd missed her. He smiled as she came in. She was dressed in black yoga pants with a long, soft, blue sweater that went down to her thighs. The color made her icy blue eyes seem bluer than usual. She stood for a few seconds, a look of uncertainty on her face.

Kevin smiled and slid to his left, making room for her next to him. He could see her body relax and she came to him, kicking off her flats, and carefully climbing in with him. She put her head on his good shoulder and one of her legs intertwined with his, just as she always did. Her right hand lay across his bare stomach.

"I missed you so much, baby," she whispered. "I thought you didn't want to see me."

Kevin ran his hand along her neck in gentle strokes. "No. I just couldn't handle talking. My brain is kind of fried."

"Well," Lindsey said in a bland voice. "Don't start thinking on *my* account."

***

I know how to help you…come take me to dinner.

Emily sent the text about an hour after she walked through the door after school. Right at six-thirty, Jarrick Nettles pulled up in front of her townhouse in a hot little green race car. The guy was full of surprises, wasn't he? Emily watched him turn the car off before she took a quick look in the living room mirror. She wore a tan maxi dress with a subtle dark brown pattern. It was a departure from her usual attire. Emily's wardrobe was geared to the sexy. She never dressed to look trashy but most of her outfits showed off her assets. Now, Emily was determined to drift away from sexy and more toward classy. It had been harder than she thought, shopping for less sexy clothing. Her eyes always seemed to stray toward the short, slinky, form-fitting outfits.

As she looked at the new Emily in the mirror, she shrugged and nodded. She could live with it. Classy was something her mother was great at. She never looked slutty, but she always looked good. Even in her professional outfits, Camila looked stunning. Maybe Emily could too. Anyhow, tonight would be a good no-pressure test…

If he ever came to the door…

She peeked out the window. What could be taking so long? She saw him practically hyperventilating, still behind the wheel. She put her fingers to her mouth and chuckled. *The poor guy.* She shook her head. She was used to having an effect on boys. In Kendall High, Emily was not just another pretty girl. There were plenty of those. To most of the student body, Emily Vasquez was a goddess. It never occurred to her what the rest of the school must think of her.

As she watched the struggling Jarrick from her living room window, Emily realized just how much she had changed in what really amounted to a few weeks. Just six months ago, a guy like Jarrick Nettles would have been little more than a means to an end for Emily. She would have used the power of her beauty and status to bend the computer geek to her will. She would have used her seductive smile and the sway of her perfect hips to mesmerize the poor kid until he did her bidding. She would have rolled her eyes at the scene outside, wondering how anyone with such meager confidence could get ever through life.

Now, Emily realized those feelings were no longer there. Her entire attitude was different. Jarrick was a sweet guy who didn't want to be humiliated in front of the prettiest girl in school. If he ever got the nerve to get out of the car, Emily promised herself she would think of him as a real guy taking her out and not a geeky computer kid who was doing her a favor. She would teach him how to handle pretty girls.

He finally came to the door and knocked. Emily answered and stood aside to let him in. Jarrick hesitated.

"Come in." She giggled. "It's okay. I promise you, I won't bite." She resisted the urge to add "*much.*" She wasn't sure he'd survive the jest.

He managed a tight grin and allowed Emily to guide him inside. She took him through the hall to the kitchen, where she poured them both glasses of iced tea. Jarrick stood, with rigid anxiety, by the breakfast bar, obviously trying not to do anything that might cause embarrassment. And it was clear he was doing everything in his power to avoid eye contact with Emily. That wouldn't do.

"Listen, Jarrick," she said, grabbing his shoulders and making sure he lifted his eyes to hers. She felt his body stiffen even more and he was unsteady, but she continued. "If you're gonna hang out with me, you need to relax. I'm over here watching you and I'm getting nervous *for* you."

He nodded and tried to smile.

"Take a deep breath," Emily said. Jarrick complied. Emily handed him a glass of iced tea. "Take a drink." After he took a sip, she smiled. "Now look at me. Girls like to be looked at. We spend a lot of time and all our money on looking good. Let us know it's working."

Jarrick seemed to loosen up the more Emily spoke, so she continued for a few more minutes, asking him about school and what he did all afternoon since they last spoke.

"Oh yeah," he said, pulling a white envelope from the inside pocket of his jacket. "I almost forgot. This is for you."

He handed it to Emily.

Emily's eyes widened. "You already did it?"

"Mmmhm," Jarrick said. "Took about thirty minutes." He nodded at the envelope. "That's everything I could find out about him, including his home address and phone numbers."

Emily was stunned. As she scanned the pages, her heart raced. She was just a step away. Now Emily was the one feeling faint.

"Are you okay?" Jarrick asked.

Emily nodded absently. "I'm fine." She stared at the pages. "I can't believe it. It's all here."

Jarrick nodded. "Everything I could find, at least." He lowered his eyes once again. "Listen, why don't you give him a call or go see him? We don't have to hang out. It's no big deal."

Emily looked up. He had no idea what to do with a pretty girl, especially one with whom he had little or nothing in common. She smiled at him and shook her head.

"You're not getting off that easy," she said, a playful smile on her face. "You're still taking me to dinner."

His eyes brightened a little. He had given her an opportunity to ditch him now that he had given her what she wanted, but she still wanted to hang out with him.

"Jarrick," she said. "Have you ever kissed a girl?"

He started getting nervous again. "I…ummm…I mean, I…"

"It's a yes or no question, Jarrick."

He hung his head. "Not really, no."

"Tell me about that one."

"What one?"

"The 'not really' one."

He shrugged. "It wasn't really a kiss."

"So tell me."

He sighed. "Well, me and a couple of my friends got invited to a party last year. We were kind of excited because that usually doesn't happen. When we got there, it turned out that they really just wanted us to help them do something for their computers."

"So there was no party."

"No, there was, and we got to stay for it, but they just used it as an excuse to get us there to help them with the computer stuff." He shook his head. "Anyway, we were all sitting around playing games when they decided that the loser of their game had to go into the closet and kiss one of us. At the time we just figured I got selected randomly, but I'm pretty sure it was rigged."

"That really sucks," Emily said. *People can be so mean.*

"So I went into this walk-in closet with this girl and we were supposed to kiss. And she was actually kissing me, but I had no idea what to do." He hung his head. "She looked at me like I was such an idiot." He looked up at Emily, his cheeks a rosy red and humiliation clear in his eyes.

Emily came closer, not taking her eyes off his. She slid put her right hand along his cheek and stood on her tip-toes to kiss him. She held the kiss for several seconds before pulling back.

"You know," she said. "It's better if you kiss back."

"Yeah, but," he began. "I mean, shouldn't we…I mean…what about dinner?"

Emily smiled, and gave his cheek a gentle stroke. "We have time. This is just practice, Jarrick. If you can kiss me, you should be able to ask Kayla out. Now kiss me, Jarrick."

He looked petrified. "I don't…I mean, I never…"

Emily stepped back and folded her arms over her chest. "Jarrick, guys usually *want* to kiss me."

"But I don't know…I mean I've never…"

"Shhh." Her voice dropped into a gentle whisper. She stroked his face with both hands before dropping them down to his chest. "Just close your eyes, and kiss back when I kiss you. Just feel it." She kissed him, pressing her lips to his just enough to make it real. "Oh, yeah," she said, her stunning eyes boring into him. "And put your hands on me."

She kissed him again, but he hesitated. She knew exactly what he was thinking. "It's okay, Jarrick," she whispered in his ear, brushing her lips across his neck and cheek. "Just keep them above my waist and off my chest and you'll be fine." She pulled back and looked at him. "Now stop *thinking*, Jarrick. I can hear the gears grinding in your head."

Emily kissed him again and felt him finally let go of his nerves. She felt his tentative hands find their way to her back. His body was stiff as a board at first, but Emily just kept gliding her hands from his chest to his arms, around his neck and through his hair. He managed to loosen up enough to at least let his hands travel all around her back. She could feel his confidence grow, and after several seconds, Emily felt him pull her close and really kiss her.

"That was nice." Emily smiled as she pulled back. She smiled at him and tapped a finger to his chin. "You have nice lips." She giggled, feeling her own cheeks heat up. "Ready to take me to dinner?"

"After that?" Jarrick asked. "I'll pretty much do whatever you want. Where do you want to go?"

"You tell me." Emily smiled. "Where does Kayla hang out?"

***

Though Jarrick's vehicle was just a simple Mitsubishi 3000GT, when Emily saw it up close, she realized that it was much more than that. The car was tricked out like a race car. The green paint shimmered in the dim lights. It had sleek black stripes down the sides. When she got inside, Emily saw computer panels embedded in the console.

"Where did you get this?" Emily asked, looking around. "It's awesome."

"Thanks," Jarrick said. "Actually, I got it pretty cheap and did all the upgrades, engine, and body work myself."

Emily looked at him. "Seriously? *You* did all this?"

It turned out, Jarrick, in addition to being a serious computer guy, was also super into cars. He loved building engines, modifying them for better performance, and then racing them. They talked about that for several minutes as they drove to their destination, but he fell silent soon after.

Emily let the silence hang and watched Jarrick out of the corner of her eye. He was an interesting guy, nothing like the boys she usually spent her time with, but he had a sweet charm. He was desperate to impress this Kayla girl. Most guys just wanted to say whatever they thought a girl needed to hear to get her to sleep with them. Jarrick just wanted her to like him, to be kind to him. He just needed a little confidence. Emily gave him a sly smile.

"I liked kissing you," she said.

His face turned bright red. "Uhhh…I…uhhh…yeah, it was nice," he managed.

As Emily hid her amusement, she noticed something different in his demeanor. She watched as he sat there, lost in thought. He seemed to be in another world. But why? Her eyes widened and a smile crept onto her face.

"You're thinking about her." It wasn't a question.

He snapped out of his fog. "What?" he asked, perplexed. "Who?"

Emily raised her eyebrows in a knowing smile. "You know who. Kayla? You feel guilty about kissing me, don't you?"

"No, I don't," he insisted, shrugging his shoulders. "Why should I feel guilty?"

"You shouldn't," Emily said. "It was just practice. You didn't cheat on her."

"I know that."

"Okay," Emily said. "But you still feel guilty?"

He shrugged. "Kind of," he said. "A little."

"But why?" asked Emily.

Jarrick shrugged again. "I don't know. Just 'cause I really like her, I guess."

Emily nodded. "That's really sweet." She reached over and brushed his cheek with the back of her knuckles. "You're a really good guy, you know that?"

"I wish *she* did."

Emily smiled. "She will. Trust me."

***

When they walked into Luigi's Ristorante, Emily felt like she was entering another world. On the outside it looked like an old style Italian restaurant, but inside, in addition to the old style Italian restaurant, one whole side of the building swarmed with young guys and girls hanging out, eating, or playing video games on huge screens throughout the room. Jarrick must have caught the stunned confusion in Emily's eyes.

"Not your normal hangout, huh?"

She shook her head. "I don't get out to Veritas all that much. I can't figure out what this place is exactly."

Jarrick nodded. "It's simple. The owner is the grandfather of a kid who loves cars and video games. Over the years, they lost a lot of business to the newer restaurants and almost went bankrupt. Rafael, the grandson of the owner, asked if he could turn part of it into a hangout. It started small, but pretty soon our entire crowd moved in. Now we all come here pretty much every night."

Emily looked around as they entered the room. "That is so cool," she said. Seeing a flash of platinum blonde out of the corner of her eye, she nudged Jarrick and pulled him toward an empty table. They took their coats off and sat down.

Emily leaned close to Jarrick. "This is a good spot. Did you see her?"

"Uh huh," Jarrick said. His fingers started doing their tapping thing. "But what are we gonna do?"

Emily smiled. "Tonight? Nothing. We're just gonna hang out, talk, laugh, and you're going to introduce me to your friends."

One thing Jarrick failed to notice was the attention he was getting from a lot of the guys in the room. He was so focused on Kayla, he forgot he'd just walked into his favorite hangout with a local celebrity. Emily got noticed wherever she went.

The rest of the evening passed with Jarrick and Emily doing little more than sitting and talking. Emily made sure to lean just close enough to Jarrick to give the impression they might be something more than friends. Whenever they walked around the room, she always made sure to maintain contact with him, either by looping her arm through his or holding his hand. Everyone who asked was told the same thing. They were just friends and Jarrick was showing her his favorite spot. Even Jarrick had no idea what was going on, but Emily was on point, an expert, laying groundwork.

Kayla, for her part, glanced up several times as Jarrick and Emily worked their way through the room. She was subtle, but her lips tightened into a thin line as her eyes followed Jarrick and Emily wherever they went. Emily saw it and knew the evening was a success. The only question was whether Jarrick had it in him to actually talk to Kayla. It was the only thing Emily couldn't control.

Chapter 7

Lindsey raised her head and looked at his eyes. Their faces were inches apart. It never got old. Kevin's eyes had the same effect on her as the first time she looked into them. Her whole body trembled. She leaned in and kissed him. She was gentle at first, then more passionate as Kevin pulled her body close. She was careful to avoid his injured shoulder, but he took her hand and brought it up to where the stitches still held the incision together. He placed her hand on his pain and it melted her to feel so close to him again.

She moved her hand in tender rhythm, exerting no pressure on his shoulder at all. But, once again, he brought his hand up and lay it on top of hers, guiding it to the incision again. He pressed down a little. Lindsey felt him tense up a bit as though it hurt, and his eyes glazed over, but just as quickly he relaxed as he held her hand pressed against his incision. He breathed out a relieved sigh.

"That feels good?" Lindsey asked, wrinkling her nose.

"Ooh yeah," he moaned. "A little pressure, for some reason, relieves the pain more than anything else."

Lindsey moved her hand from place to place on his shoulder, exerting slight pressure and seeing which spots were the most sensitive. None came close to the area around the incision. She was amazed at the difference when she applied a little pressure. It was like all the pain receded and the color returned to his face.

"Don't you have painkillers?" she asked. "They had to give you something."

"Yeah, I have some. I just don't want 'em."

"Ohhhh, so, you're an idiot." She shook her head. "But we already knew that, didn't we? Who goes out and plays football with a dislocated shoulder, anyway?"

"Thank God I have a girlfriend who thinks so highly of me," Kevin snorted. "What would I ever do without your encouraging words?"

"Hey!" Lindsey objected. "I think very highly of you. It's just that…" She looked him over with a skeptical frown.

"It's just what?" he asked with his eyebrows raised.

She shrugged. "Well, you're not really all that useful to me like this." She grinned.

"Useful," Kevin repeated. "You mean…"

"Exactly."

"Of course." Kevin grew silent.

Lindsey's teasing grin faded as the atmosphere between them darkened in an instant. She continued to run her hands over his shoulder, pausing now and then to apply gentle pressure over his incision. There was a long period of silence and she noticed he wasn't even reacting when she pressed on his wound. He seemed far away.

After a few moments, she couldn't take it, and broke the silence. "You still with me?"

Kevin blinked and nodded, but said nothing. More silent moments passed.

"What are you thinking about, Kevin?" she asked, continuing to move her hands over his shoulder. By now she had moved behind him and massaged the rest of his back. It wasn't hard to see what areas to be careful around. The entire upper left quadrant of his torso was discolored in front and back. It looked like someone had beaten his shoulder with a baseball bat. Lindsey slid her hands over his skin, relishing the dips and peaks of his muscles.

"I'm thinking about the first day I saw you last summer."

Kevin's head was down, his chin to his chest as Lindsey massaged the muscles in his neck. They were knotted up worse than ever, probably from him lying in bed so much, but also from the pain.

"Remember?" he asked. "We sat out on your back deck for the whole afternoon."

She smiled at the recollection. "Yeah," she said, her voice fading as her mind drifted back in time. "That was a nice day."

"I miss that," Kevin said in a soft voice.

"Miss what?"

"I miss just being with you."

Lindsey frowned. "We're together all the time."

Kevin shook his head. "It's not the same."

Lindsey's mind scrambled to decipher his cryptic and evasive tone. "Kevin, is something wrong? Did I do something?"

He shook his head. "No." Kevin stretched his neck and she heard the *pop* that always made her skin crawl. "I'm missing the way we used to be together before we—"

"What, Kevin?" Lindsey prodded. "Before we what?"

"Before we started sleeping together."

Lindsey's heart dropped. For a second, she lost feeling in her hands. She recovered, and continued moving them in gentle circles around his back. It took a few moments for her to find her voice.

"You don't like being with me?" Lindsey asked. She wasn't certain she wanted to hear his answer, but had no control over the thoughts tumbling out of her mouth. "I mean…sexually?"

Kevin shook his hand. "No, I don't mean that. It's not really about the sex; at least I don't think it is. I just think…Lindsey, we never talk anymore. Not like we used to. We spend all our time hooking up and no time talking or just being together."

Lindsey sighed. It wasn't like she hadn't felt the distance, but why did everything have to be so serious all the time with this guy?

"Can't we just have fun, Kev?" she asked. "I mean…do we have to take everything so serious?"

He shrugged. "I'm not really like that, Lindz. I *do* think about things seriously. Sex with you meant something to me, and at first, it wasn't a small thing for you, either."

"So," she said softly. "You *do* regret being with me."

"It's not like that." He turned to face her. And she saw the worry on his face. "I love you, Lindz. But this…" He shrugged. "What we've got going on between us…it's not good. And it's not just about sex. It's about everything else. That's what's changed. Sex was just the catalyst for that change."

"Catalyst?" Lindsey raised her eyebrows. "Are you going to give me a science lecture now?"

Kevin sighed and turned around. Lindsey shook her head and

"Hey, I'm just kidding," she said, leaning forward and sliding her hands under his arms, careful not to press too hard on his sore ribs. She pulled him back into her body and ran her hands over his chest and stomach. *Oh, my GOD, this feels good!* She felt passion begin to take control of her mind and grappled with it for control. It was exactly what Kevin was talking about. She took a deep breath and rested her head on his back, breathing him in and savoring the closeness…the non-sexual closeness.

"So, what do you want to talk about?"

***

"Okay now," Emily said. "Just play it cool and don't look at her."

It was almost lunch time. Emily and Jarrick were about to have lunch together and continue to subtly push Kayla's buttons. The goal was to push Kayla into some sort of a move. Emily saw the irked expression on Kayla's face at Luigi's the other night. She figured it might be easier to get Kayla to make the first move than Jarrick.

"Yeah, and don't be too obvious about it, either," added Lindsey. She thought the plan was stupid and childish, but she liked the computer guy and wanted to see him get his girl. "You don't need to make a scene. If she's as into you as Emily says, she'll know as soon as you walk into the room. This is a less-is-more situation."

Jarrick looked less than convinced. "What if she's not as into me as Emily thinks?"

"Blasphemy," replied Lindsey in a stern voice, looking right into his eyes with her patented ice-blue stare. "Emily is *never* wrong."

He shut up and nodded. Emily turned her head and chuckled to herself. The poor kid was petrified of Lindsey. Maybe it was because her boyfriend had the reputation of being just a notch below certifiably insane and could snap a guy like Jarrick in half. Emily knew Lindsey just liked being feared.

Emily spun him toward the door and looped her arm through his. She held his arm, not like they were intimate, but enough to imply they were not just friends having lunch. They could be dating, but maybe not. They came off as a casual couple enjoying a casual relationship. Neither of them looked around the room as they entered the cafeteria, claimed a booth, dropped their backpacks, and got into line. They didn't have to.

"She's watching," Lindsey whispered to them in passing as she took her place in line, several spots behind the phony couple. Lindsey watched Kayla to see if the new couple garnered any attention, and she was not disappointed. Kayla's eyes followed Jarrick Neddles' every move.

Emily and Jarrick spent lunch laughing together while Lindsey joined a few of her recent acquaintances and kept watch. She was amused at Kayla's interest in Jarrick's apparent new love life. The two were hot for each other. Why not make a move? What if Emily was really into Jarrick? Kayla would have missed her chance.

Not that Lindsey was some sort of move maker. As she sat and watched the jealousy build in Kayla's eyes, she wondered if she would have the nerve to make a move if she were in a similar situation. She wondered if indeed she and Kevin broke up, would she even want to consider a new relationship? She doubted it. Relationships were heartache waiting to happen.

Emily leaned across the table, close to Jarrick's head. She used the proximity to keep up a constant chatter about how he was doing and what to do next, and more importantly, what *not* to do, like look at Kayla and give away their plan.

"Just keep doing what you're doing and eat your food," she said with a soft smile. "You're doing great."

"Is she still looking?"

"Oh yeah," Emily replied. "She's not happy."

"Maybe I should go talk to her now."

Emily wanted to slap him. "You'll do *nothing*. Don't blow it, Jarrick. We're putting the ball in *her* court. It's up to her to make a move. If she asks you, you know what to say, right?"

He nodded. Emily knew he was desperately hoping Kayla *didn't* ask him. Emily agreed. She hoped Kayla would come to *her* instead of Jarrick. He was liable to blow the whole thing in a single conversation.

The bell sounded the end of the period. Emily signaled to Jarrick to leave. He rose and kissed her on the cheek. Emily smiled up at him as he walked out, and gathered her things. She opened a small compact and touched up her makeup before getting up to leave herself.

As she did, she heard a voice behind her.

"Excuse me?"

Emily, with her back to the speaker, smiled. *Gotcha.* She turned and came face to face with Kayla Helmsley, who looked as nervous as Jarrick had before he kissed Emily on the cheek.

"You're Emily…right?"

***

Matt sat in Pastor Peter Morgan's office. The pastor sat behind his large mahogany desk, which was almost clear but for a closed laptop off to one side. The top of the desk was polished to a mirror shine; there wasn't a fingerprint to be seen.

"So…" The pastor smiled. "With everything that's gone on, your head must be spinning a little."

"It is," Matt replied. "To be honest, I'm just really happy right now."

The pastor nodded. "I can't blame you for that. What are you happiest about?"

Matt shrugged. "Do I have to pick one thing? I'd say I'm happiest about how things ended up with Tracey and me, but if you're asking me what I'm most thankful for, I'd say that I'm most thankful I met *you*."

"Me?" Pastor Morgan wrinkled his forehead. "Why on earth would you say that?"

"Because if you hadn't taken me to dinner the night I was trying to talk to Tracey, I doubt I'd have ever accepted Jesus as my Savior."

If there was one thing Peter Morgan had learned about dealing with young people, it was that they'd give it to you in blunt honesty. It never got old having people tell him how grateful they were for salvation. He didn't want the credit, like Matt had just given him, but loved to know Matt was moved by what Jesus had done for him.

"Well, that warms my heart, Matt." Peter got up and came around the desk, taking the chair next to Matt, and patted him on the knee. "Remember though, Jesus did all the work. All I did was tell you about it."

Matt had questions, and they sat for an hour in close conversation about everything from basic life questions to more complex theological concerns. Peter Morgan's method of answering his questions was really an exercise in how to research scripture. For every question Matt presented, Peter responded, not with the answer, but with several references in scripture for Matt to research when he was alone. The pastor was teaching him something, but Matt was struggling, which to Peter Morgan, was the best place for him to be.

"I get the sense that you want me to learn something that you're not telling me," Matt said.

Peter smiled. "What I'm trying to teach you is how to search scripture for answers. It's not a problem if you get stuck and have to ask, but you learn so much more by seeking out the answers for yourself."

"You mean there's more to it than just the gospel and how to live life?"

Peter chuckled. "That's just the beginning, Matt. The gospel is what saves you, but then it's about a relationship with your Savior. That's the ultimate goal. And that's really the best part because it's what we were created to do."

***

"Honey!" Karen called up the stairs. "Dinner's ready!"

"Okay, Mom! On our way!"

Lindsey helped Kevin out of bed. He pulled her close and kissed her. That made her happy. For three days in a row, Lindsey spent her afternoons with her boyfriend in her arms and tried to regain the missing piece to their relationship. She was tentative about intimacy ever since he'd expressed his feelings the other day. She didn't know when to touch him or when to get close anymore. At least he didn't completely shut her out. For now, she'd just follow his lead and hopefully things would snap back when he was feeling better. Once he was on his feet, he could move around without help, but Lindsey held his arm and guided him. She just wanted contact.

They devoured the lasagna in record time. Kevin and his step-father, Jeff, always demolished Karen's lasagna, so the scene was nothing new. She and Lindsey exchanged amused glances throughout the meal.

"Maybe you guys should come up for air," Karen said.

"Can't." Jeff shook his head, gesturing to Kevin. "He'll eat it all."

Kevin shrugged. "I need my strength if I'm gonna get better."

"Well, I'm just glad you have an appetite tonight." Karen laughed. She looked at Lindsey. "He hasn't eaten much since the surgery."

"It's that stupid medicine," Kevin said. "That's another reason not to take it."

Before Karen could retort, the phone rang. She sighed. "Here we go again," she said. "People won't stop calling for you, Kev. They want interviews and photographs…" She picked up the phone. "Hello?" Within a few seconds, her expression changed. She glanced at Kevin and then at Jeff. "Yes, I'll accept the charges."

After a few seconds of waiting, she responded, "Duncan, hello."

Lindsey felt Kevin's mood shift. She turned to him and saw his emerald eyes staring daggers at the phone in his mother's hand. It was amazing what those eyes revealed. One moment they could be filled with mischief and she just wanted to be around for the fun. The next moment they looked at her with such passion she felt like the sexiest girl in the world. When he played football, they were so intense; she often worried about the opposing players. Now, she saw something different in his eyes, something she had never seen before. Hatred.

Lindsey put her hand on Kevin's and gave him a quizzical look. He never took his eyes off the phone.

"It's my father," he said through clenched teeth.

Lindsey nodded. Kevin never talked about his dad. She knew he was jail for almost killing someone while driving drunk, but that was about it. Kevin never brought him up and Lindsey hadn't asked about him in a long while.

Karen explained some of the details of Kevin's injuries and what he had in store for him over the coming weeks. She glanced at Kevin a few times, raising her eyebrows. Kevin just shook his head every time, his eyes never changing and never moving from the phone. Lindsey ran a hand over his back and tried to keep him calm.

"Okay," Karen said into the mouthpiece. "Hold on and I'll get him." She put her hand over the mouthpiece and held the phone out for Kevin. "Talk to your father, Kevin."

"I have nothing to say to him."

"Kevin," his mother replied. "The man's in jail and hasn't seen his only son in years. He just wants to congratulate you and tell you how proud he is. Now, talk to him for a minute."

Kevin's voice rose. It was a slight increase in volume, but it conveyed his message. "I said I have nothing to say to him. Tell him to stay out of my life."

"Kevin," Karen Timmons held out the phone. "If you want to tell him that, then tell him yourself. I'm not your messenger."

Kevin shook his head, but got up and circled the table. "You're right." He took the phone from his mother's hand and, without so much as a second's hesitation, pressed the "END" button. He placed the phone in the charger and went out the back door, across the driveway, and into his wood shop, leaving everyone in the kitchen shaking their heads.

Chapter 8

Kevin threw some scrap wood into the woodstove, on top of some wadded up newspaper, and lit a fire. After several moments, the wood began to catch and Kevin stood back and watched the flames grow. He shivered. He'd walked out of the house, burning with rage, but his anger wasn't enough to keep him warm on a freezing January evening. His shop was always a refuge, but he needed to get some heat going. He was dressed in a pair of Kendall High sweat pants and a tank top Lindsey helped him put on before going down for dinner. Other than that, all he had on was a pair of flip-flops. With his good hand, he dragged a large piece of a log over in front of the fireplace and sat on it. He'd been saving it for a large vase he intended to make over the winter, but for now, it was perfect for sitting in front of a fire.

He knew his mother didn't approve of the attitude he took toward his father. He didn't understand her. The man had done nothing to earn even a moment's thought from her, yet she still cared about his relationship with Kevin. As far as Kevin was concerned, Duncan Sinclaire was not his father. He didn't care what it said on his birth certificate or what DNA could prove. Fatherhood was about more than biology. Jumping into bed with a girl might be all it took to create a child, but it didn't make a guy a father.

What kind of man cheats on his wife? Kevin's attitude toward unfaithful people bordered on the psychotic. He knew he had an irrational hatred for infidelity, but he couldn't help it. The mere thought of a woman sitting home in tears while her man was out with another woman drove Kevin to violent rage. It was one reason he had thought Lindsey was nuts when she was so concerned he would cheat on her once he got popular. Had she considered for a moment his disdain for guys like that, she'd be able to rest easier and they wouldn't have rushed their relationship so much. As his thoughts bounced back and forth between his girlfriend and his father, Kevin wondered what he was most upset about, his relationship with Lindsey, or his father thinking he could just call and talk to him whenever he wanted.

The door opening behind him interrupted his thoughts. He glanced back as Lindsey closed it and came toward him. He refocused his eyes on the fire.

"I don't feel like talking about it," he said.

Lindsey nodded to the back of his head. What could she say? She stepped close, behind him as he sat, staring at the flames, absorbing their warmth. She placed her hands on his shoulders. She wanted him to know she cared, to know she was there for him. The truth was, she couldn't keep her hands off him. She loved the way he felt beneath her fingertips. Her heart raced as she massaged his neck, and raced even faster when he lowered his head, granting her fingers full access. Lindsey breathed a soft sigh of relief.

After several minutes, she took a break to rest her hands. She sat on a stool, still behind him, and stared at the love of her life. Though she couldn't blame him for his anger toward his father, something continued to nag at her as she considered her own family. She knew the best thing to do would be to sit in silence and let Kevin work through his anger, but Lindsey wasn't built that way. She couldn't—wouldn't—remain quiet when she had an opinion. Plus, he was the one who wanted more and deeper communication, wasn't he?

"I told you, my dad left us a few years ago." She saw his head nod once. "But I don't think we ever talked about why he left."

Kevin remained silent. He wasn't ignoring her; he was waiting. Kevin was great to talk to because he didn't interrupt a person with unnecessary comments to fill brief moments of silence. If he had something to say, he'd say it. Otherwise, he was content to listen, and even though his eyes were on the flames and his back to her, Lindsey knew she had his full attention.

"The truth is my mom threw him out, which is kind of a stretch to say, because the reality was he was never home." She looked at her hands. It was depressing. "My dad really only cares about one thing…his work. He's a brilliant scientist, but has no family skills to speak of. It's like any love or passion he has inside him can only be directed at his projects, his classes, all that."

Lindsey paused and bit her lip as she studied Kevin's posture. His head was tilted to one side, just enough to be obvious. He was waiting for her to continue. She could never claim her boyfriend wasn't interested in what she had to say. He soaked up every word. If he were looking at her, his bright green eyes would be boring into her soul, embracing her every emotion.

"For the longest time, we'd have no idea when he was coming home, if at all. He wouldn't call, wouldn't answer, wouldn't respond, not even to an email. One day, my mother had enough. I remember she cried her eyes out, called us together, and told us Daddy would no longer be living with us. I remember Tracey and me laughing at that because we hadn't seen or heard from him in a little over a month." Lindsey chuckled in wry remembrance.

She paused for a moment and moved closer to the fire, kneeling in front of Kevin and putting her hands out to warm them.

"Anyway," she said, staring into the flames. "Nothing really changed as a result. He was never around before they split, and he wasn't around after. He'd left us long before Mom made her decision. Sometimes we see him on holidays, or once in a while a birthday. Mom texted me a while ago that there was a card in the mail addressed to us in his handwriting. There's probably a pretty big check in there for us to split. He didn't bother to come down or even call on Christmas. We tried to call him, but had to leave a voicemail."

"That sucks," Kevin said. "I'm sorry. You deserve better than that…Tracey too."

"Tracey pretty much hates him," Lindsey said. "I mean, she doesn't hate him really, but she won't allow herself anymore disappointment, so she doesn't even expect him to be a part of her life. She hasn't even told him the news."

"Would he respond if she told him?"

"I don't know." Lindsey shrugged. "Probably not. I mean, he might come down and see her, but that'd be about it. Whatever his response, it wouldn't last."

Kevin shook his head. "What's wrong with these people?"

Lindsey was silent for a few minutes. "Want to know something?"

Kevin looked at her and nodded.

She let out a short sniffle. "Even if he only came once or twice, I'd still take it. I miss him so much. I wish he were here so I could tell him all about my boyfriend, Emily, everything that's happened to me since school started."

Kevin nodded. "I get that."

Lindsey turned and watched his eyes. He wasn't getting it. "But you don't feel that way about *your* dad."

All of a sudden, Kevin's eyes shimmered with understanding. He sighed and shook his head. "So the point of that story was really to get me to talk about my dad?"

"I'm just trying to understand, Kevin. Your attitude doesn't make any sense."

"It doesn't *have* to make sense to you!" he shouted. "You want to know about my dad? He's a scumbag, Lindsey. From the moment I was born, he's done nothing but cheat on my mom. He cheated on her while she was pregnant, after she gave birth to me, and the whole time she was raising me…all by herself, because that cheating jerk would rather go get laid than be at home with his family. When she finally had enough and kicked his lying, cheating butt out, he tried to buy me off with expensive gifts and crap like that. He'd go out and get the latest video game system and show up on my birthday with it and five hundred dollars' worth of games, thinking his gift would outshine hers."

He shook his head. "Like I'd forget that he ripped my mother's heart to shreds a thousand times. Like I'd forget that she was the one who really loved me. And all those gifts? I never asked for any of them. I don't play video games. Anyone who knows me knows I'm not into that stuff and never have been. How can a man not know anything about his *only* kid?"

Lindsey was stunned into silence. Kevin's emotions rarely bubbled to the surface. Usually he was a portrait of calm and control. Even his anger was controlled, like on the football field or when someone picked a fight with him. But when it came to his father, he was a different person. His green eyes darkened, almost black. He stared with rage in his eyes.

"Anyway," he said, after a moment. "I have no interest in speaking to the man…ever."

"Even if he's sorry and wants to know you for real?" Lindsey asked.

"Of course he feels sorry, Lindz. He's been in jail for a long time. What else can he do but sit there and think about all the crap he's done? Sure, he wants to know me. In fact, he's probably getting out sometime soon and will try to see me. That won't go well, I promise you."

"He's still your father, Kev. I'd give anything for my dad to pay even a little attention to me."

"Well," Kevin replied. "You *like* your dad. I hate mine. Your dad doesn't sound like a bad guy. He's just got his priorities screwed up and needs to make some changes. My dad's a piece of crap who deserves to be beaten with a baseball bat."

"You know," Lindsey said, standing up. "I've never seen you like this."

"Like what?"

"Irrational." She stretched and rubbed her knees. "This isn't you, Kevin. This kind of uncontrolled…what*ever*…it's not you. It's beneath you."

Kevin looked at her, his eyes blazing. "You know what, Lindsey? You don't know what you're talking about. You don't know me. If you knew me, all this crap we've been going through for the past six months would never have happened. So stop pretending you have some kind of insight into my psyche, okay? Just stay out of it and mind your own business."

Lindsey felt an inch tall. He had never spoken to her like that in the entire time they'd been together. Tears filled her eyes. Her heart pounded in her chest and she felt it shatter with every pulse. The truth had finally come out; his true feelings regarding their relationship were now in the open. He had been trying to tell her gently for weeks, maybe even months. Now, there was no doubt and no illusion left for her.

She gathered her thoughts, but decided against any response. She was about to burst into tears anyway. She turned to leave.

"I'll wait inside for my mom," she said, and headed out the door.

Twenty seconds after the door closed behind her, Kevin's response finally reached his lips. "Yeah, Lindz," he mumbled. "You do that."

***

"I think you're overreacting."

"I'm not overreacting, Emily." Lindsey paced the floor in Emily's living room. It was Saturday night and they had a girls' night all planned. Now that the Kendall Cobras' season was over, there would be fewer parties and life would slow down a bit. Lindsey and Emily hadn't seen much of each other since Emily broke up with Tony and withdrew from the social circus of Kendall High. It was annoying. Lindsey had finally embraced the whole scene, and *poof*, they were no longer the dynamic duo at parties. Lindsey had been on her own in recent weeks. "I haven't even told you the worst part yet."

"Uh oh."

"Yeah," Lindsey agreed. "We're sitting at dinner and everyone's in a great mood, joking and laughing. Then the phone rings and it's Kevin's dad, calling from jail."

"Jail? He got arrested?"

Lindsey shook her head. "No. He's *in* jail. He has been for like five or six years. He almost killed a guy driving drunk."

Emily shook her head in stunned silence. "I never knew that."

"He doesn't talk about it," Lindsey said. She told Emily about the scene at dinner. Emily's eyes became glassy. Lindsey frowned, but had too much on her own mind to ask what the strange look was all about. Emily seemed to snap out of it as Lindsey continued. "The man just wants to say hi and congratulate his son. Isn't that sad?"

Emily gave her an absent bob of the head.

"Next thing you know, Kevin takes the phone and hangs up on the guy. Then he just goes out into his wood shop."

"Did you talk to him about it?" Emily asked.

"I tried, but everything came out wrong." Lindsey shook her head. "I was so upset, I think I went overboard and told him how awful it was to reject your father when some of us have fathers who couldn't care less about them and never come around even though they're walking around, free as a bird."

Emily gritted her teeth and Lindsey realized the conversation was hitting a little close to home for her best friend. She wondered if Emily's reaction would have been similar to her own had she been in the woodshop with Kevin instead of Lindsey.

"So you guys had a little fight." Emily shrugged. "Trust me, he'll get over it. Kevin's not that shallow."

"That's just it," Lindsey groaned. "He thinks *I'm* shallow."

"*You're* shallow? Why?"

Lindsey shook her head. She was pretty heated herself. Kevin had implied some pretty harsh things. "He said he misses the old Lindsey." Her arms began to come up when she said "old Lindsey," but she caught herself and dropped them back to her sides.

Emily didn't miss it. "Oh, my God!" she giggled. "You were about to make quote marks in the air!"

"No, I wasn't," Lindsey said.

"Yes, you were," Emily said, pointing her finger at Lindsey. "Don't even try it."

"Will you stop being stupid and tell me what to do?"

"About what?" Emily shrugged. "Lindsey, the guy is in love with you. He's in love with the *real* you, the *real* Lindsey, the one he started this school year with. Just be yourself. Stop trying to be some sex goddess."

Lindsey flopped down on the love seat across from Emily and closed her eyes.

Emily shook her head, chuckling. "You know…this doesn't have to be so complicated."

"Well then…" Lindsey spread her arms in frustration. "What do I do?" Lindsey shook her head. "God forbid a girl shows a little confidence and enjoys sex…"

Emily shrugged. "Good guys like good girls. And before you object, it doesn't mean no sex. It just means that there has to be more than that…a lot more. Shouldn't sex be special, Lindz?"

Lindsey shook her head. "I don't know. Who cares? Was it all that special for *you?*"

"Not really, and that's my point," Emily replied. "For me it was always about the moment, having fun right then and there. By the time I realized how special it *could* be and *should* be, I had a reputation that kept me from having the kind of relationship I really wanted."

Lindsey opened her eyes and sighed at the lingering sadness in her best friend's expression. Emily was the *real* sex goddess of Kendall High, but she lost the love of her life to Tracey, Lindsey's sister. The experience changed Emily; there was a spark missing where once there was fire. There was seriousness where once there had been seductiveness. Lindsey missed the super-sexy Emily. Kevin wanted the old Lindsey? Well, Lindsey wanted the old Emily.

"You just have to get back out there," Lindsey said, nodding. "There are a lot of really hot guys in Kendall High."

Emily shook her head. "I don't think so. I'm taking a break. I'm going to focus on school and being your best friend. That's all. No guys for a while."

"Wow," Lindsey retorted. "That sounds like loads of fun."

Emily lay back on the couch. "I don't think my heart can take any more pain right now."

Lindsey sighed. "Maybe you have the right idea. Maybe we're both better off single."

Emily rolled her eyes. "You and Kevin will fix things."

"You didn't hear him last night, Em." Lindsey closed her eyes and tried not to cry. "He really told me what he thought of me…of us."

Emily got up and sat on the love seat so Lindsey could lie on her lap. "It's okay, sweetie. We'll fix it. I promise."

Lindsey sighed and sniffled. She had no doubt Emily could help her fix it. At this point, the question was, did she really want it fixed?

Chapter 9

Kevin was in his room resting when his mother walked in. The whole mess with his father and then the ensuing fight with Lindsey caused a mood to settle over Kevin making him all but unapproachable for the past few days. Karen Timmons knew better than to try to talk to him when he was in one of his moods, but enough was enough. Kevin needed to deal with his feelings for his father. Duncan Sinclaire would be out of prison soon and wanted to reconnect with his son. Karen was determined to stay out of it; she wouldn't be the one to tell Duncan his son didn't want to talk to him. Kevin would have to do his dirty work himself. And while he was at it, he could think about apologizing to his girlfriend for treating her like dirt.

"Hey, kiddo," she said, sitting on the side of his bed and inspecting his shoulder. "How you feeling?"

"Not too bad. The swelling's starting to go down a little."

"Mmmhmm." Karen looked at the incision. "This looks pretty good. Not infected, at least. The stitches come out in a few days, right?"

"Yeah," Kevin said with a chuckle. "Just in time for another surgery."

Karen raised her eyebrows. "No complaints. This was *your* choice."

"I know, I know."

Karen changed the subject. "Have you been doing your school work?"

Kevin nodded. "All caught up. I just need to get it to the school. Maybe one of the guys can swing by."

"Or Lindsey," his mother said with a pointed expression.

His eyes shifted away from her. "Right," he said, gazing at the wall. "Lindsey."

Karen put her hand on his knee. "Kevin, you should call her."

"It's not like she's been calling *me*."

Karen sniffed. "Part of being the man in a relationship is putting the girl first, swallowing your pride, suckin' it up…how do you kids say it these days, anyway?"

Kevin chuckled. "Are you trying to tell me to man up?"

Karen raised her eyebrows. "*Man* up?" She nodded. "I like that. That's good. Now, *man up*, and call Lindsey."

Kevin gave her a wry smile and shook his head. "Sorry, Mom. It's not about pride or anything like that. It's more about whether we really want to be together at this point."

"Really?" Karen frowned. "Everything seemed fine the other night until your father called." She looked at him. "Anything you want to talk about?"

Kevin shook his head. "It's not really something you talk to your mom about."

Karen nodded. She wondered if Kevin thought she was stupid, but it really didn't matter. He was brilliant, and at his age, high intelligence came with an unusual amount of arrogance. What he didn't realize was experience counted. Kids always thought their parents were in the dark.

"Why not, sweetie?" she said. "Because you two are having sex and things are getting complicated?"

She had to give him credit. He didn't react…much. Kevin had extraordinary control over his emotions, but she saw the slight flicker in his eyes. She never took her eyes off his. Kevin's eyes were the key.

Karen stared at him. "Don't play dumb with me, Kevin. I don't need to be in the room with you guys to know what's going on.

All I need is to see the look in her eyes when you're with her. It's hard for a girl to disguise it when her innocence is gone. They never look at boys the same way again."

Kevin shook his head. He thought for a second about denying it. Deny. Deny. Deny. That's what the accused was supposed to do, right? But what was the point? If his mom thought he was having sex, she would do whatever she was going to do whether he admitted it or not.

"Okay, fine, Mom. You got me. Lindsey and I had sex and now everything has changed and I can't stand it."

Karen closed her eyes and fought back the tears. *Lord, what kind of a parent am I?* She dismissed the thought as soon as it entered her mind. There would be plenty of time for self-examination later. She took a deep breath.

"Tell me."

"Mom," Kevin said. "The last thing a guy wants to do is talk to his mother about sex."

"Well," Karen said. "You're gonna have to…"

At that moment, the house phone rang. It was merciful in its timing, making Kevin feel as though maybe there really was a supernatural being in his corner. Karen picked up the extension in Kevin's room.

"Hello? Yes, this is she…really? He's doing well. He's still pretty banged up, but he'll make it, I think. Okay…" Her eyes widened. "Wow! I think…actually, I *know* he'd be *very* interested. He's right here if you want to ask him yourself."

She handed the phone off to Kevin. "You're not gonna believe this. His name is Andrew Michaelson…from *Princeton*!"

Kevin frowned, but took the phone. "Hello?"

"Mr. Sinclaire, I am Dr. Andrew Michaelson, and I run the physics department at Princeton University. Are you familiar with our institution, son?"

Kevin almost burst into laughter. "Am I familiar with the number one university in the world for the physical sciences? It rings a bell."

Dr. Michaelson laughed on the other end of the phone. "Okay, I'll get right to the point. Believe it or not, we know about you up here. I'm reviewing your academic accomplishments…a perfect sixteen hundred on your SATs at age twelve. I also caught the state championship game on TV. Congratulations. That was the gutsiest thing I've ever seen."

"Thank you, sir."

"According to my sources, you have an interest in Princeton."

"Yes, sir. It's my first choice."

"That's great to hear, Kevin." Dr. Michaelson paused. "I wonder if you'd indulge me. I have a proposition I'd like to make to you. Do you think you'd be interested in coming up here tomorrow and talking to me?"

Kevin agreed to meet with Dr. Michaelson and handed the phone back to his mother. Karen spent the next several minutes discussing what the meeting would entail and finally hung up. She turned to Kevin and let out an excited squeal.

"Oh, my Lord in Heaven!" she cried. "My son's going to *Princeton*!"

"Just for a visit," Kevin said. "I'm pretty sure they make you apply and get accepted these days."

"Oh, man, this is so exciting." Karen looked at Kevin. "Don't think I've forgotten about our talk, Bub. Rather than ruin my mood today, I'm going to put it on hold until after the meeting tomorrow."

She was about to leave the room, but then stopped at the door. "Hey," she said. "Doesn't Lindsey's father teach at Princeton?"

Kevin nodded. "Why?"

She thought for a moment. "Call her. See if she wants to go up with us. I'll talk to Abby and make sure it's okay if Lindsey skips school for a day."

"Mom, why?"

"Because she's your girlfriend and you're going to be on the same campus as her father. Ever think she might want to see him? How will she feel if you go up there and don't even mention it to her?"

***

When they pulled up in front of the Overton house, Kevin felt a tinge of nerves. He and Lindsey hadn't spoken since their argument over the weekend. When he called and invited her to make the drive to Princeton, she sounded excited for the opportunity to see her father, though Kevin sensed the invitation didn't erase their problems. The phone call was quick and to the point. They didn't talk about much. Now, Kevin wished he'd at least made the effort to ease the tension between the two of them. It would be an uncomfortable drive with his mother sitting in the front if they weren't at least on speaking terms.

Kevin hopped out and went to the door. He wanted to speak to Lindsey alone before getting into the car with his mother. When the door opened, Mrs. Overton was standing at the threshold with a smile on her face.

"Hello, Kevin," she said, waving to Karen. "Come in. Lindsey's just about ready."

Kevin entered the Overton home and Abby closed the door. He trudged up the stairs and knocked on Lindsey's door. He couldn't believe how nervous he was. How many times had he run up those steps and knocked? He was never anxious before.

"Lindz?" he said softly, pushing the door open.

She sat cross-legged on her bed. "Hey," she said, her eyes trained right on his, conveying a confidence he knew wasn't there.

"Hey," he responded. "I just wanted to see you before we leave. Make sure everything's okay between us."

She folded her arms across her chest. "*Is* everything okay between us?"

He looked at the floor. "I guess not."

"How could it be?" she said. "You got mad and shut me out of your life."

Kevin could have mentioned the main problem they had was a lack of any substantial conversation due to Lindsey's recent obsession with sex. He also could have pointed out that the phone worked both ways. She hadn't called him either and it was Lindsey who started the argument the other night. But he didn't. Instead, he did exactly what his mother advised. He manned up.

"I'm sorry," he said. "I got mad and took it out on you. You didn't deserve it."

Lindsey's eyes softened and she smiled. "Apology accepted."

The trip to the Princeton Campus took nearly two hours. Karen encouraged Lindsey to establish communication with her absentee father. During their conversation, Lindsey's eyes teared up. The emotional effect of not having her father in her life overtook her. Kevin, sitting next to her in silence, reached over and took her hand in his. Lindsey cheered up and felt a weight lift. Her eyes found his in a moment of unspoken love. It was the kind of look they'd shared a million times in the past, though not all that often in recent weeks.

He still loves me, she thought. *I wonder if love is enough…*

They found the right building and made their way to a large outer office where a secretary as ancient as the buildings on the campus, greeted them before they could say a word. "Kevin Sinclaire?" she asked, looking right at Kevin.

"Yes, Ma'am."

She nodded with a smile, strode to a large, ornate wooden door, and poked her head in, announcing the visitors. Kevin's eyes were drawn to the door. It was vintage, handmade, probably by a master craftsman, considering the detailed carvings. He wished he could take some time to inspect it in greater detail, but Dr. Michaelson appeared in the doorway.

"Kevin!" he almost shouted, extending his hand. Dr. Michaelson was nothing like what Kevin expected. He was tall and broad-shouldered, more like a ball player than a college professor. Kevin shook his hand and turned to the ladies.

"This is my mother, Karen," he said, gesturing to his mother.

Dr. Michaelson shook her hand. "Andrew Michaelson. It's a pleasure."

"And my girlfriend, Lindsey."

"It's nice to meet you, Lindsey." He shook her hand as well. "I bet you ladies are pretty proud of this guy, aren't you? That state championship game was the most amazing thing I've ever seen in sports."

"Thank you, sir."

Karen gestured to Lindsey. "Dr. Michaelson, Lindsey's father is a professor here. Dr. Everett Overton?"

Dr. Michaelson's eyes widened. "Everett is your father?"

Lindsey nodded. She wasn't sure if she should be embarrassed or proud of her father.

"Well," he said, smiling. "It's an even bigger honor. Everett is a brilliant scientist. We're proud to have him on staff." He turned to his secretary. "Alice, would you pull up Dr. Overton's schedule for today?"

"Certainly." With deft fingers, she brought the schedule up on her computer screen. "It looks like he's just finishing up a class and then he's got ninety minutes until the next one."

"Perfect timing," Dr. Michaelson said. He went over to the large picture window. "See that building across from us? His office is on the second floor. Everyone knows who he is. Just ask for directions when you get over there."

Karen nodded. "I'll walk over with you, Lindsey." She turned to Michaelson. "Unless you need me here."

He waved a hand. "Not at all. I can show Kevin around and chat a little with him, and we can all meet up for lunch. You and I can talk a little then. Sound good?"

They all agreed and Karen and Lindsey walked together across the grass. Fortunately, it wasn't windy so the cold air was not oppressive. They took their time. Lindsey wasn't in a big hurry anyway.

"Are you nervous?" Karen asked.

Lindsey shrugged. "A little, I guess. What if he doesn't really want to see me? I mean, it's not like he's made any effort at all to see us or talk to us. Maybe it'd be better if I just take a hint, you know?"

Karen shook her head. "You shouldn't have to 'take a hint' when it comes to your parents. If he really doesn't want to see you, he ought to be man enough to look you in the eye and tell you. Though I doubt that's the case."

Lindsey shrugged. Her father clearly hadn't received the memo on being a man. He never came clean with his intentions. All he ever did was tell his family what they wanted to hear.

"Lindsey," Karen said, putting her arm around her. "Whatever happens when you talk to him, remember this: Your mother and sister both love you. Kevin loves you. I love you. You deserve your father's love, but if he won't give it, we'll all be here for you."

***

Lindsey made her way to the second floor and wandered through the hall, ignoring the looks from many of the boys. Even without putting on makeup and getting dressed up, Lindsey guessed she looked old enough to be in college. It was her figure. It overshadowed her youthful face. She could probably pull off being a college freshman. She wondered if Emily ever hung out with college guys. What would that be like?

Before she realized where she was, Lindsey stood in the doorway of his office. He was leaning over his desk, pointing to a page in a book, and finishing up a conversation with a student, so he didn't see her right away. She had time to collect her thoughts. Seconds later, the young man stepped out of the office, leaving no one between her and the professor. He didn't look up, probably assuming she was just another student stopping by to ask him about the week's assignments. She stepped into the office.

"How can I help you...?" He stopped as his eyes lifted. His mouth hung agape. He finally managed to react. "Lindsey?" he said, standing up straight.

She nodded. "It's me, Dad. How are you?"

His face continued to register his shock. "I'm fine," he said, coming out from behind his desk. He laughed, smiling with more ease. "I'm fine. How are you? What are you doing up here?"

She stood still and allowed him to hug her. It felt good to feel his arms around her again, and he seemed genuinely happy to see her, but her guard was still up.

"I'm okay," she said. "Why haven't you called?" *No sense beating around the bush...*

He stepped back with a quizzical expression. "Well, I've been pretty busy. I have two projects I'm heading up, and my class schedule, grading papers, speaking engagements, writing papers for publication. It's a lot of work. It takes a lot of time." He gripped her shoulders and smiled. "But I'm glad you're here. It's great to see you. I've missed you. Where's Tracey? Is she here too?"

Lindsey shook her head. "Tracey didn't come. I came up here with my boyfriend and his mother."

"Oh, that's nice." The professor nodded. "Well, tell her I said hello."

"Why can't you call her and tell her yourself?" Lindsey asked.

Her father shrugged. "I always mean to," he said. "I just get caught up, and the next thing you know, it's midnight."

Was he serious? Lindsey didn't know how she ought to respond. Was it strange to expect a man in his position to call his kids once in a while? How do you talk to a person who doesn't seem to exist on the same plane as everyone else?

"Sit down. Sit down," he urged. "Tell me what's been going on. How is high school?"

Lindsey sat and told him all about Emily and how the two of them had become such close friends. He asked questions and listened as she responded. The genuineness of the moment felt so surreal to Lindsey, she began to wonder if she was dreaming. This was the father she wanted, interested and caring. *Then why the heck doesn't he ever call?* The whole thing was maddening, but Lindsey was determined to at least enjoy the little time she had with him.

"You mentioned a boyfriend?" he said.

"Kevin," Lindsey said. "I've been with him for about nine or ten months now. He's meeting with Dr. Michaelson right now. I tagged along with him. That's why I'm here."

"Wait," Dr. Overton said. "You're dating Kevin *Sinclaire?*"

"Yeah." Lindsey nodded. "You know who he is?"

"Are you kidding?" Her father chuckled. "Michaelson can't stop talking about him. The kid's a genius. He played in that amazing state championship football game. I couldn't believe what I was watching."

Lindsey's eyes widened. "You *saw* that?"

"Sure! My home town school was playing for the title. Of course I watched."

Lindsey couldn't believe her ears. He had time to watch a football game but no time to call his children? One second he seemed perfectly normal and eager to know all about her, and the next he was a complete flake who didn't even relate to how his girls felt. How could he act like everything was normal and acceptable? He didn't seem to see himself for what he was. He seemed to think his explanations were reasonable and acceptable. They weren't.

He went on about Kevin for several moments, expressing his admiration for his abilities as well as his mind. He was as eager as Michaelson to get Kevin up to Princeton as soon as possible. Is that what the whole trip was about? Were they going to try to get Kevin to skip out on high school and come to college next year? If so, they would be sorely disappointed. What Kevin cared most about was playing football. Just watching him play in the championship should have told them that. Kevin wouldn't give up immortality for college. Or would he?

"Are you okay, Lindsey?" Her father looked at her with a furrowed brow.

She shook her head. "I'm sorry, what was the question?"

"I was asking about lunch. Are you hungry?"

"Yeah, I guess so."

"Great." He grabbed his cell phone and tapped the screen before holding it up to his ear. After a moment, someone picked up on the other end. "Allan?" her father said. "Could you take my next class? My daughter's here and we're going to lunch. Thanks."

Lunch was more of the same surreal conversation. Lindsey realized she wasn't going to get anywhere trying to steer him into an understanding of how she and Tracey felt about his absence. She decided to take a more direct approach.

"Dad," she said. "We miss you." She looked him in the eye. "Tracey and I both miss you and we want you to start making time to see us."

He looked at her. "It's just that I don't know how I can. I have so much going on..."

She shook her head. "You just picked up the phone and told someone to teach one of your classes. You watched the championship game a few weeks ago. That game was double the normal length of a game. It seems like you can make time for anything you *want* to make time for. I'm just asking you to make some time for your daughters who miss you. You didn't even call on Christmas."

He looked down. "Look, Lindsey. I'm sorry I'm not the best father, but my work is important. Sometimes, we all have to make sacrifices to do what we were born to do."

Lindsey nodded. "Tracey and I aren't making any sacrifices. A sacrifice is something you do willingly. We haven't been given a choice. Instead, we're being cheated out of a parent."

"Lindsey…"

"No," she said. "Don't bother. I'm finished begging you for your time. I came up here to see you and ask for just a little bit of your time, but your work is too precious…too vital to mankind. Who do you think you are? The world can't do without you for a few hours while you take your daughters to dinner or open up Christmas presents?"

He started to speak, but Lindsey's emotions poured out. "No, that's not the problem. The problem is you just don't care about us and you never did. But that's okay. There are people who *do* care about me, so don't worry. Tracey too. She's got a boyfriend who loves her and wants to take care of her…*and* her baby."

He looked up, his eyes wide in stunned disbelief. Lindsey put her hand to her mouth in mock surprise. "Oh, my!" she said. "Did I just say that? No worries, Dad. No one's asking you for a thing. Notice nobody bothered to mention it to you before now. She's almost five months along now, not that you care. She thought about having an abortion, which you'd probably support, being a heartless scientist with no regard for his family, but she decided against it. Know why? This is gonna make you laugh. The *father* stepped up! Isn't that a riot? The father actually stepped up and told her how much he loved her and has been by her side *every day* since, and will marry her someday."

She stopped her tirade and took a breath, staring daggers at her father, who sat speechless. She looked around the room. Some people were trying not to stare at her. She didn't realize she had raised her voice so much. "Anyway," she said in a lower tone, as she stood up. "That's what I came to tell you." She pushed her chair in. "Thanks for lunch, Dad. Have a nice life."

She began to walk away when another thought occurred to her. She turned back. "Oh yeah, I forgot to mention. Tracey's a Christian now too. Bye."

Chapter 10

"Wow." Vivian shook her head. "This is a lot of information."

Emily nodded. "I know. All I really wanted was the address, but reading all of this makes me feel like I kind of know him, you know?"

Vivian blew out a long breath. She came right over after school at Emily's request. They organized and read through all the documents Jarrick had provided. He found everything, from Robert Armand's college transcripts, to his record as a public defender, all the way up to his current job as assistant county prosecutor. Emily had plenty of information about him now, assuming they had the right Robert Armand.

"Whoa!" Vivian said, holding up a 5x7 photo. "Did you see this picture?"

Emily nodded. "Yeah, I spent an hour staring at it last night."

"He's hot," Vivian said. Then she winced. "Sorry, Em. That was weird. He's your dad."

Emily giggled. "Don't worry about it. I had the same thought myself when I first saw it."

Vivian laughed. "I guess I shouldn't be surprised. A gorgeous mom, a gorgeous dad, and you were the result."

"If it's the right guy," Emily said, taking the picture. "Do you think I look like him at all?"

Vivian held the picture next to Emily's face. "Yeah, I can see it. Same nose. Same forehead. You could definitely be his daughter." She looked at the papers spread out on Emily's bed. "Look, it's gotta be the right guy. Everything matches up."

Emily nodded, breathless. "I know, but there's only one way to know for sure."

Vivian looked at her. "Are you ready for that, Em? You need to be ready, not just for a happy reunion, but for what*ever* might happen."

Emily nodded and sighed. "I know. Maybe he doesn't want to know me. But at least then I'll know, and I can live with it even if he hurts me."

They waited until after dusk, hoping Robert Armand's schedule brought him home at a reasonable time each evening. Vivian drove in silence while Emily sat, fidgeting in the passenger seat with her leg bouncing up and down. She didn't know whether to be excited, anxious, or scared.

"Well," Vivian said, turning onto a side street in one of the newer areas of town. It was an area where the houses were nice, but too close to one another, making everything seem squished together a little too much. Vivian pulled to the side of the road and put the car in park. She turned to Emily.

"It's right across the street," she said.

Emily nodded and gulped. Her heart raced as she surveyed her destination. Now that they were there, she wasn't sure she could make it to the front door. Vivian placed her hand on Emily's.

"It's okay, Em. Just take your time."

Emily nodded. She wished Lindsey was there. She would make some smart-aleck comment about being a sissy girl or something, and Emily would laugh, but it would calm her down and give her confidence. With Lindsey's recent disappointment concerning her own father, Emily didn't want to involve her in another potential disaster. Lindsey didn't need to feel Emily's pain if things went south, and if things went well, Lindsey might feel even more depressed about her own father. Emily would tell her all about it later.

After several more minutes and countless deep breaths, Emily pulled down the visor and checked her appearance in the mirror one last time. She turned to Vivian.

"Okay," she said. "It's now or never. Wish me luck."

"Luck." Vivian smiled as Emily opened the door and got out into the cold night air.

As she approached the front door, Emily's throat tightened. Her heart thudded like a hammer in her chest and her mouth was like cotton. She wondered if what she felt was anything like what boys went through when asking a girl out. If so, she was glad she wasn't a boy. She shook her head and wondered where that idiotic thought came from.

When she reached the front porch, Emily rang the doorbell. She did it before she could think twice about it and regretted not taking a moment to compose herself. She stood up straight and tried not to look too petrified. She heard footsteps and hoped it wasn't the wife. She hadn't considered that possibility. What would she say if a woman opened the door?

She heard the lock click open from the inside and then the door opened. After sixteen years, Emily stood face to face with her father for the first time. At least she *thought* it was her father. She couldn't breathe. She just stared at his eyes, willing him to love her. He stared back in confusion, waiting for an explanation. She tried to speak, but words failed her.

"I'm…I mean…you're…" she stuttered.

His eyes narrowed and a glimmer of recognition came over his face. "Emily?" he asked, stunned disbelief washing over his face.

Her heart soared. It was all the confirmation she needed. He *knew*! He had never seen her before, but somehow he knew exactly who she was. But still she couldn't speak. All she could do was nod, her eyes never leaving his.

He didn't move toward her. He stood rigidly in the doorway. "Is your mother okay?" he asked.

Emily nodded.

"Does she know you're here?"

She shook her head. Her thoughts were a jumbled mess of emotions and she couldn't get her brain to slow down. Why didn't he reach for her? She longed to feel her father's arms around her.

Robert seemed to stiffen even more. "Emily," he said, shaking his head and looking up and down the street. "You can't be here."

What? The words didn't register right away. Emily stared back at him.

"Your mother…" he started, but clamped his jaw shut. "Look, my wife will be home soon. She doesn't know about you. This is the worst possible timing."

Emily stood frozen in shock. She felt a familiar coldness begin to surround her heart, which she knew was about to break in ways she had never imagined. She backed down the steps in stunned disbelief, somehow managing to do so without falling backward off the porch. She was on the verge of a complete breakdown, so she forced herself to turn around and run across the yard toward the street.

"Emily!" Robert called out.

She ignored him. He wasn't going to get to see her tears. She ran across the street to Vivian's car, opened the door, and got in. She didn't care that she'd ended up in the backseat.

"Go," she said, looking back across the street and seeing Robert hurrying toward them across the grass. Vivian's mouth dropped open. Emily responded by slapping the back of her seat. "*Just go!*"

Vivian put the car in gear and peeled away, leaving Robert standing at the curb, watching the car disappear around the corner.

***

Everett Overton sat, staring at a photo on his desk. He couldn't remember when it was taken, but the girl who'd stormed out of the cafeteria three hours before was not the same girl as the one in the picture. When did sweet little Lindsey turn into such a cynic? And when did she start to hate him so much? She understood how important his work was. The little girl in the picture told him she understood. She knew he worked on things the world needed. The kids he taught, mentored…they were some of the finest minds on the planet. The country…the *world*…needed them. At least, that was what he'd told himself all these years.

Now, he realized, all the things in which he'd invested so much time and energy were losing their value. Where his research led over the past several years had, bit by bit, shaken him to his core, and just as he was coming to some truly depressing realizations, his daughter showed up and added new fuel to an already out of control fire.

So now one daughter is pregnant and the other hates me. Actually…they both probably hate me at this point.

Strange as it was, the thought didn't bother him. He no longer had the capacity for those kinds of feelings. He wondered if he'd *ever* had it. At some base level, he knew there had to be something wrong with that, but it was his default emotional setting. It was what made him who he was. His detached nature is what he believed made him successful, but he wasn't so detached that the reality of Tracey's pregnancy escaped him.

"Fifteen years old and pregnant," he mumbled and shook his head. *Or was it sixteen?*

***

His thoughts were interrupted by a light knock at his open door. He glanced up to find Andrew Michaelson leaning against the doorframe. Everett lowered his eyes and returned his gaze to the photo.

"Got a minute?" Michaelson asked, coming in.

Everett gestured to the seats in front of his desk and Michaelson sat down. He nodded at the picture in Everett's fingers.

"Surprise visit stirred up some memories, did it?"

Everett looked at the picture once more and tossed it aside. "A little, I guess."

Michaelson nodded and took a deep breath. "So," he said. "Things got a little tense with your daughter? Lindsey, was it?"

Everett nodded. "A little, I suppose."

Michaelson tapped his fingers on the desk. "I understand your other daughter is pregnant."

"Tracey." Everett drew a short, annoyed breath. "Her name's Tracey. And yes, it appears so."

Michaelson's fingers continued to tap. "Are you going to go see her?"

"No." Everett shook his head slowly. "There's no point."

"Really?" Michaelson gave him a bewildered stare. "You don't think your daughter's pregnancy is worth a trip home? That seems insane."

Everett was losing his patience. "Why? What good would it do? I can't change the fact that she's pregnant. It's not like they need me. Hell, they don't even *like* me!"

***

Emily was inconsolable and Vivian knew there was nothing she could say to help her. She had no idea what happened, only that it had gone terribly wrong and whatever the guy said to her, it had been quick and not fatherly. The only thing Vivian knew was it was going to be a long night and she would need reinforcements. She pulled her phone out and called Mike.

"Hey, baby," she said when she heard his voice on the other end. "I'm not gonna make it tonight. Emily needs me…yeah, it didn't go well. I want to stay with her. I'll call you later. Love you!"

Next, she grabbed Emily's phone from the center console and scrolled through until she found what she needed. She tapped the name. The phone rang twice on the other end.

"Hey, Em," Lindsey said.

"Hey" Vivian answered back. "It's not Em, though. It's Vivian."

"Vivian? What are you doing with Emily's phone?"

"She's here with me," Vivian answered, glancing over at Emily, still weeping in uncontrollable gasps. "Listen, she needs you. Are you home?"

"Right now I am, but I'm going out in a little bit. What's the matter?"

"Change of plans, honey. We're on our way to pick you up. You're gonna need clothes for tomorrow."

"Why? What's going on? Let me talk to Emily."

Vivian shook her head. "Emily can't talk right now because she's melting down in my backs seat. Now get your things together and be ready when I pull up in six minutes." She hung up before Lindsey could say another word. She tossed Emily's phone onto the passenger seat and reached back with her heand for Emily to take. "Don't worry, Em. We'll be with you, okay?"

***

"What happened?" Lindsey demanded.

She stormed out of her house as soon as Vivian pulled to a stop. She had a black onStage duffel bag slung over her shoulder. She glared at Vivian as she hurried across the lawn and looked through the back window.

"Emily met her dad for the first time tonight," Vivian replied and gestured to the backseat. "And this was the result."

Lindsey's eyes widened. "What?" She looked into the car, and then back to Vivian. "She *found* him? He's local?"

"Yep."

Lindsey looked into the window once again. She shook her head. "Unbelievable."

She tossed her bag onto the front seat and climbed into the back with her friend. Emily looked up, and threw herself into Lindsey's arms. Her crying intensified. Lindsey wrapped her arms around her best friend. It was all she could do.

She buried her face in Emily's hair and whispered, "I'm here for you and I love you."

By the time they pulled into a parking space in front of Emily's townhouse, she was calm, yet still sobbing and sniffling, in Lindsey's arms. Inside, Lindsey guided her to the living room and continued to hold her on the couch, while Vivian got her a glass of water. Emily was silent, staring in absent despair, off into the distance. Emily's eyes were vacant, devoid of life, and Lindsey worried Emily was falling into an irrecoverable depression. What the evening needed was a little fun and laughter. Vivian had the answer.

"Hey," she said. "I'm going out for supplies. This is gonna be a girls' night in, and we're going to eat a ton of junk food and watch movies all night." She mouthed to Lindsey, *Talk to her.* Lindsey nodded.

***

When Vivian left, Lindsey pulled Emily into a seated position and knelt on the floor in front of her. She held both of Emily's hands and caressed them with her thumbs. She couldn't stand to see so much pain in her friend's eyes. It broke her heart. Hadn't Emily been through enough for one school year? How much heartbreak did one person have to suffer? Now, someone who should have provided unconditional love had hurt her as well. Thoughts of revenge floated across Lindsey's mind, but she would save that for later.

"Talk to me, Em." Lindsey's eyes never left Emily's.

Emily sighed. "There's nothing to say. I found my father and he doesn't want me."

Lindsey nodded. It was something they had in common. Her own father had blown her off with such ease she had no intention of ever making the effort again. Everett Overton rejected his family long ago. The pain never went away, but it dulled over time. The more recent rejection created a new and profound hurt because Lindsey had allowed her hopes to rise. It was a mistake, and she knew Emily had done a similar thing to herself. If they weren't two peas-in-a-pod…

"I don't know what I was thinking," Emily said, shaking her head as tears threatened to pour out once again. "It's not like he was trying to find me or know me. He was perfectly happy with his real family. He doesn't need me."

Lindsey shook her head. One thing she was not going to do was allow her friend to put any blame on herself.

"Knock that off," she said in a tone which could have and should have been less intense. "This says *nothing* about you. It's all about him. He's selfish and cruel, and you don't need that kind of man in your life, trust me. My dad's the same way. He'd rather spend all his time in a lab than see us even once a month." Lindsey shook her head, feeling a twinge of sadness despite herself. "Screw 'em," she said in a softer voice. "Screw both of them." She looked up at Emily, her eyes filling with tears of her own. "*I* love you, Em. I love you more than anything in this world. You will *never* lose me; do you understand?" Lindsey grinned. "Even when I hate you, I'll still love you."

Emily pulled Lindsey close. "You're beautiful. You know that?"

Lindsey pulled away slightly, a look of mock discomfort on her face. "Is that some kind of freaky come on? 'Cause if it is, I'm not into it."

Emily sighed and launched herself at Lindsey, tackling her to the ground. The two wrestled for several minutes, howling in laughter as the front door opened. Vivian stepped in with two bags full of groceries. She surveyed the scene with the two girls now laying side by side on the floor, out of breath and hair everywhere, but giggling up at her like children.

"Okay," she said, holding up the bags. "I have Rocky Road, Fudge Ripple, Mint Chocolate Chip, and Cookie Dough…*and* a million toppings. I say we load up and watch something on TV."

Lindsey got up and pulled Emily to her feet. "Something with shooting and explosions and stuff."

Emily nodded as she wiped the joyful tears from her face. "Absolutely."

***

While the girls ate scrambled eggs the next morning, Emily sat alone in her room, at her computer, with a blank document open on her screen. She thought about what she wanted to write for a few seconds and then began to type.

Daddy,

She quickly backspaced over that. He didn't deserve the title. She began again.

Mr. Armand,

That would send the message. As she typed, the words began to flow. It didn't take long. Her thoughts were clearer than they had been the previous night. Thank God for friends. Vivian had gone above and beyond, but Lindsey was her rock. It took her only ten minutes or so to complete the letter.

Emily read it over several times and then printed it out. She almost signed it, but then changed her mind. Pulling out a stack of heavy, high quality paper, she found a nice pen, one Kevin made for her some time ago when she pestered him for a handmade fountain pen. Emily had pretty handwriting, and had once taken up calligraphy. Though she was out of practice, she still knew how to hold a fountain pen. She copied the letter onto the heavy paper. Even without lines on the paper, her sentences were straight and written in beautiful flowing cursive. When she was finished, she waved it in the air for a few seconds to ensure the ink was dry. Rather than fold it up, she slid it into the envelope on top of the rest of the letters and cards she had made over the years and sealed it.

Chapter 11

Robert Armand returned to his office in time to see a flash of red hair disappear around the corner. He had a fleeting moment of recognition, but dismissed it with a shake of his head and entered his office. A large envelope sat prominently on his desk. He looked around. It was addressed to Robert Armand, in spectacular handwriting. There was no postage, so it hadn't come in the mail. He picked it up. It was pretty thick. He opened it and pulled out a sheaf of multi-colored papers. Some were construction paper, while others were notebook paper, but it was the letter on top which caught his eye. Like his name on the envelope, it was written in beautiful script.

Mr. Armand,

I write this letter to apologize for surprising you the way I did. Showing up on your doorstep was clearly not the best way to introduce myself, but for some reason I thought a girl coming to meet her father for the first time would be excused for such a mistake. Just know that all I wanted from you was a hug and a promise that we could get together and talk sometime.

Though you made it perfectly clear you have no interest in seeing or knowing me, I still feel the need to introduce myself, even if it is just for my own closure. My name is Emily Vasquez and I am your daughter, but you already knew that. I realize life sometimes causes us to make decisions that seem good and right at the time, but later we realize just how mistaken we were. I hoped seeing me would remind you that there was a girl out there in the world who needed you. I hoped that by coming to see you myself, it would show you that I want to know you, and I want you to know me. And, to be perfectly honest, I really hoped you would love me.

While I can't blame you for not wanting to begin a relationship with a long-lost daughter this late in her life…what am I saying? Of course, I can blame you. This is shameful. The way you've ignored me, the way you humiliated me on your doorstep, makes me wonder how my mother could have ever been with such a cruel and heartless man. All I'm saying is that you could have treated me with a little decency.

I have spent my whole life not knowing who my father was. I have asked, but never gotten a good answer. There is obviously a great deal of pain on my mother's part. I see it in her eyes whenever the subject comes up. Over the years, I have drawn you pictures, made you cards, and written you letters. Every one of them is in this envelope. Since you have no desire to know me personally, maybe you can know me through them. Writing them gave me hope that one day I would meet you and hand them to you, and we could look through them together, and I could tell you all about my life. Now, they are nothing more than a stack of wasted wishes and I can't stand to even think about them anymore.

I would burn every one of them, but I can't bring myself to do it. The truth is, they're not mine. They're yours, so I'll give them to you and let you discard them…like you did with me…twice.

Your daughter,
Emily

He sat back in his chair and closed his eyes, squeezing them shut in an effort to stave off the monster headache he knew would soon emerge. He knew his words had hurt her, but she took off so fast, he couldn't recover. The shock of seeing her on his porch and the inevitable fight he would have with his wife Janice over it caused him to react on impulse, and he had been unforgivably abrupt. But he couldn't do anything about it. He had no current contact information for Camila or Emily. He'd spent the night trying to figure out how he could contact them and how to tell his wife. They were barely on speaking terms as it was.

In the end, he just came right out and told her. It was as explosive as he'd feared, but the fight was just a rehash of their previous fights. Their marriage was in tatters and a long-lost daughter was just more fuel on the fire. When he stopped to think about it, Robert was more upset over how he'd handled Emily than he was about the fight with his wife.

"She really thinks I don't want to see her," he mumbled. He suddenly had an urgent need to find Emily, but he knew he had to first locate and speak to Camila. A thought occurred to him. He leaned out the door of his office. "Jenson!" he shouted. A young, well-built man came around the corner.

"Yes, sir?" he asked.

Robert smiled at him. "Hi, Steve. I need you to track down a number for me. It's a personal matter…"

Within a half hour, Jenson had Camila's work, home, and cell numbers. Robert figured the safest number to start with would be the cell. Less chance of getting her in trouble by calling her at work, and less chance of Emily picking up by calling her on the house phone. He dialed the cell number and waited as it rang. After several rings, a sleepy female voice answered.

"Hello?"

A wave of nostalgia hit him like a tsunami. She sounded just like she used to. "Camila?"

"Yes. This is Camila."

He took a deep breath. "Camila, it's Robert…Robert Armand."

"Robert?" she said, her voice dropping into a gentle whisper.

"I'm sorry for calling you out of nowhere like this." He paused. "Um…have you spoken to Emily since last night?"

***

She found the girls watching television, sprawled out on couches in the living room. Camila could see the sadness in her daughter's eyes the moment she walked into the room. She often doubted whether her decisions over how to handle Emily's father had been wise, but for the first time she felt real regret. She hated to see her daughter hurt. It pained her to know Emily had been hurting for so long.

"Girls," she said, entering the room. "Lindsey, would you mind if I spoke to Emily alone for a few minutes?"

When Lindsey had gone upstairs, Camila looked at her daughter, trying to convey her eternal love in her expression. Emily did her best to look normal, smiling as best she could as she returned her mother's gaze. Camila went to her and sat beside her, taking Emily's hand.

"Mija," she began. "I just had a phone call…" She hesitated, looking into Emily's eyes. The sadness was still there despite her efforts. She could never hide her feelings from her mother. "It was your father."

Emily's eyes widened. She lowered her head. "I'm so sorry, Mama."

Camila pulled her daughter into her arms. "Oh, my sweet girl. *I'm* the one who is sorry. We should have had this conversation long ago. You deserved better from me."

Emily's tears flowed. "I just wanted to meet him, Mama!" she cried. "Just to see if he cared about me at all."

"I know, Mija, and he does."

Emily pulled away and shook her head. "No, Mama. He doesn't want me. He told me I couldn't be there."

"I know." Camila nodded, pulling Emily back into her embrace. She stroked her hair like she did when Emily was a little girl. "He panicked. His marriage is in trouble and you caught him off guard, just as he was expecting his wife to come home. He just panicked, that's all."

Emily cried on her mother's shoulder. Camila squeezed her as though she could make all the pain go away by doing so. If only life were that easy.

"I want to tell you a story, Mija." Camila released Emily so that she could sit and talk. Emily wiped her tears and regained her composure.

Camila took a breath. "When I was about a year older than you, your father and I dated. It was near the end of the school year, just in time for the senior prom. He was a senior and very handsome. He was also an athlete, got good grades, and all the girls wanted to date him, but he chose me. I fell in love with him, but soon found he was not interested in a relationship. The night of the prom, he told me he wanted to see other people. When he told me this, I got so angry with him I told him I never wanted to see him again. A few weeks later, I found out I was pregnant. By then it was summer and Robert had already moved on to another girl who was going to the same college as him. In fact, they met at some freshman event over the summer."

Emily could see the pain the memories caused her mother, but she was fascinated. It was all new to her, but she could see it was opening old wounds for her mother. Camila dismissed the pain and continued.

"I finally got up the nerve to call him and tell him, but before I could tell him, he told me this other girl was pregnant and they were getting married. He sounded scared, but also happy and excited. I couldn't bring myself to tell him. He must have put two and two together, though, because a couple of weeks later he showed up. Of course, I was looking more and more pregnant every day. He got very upset with me for not telling him. He hadn't told his fiancée about me and he wanted to try to keep it all quiet and separate. I told him if he wanted to be in your life, he needed to be open and honest about it, otherwise he should just leave and forget about us." Camilla looked at the floor. "He chose to leave."

Emily shook her head. "How could he do that?"

Camila shrugged. "He was young? He was scared? He was stupid? What difference does it make? He didn't want to risk losing his fiancée, so he took the easy way out." She smiled through moistened eyes. "I do wonder though…"

"What might have happened?" Emily asked, staring at the floor, like her mother. "Me too."

Camila smiled at Emily. "I think we turned out okay, no?"

Emily put her head on her mother's shoulder. "I do. I'm so lucky you're my mama." She sighed. "I just wish he was in my life too. The other girls love their dads so much."

Camila nodded with a sigh.

"So what happened?" Emily asked. When Camila looked at her, Emily said, "With Dad. You guys had one fight and he just stayed away? That's it?"

Camila chuckled. "No, not exactly. He checked in when he heard you'd been born. Since he hadn't told his wife about you, I wouldn't let him come see you. That might have been wrong, by the way, but I couldn't let him live a double life, coming to see you in secret once in a while and then going back to his "real" family. It wouldn't be fair to you. I don't know if I was right, but it seemed right at the time. I was young too." She rubbed Emily's shoulder. "Anyway, you surprised him and he panicked. He feels awful and he would like to see you tomorrow for dinner…if you'd like to give him another chance."

Emily's eyes sparkled. "Really?" Her tears returned, but this time she was joyful, like a heavy weight was lifting. "He wants to take me out?"

Camila smiled. "Yes. Just the two of you. Your first father/daughter date. That's what my Papa used to call it when he took me out with him."

Emily leaned back on the couch. "A father/daughter date," she said, a beautiful smile taking over her face. "That sounds nice." She looked at her mother. "So, what do I have to do?"

***

"And he hasn't returned a call or text all weekend." Lindsey was in a mood alternating between hysterical anger and hysterical sadness. "What am I supposed to think, Emily?"

After seeing Kevin earlier in the week, she assumed things would get back to normal, but he remained sporadic and aloof. One minute he was holding her, telling her how much he loved her, and how important she was to him, and the next minute he was ignoring her. Then he disappeared Friday night and Lindsey hadn't heard a word from him since. Not a peep. Not a text…nothing.

"Just relax, Lindz," Emily said. "He'll call. His life is messed up right now with all the surgeries and stuff. He's probably on pain killers and foggy, and I bet he's not sleeping on his normal schedule. Who knows, Lindz…"

"Exactly!" Lindsey shouted. "Who knows? Not me! Because he never tells me anything! I'm not even his girlfriend right now. I'm just another girl trying to get his attention. This sucks."

"I'm sorry, Lindz. I wish I could hold you right now."

"No, I'm sorry for dragging you down." Lindsey breathed a long sigh. She moved on to happier topics. "Today's your first father/daughter date. You must be so psyched."

"I *am* psyched. But you come first. If you need me, just say the word and I'll be there."

"Don't even think about blowing off your father. I'll be fine. Call me later and tell me all about it. I'll be up all night pissed at my soon to be ex-boyfriend."

"Don't say that, Lindz. It will all work out. I promise. He loves you. Just think about that."

Lindsey hung up the phone and leaned back in her bed with a wistful expression. Her relationship with Kevin materialized out of thin air one day when he just made it happen. She was at first unwilling to let anyone get close. She just wanted to be left alone, but Kevin wanted to be close to her, to know her.

The next thing Lindsey knew, she was infatuated with a green-eyed genius. He never made her feel anything but perfect. He made her feel beautiful, wanted…adored, like she was the only girl on the planet. When he looked at her, the world melted away.

Now, things were different. And it was her fault. She shouldn't have rushed things with sex. Instead of bringing them even closer together, it created a chasm between them. She hated that space, but had no idea how to bridge it.

She let out a huff and shook her head as a knock came from her door.

"Lindz?" Tracey poked her head in.

"Hey," Lindsey said. "Everything okay?"

Ever since Tracey made the decision to keep her baby, Lindsey felt a change in the way the two sisters related to one another. It was a startling reversal of attitudes for her. She and Tracey had never been close, but it was all different, and Lindsey liked the change.

"Everything's fine with me," Tracey replied, sitting on the end of Lindsey's bed. She looked at her little sister with concern. "What's wrong with you?"

"What are you talking about?"

Tracey rolled her eyes. "You're angry and sad."

"Like that's anything new."

"I'm not talking about the usual Lindsey. We might not be super close but you're still my sister and I still know you better than everyone else."

Lindsey thought about that for a moment. It wasn't worth debating. "I guess."

"So?" Tracey said. "Spill. Talk to your big sister."

Lindsey didn't really want to get into it with Tracey. It was far better talking to someone who was as much a mess as she was, at least when it came to guys. Tracey had been on cloud nine ever since Matt came back into her life. Tracey was pretty much right where she wanted to be. Talking to people who had no complaints was a miserable thing to do, in Lindsey's experience.

"It's nothing," Lindsey said, trying to sound convincing. "Just a bad day."

Tracey shook her head with a smile. "Uh uh. Not buying it, Lindz." She stretched out on the bed. "I guess I can stay here all night until you cheer up."

"Get out of my room, Tracey."

"Oh, wait! I know." Tracey popped back up. "We can watch some chick flicks. I have a bunch saved. Where's your remote?"

"Tracey…"

"Hold on! I'll go make popcorn!" Tracey jumped up. "I have a bunch of different powder toppings for it."

Lindsey scrunched her forehead despite herself. "Powder toppings?"

"Yes. They're awesome. I'll bring them up."

"For popcorn?"

"Of course." Tracey started ticking them off on her fingers. "We have Butter, White Cheddar, Caramel, Taco, Pizza…"

"Pizza?" Lindsey cried. "Taco? For *popcorn?*"

"Trust me, Lindz, they're aaaaamazing!" Tracey sang the last word.

Lindsey grimaced. The night was approaching worst-case scenario proportions. "Yeah…trust a pregnant maniac about what tastes good. No thanks. Plus, I'm not watching those stupid movies with you."

"Then tell me what's going on with you."

Lindsey shrugged. It was pointless to argue. She started from the beginning, talking about how she used to feel with Kevin, when he looked at her, when he held her, when he kissed her. She told Tracey how hard it had been to watch him leave for Japan last summer and then how wonderful it was when he finally came home. But then high school began and things changed.

"What changed, Lindz?"

Lindsey took a breath. "I just didn't like all the girls trying to get with him. It felt like I'd lose him any day because these girls were willing to sleep with him."

"Oh." Tracey nodded, a knowing look coming over her face.

Lindsey raised her eyebrows and shook her head. "I spent most of the season struggling with whether or not to sleep with him."

"And what did *he* have to say about it?"

"He kept telling me how he didn't care about all that and he was in no rush."

Tracey wrinkled her forehead. "That's good, isn't it?"

"I guess." Lindsey shrugged. "These girls…I swear they literally threw themselves at him every day. They'd even tell *me* all the things they were going to do to him. It was horrible having to hear that every day."

"I bet."

"So I figured if I wanted to keep him, I'd have to sleep with him."

"Oh, Lindsey. Why would you—"

Lindsey waved her hands. "It didn't happen that way. We didn't actually do it until way later…on his birthday. I actually tried the week before, but you had just told me you were pregnant and I fell apart in his arms. We ended up just sleeping…which actually was really great, by the way."

"It always is," Tracey replied with a wistful smile.

"But ever since we did it, it seems like I've been more and more into him. You know, I always want him now. It's like a switch flipped inside me and now I can't get enough of him."

Tracey nodded. "So, what's the problem? It sounds like a fairytale so far."

Lindsey let out an exasperated sigh. "I don't know *what* the problem is exactly. He says we don't talk anymore. He misses the way we used to be." Lindsey shrugged. "I guess now I'm a slutty girl who only thinks about sex all the time."

"He *said* that?"

"Not exactly. But that's how he makes me feel."

Chapter 12

Emily looked at the clock on the wall. She had fifteen minutes before her father picked her up. Her *father!* Emily shopped for a new outfit for the occasion, courtesy of her mother. She settled on an emerald-green cocktail dress that felt amazing on her skin but was not too slinky. It was perfect for a date with Dad. *And* she found a great pair of wedge-style sandals in a color very close to the darker green trim of the dress.

She'd even gotten her hair done. She had her brown locks trimmed and had the stylist add fresh blonde highlights. As she stared at herself in the mirror, she wondered if her appearance would even matter to her father. Do dads care if their daughters are pretty? Do they worry more about the pretty ones who are popular with the boys, or do they worry more when they have a daughter who is unpopular and not as pretty?

Emily figured dads worried about their daughters no matter what. Maybe they didn't even see how pretty or not pretty their daughters were. Maybe all fathers thought their daughters were beautiful. What would Robert Armand think of *her?* Would he worry about her? Would he ask questions about her life? Maybe he'd be like the dads on TV who didn't want to know too much about the girly stuff and lived in blissful ignorance about what their daughters thought, said, and did. When the doorbell rang, her mind went blank and her heart pounded once again.

"This is it," she said to herself, taking a deep breath and a final look at her reflection in the mirror.

It's strange when a lifelong dream comes true. He greeted her at the door in an awkward, almost formal, approach, but with a warm smile. Emily had to resist the urge to leap into his arms and hug his neck. Instead, she played it cool, a lot cooler than she felt, and after he opened the car door for her, like a true gentleman, they drove in awkward silence to the restaurant. When they arrived, he turned to her and promised that their car rides in the future would not be so uncomfortable.

The *future?* That had to be a good sign. He was already talking about taking car rides together in the future. That meant he intended to know her, at least enough to get together and drive places. Emily couldn't believe how desperately she wanted that, to take a drive with her father. She didn't care where they went. They could go grocery shopping for all she cared. Daughters did that with their dads, didn't they?

"So," Robert said. He looked uncomfortable sitting across from Emily. "This is a lot more awkward than I'd hoped."

Emily forced an anxious smile and nodded. "I guess it is."

"It's my fault," he said. "I know I hurt you the other day and I pray you can forgive me for that."

"I do."

He sighed. "I was too afraid to do the right thing." He shrugged. "I took the easy way out and this is where it got me…us."

Emily nodded. She wanted to cry. She wanted to be in her father's arms. But she also needed answers. She lowered her eyes to the plate in front of her. "Did you ever think about me?"

Robert closed his eyes and struggled for control. He nodded. "All the time, in the beginning. But as time went on and your mother refused my terms, I did my best to put you out of my mind. It wasn't that I didn't care. I just didn't know what to do. Does that make any sense at all?"

Emily nodded sadly. "I guess it does." She shook her head. "Well, not really, but I don't want to talk about sad things tonight."

"Really?" he asked in surprise. "I assumed you'd want answers. I mean, you deserve them."

"I know," she said. "And I do, but can't we just talk about all that later and have a pleasant, happy conversation tonight?"

He smiled. "I think I can manage that." Relief flooded his face. Robert sipped his diet soda as he looked at his daughter over the rim of the glass. He couldn't help but smile.

"You look just like your mother," he said.

"But I have your eyes," Emily said. "I noticed that when I saw your picture."

"What picture was that?"

"Um…I don't really know when it was taken. We just found it online."

"Online?" Robert's forehead crinkled. "Where online?"

Emily realized she might have made a mistake. She wasn't about to tell him about her hacker friend from school. What Jarrick had done was still illegal and Emily couldn't allow him to get in trouble on her account.

"Just online," she said. "I don't know where exactly." It wasn't a lie. She had no idea where Jarrick found the information.

Robert leaned forward. "You know I make a living getting information out of people, right? Is there something you're not telling me?"

She sighed. "Yes, but please don't make me tell you the truth."

"Okay," he replied with a suspicious expression. He pursed his lips and crinkled his forehead. "You did what you had to do. Why don't we just leave it at that?"

Emily blushed and breathed a sigh of relief. "Thank you."

He gave her a stern nod but she saw the twinkle in his eyes. He shook his head with a chuckle. "But keep it legal from now on, huh? I *am* supposed to be a prosecutor."

She smiled. "Promise."

"Good. Now tell me about yourself."

Over the next hour, Emily told him all about her schooling, her likes, dislikes, favorite foods, movies, books, favorite color, and on and on. She asked Robert a million questions about his family, her grandparents, and he answered them all with enthusiasm. Before long, they were as comfortable together as old friends. Emily felt like any other daughter out for dinner with her father. It made her happy.

"And what about boys?"

And then he asked *that*. Just when things were going so well. One thing she didn't want was to discuss her love life. But fathers were allowed to ask about boys, weren't they?

"Your mother tells me you've had a rough school year so far."

Emily's eyes widened but she kept her surprise hidden. When did this happen? "I guess I have."

He nodded. "Yeah, boys'll do that to you."

"No kidding." Emily's voice was sarcastic but her face betrayed the sadness lurking underneath her tough façade.

Robert looked at her with compassion in his eyes. "I can't imagine there's a shortage of boys interested in you."

Emily chuckled. "I guess not," she mumbled, lowering her eyes.

"Ahh." He nodded in silent understanding. "Just not the one you want."

It was a statement rather than a question. Emily folded her arms across her chest, as if that could protect her. Robert smiled. She felt like he knew her every thought. Was this some kind of prosecutor mind-reading technique?

Robert laughed. "I'm sorry. I'm not sure how far to pry. It's so different with girls. I don't know what to say any more than you do."

For whatever reason, that made Emily feel a little better. Though she really didn't want to talk about boys, it might be good to talk to someone who wasn't so…involved. She started with superficial details, but eventually told her dad everything…well, not *everything*. She left out the gory details and tried not to make herself seem like too much of a slut, but the way she felt about herself made that hard. She was starting to realize she might have a self-esteem problem.

Her father leaned forward. "Emily, I'm here for you, okay? I don't really know everything I'm supposed to do for a sad and lonely daughter, and I know I haven't been there for you. I am so sorry for that, but I am here now. And I'll be here for you whenever you need me." He pressed his lips together. "I want to hold you right now, but I don't want to freak you out in the middle of a restaurant."

Emily giggled. "You know, for the first time since I came to see you, I feel like you're really my father…like you really care, and not just because you're obligated or anything."

"I'm glad." He smiled. "Because I really do love you, Emily. And I'm going to love getting to know my daughter."

***

When he dropped Emily off, Robert walked her to her door and waited until she unlocked and opened it. He wasn't sure what to do at this point. She was practically a grown woman and he hadn't spent any time with her in the past sixteen years. Would it be weird to try to kiss her and give her a hug?

Emily stood smiling at him, her cheeks flushed. She was as nervous as he was. Even though he was her father, this was the first time they'd ever been together. What was he supposed to do? Ultimately, Emily made the decision for him. Taking a breath, she closed the distance between them and put her arms around his neck. He wrapped his arms around her slender body and squeezed. He squeezed her for every moment they'd spent apart, for every missed bedtime story, for every missed birthday. He squeezed her close and let her hold him as tightly as she needed for as long as she needed.

"Thank you for dinner…Daddy."

***

By Monday morning, Kevin was going out of his mind with boredom. While he enjoyed sitting around a quiet house reading all day, he was not the type to sit idle for long. As an athlete, nothing bothered him more than inactivity. The problem was, he'd gone through another surgery on Friday night and was supposed to stay in bed for two more weeks. Then, he might have to have a *fourth* surgery, which would mean even more time in bed. To Kevin, it was unacceptable. He could deal with the pain and inconvenience; that was well worth a state championship. What he couldn't deal with was another day in bed.

He was up early and dressed in jeans and a t-shirt. Since the temperature was reading in the single digits, he found a heavy sweater and began to work it onto his injured arm. He'd just started struggling with it when his mother passed by his doorway.

"What are you doing?" she asked.

"It's Monday," Kevin replied. "I'm getting ready for school."

She shook her head and smiled. "Come on, sweetie. Take some time to heal. I don't want you to cause any more damage."

Kevin continued to work the sweater over his shoulder, wincing at the effort. "I'll take it easy." He looked at her. "Please, Mom. I can't sit around anymore. It's killing me."

Karen shook her head and took the sweater in her hands. She worked it over his shoulder and head. "There," she said, looking at him and again shaking her head. "You know the doctor hates you, right?"

"I know."

"You don't take pain medication. You ignore his advice about resting."

"I know, I know," Kevin droned. "Tell you what…I'll buy him a nice fruit basket."

"Very funny. I'll make you some eggs and then drive you to school."

"Actually, I was thinking about running to school today," Kevin said with a straight face.

"What!" Karen whirled around with a look of horror on her face. "You can't be serio—" She caught the smile tugging at the corners of his mouth. "Oh, real cute." She shook her head as she headed down the stairs. "You're not as funny as you think you are."

No one knew of his plans to be in school this morning. It was a snap decision Kevin made when he woke up. When he took his time, and gingerly stepped out of the car in front of Kendall High School, a hush fell over the students as they realized he was among them once again. He adjusted the sling over his left arm and made his way across the quad. Most of the kids just stared as he walked by, unsure of how to act. Kevin Sinclaire transcended legendary status in Kendall Township.

As he approached Tony and Brittany, hanging out in their usual spot on a bench near the flag pole, he saw Lindsey and Emily heading toward him. Emily was trying to hold Lindsey back to no avail. Lindsey looked displeased. He knew she'd be pissed. He hadn't returned her late night texts and hadn't answered the phone when she tried to call. After Friday's surgery, his throbbing shoulder made him miserable, but that wasn't the reason he didn't want to talk to her. Things were so off between them he was having trouble pretending everything was okay. She made a beeline for Kevin, and intercepted him.

"Hey, *stranger*," she said.

Though her tone was sweet and enthusiastic, Kevin knew it was put on. He could see her eyes blazing and he really couldn't blame her.

"Hey, Lindz."

She nodded. "So…you can't even give your *girlfriend* a call to let her know you'd be coming back to school?"

He shrugged, putting a bored look on his face. He knew it was wrong, but he wasn't in the mood for attitude.

Lindsey stood there, shaking her head in disbelief. "Kevin, you haven't called for five days. What's going on? You complain that we don't talk but you never call anymore, and you don't answer when I call. Should I be taking a hint here?"

Kevin shook his head in a weary sigh. "Honestly, Lindsey, I don't know what to tell you right now. I had surgery Friday night, so I was a little out of it until yesterday. I didn't know I was coming to school 'til this morning, so I didn't call anybody."

Lindsey's eyes widened. "Oh, my god! You had surgery Friday!" Her hand went to her mouth, which dropped wide open. "I *totally* forgot. I'm sooo sorry, baby. Do you hate me?"

Kevin chuckled at the mortified expression in her eyes. As bad as their relationship had gotten, he still couldn't resist her icy blue eyes. "*Hate* you? That could never happen. Come here." He held his good arm open for her and she came to him. She placed her hand gently on his bad shoulder.

"How does it feel?"

"Like someone tried to cut it off."

Lindsey grimaced and looked around. "Uh oh. I think the natives are getting restless. Everyone wants to say hi, so I'll leave you to it." She kissed him on the lips. "I'm sorry again. I'm such a psycho."

"I won't argue with that," Kevin said with a wry grin. Sometimes he still felt like they were meant to be together.

"So, the prodigal son returns," Tony came over and put an arm around Kevin's neck, pulling him in close so he could kiss Kevin on the head. It was the kind of thing only certain guys could get away with in high school. Everyone knew both Kevin and Tony were crazy, so kissing Kevin on the head was pretty tame in the grand scheme of things. "Good to see you up and out of the house, brother."

"Thanks, man." Kevin turned to Brittany and gave her a kiss on the cheek. "Hey, Brit. You taking care of our guy here?"

Tony squeezed Kevin's neck. "Buddy, we're doing just fine. It looks like *you* have more trouble than we do. What's up with Lindsey?"

Kevin shook his head and ran his fingers through his hair. They strode into the school as the five-minute bell sounded. "We're in a death spiral. I don't think we're gonna make it."

"Aww, that's sad," Brittany said. "I know you really love her, Kev. Don't give up on her."

Kevin shrugged. "I might not have a choice. I think she's looking for a way out."

***

The news of Kevin's return to Kendall High spread like wildfire throughout the school. No one in the school could pay any attention to class work. All they wanted to do was see and talk to their hero. Crowds of students followed him everywhere he went. Some approached and shook his hand or gave him a high five, but most just stared at him in awe. A few were brave enough to ask for a selfie with him.

By lunchtime, Kevin had been greeted by pretty much everyone in the entire school, including the principal and his staff, all the guidance counselors, most of the teachers, and even the members of the custodial staff. When he finally made his way to the cafeteria, he found a table, and dropped into a seat with a weary sigh. His shoulder throbbed. He fought against taking his painkillers, but he was about ready to give in. Tony and Brittany strolled in moments later and dropped their backpacks on the floor next to the table.

"You look like crap, Kevo," Tony said.

"Oh good," Kevin said. "At least I look better than I feel."

Brittany laid a hand on his good shoulder. "Too soon."

Tracey and Matt came in and sat nearby. Soon, the tables around Kevin filled with Cobra football players, cheerleaders, and Brette Girls, all clamoring for Kevin's attention. Kevin downed a half of one of his painkillers and felt a little better. It made it easier to socialize with his friends, and as long as the pain didn't totally go away, he figured he wasn't overdoing it with the powerful narcotics.

"So," Tracey said to him, sliding into the seat next to him. "How are you feeling?"

"I'm hanging in there. I couldn't really sit in bed another day, but today has already been way too intense and I'm only halfway through it."

"Yeah," she grinned. "Everyone loves you."

Kevin looked around. "It's nice to be appreciated."

"Listen, Kevin." Tracey put a hand on Kevin's. "I wanted to say thank you."

"For what?"

"For being a friend to me." She sighed and looked around. No one payed them any attention. "I think you're probably the reason Matt and I got back together."

Kevin shook his head. He didn't know what to say. It was amusing. Here he was, receiving praise and gratitude from two people he had helped get back together and yet he felt powerless to do anything about his own relationship with Lindsey.

He chuckled. "I doubt that, but I appreciate you saying so."

Tracey squeezed his hand. "No, really, Kevin Sinclaire. The father of my child is with me because of you." Her eyes were teary.

"You look really happy."

She laughed. "I am. I'm still scared out of my mind, but I really am happy because whatever happens, Matt is going to be with me. And I suspect you made that happen." She looked him in the eyes, something she'd never been able to do before. "And I'll always love you for that."

Chapter 13

Dr. Everett Overton took the elevator to the top floor, and carried his lunch through the halls to the service corridor. He nudged open the door to the rooftop staircase. He climbed the remaining steps and pushed through the door that led to the roof. No one gave him a second glance. He'd taken his lunch to the roof overlooking Lewis Library for years. Even in the brisk cold of winter, the professor preferred to be alone and outdoors, high up where he could watch the people bustle about below.

Plus, he loved the cold. No season more invigorated the fifty-one-year-old professor. He loved breathing in the frosty air and battling the icy breezes with his thermos full of steaming-hot soup, usually something hearty and full of vegetables. He also had a small salad which he always devoured in haste before opening the thermos and pouring some soup into the cup. He took his time eating and tried to refocus his mind. He was more frustrated than ever before and now his work was beginning to suffer. Ever since Lindsey's surprise visit, and the ensuing conversation with Dr. Michaelson, Everett's mind had been a cluttered mess.

Why did she have to come here? Instinct told him there was something wrong with that thought, but nonetheless, he harbored resentment toward his daughter for interrupting his life. He hated all the phone calls and emails, not to mention the voice messages begging him to come see them. Couldn't anyone understand he was working? He wasn't playing games and indulging himself. There was serious, real-world work to be done, and fewer and fewer young people entering the scientific fields to do it.

In the past, Dr. Overton would brush aside the calls and messages, and go about his business, ignoring such trivialities. People seldom asked anymore about his family and he never talked about them. Work was all-consuming and he never gave his personal life a second thought, but in one day, all that changed. With one visit, his youngest daughter so disrupted his life, even his colleagues were beginning to think he needed some time away from his office and his labs. It was offensive that other people would presume to know what *he* needed.

A cloud of depression began to consume him. Depression was nothing new to the professor. He'd always suffered from vast mood swings. His euphoria almost always came from his work, which made sense as it was his greatest passion. Almost everything else about his life depressed him to no end. Even the joyful things in life, such as a loving and caring family, only served to drive him deeper into depression. Abby had mentioned once to him how incredulous it made her to think that a biologist, a man who studies life for a living, could be so unfazed by the miracle of the two lives they had created together.

It *was* inexplicable. The professor knew it, but he couldn't reverse the notions in his mind no matter what he did. He wasn't even sure he wanted to. Evolution hardwired him that way. What good would it do to fight science? So he spent his days and nights immersed in his work, devoted to the study of life, uncovering the answers to life's greatest mysteries.

Only now, even *that* was tedious and unfulfilling. His eyes found the edge of the rooftop. He was twelve stories up. He stood and studied the scene below, as he often did. Students and faculty moved about in their daily routines, some hurrying to class, others off to lunch. Even that depressed him.

Is this all there is?

Of course it is. Science was clear. We're born. We live. We die. Life continues. There is nothing else. There doesn't *have* to be anything else. It just is. He looked straight down over the edge again. He could do it. He was capable of taking that last final step into oblivion. How peaceful would that be? No more stress about families, or the collapse of society, or the battle between religious fundamentalists and scientists. All of that would be someone else's problem. He could finally sleep…

"Nice day, ain't it?"

The voice rang in the professor's ears just as he was preparing to ease his right foot forward. It startled him, but it was also enough to keep both his feet planted rooted in place. Who the hell would be up here? He wanted out of his life, but he didn't want an audience. He turned his head a little.

The voice continued. "Yeah, it's a little cold, but you know what I think? I think the cold makes a man feel alive."

If you only knew…

The professor stepped back from the edge, turned and saw a bundled up black man, about his own age, sitting, and eating a sandwich wrapped in deli paper. He sat not twenty feet from where the professor had been eating his own lunch. Focused on his own bitter thoughts, and in the throes of deep depression, the professor must have missed the man when he came up.

He was still talking, a Deep South twang accenting his words. "You know, breathin' in that chill…feelin' the cold in my lungs. Whew! Always makes me smile."

With a sigh, and an internal roll of the eyes, Everett took his seat and resumed eating his soup while the man chattered on. "Yeah, this is my favorite time of the year, when I can see my breath in the air." He was looking at Everett. "How 'bout you, Professor?"

Everett turned to look at him. "How do you know I'm a professor?"

"Well ain'tcha? You look like a professor." He laughed, a loud knee-slapping guffaw, like he'd just uttered the funniest thing he'd heard all week. "Now, I know we ain't supposed to judge a book by its cover an' all that, but by an' large, professors all look the same."

Well, there's a real encouraging notion. I even look *like everyone else?*

"So, how 'bout it, Professor?"

"How about what?"

"What kinda weather you like?"

"I really don't care." Everett spooned a mouthful of soup, chewed, and swallowed as the man stared at him with a frown.

"Don't care? How that be? Everyone has a favorite season."

The professor sighed. "Well, I don't. I like the change of seasons."

"Oh," the man said. "So, you one a those."

"One of what?"

"One a those people who act like they ain' affected when things change, like the seasons. They act like they like it an' all."

"Well, I don't act. I just like the change of seasons. It's the cycle of life."

"Mmmhmm."

They sat in silence for several moments. The professor hoped the guy would finish his lunch and go away so he could get on with it, but time passed and the man remained.

"You mind if I ask you a personal question, Professor?"

Sigh. *Here we go…*

"Why not?"

"I'm asking *you* why not."

Everett shrugged in bewilderment. "Go ahead and ask."

"If you a man likes the change of seasons, why'ns you about to hop off this here roof?"

Everett was confused. "What does one have to do with the other?"

The man frowned. "Well, if you ain' like the cold, Professor, you knows all you gotta do is wait a little while 'cause it's fixin' ta change. You just said yourself it's the cycle a life."

Everett considered. He had to admit, the man was pretty perceptive. "Well, I've been waiting for it to change for a long time now and maybe I just don't feel like waiting anymore."

"*Maybe?*" the man said, raising his eyebrows. "You *maybe* don't feel like waitin' no moe? Ain'tch you think it'd be a good idea to wait till you was *sure* you don't feel like waiting no moe?"

Everett shrugged impatiently. "What difference does it make?" He shook his head and sighed as the man stared at him with a quizzical expression on his kind face. He didn't look at all disturbed by the fact that a man was prepared to jump off a roof right in front of him.

"Pshhh!" The man shrugged and smiled. "Shoooot, it don't make *no* difference to me. I'm just settin' here wonderin' how a man can step to the edge when he ain' eem sure he wanna join the majority."

"Join the majority?"

The man smiled. "You like that?"

Everett shrugged. "It's pretty funny."

"I don't suppose you in the mood to share what's goin' on in your head to make you wanna splatter youself all over the ground down there."

Everett frowned at the image, but he just focused on his thermos of chowder. It was still hot, so he poured himself another mug and ate in silence for a minute. *How did I not see him?* Was he so caught up in his own mind that he failed to notice an onlooker sitting not twenty feet away? He may be task driven, but he was still observant. He turned to face the man.

"Were you really up here the whole time I was?"

"Been settin' here for over a hour," the man replied, taking another bite of his sandwich. "Jus' takin' in the sunshine…'til you showed up and made the day a whole lot more excitin'."

Everett shook his head. "I suppose you think you saved me."

The man held up a finger and shook his head. "I ain' saved no one."

"Then why did you interrupt me? Why not just let me fall in peace?"

The man shrugged. "Just got a feelin' you was someone shouldn't be up here."

"You got a *feeling*?"

"Yep." The man bobbed his head up and down. "God sometimes just steps in when we don't 'spect Him to."

"God?" the professor asked in his distinct monotone reserved for those he particularly loathed. "You think God told you to stop me?"

The man shrugged. "Now I ain' say all that. I just said I got a feelin' boutchyou."

"But you think the feeling came from God?"

"Well now, I can see in your eyes how you feel about *that*, so let's just leave it at I got a feelin'."

The professor nodded and chuckled.

"What's so funny, Professor?"

Everett ate some more of his soup. "Nothing really. I was thinking about how people who believe in God usually want to tell me all about it and try to save me. You don't seem to want to talk about it."

"Now wait a minute," the man said. "I'm happy to talk about it. Lord, I'll talk about it all day long." He let out another joyful laugh. "There ain' nothin' I'd rather be doin' than talking 'bout the Lord."

"But you didn't tell me what a sin it would be to kill myself. You didn't tell me all about how Jesus loves me and all that nonsense."

"Well now, I jus' figured you done already heard all that and wasn't no point in talking 'bout sin and punishment. Sides, if you fenda off youself, my guess is you ain' all that concerned 'bout Jesus. Am I right?"

Everett nodded. "You are absolutely correct."

"See that?" the man grinned, his dark eyes gleaming in the sunlight. "We agree."

Everett shrugged. There was silence between them for several moments.

"So you probably think God sent you up here today to save me." He looked over at the man and saw him think about it for a second or two before shrugging.

"Shoot," he said. "I don't know what God did or ain't do. I just know I was here and you was here. Some folk might call that fate. Some might call it the sovereignty a God."

Everett almost spit out his food as he let out a scornful laugh. "The sovereignty of God? That's a good one." He shook his head. Christians were always telling him how God was in control of everything. "What about plain old coincidence?" he asked.

The man wrinkled his forehead. "What about it?"

"You don't think that some things just happen purely by chance?"

The man shrugged. "Sure I do. Don't mean God ain't in control of 'em."

"That's exactly what it means."

"No, it don't."

Everett sighed. "The word 'coincidence' means events occurring without causal connection."

"Whew!" the man took in a breath, smiling once again. "That sho' is a mouthful, Professor. Talkin' 'bout causal connection an' all that." He laughed. "Now I don' know nuthin' 'bout no causal connection, but I sure do know that things can happen by chance and *yet* God still be in control. Just because He don't *make* the things happen don't mean He gotta *let* 'em happen."

"So you're saying God let's everything happen."

"Not *everything*. He *makes* some things happen. Just not all things."

"That doesn't make any sense."

The man frowned and chewed in a slow, deliberate rhythm. "It don't?"

"No." Everett shook his head in frustration, though he felt strangely alive. Considering the decision he'd recently come to, it was an unexpected feeling, but there nonetheless. Maybe all he needed was a good debate. "You can't attribute just the things you want to God and then say He simply *allows* the rest to occur."

The man stopped chewing and stared at Everett. "I can't?"

Everett stared at him. "No!"

"Why not?"

"Because." Everett spread his arms. "Don't you think that's a little convenient? You Christians get to say that the good things of the world are all the work of this wonderful God, but then blame the bad things on all us sinners."

"Ain' nobody blamin' you for the bad things."

"But if God wanted to wipe all the evil and bad away, He could just go ahead and do it, couldn't He?"

"Sure He could!" the man exclaimed. "He done did it one time already."

Everett rolled his eyes. "Oh, please, not the Flood." Everett shook his head. "I'm sorry to tell you science doesn't support your theory."

The man feigned a look of shock and sadness. "It don't?"

"No."

The man considered for a moment. "Well, then I suggest you go back and start from the beginning, Professor, 'cause your science is wrong."

Everett had to laugh at that. "That's it? That's all you have?"

The man frowned. "How much more I need?"

Everett laughed. "Well, I'd say you need a lot more than "science is wrong" if you're trying to tell me that something happened that science says most certainly did *not* happen."

"Oh." The man shrugged. "Well, you got your science, written by men…sinful and corrupt men, by the way, 'cause there ain't no other kind, an' I got this." He held up a well-worn, leather-bound book.

"The Bible," Everett said.

"Yep. That's all I need. If it says it in here, it's the truth, an' you don't need ta look no further."

Everett shook his head and sighed in derision. "That's ridiculous."

The man tilted his head. "Yeah, well, I can see how a man like you might get ta thinkin' so."

"A man like me?"

The man forced a grim smile. "Tell me somethin', Professor. If your way so right and smart, how come you the one fenda jump off the roof?"

***

Kayla was nervous. It was doubtful Emily Vasquez would pass over all the super-hot jocks and end up with a computer geek like Jarrick Neddles. Then again, she claimed they kissed. Did Jarrick really kiss Emily? Would he? Oh, who was she kidding? Of course he would. What guy wouldn't?

"Heck," Kayla muttered to herself as she walked through the halls. "*I'd* probably kiss her." She almost burst out laughing at the absurdity of the thought. Emily was so beautiful and sexy, Kayla figured three quarters of the school would probably kiss her without a second thought. The school was more than fifty percent female, so the math was clear.

But the question wasn't whether or not Jarrick would kiss Emily. It was whether *she* would kiss *him*. Would she? And what's more…*did* she? And if so, how did Kayla feel about *that*? It wasn't like she and Jarrick had ever been together. In fact, they hadn't even spoken much because he was too scared to make a friggin move.

Kayla was usually shy and timid. Boys sometimes approached her, but she was always too anxious to respond. Getting up the nerve to approach Emily had taken an awful lot of determination on her part. It took her the rest of the week to muster the nerve to approach Jarrick. He was alone for the first time all week. He walked the halls just like always. He hung around his friends. Everything seemed back to normal.

Kayla wasn't going to let any more time pass. Jarrick had been staring at her all year. She'd been waiting for him to talk to her and he just never did. It was up to her, just like Emily said. She saw Jarrick alone at his locker and took a deep breath before walking up to him.

When Jarrick realized who stood in front of him, his eyes widened and he swallowed really hard. Kayla wondered if it hurt. It looked like he swallowed a golf ball. She tried to relax.

"Well?" she said after staring him in the eyes for several seconds.

"W-w-well w-what?" Jarrick looked confused and petrified.

Kayla shrugged. "Oh, I don't know. How 'bout I've been waiting the whole year for you to ask me out and now you're running around with Emily Vasquez?"

He grimaced. "Oh."

She stood there in disbelief. "*Oh?* What does that mean, 'oh'?"

"I'm sorry?"

"You're *sorry?*" She pushed him in the chest. "You waste half the year. We missed the winter formal, and now you're with Emily."

Jarrick protested, "I'm not with—"

"No? Then what is it with you two?"

"W-w-w-we're just friends. I promise." The poor guy was ready to blow a gasket. Kayla had to stifle a smile. "She's just a friend."

Kayla nodded. Her expression softened for a moment. "Okay. I believe you."

He breathed a sigh of relief. But then she pushed him again.

"Do you have any idea what it's like for a girl to spend half a year waiting for a guy who *Never. Makes. A Move?*"

With his back against the lockers, Jarrick fumbled for words to say. All he could come up with was, "I'm s-sorry."

She lightened up and crossed her arms over her chest. "Why didn't you ask me out, Jarrick?"

He shrugged and lowered his eyes. "I thought you'd say no."

"Hey," she purred, taking his hands in hers. "Look at me."

When his eyes met hers, she smiled and pulled him closer. She closed the distance between them and ran her right hand behind his head. She pulled his head to her and met his lips with her own in a sweet, soft kiss. He brought his hands up to Kayla's back, running them softly over her shoulder blades. She reacted to that by deepening her kisses and running her fingers through his hair.

When they separated, Kayla smiled and said, "Sit with me at lunch?"

***

As Kayla walked down the halls, Emily fell into step beside her.

"Wow," she said, shaking her head and putting an arm around Kayla's shoulders. "That's one way of doing it."

Kayla couldn't keep the smile off her face. "I fell for him a long time ago. It just took this long to get up the nerve to do something about it."

Emily laughed. "My work here is finished."

Chapter 14

"This is *sick!*"

Tony spoke for the entire team; heads nodded all around him. With Kevin back in school, the town was finally getting its championship parade. They'd put it off because no one wanted to celebrate without the player who brought it home for the Cobras. Kevin had been through four surgeries and weeks of painful recovery over the past two months, but he was up and around, and able to stand on a giant black and silver float as it moved through town at the breakneck speed of eight miles per hour. He had one good arm, which he used to wave to the maniacal people of the community, who lined the streets, screaming their appreciation, twirling their Kendall Cobra rally towels, and chanting *VE-NOM* over and over again.

The streets were decorated in silver and black with the various Kendall High and Cobra logos prominent on every block. The Venom Cobra logo was everywhere, in just about every storefront. As the float moved from block to block, the citizens showered the team with black and silver confetti, streamers, flowers…yes, they were throwing black and silver roses. How they managed to get the roses silver was anybody's guess, but there was an even bigger question:

Who paid for all the flowers?

***

As Emily strutted through the party, she was greeted by several Kendall Cobra fans. The adults all knew her because of her relationship with Matt Kildare, and more recently, because she was best friends with Lindsey, who dated their new hero. Now that she was sixteen, she could work over the summer for one of Kendall Township's many business owners. They all let her know they'd have a summer job for her if she was interested. She smiled and thanked each one, and made mental notes of the jobs she was interested in. She'd have to give some thought to the idea of getting a job. She didn't want her mother to have to keep giving her an allowance when she could be working and making her own money, and she'd be getting her license before long. Gas wasn't free.

One offer, in particular, captured her attention. Lyle Garrity was a Kendall Township native and a rabid Cobra fan. He and his wife Sara had been high school sweethearts and went on to start a small but successful talent management firm. They took on clients from many different areas. Athletes, musicians, and writers were just some of the areas they represented. They also represented models, which was why Sara Garrity had been focused like a laser on Emily for years. Before Emily could get sucked into a conversation with another restaurant owner who was looking to have the prettiest girl in Kendall Township standing at the front of his restaurant, Sara pulled her aside and they sat at a table near the back where it was a little quieter. She talked a mile-a-minute, and made it seem like Emily was in on a joke that was just between the two of them.

"You're gorgeous," she said. "That's why they all want you working for them…so you can stand up front and look pretty." She grinned at Emily. "Well, if you're going to take a job being pretty, then I say get paid real money for it!" She laughed and sipped her drink.

Emily smiled and bit her bottom lip. "Modeling?"

"Absolutely," Sara replied, taking Emily's chin and looking at her from different angles. "You're stunning, Emily. You're absolutely perfect. You've got it all…the face, the body, the eyes. My God, those eyes are amazing! You really need to get with a photographer and put together a portfolio. I'll get you a list of local photographers. I'll have you doing make-up, shampoo, runway…"

"Not lingerie," Emily protested. "Please don't say lingerie or swimsuits."

Sara laughed and patted Emily's hand. "Don't you worry, sweetie. I wouldn't even take their calls."

"Really?" Emily wrinkled her forehead.

"Of course not." Sara frowned. "You're sixteen. I wouldn't let my *sixteen*-year-old client *near* a lingerie shoot…*or* a swimsuit shoot, but there's plenty of money elsewhere. No need to take it all off. I'd rather let that beautiful face take us where we want to go."

"That sounds really great." Emily was getting excited. *Where* do *I want to go?* It might be time to start thinking about a future beyond Kendall Township. The coming summer began to look promising, both financially and professionally. *Professionally?* Really? She needed to find Lindsey and tell her everything.

She ran into a beaming Jarrick Neddles and Kayla Helmsley. They were holding hands like they'd been together for years. Kayla looked cute in a simple floor length black dress with a silver pattern that looked a little like thin leaves falling through the air. Her turquoise-tipped platinum hair gleamed in contrast to the dark outfit. It was an unusual look for a typical Kendall party…goth, though not too goth, and Kayla had the personality to pull it off. Jarrick wore a dark jacket over a t-shirt with some computer geek phrase on the front. He sported black jeans and a pair of black Chucks. Emily wanted to slap him. He looked cute enough, but it wasn't a school dance. Her work might not yet be done with him.

"Hey, guys!" she said with a bright smile. "You look great together!" She resisted the urge to grab Jarrick by the scruff of the neck and drag him off to comb his hair. As they approached, she could see he probably did little more than run his fingers through it. "Are you having a good time?"

"Great," Kayla replied with a giggle. "…thanks to you."

Emily smiled. "You make the cutest couple."

Kayla looked down. "Thank you." She looked Emily in the eye. "Really. Thank you." She turned to Jarrick. "I'll go get us some punch."

When she left, Emily turned to Jarrick and touched his jacket. "I should slap the geek out of you."

"Why?" he asked, stepping back and bringing his hands up in a defensive posture. "What did I do?"

"How can you let her dress so beautifully and you wear a stupid t-shirt?"

He looked down sheepish frown. "I don't…I mean…I never…" He sighed. "I don't think she really cares."

Emily chuckled. "You're probably right. She's sweet." She poked a finger into Jarrick's chest. "And you better be good to her."

Before he could respond, Lindsey appeared and looked Jarrick up and down with a skeptical smirk. She reached out and felt the lapels of his jacket, shaking her head as she opened the jacket up to look at his t-shirt. She sniffed, and the corners of her mouth twitched, but she remained impassive.

"What a slob," she muttered. "What does that girl see in you?"

Emily stifled a giggle and held a hand in front of her mouth as Jarrick squirmed under Lindsey's icy gaze. Though he had warmed up to Emily and could bring himself look her in the eye, and even talk to her with some degree of focus, he was still terrified of Lindsey, and she did nothing to assuage that fear. She treated him like a moron. He failed to comprehend that it meant she really liked him.

Without waiting for an answer, Lindsey turned to Emily. "I need you."

Jarrick took the opportunity to make his escape and went off to rejoin Kayla.

"What's the matter?" Emily asked. She read the look in Lindsey's eyes before she said anything. "What did he say?"

Lindsey shook her head. "It's not what he said. He *said* all the right things. He keeps telling me he loves me and he's not mad at me and all that." She shrugged, with a helpless look in her eyes. "But then, he doesn't really touch me. He doesn't put his arm around me or hold my hand. It's like he's trying to keep his distance."

Emily frowned. It did sound bad. Kevin wasn't an all-over-his-girl kind of boyfriend, but she'd never seen him leave Lindsey hanging. He was always her rock, the one she could always depend on. If Lindsey felt awkward around him, something was wrong.

"Maybe he just needs some time to get his feelings straight. You guys have been going hot and heavy for weeks now. He's hurt and probably on meds and stuff."

Lindsey sighed in frustration. "If he's so smart, Em, why can't he see how much I love him?"

"He sees it. He's just confused right now. Don't push him. Let him work it out."

"Ugh!" Lindsey slumped and put her forehead on Emily's shoulder. "This totally sucks. Just sitting there next to him, all I wanted to do was sit on his lap and kiss him." She stood up straighter. "But if I did that, he'd probably think I'm just being manipulative and trying to fix all our problems with sex."

"That's not what he'd think. You can kiss your boyfriend, Lindz."

"You sure about that?" Lindsey shot back. "Because when I'm with him, it feels like I can't even *touch* him."

***

"You mind if I ask you a personal question, Professor?"

"*Another* one?" Everett shook his head. It seemed as though all they ever did was talk about his personal life.

"Well, seein's how we getting ta be friends an' all…"

"We are?" Everett frowned.

"Well, ain't we?"

"I wouldn't know."

It turned out the man's name was Earl. Other than all the religious nonsense, it was about the only thing Everett knew about him. Somehow, Earl managed to convince Dr. Overton to come over to his apartment for dinner. Now, he wrinkled his forehead in amusement.

"What? You ain' got many friends?"

Everett shook his head without emotion and shrugged a shoulder. "Not really, no."

"Hmmm." Earl frowned and leaned back in his chair, watching the professor's face.

After a moment of uncomfortable silence, Everett asked, "What did you want to ask me?"

"Oh yeah." He paused and thought for a minute. "I guess I was just curious what it was you believed in. I mean, you said you ain' believed in God, so…what *do* you believe in?"

Everett looked down and shook his head. "Not much, I'm afraid. In fact, I don't think I believe in *anything* anymore."

Earl looked stunned. "*Nuthin*? You sayin' you ain' believe in nuthin' at all."

"I'm afraid so." Everett shrugged. "The things I did believe in…" He shrugged again and spread his hands a bit in a gesture of resignation. "…weren't as solid as I'd thought."

Earl nodded in understanding. "I get it." He leaned forward. "These things you say you used to believe in…they still around?"

Everett looked confused. "Of course."

"But you ain't believe in 'em anymore."

"Not really, no."

"Well," Earl pressed, leaning forward with an intent gaze. "What kinda things we talkin' 'bout?"

"Just things."

"Gimme a for instance."

"Well, science for one."

"Science." Earl nodded in appreciation. "Science is a good one to believe in, ain't it?"

"Don't be so sure."

"Why? A lotta good, smart people become scientists, don't they?"

Everett sighed. "Yes, they do, for all the good it does."

"They don't do no good?"

Everett shrugged. "They do some good, I suppose, but in the long run, answering the bigger questions…we're woefully inadequate."

"Ahh, the bigger questions." Earl leaned back in his chair with a contemplative look on his kind face.

"Yes, the bigger questions. Like how life began. Why are we here? All the stuff people look to science to answer for them."

"And you ain' got no answers for 'em?"

"Not anymore I don't." Everett let out a long sigh. The weight of it all was more than he ever realized. Talking about it seemed to lighten the load. "At one time, I thought we did. But unfortunately, I've lived long enough to watch that façade begin to crack and crumble."

"Really?"

"Really." Everett shook his head and swallowed hard. "A colleague once asked me, in confidence, how I felt about being around to witness the death of science. At the time, I thought he was crazy. Now I realize he was absolutely correct. The quest for knowledge, for truth, for answers…it used to have value to people…to me. People have stopped valuing truth and knowledge. Now it's all agenda-driven pap. No one wants real answers anymore and no one wants to be the one to stand up and buck the system, which is broken beyond any point of repair. The world as we know it is mostly destroyed, and soon, it will be completely destroyed."

Earl bit on the end of his thumb and raised his eyebrows. "I don't quite know what to say to that, Professor. I don't think I'm followin'."

"The things I love are not as sturdy and powerful as I once thought. They're very frail. I didn't know that. I thought they were indestructible. I thought science was unassailable, that logic was the ultimate wisdom, and the human mind the most powerful thing in the universe. I thought things like culture and books, art and music, were foundational to civilization. I thought evolution had finally brought us to a point of awareness that would lead to even greater heights." He breathed in, held it, let it out in a long, slow, breath, and nodded to himself. "But I was wrong. I was dreadfully wrong."

***

"Killer fiesta, boys. This is the life."

Once again, Tony spoke for all of them. He'd already downed a twelve-ounce filet and was elbows-deep in a pile of hot-wings. The rest of the Cobras joined him in putting away copious amounts of food. No expense was spared for the evening's festivities and that included all-you-can-eat steaks, wings, burgers, lobster tail, shrimp, and loads of other items. The buffet tables stretched across the two entire sides of the room and hundreds of guests rotated back for seconds and thirds.

"You ain't kiddin'," Anquan Griffin said, holding out his fist for Scott to bump. "Glad we got one 'fore I bounce outta this place."

"We're gonna miss you next year, Quan," Kevin said, gripping the big running back's shoulder. "The Tide is lucky to have you."

It was a bittersweet moment for the Cobras. While the party was a celebration of a wonderful accomplishment, it also marked the end of a season. It was the last time that Cobra team would be together in one place. Next year, the seniors would be off to college, some on football scholarships. The rest of the graduating class will have likely played their last game. If that were the case, what a game to go out on!

Matt Kildare stood up and raised a glass. Kevin thought he looked a little misty-eyed and wondered if he'd managed to sneak a few adult beverages when no one was looking. It wouldn't be the first time.

"I just want to say, before we really get partying, that I've been friends with Quan since grade school. We've been playing football together for over ten years. Next year, we won't be taking the field together, but I'll be with you in spirit, brother." His eyes really were moist now, there was no doubt about it, but Matt didn't seem to care. He let the tears roll down his cheeks. Tracey took his hand.

Lindsey put her hand on Kevin's shoulder and squeezed. Everyone at the table choked up as the two friends shared their last evening together as teammates.

"Now," Matt finished. "Before I embarrass myself and cry…" He couldn't go on so he just came over to his friend. Anquan jumped up with tears streaming down his face. The two friends collided with more force than necessary and embraced, gripping one another and holding one another up. The table let out a cheer and clapped.

After the plates were cleared and everyone was served dessert, the program began. There were the expected speeches by the school officials, the principal, the superintendent, and finally, the mayor. All were enthusiastic in their praise for the Cobras and each one told stories about their experiences throughout the season and the thoughts they'd had as the season progressed from one win to the next. They were all vivid in their recollections of the snowy championship game where Kevin's heroics made this evening possible. Even the governor got in on the act, calling Kevin's performance the single most courageous thing he'd ever seen in an athletic event.

Next came the awards. Kevin was the shoo-in for team MVP. He was also recognized for breaking several school and state records. All the seniors were recognized and they all gave short speeches, mostly talking about their memories as Kendall Cobras. Those who had committed to colleges for next year announced their intentions, and those with athletic scholarships were roundly cheered.

Finally, all the talking was done and all the awards had been presented. It was time to party. At that point, most of the adults found a reason to exit, but a number remained to party with the state champions for a while longer. As the music from the DJ booth cranked up, the dance floor began to fill and the party was under way.

***

Kevin leaned back in his chair and watched as his teammates got crazy on the dance floor. Tony was like the Tasmanian Devil. Lindsey sat and watched for a minute, but then turned her gaze on Kevin. She didn't know what to think, or what to say, but she knew whatever was going on wasn't good. Emily had tried to give her some encouragement but Lindsey felt it in her gut.

"We're not okay, are we?" she shouted over the music.

Kevin turned to her but quickly dropped his gaze to the floor. He shrugged and shook his head. "I don't know, Lindz." He looked back up with tired eyes. "I mean…I know I love you. I just…I don't know how to get us back to where we were before all this…"

"Before sex," she finished.

"Yeah," he replied. "I guess. I just want us to be great together…like we were before things got so serious."

"We've always been serious, Kev."

"Yeah, but we still had fun. Now it's all serious…intense. I used to like laying with you and feeling you next to me. I don't want to feel like we have to peel off our clothes and have sex every time we're alone together. You want a different kind of relationship than I do."

Lindsey sat back. She hadn't thought about it in those terms before. One thing she never wanted to be was a high maintenance girlfriend. Their relationship was always relaxed. Kevin was right. They used to lay together, his hands running up and down her legs, not even in a sexual way…okay, well, maybe it was a *little* sexual, but they weren't having sex then and he wasn't trying to *get* her to have sex. He just loved to touch her, and she loved his touch. Why in the world did she insist on changing that?

Oh yeah, because a thousand half-naked girls throwing themselves at her boyfriend had driven Lindsey to the brink of insanity. She wondered if they could *ever* get past the valley they'd wandered into. Maybe Kevin was right. Maybe they were heading in different directions. Perhaps it was the end and they were hanging on out of sheer habit…or fear. The slightest thought of ending things with him made her stomach hurt and caused a dull ache to settle in her chest. She couldn't help but feel like the biggest fool in the world. The one thing she'd thought would save their relationship would be the thing that drove them apart. She wanted to cry.

Chapter 15

Earl sat in silence. His eyes never left the professor. Sometimes words were inadequate. He could see the torture his new friend put himself through but doubted his ability to work through it with him. Only God Himself could answer those kinds of questions. Only God could relieve the dread that plagued a man's soul.

After a long pause in the conversation, he spoke. "What happened, Professor?"

Everett looked up. "I just told you."

"No." Earl shook his head. "Somethin' must've happened. All that stuff you mentioned, the world's destroyed an' all…you already knew that. So, what was it, Professor?"

Everett shook his head. "You're very perceptive, Earl."

"I got my moments."

Everett stood and walked to the window. "Something happened recently in my work that…" He shook his head as he peeked out the curtain. It was dark.

"Drove you to the edge?"

"Yes, if you like." Everett turned from the window and took a seat across from Earl. He sighed and ran a hand over his chin. "I've studied the origins of life from every angle. I've always believed in Darwinian Evolution. It makes the most sense logically and science bears most of it out." He pinched the bridge of his nose. "At least that's what I thought."

"But you don't think so no more?"

Everett dropped his hand and shrugged. "A colleague of mine challenged me to start from the beginning and construct a framework of questions that, if all of them could be answered, would confirm our claims about evolutionary biology."

"And this framework…was it questions the two of you came up with together?"

"Yes."

"And this other colleague…was he a Christian?"

Everett raised his eyebrows. "Actually, no. He was an Intelligent Design advocate, though."

Earl nodded, a thoughtful expression on his face. "So…you got this framework?"

"Yes. It is a complicated series of questions and benchmarks, and I set out to answer each one. It would be my life's work. It *has* been my life's work. But it's dead. Science is dead."

Earl nodded. "So, you set out to prove what you believe and what happened? You couldn't do it?"

"Oh," Everett cried. "I wish it was just that I couldn't prove it. That would be fairly normal. We can rarely prove a theory to be absolutely true. We usually just run out of ways to attempt to disprove something and then we consider the theory proven, but it's never an absolute certainty."

"So what happened?"

And then he saw the sorrow in the professor's eyes, the defeat, the shame.

"Oh," Earl said in a reverent whisper. "You set out to disprove *God*, didn't you?"

Everett was silent, but it didn't matter. His face told the entire story. He had set out to be the man who destroyed God and God responded.

Earl sat back in his chair and nodded in understanding. "What did you find out?"

Everett looked at him. "I found out that my life's work, my life's ambition…is a complete and utter waste."

"And that's what made you step to the edge of that building? It wasn't something in your personal life that did it?"

"Personal…professional." Everett waved a hand, dismissing the differences. "It's all the same. That's the problem with being highly educated. Everything becomes very, very personal. The world becomes personal. I study the world. It's a part of me. When the foundations of what I believe about the world began to crack and crumble, I got nervous. When I saw the foundation fall apart, I…well, I just wanted out."

"Hmmm." Earl squeezed his lips together and frowned. "Strange."

"What's strange?"

You got yourself some lofty notions, Professor. Them's big ideas…*educated* ideas."

"I suppose. What's your point?"

"I guess I wonder what good is it having them kinds a ideas if all they do is make you wanna jump off the roof?"

Everett rolled his eyes. "If you're trying to tell me that I'm depressed because of my education, it's ridiculous."

"Ha!" Earl rolled back in his seat in laughter. "Maybe it is, Professor, but you gotta admit one thing."

"And what might that be?"

Earl jumped up and stepped to a small bookcase. He picked a Bible off the top. "Right here in the beginning, it talks about knowledge and how it kills."

"Oh, here we go with the Bible verses."

"You got something against Bible verses, Professor?"

Everette sighed, long and loud. "Why is it that you people can't just accept that some of us don't have the slightest desire to believe in a god of any kind?"

"I can accept that, Professor."

"Really?"

"Sure. It would be kinda hard to deny something I see every single day of my life. I mean, we *are* on a college campus."

"Very funny," Everett sighed again. He'd been sighing a lot since meeting Earl. "So, if you can accept that, then why do you feel the need to torture us? Why not just leave us alone?"

"So you can leap off the roof in peace?"

"If that's what we want to do, yes."

Everett sighed and put his head in his hands.

Earl stared for a second before commenting. "Must be something in the world can make you happy."

"Oh God!" Everett let out a sardonic chuckle. "Please! Happy?"

"What's the matter with bein' happy? You got a problem with happy people?"

"Oh, Good Lord." Everett rolled his eyes and shook his head. "There's no such thing."

"No such thing?" Earl couldn't disguise his shocked expression. "Not for nobody?"

"Absolutely not."

"Now, why would you think such a thought?"

Everett chuckled as if the answer was as plain as day. "Because human beings were born to suffer. It's just the way it is."

***

Tracey had not been told about Lindsey's trip, so when Abby brought it up the next day, she was stunned, and pissed. Her father's departure and subsequent failure to even attempt to maintain a relationship with his daughters was an open wound in Tracey's heart. She'd spent countless hours crying over missed birthdays, holidays, and other important milestones. He wasn't there when she danced her first solo in onStage's annual program. He wasn't there when her competition dance team won the state championship for the first time. They went on to win three in a row since and he hadn't shown up for a single one, even when the event took place less than fifteen minutes from his office on the Princeton campus.

He hadn't been to a single birthday party in the past five years for her or Lindsey. That was the real surprise…his neglect of Lindsey. Lindsey had always been his favorite. She was the intellectual; she spoke his language and understood him. She was always interested in his work and asked a million questions, ingesting all she could of his world. He didn't even bother to make an appearance when Lindsey competed in the state gymnastics competition two seasons ago. Lindsey would never admit it, but Tracey knew the heartbreak of his failure to show up was responsible for Lindsey only coming away with a silver medal. It was also the most probable reason she'd all but vanished from the onStage gymnastics program afterwards.

Now, it looked as if their delinquent father claimed yet another part of her little sister's heart. Tracey could tell she was crushed. Lindsey was a stoic when things were going bad. She didn't open up, especially to Tracey. She usually just turned sullen and withdrawn, which was a default for Lindsey, so it was difficult to know if there was ever something wrong, but Tracey could always tell by looking in her eyes. Lindsey tried to hide it with makeup, but her pain showed despite her efforts.

At some point, Tracey made the conscious decision to eliminate all thoughts of her father from her mind. She would go on as though he passed away. She still missed him, but she assumed she would never see him again and acted that way whenever the subject came up. Whenever Lindsey or her mother spoke of him in conversation or try to call him on holidays, Tracey would shake her head at them, treating them the same way she would treat a person who was desperate to communicate with a dead loved one. As far as Tracey was concerned, her father *had* died, at least to them. Lindsey and Abby just hadn't accepted it yet.

***

"Sweetheart," Abby said. "I wish you would eat something. You can't let yourself fall apart over this."

Lindsey pushed her food around her plate in circles, disinterested in everything going on around her. Her mind floated in and out of dreary, depressing sadness and violent, white-hot rage. She felt if she began talking about it, she would snap. What kind of father acted like that? On TV, or in the movies, fathers loved their daughters more than anything in the world. Daughters were treasures the father protected and doted on, worried about, fretted over. Fathers were the ones with advice and loving arms to hold. But not *her* father. No sir. He was too busy doing important work.

"No one else can take up the slack for a day or two a month while he visits with his children?" she blurted. "Really? What a silly thought, right?"

"Lindsey…" Abby reached across the table to try to take her daughter's hand.

Lindsey pulled her hands away and stood up. It was like a pressure relief valve had just blown. "No. I mean, really…what the hell is wrong with this guy? All I want is a few hours of his time once in a while! Is that so much to ask? I'm his *daughter*! He's supposed to *love* me!"

"I know, sweetie, he's just—"

Lindsey held up a hand. "No, Mom. There's nothing you can say. My own father looked me in the eye and told me flat out that there are more important things than family…than his *children*!"

"I understand, but you can't—"

"I can't what, Mom? What can't I do?"

"You can't let him tear your heart out like this, baby."

Lindsey spread her arms, her tears streaming down her face. "Mom, we're long past him tearing my heart out." She started to walk away. "You know," she said, shaking her head. "I don't even care anymore."

"*Now* you're getting it," Tracey said, nodding.

Was that necessary?

"Shut up, Tracey," Lindsey and Abby said in unison.

Tracey shrugged. "What? You guys always get your hopes up that the guy is gonna change. He never does and it always ends up like this, only *I'm* usually the one in tears. Now, I don't care if I ever see him again, and I don't get all screwed up when he doesn't call."

"Yeah, well, that's great for you," Lindsey said with a smirk. "You'll be glad to know he doesn't care about his grandchild either, then."

Tracey's eyes widened. "You *told* him?"

Lindsey shrugged. "It just kind of came out when I got pissed."

"No it didn't." Tracey shook her head. "You had no right to go around yapping about *my* business. I didn't want that prick to know."

"Oh Tracey." Lindsey smirked. "You and your secrets."

"*My* secrets? What about *you*, Miss Can't Keep My Hands Off My Boyfriend Now That We've Finally Gotten Around To Doing It?"

Uh oh! Did I just say that out loud?

That stopped Lindsey in her tracks. "Oh, that's real cute coming from you, Miss OMG I Just Screwed A Guy And Had To Run Out Of The House!"

I guess we're going there…

"Girls," Abby warned.

"Really?" Tracey shouted. "Miss WTF, Everybody Wants To Screw My Boyfriend So Let Me Beat Them To It…"

Geez, and in front of Mom?

"How original, Miss…"

"All right! Stop talking!"

Abby's voice cut through the quarrel and ended any further comment. "We are *not* going to do this, girls! We are not going to go round and round, beating each other's heads in for the next half hour, because we're just going to end up hating each other and we'll still have the same problems. You two need to make up right now."

Lindsey and Tracey stared at one another, tears on both their faces. Lindsey's heart grew more defiant with every passing moment, while Tracey just stared back at her. Neither moved. Finally, Lindsey tore her gaze away, glanced at her mother, and walked away. Insults were fair game in their sisterly spats, but bringing her sex life up in front of their mother was borderline unforgivable.

***

Tracey and Abby stood in silence for a few moments before Tracey rubbed her belly and reassured herself everything was okay. Then she slumped down into her chair and cried. A huge wave of self-loathing crashed over her. She regretted every word. What kind of a sister…?

Abby sat and sighed. "Is it true?" she asked, her head tilted over the back of her chair, stretching her slender neck.

"Mom, please," Tracey begged. "Don't make me talk about Lindsey behind her back."

"Is she having sex with Kevin?"

"Mom…"

"Is she?"

Tracey sighed. "She's in love with him, Mom. It was going to happen sooner or later."

Abby's breathing became erratic again. Tracey stood and got her a glass of water. She took some deep breaths and shook her head in sadness. "I was kind of hoping for later rather than sooner, if you want to know the truth…for both of you."

Tracey lowered her eyes, feeling the sting of shame. She had all but gotten over that, but it still crept back in on occasion. "I'm so sorry, Mom."

"I don't need an apology," Abby said with a shrug. "You're both big girls. But *this*," she pointed to Tracey's stomach. "And now her," she gestured upstairs, "makes me feel like such a failure."

"You're not a failure, Mom. We're both going to be fine."

Abby shrugged. "Maybe. You girls know I'm not a helicopter parent. I've always wanted to give you the freedom to experience things for yourself. But with sex, I just thought I taught you both the importance of being sure, being with the right guy, and having all the emotional support you need before sleeping with a boy."

"You did," Tracey said. "And I think Lindsey followed that advice."

Abby shook her head. "Tracey, if you can't see she's messed up right now, you're blind."

"That's just the whole thing with Dad."

"No," Abby said, holding up a finger. "She's using the situation with your father to vent everything. She's hurting, Trace. I don't think she'll talk to me right now, though."

Tracey shook her head. "She won't talk to *me*, that's for sure."

"Go try," Abby said. "For me? Just tell her you love her and you're there for her. Don't let her go through it alone."

"I'm sure she's talking to Emily. She's not alone."

Abby nodded and sighed. "Emily is a good friend to her, but I want Lindsey to know her *family* is here for her as well. I feel like I'm losing her, Tracey." She stood up. "I'm going to go talk to her. Promise me you'll do what you can to patch things up."

***

Abby poked her head into Lindsey's room. "Hey, baby girl. Can I come in?"

Lindsey reclined on her bed. She sat up and nodded. "Sorry about all that down there. We just got a little crazy. It's my fault. I shouldn't have told Dad about the baby."

Abby came in and put her arm around her youngest daughter. "Sweetie, I know this is all very hard, and that you're hurting right now." She pulled Lindsey in close so their heads touched. "And I know it's not just about your father."

Lindsey's body stiffened. "Can we not talk about sex right now?"

"We can put it off for a day or two, but it's a conversation we *are* going to have and very soon."

Lindsey nodded.

"Does Kevin's mother know about the two of you?"

Lindsey nodded. "I think so. I'm pretty sure he's waiting for the same talk you're going to give me."

Abby considered for a moment. "I think I need to talk to Karen."

Lindsey lowered her head even further. "Seriously, Mom? I can take a lot of humiliating things, but our parents discussing our sex lives is a little over the top, don't you think?"

Abby sniffed. "I think two freshmen sleeping together is even more over the top. You two aren't going to be allowed to roam free doing whatever you want, I can promise you that."

Me: Life is about 2 get suckier.
Kev: Huh?
Lindsey: Parentals about 2have a confab.
Kev: Huh?
Lindsey: About US stupid.
Kev: Huh?
Lindsey: About us and SEX. r u really this dense?
Kev: Oh…that does suck.
Lindsey: So…
Kev: So wat?
Lindsey: Wat r we gonna do about it?
Kev: about wat?
Lindsey: Ur very close to being beaten to death.
Kev: about parentals talking??? Nothing to do.
Lindsey: Thats real proactive…
Kev: I think we r screwed.
Lindsey: No pun intended? 😉
Kev: lol

Tracey knocked and pushed open Lindsey's door. "Hey," she said. "Got a minute?"

"I guess."

Tracey came in and sat on the bed. Lindsey had her head and shoulders propped up against the headboard and her tablet against her thighs. She was probably texting with Emily or Kevin.

"I just wanted to tell you I'm so sorry for spilling your secret in front of Mom. That was totally wrong of me."

Lindsey stared at her tablet and continued to tap on the screen. "You're right, it was."

"So," Tracey continued. "Do you think you can forgive me?"

Lindsey pursed her lips and thought for a minute before shaking her head. "Nope. Not yet, anyway."

Tracey frowned. "What is that supposed to mean?"

"Not 'til I get revenge." Lindsey swiped and tapped. Was she playing a game?

"That's real mature, Lindz. Any idea when this revenge will take place?"

"Nope, I have to wait for you to secretly do something really embarrassing and humiliating so I can tell everyone about it."

Tracey giggled. "Oh, I see. Then you'll forgive me?"

"Maybe." Lindsey squinted at her tablet and tapped some more.

"Okay then." Tracey stood up.

Lindsey tossed her tablet aside and swung her legs so they were dangling over the side of the bed. "Tracey, don't go." When Tracey turned back to her, she said, "I'm sorry too…about what I said. It was really mean, especially since you have my little niece in there."

Tracey rubbed her belly. "Oh, so it's a niece?"

Lindsey reached out and placed her hand on Tracey's belly. "*I* think so."

Tracey took her hand. "You know I love you, right, Lindz?"

Lindsey nodded and smiled. "Now I do."

Tracey turned to leave.

"But I'm still getting revenge," Lindsey muttered just loud enough for Tracey to hear.

"Of course you are."

Chapter 16

They are having sex.

The thought gnawed at her mind all day. It was a nightmare for any parent, but for Karen it was especially disappointing. Kevin, for all his arrogance and stubbornness, had always demonstrated a respect for girls that bordered on reverence. She knew, whatever the situation, Kevin would put a girl's feelings and insecurities ahead of his own desires. She'd watched him with Lindsey over the past year and he never disappointed. He was always careful with his lady, always gentle and adoring, but never in a way indicating he had ulterior motives.

When they'd first started spending a lot of time together, Karen sat Kevin down and spoke about what it meant when a girl allowed herself to be alone with a boy, especially at their age. It was a big deal because it took trust, even if the girl didn't realize it, and his job was to be worthy of her trust. Groping her body and trying to push her into going further than she wanted to go was a betrayal of her trust and made him unworthy of her.

That kind of language always affected Kevin. Trust...worthiness...betrayal...concepts like those got into his head far better than the standard teen lectures about sex and being careful and waiting. At the time, Kevin's reaction was so reassuring, Karen thought everything would be a snap from then on. That was her first mistake. It was so easy to trust Kevin because he always had the right words. Boy, could he talk. He'd been stunned she would think he was capable of pressuring his Lindsey like that. He actually said that. *His* Lindsey. But he meant it. He went on to tell his mother he didn't care about sex and could wait until Lindsey was ready. It wasn't exactly what she wanted to hear, but Lindsey was so sweet, shy, and innocent. Karen figured if Kevin wasn't pressuring her, there would be plenty of time for more discussions. Another mistake.

I'm the worst parent in the world.

She pulled into the parking lot at Grace Gospel and hurried inside to the church offices. She was right on time for her appointment with Pastor Peter Morgan and Youth Director Gavin Dalyrimple. Karen didn't know Mr. Dalyrimple all that well, but when Pastor Morgan suggested he sit in on their conversation, she consented. Anyone willing to help was welcome; Karen was near the end of her rope. Both men were already in Pastor Morgan's office when she was shown in by the pastor's secretary. They stood and Pastor Morgan took her hand and guided her to a seat in front of his desk.

"You know Gavin, right?" the Pastor gestured to Dalyrimple, who also shook Karen's hand.

When they were all seated, Pastor Morgan wasted no time on pleasantries. He started their meeting off the same way he opened any meeting, with a prayer. He asked God for guidance in their discussion and for peace and an increased faith in God's ability to work in her family. After the prayer, Karen felt more settled. She had prayed all the way over, in between bouts of self-loathing and regrets over her parenting skills, but it always felt better when someone else prayed with her.

"So, Karen," the pastor began. "You mentioned having some issues with Kevin, so I thought having Gavin here might be a help. He has a great love for the kids and already has a relationship with your son."

Karen nodded but hesitated. Once it's out there, she couldn't take it back. She didn't want to embarrass Kevin, but she didn't know what else to do. "Kevin is having sex." There. What's done is done. He brought it on himself.

Both men took the news in stride. It didn't even seem to faze them. They nodded, each with a look of concern. Karen hung her head in shame. "I should have seen the signs. I'm not ready for this."

"We never are, Karen." Pastor Morgan shook his head with a sympathetic smile. "But this isn't your fault. You can't control what a teenager does every minute of his life."

"So, it's hopeless?" Karen scowled. "There's nothing I can do?"

Gavin shook his head. "No. There's a lot you can do. You just have to understand, what Kevin needs most of all is prayer and a change of heart. That's really the only way his behavior will change. He has to *want* to change it. And that doesn't usually happen without a change of heart."

Karen sighed and shook her head sadly. "Well, I think Kev's a long way from that."

Pastor Morgan nodded. "Maybe he is, but that just means we have to meet him where he is."

"Sure," Karen spread her arms in a helpless gesture. "But what can I *do*? I mean, I still have to worry that he's going to go out and get some girl pregnant."

"Well," the pastor said. "Maybe you need to set some new ground rules.

***

Kev, be home when I get off work. We need to talk.

The text came during Kevin's lunch period. He was sitting with Scott, Tony, and Brittany. When he read the text, a grim smile came over his face. He knew the topic of discussion. He also knew the only recourse she had was to ground him from parties and evening social functions. She could get extreme and try to forbid him from seeing Lindsey, or any other girl, but she would pull her hair out enforcing that. He leaned back in his seat and rolled his eyes, imagining how ridiculous the conversation was going to be.

"What?" Scott asked. "Bad news?"

"Nah. Just count me out for tonight." Kevin shook his head. "My mom wants to talk to me."

Tony frowned. "She wants to talk to you *all night?*"

"No," Kevin replied. "She wants to talk to me after she gets off work. It's just going to end with me being grounded…probably." He chuckled at their disbelieving expressions. "She's going to have the Sex Talk with me."

"*Really?*" Brittany blurted. "She *said* that?"

Kevin shook his head. "She didn't have to." He told them about the conversation interrupted by the call from Princeton. His mother never reopened that talk and now she wanted a sit down.

Brittany's mouth was open. "So, she knows you and Lindsey are having sex." It was a statement, not a question, and she lowered her voice for the last part of the statement. That always made Kevin laugh.

"Yes," he whispered, mimicking her hushed tone.

She ignored his jab. "So, what do you think she's going to say to you?"

He shrugged. "Typical stuff probably, about how I'm too young and she's too young and how if we really loved each other we'd wait until we were married."

Brittany nodded. "She's right about all that, you know."

Kevin looked at her. "I know *you* think that."

"You know the truth, Kev." Brittany shrugged. "You don't fool me with all your philosophies."

Kevin laughed. "There she is, the condescending church girl." He leaned forward. "I love you, Brit, but you have this sad habit of telling other people what *they* believe, and it always matches up perfectly to what *you* believe. Now tell me, how is it that everyone believes the same thing you do and yet you're the only one who lives by it?"

Brittany shook her head. "Stop trying to turn it back on me, Kevin. I'm not talking about everybody else. I'm talking about *you*. I've known you for your whole life. I know how you were raised. I know what you know and I know you believe it. Maybe you don't care about it right now, but you know the truth."

He shook his head. "Well, here's some truth for you, Brittany. I *do* love my girlfriend. Having sex with her hasn't changed that."

Brittany shrugged. "Maybe, but I happen to know she's been going out a *lot* lately, and not with you."

Tony and Scott both exchanged glances and raised their eyebrows.

"Sooo…what?" asked Kevin. "Are you saying she's seeing other guys behind my back?"

"I'm not saying anything," she replied, shaking her head.

"Well," Kevin said. He could feel his blood pressure increasing. "You're saying *something*. Either you know something or you don't. Lindsey hanging out with other people doesn't equal cheating."

"I didn't say anything about her cheating on you, Kevin. I just said she's been going out a lot lately without you. You guys were going hot and heavy for a good long while there and now…what? Maybe you're both finding out sex isn't the answer to all your relationship problems. "

"No one ever said sex was the answer for *anything*," Kevin said, though he had to admit, Lindsey certainly thought sex was the answer for *some* things. Brittany wasn't far off, but it was really none of her business.

"The point is, you and Lindsey used to be inseparable. Now you seem to be going your separate ways."

Kevin stared at her for a long moment before getting up and leaving without a word. Tony made a move to follow, but Brittany laid a hand on his wrist. She sighed and patted his hands.

"I'll go," she said softly.

Brittany caught up to Kevin outside on the front quad. She looped her arm through his and laid her head on his shoulder as they walked. Kevin didn't react at all and they just walked for a few seconds in silence.

"I'm sorry, Kev."

"Don't worry about it."

Brittany sighed. "It's just that I care so much about you…*and* Lindsey. I pray for you two every day. Did you know that?"

Kevin shook his head.

She kicked at a rock on the ground. "Can't you feel God drawing you to Himself at all?"

Kevin shrugged. "Honestly...I don't know what I feel right now."

Brittany prayed silently in her heart, *God, don't let me screw this up. Just help me!* She didn't know why she phrased it like that. Christians were always scared about messing up someone's salvation, as though God was dependent on humans to persuade people to believe. One of the biggest fears Christians had is that they would somehow fumble their words or say the wrong thing and the potential convert would run away screaming. Brittany knew it didn't work that way, but she still prayed the same prayer every time she witnessed to someone.

Kevin sighed and shook his head. Brittany looked at him with tears brimming in her eyes.

"Can I ask you something?" she said, blinking and wiping her tears away with her sleeve.

"Anything."

"You knew I liked you, right? I mean...before...you knew, right?"

Kevin shrugged. "I guess I knew we both liked each other."

Her eyes widened. "*You* liked *me?* You never said anything."

"No," he said. "First, I'm all wrong for you, and we both know it. Second, my best friend has been in love with you since forever."

She nodded and grinned. "So, you were saving me for *him* all this time?"

"Actually," Kevin replied with a laugh. "I never thought you and Tony would really get together. It was like a fantasy for him...until you said yes."

She nodded slowly, taking it all in. It was amazing how God worked. She knew, had Kevin ever asked her out, she would have probably said yes. She knew if he ever tried to kiss her, she would have kissed him back. She also knew what she always felt just sitting next to him was as frightening as it was exciting, and Kevin could have probably gotten her to go even farther than kissing if he'd ever tried. She was grateful he never did. She thanked God every day for Tony, who never pressured her or made her feel like her kisses weren't enough.

***

"It's not like you haven't already admitted it to me, Kevin."

His mother sat across from him at the dining room table. Kevin had zero interest in a conversation about sex. Who wanted to sit down with his mother and discuss his sex life?

Kevin shook his head. "What do you want me to say?"

"Fine," Karen said. "Here's what I'm going to assume. I'm going to assume that you and Lindsey are having sex regularly. Is that fair?"

Kevin shrugged. "Sure." He really didn't care about what assumptions she made. As far as he was concerned, an arbitrary assumption was as good as the truth. He wasn't about to discuss Lindsey with *anyone*, especially like this.

Karen nodded. "And you know you were raised differently." It wasn't a question, but she still waited for a response. Kevin didn't provide one.

"Kevin," Karen said, squeezing her hands together. "Sitting there like a criminal and pleading the fifth won't get this over with any faster than honest answers."

Kevin shrugged. "This isn't about what I say. You're not interested in a discussion. You're going to tell me how it is…or how it's going to be."

"You know what?" Karen nodded. "You're absolutely right. I *am* going to tell you how it's going to be, but your attitude might influence who you're allowed to hang out with…*and* who you date."

Kevin couldn't keep the smile from his face. He shook his head. "So basically, you're telling me that I'm confined to this house for the next three years and you're going to homeschool me." He said it as matter-of-factly as he could.

"What?" She frowned and leaned back. "Homeschool? What are you…?"

"Because that's the only way you can enforce what you're suggesting." A voice in Kevin's head told him to shut up, but he plowed forward anyway. "If you tell me I'm not allowed to date Lindsey, the only way to enforce that is to keep me inside this house, because there's no way I'm breaking up with her. The same thing goes for my friends. I'm not changing my friends. All you can do to me is ground me for three years. And then after those three years, you'll never see me again."

"Shut up, Kevin."

His mother was used to his extremes. He expected such a response. It didn't mean she didn't believe him. She just refused to let him have the upper hand. He didn't care.

She pointed a finger at him. "You're not going to threaten me into just letting you do whatever it is you want. My responsibility is to raise you in a scriptural way. Your stupid threats won't make me change."

"Fair enough." Kevin shrugged. "So, what's the bottom line?"

"You and Lindsey are through with sex. Your word is enough for me."

Kevin chuckled and shook his head.

"It's not funny," his mother said in a firm tone. "And if you don't wipe that cocky grin off your face, I'll knock it off with a rolling pin."

Kevin controlled his facial expressions. His mother wasn't abusive but Kevin knew how to push her buttons. Push the wrong one, and that rolling pin might actually come out. It wouldn't be the first time. What would he do then…fight his mother? Not likely. He'd never raise his hands to her. Jeff maybe…definitely…but not his mother…not ever. And rolling pins *hurt*.

She looked him dead in the eyes. "What's it gonna be?"

Kevin shrugged. "Mom, that's not something you can enforce."

"I don't have to enforce *anything*." Karen grinned. "You're going to make a promise, and I'm going to trust you to keep your word of honor."

He gritted his teeth. She knew his buttons as well as he knew hers. His "word-of-honor" was nail number one in the coffin of his sex life. It wasn't a promise he could make because he was pretty convinced he was incapable of keeping it. As much as he hated what he and Lindsey had become, he still loved her. If she wanted him, he couldn't resist her, couldn't deny her. It was the reason he had to maintain distance from her. All it took was a look, the touch of her hand on his chest or face, and she owned him.

It wasn't that Kevin couldn't tell a lie. He made up stories all the time about where he was going and what went on. A promise was different. And of course his mom broke out the "word-of-honor" card. That was cheating and his mother knew it. Honor was Kevin's kryptonite. He was now stuck in a textbook rock and hard place situation.

He shook his head. "Mom, there's no way I can make that promise. I can't guarantee the two of us won't ever do it again. That's not trying to be cocky or arrogant. It's just that we're long past that point in our relationship. We can't go back."

She shrugged. "Well, you better figure out how to go back, Kev, because if you two *both* won't make that promise, you won't be together at all."

Kevin stared at her. "And you really think we'd ever stay apart? Again, not to be cocky, but unless we're going to be locked away, we'll see each other every day."

"But you won't be in bed together."

Kevin nodded, keeping his eyes down. Karen must have caught him trying to hide his expression.

"What?" she said. When he didn't reply, she slumped her shoulders in defeat. "Tell me this is going on in school too."

Kevin chuckled. "No, Mom, we're not having sex in school." He shrugged. "Then again, we've never been put in a position where we only saw each other in school, so who knows?"

Karen shook her head. "Well, you gotta do what you gotta do, right, Kev?" She sat back in her chair. "You're right. I can't stop you two from doing what you want to do, but I won't make it easy for you. If I can't get you to do the honorable thing, then as of right now, Lindsey is no longer your girlfriend as far as I'm concerned. I don't care what *you* think about it. She is not allowed in my house. You will not be going out on dates. And don't plan on any nights out with friends for the time being, either."

Kevin nodded. "So, I'm grounded indefinitely." He started to get up. "Is that all?"

"No," Karen said. "You will see Pastor Morgan once a week, beginning next Monday. You will be attending Wednesday evening in either the Youth Center or the Bible study. Don't even think about playing any sports this spring. It's not gonna happen."

Kevin nodded, considering everything she had just dumped on him. "Okay," he said. "What about work? Am I allowed in the shop? What about shows?"

"You can do your work. There's no reason to…" She looked him in the eyes. "Kevin, I want you to know this isn't a punishment. I'm keeping you from destroying your life by limiting your access to temptation while you struggle with it."

Kevin almost burst out laughing, but made sure he didn't. Instead he shrugged. "Honestly, I don't care, Mom. Grounded is grounded no matter what the reason. And making me see the pastor is just a waste of everyone's time, which doesn't matter to me, since I'm grounded anyway, but you shouldn't be wasting *his*. There's no way I'm going to discuss sex with him…or anything else, for that matter."

Karen shrugged. "You'll still show up and sit there. If that means he does all the talking, great. Then you'll be hearing God's Word instead of talking the whole time. Either way, it's a good idea."

Chapter 17

Lindsey was blindsided by her mother, Abby, who stopped her from leaving the house before dinner. She announced Lindsey would be staying in for the evening and there would be new rules at the Overton house. Lindsey sat and did what she could to control her temper while her mother lectured her.

"You're not even fifteen yet, Lindsey, and you're already sleeping with your boyfriend?"

"What difference does it make, Mom?" Lindsey asked with her arms spread. "Every girl in the school is sleeping with their boyfriend."

Abby folded her arms. "First of all, that's not even close to true. And second, I'm not here to talk about other girls. This is about you. And after what happened to your sister, how could you be so quick to jump into bed with Kevin?"

"Don't bring Tracey into it," Lindsey said. "She got pregnant because they were reckless. It's not like that with Kevin and me."

Abby shook her head and waved her hands in front of her. "I'm not just talking about pregnancy. What about all the heartache she went through? You and Kevin were perfect together! You told me one of the reasons you loved him was that he wasn't in a hurry to sleep with you. What happened?"

Lindsey shrugged. "I guess *I* happened."

"And what does that mean?"

Lindsey explained about how she had entered high school not planning on having sex for a long time, but when all of the girls, including upperclassmen, began throwing themselves at Kevin, she got scared that she was going to lose him if she didn't change her plans.

Abby closed her eyes. "So Kevin started pressuring you?"

"Not even a little bit," Lindsey said. She realized she was going to come out of this looking like a world class slut. There was no way to explain it without admitting *she* was the one who pushed sex. "Kevin always said he was fine with waiting, but how much can a guy take?" Her eyes pleaded with her mother to understand.

Abby shrugged, trying to follow along. "Before he cheats on you? Or breaks up with you?"

"Yes!" Lindsey nodded with more urgency than she should have. Somehow, the need to make her mother understand overwhelmed her. "I didn't want to lose him, so I started working up the courage to do it. Finally, we did it."

"And now?" Abby asked. "You're still doing it?"

Lindsey nodded, feeling sluttier and sluttier. "Yeah, well, it didn't make sense *not* to do it once we did it the first time."

Abby sighed. "Amazing," she said. "The two of you are so smart and yet so incredibly stupid." She looked at her daughter in disbelief.

The disappointment in her eyes made Lindsey feel even smaller. "I'm sorry, Mom. I didn't think it was that big a deal. It's *my* body. I was ready and I made the decision."

"Don't you get it?" Abby replied. "You don't get to make that decision at your age."

And on and on it went until Lindsey thought she was going to die. On one hand, she felt like she had let her mother down by choosing to grow up. To her mother, she had always been quirky and sometimes sullen, always cynical and sarcastic, but never disappointing. When Tracey had gotten pregnant, she fell from the perfect daughter status and Lindsey had enjoyed a little time being the good daughter for a while, but that was over now. Not only had Lindsey made a bad decision in her mom's eyes, but unlike

Tracey, she continued in it. At least Tracey learned from her mistake and changed course.

In the end, she was grounded, like Kevin. Tracey stepped in and tried to mitigate the punishment, but Abby told her to stay out of it. Lindsey stormed up to her room since she wouldn't be going out any time soon.

Me: Grounded 4ever.
Kev: U2?
Me: Yep. Hate this.
Kev: I know. Least u don't hav 2 go 2 counseling at church.
Me: That sucks.
Kev: Tell me about it.
Me: Let's run away.
Kev: K
Me: I'm serious.
Kev: K
Me: u think I'm not serious???
Kev: ;)
Me: u want to get hurt, don't u?
Kev: ur so sexy wen ur mad.

***

The phone rang for the eighth time with no answer. Lindsey tapped the END button without leaving a voice mail. Instead, she switched to text mode.

Me: Ur not answering.

Not surprisingly there was no immediate return text. It was suspicious. Emily never strayed far from her phone. Lindsey gritted her teeth.

Me: Answer…now.

Nothing.

Me: I neeeeeeeed youuuuuuuuu.
Emily: Hey, girlie, wassamatter?

Lindsey's eyes widened in relief.

Me: Call me. I need to talk.

Seconds later the phone chirped and Lindsey swiped across the screen to answer.

"I hate everyone," she said as soon as the line connected.

"Me too," replied Emily without hesitation. "Why do we hate everyone?"

"Because of sex!"

"Oh?" Emily chuckled. "In that case, I *don't* hate everyone."

"Guess what?" Lindsey asked. She shook her head in frustration. "No, don't bother. I'm basically grounded."

"Why? What'd you do?"

"I had sex with Kevin."

"And you got *caught?*" Emily giggled. "Where were you? Did your mom walk in on you? That's so embarrassing."

"No, we didn't get caught *actually* doing it. Kevin's mom figured it out and talked to my mom and they combined to ruin our lives."

"Well," Emily said. "Grounding you isn't the end of the world."

"They want us to promise not to have sex again."

"So promise."

"That's what *I* said, but Kevin won't make a promise he has no intention of keeping."

"Oh." Emily was silent. "Hmmm."

"What?" Lindsey frowned.

"Nothing," Emily replied. "It's just…"

"Just what?" Lindsey snapped. "Spit it out."

"Well, you made a mistake, and it's killing the two of you, and you won't admit it." Emily sighed. "Take this as an opportunity for a reset."

"A reset?" Lindsey asked. "What are you talking about?"

"Just admit you were wrong about having sex so soon and then you and Kevin can start over on the same page and fix things."

"No," Lindsey argued. "Because I wasn't wrong. Maybe I could have handled things differently afterwards, like not get so into the physical stuff…"

Emily interrupted. "Knock it off and just admit that the root of all this is that you rushed sex with your boyfriend…your totally hot and gorgeous and sexy boyfriend who I would never be able to keep my hands off, if I was in your shoes."

Lindsey would have laughed at that, but she was far too irritated. "Look, Emily, I didn't make a mistake. And stop talking sexy about my boyfriend."

"Oh, so he's *not* totally hot? And now I'm not allowed to be totally jealous of my best friend?" Emily laughed. "But if you can't admit it when you're wrong…"

"I can admit when I'm wrong." Lindsey huffed. "I know I'm fallible and that I make mistakes and I have the capacity for error. Not everything I do is good and right and fair and all that."

"So admit that you might have made a mistake having sex with Kevin?"

Lindsey wrinkled her forehead. "Of course not."

"So," Emily replied with a snicker. "This is more of a theoretical capacity for error and not really a practical one."

"Exactly."

"You're hopeless."

***

"I think you look hot."

Lindsey stood in front of her mirror, shifting from her right side to her left side. The silky charcoal-colored skirt fell all the way to the floor. The light gray top with the bluish pattern running through it was nothing special but worked with the darker skirt.

She frowned as she inspected the way the fabric slid across her curves.

"I don't *want* to look hot," she said, holding her hair up in various styles to see which worked best with the non-sexy outfit. "I just want to look good. Nothing sexual…just classy and non-tempting."

It had been almost two weeks since Kevin and Lindsey were grounded. Their united front kept them apart outside of school. They were only allowed to see each other that night because it was Lindsey's birthday party and their parents would be present.

Emily laughed and stretched her arms over head as she lay back on Lindsey's bed. "You look perfect…totes cute. "

Lindsey dropped her hair and turned to her best friend with a sigh and a look of distaste. "Totes?"

Emily nodded with an ultra-serious expression. "Look, if you want to be non-sexy, just use junior high words."

Lindsey shot her a blank stare.

"It'll work," Emily said with a straight face. "You can't be sexy and totes cute at the same time."

Lindsey pushed out her bottom lip as if to consider the ridiculous comment.

"Just try it, Lindz. Try to be hot and say something junior high."

Lindsey shook her head and sighed again. "I can't stand you sometimes." She looked back in the mirror. "Okay fine," she said, seeing the pout on Em's face. She put on her most seductive face, and in her best sexy voice said, "Whoa, dude! I should def wear this outfit. It's totes cute!" She turned back to Emily. "I can't believe I just did that."

Emily giggled. "Me neither. I totally should have recorded it."

"I think I must be losing my mind." Lindsey shook her head and leaned against the mirror with her forehead. "Maybe Kevin and I should just break up."

Emily's eyes widened in disbelief. "Whoa, sister! Slow down. Break up? Why?"

Lindsey shrugged. "If we can't be together, what's the point?"

It was brand new territory. Emily had never heard Lindsey talk about breaking up with Kevin. Well, there was the day the Brette Girl Calendar came out, but that didn't count because all Lindsey did about that was pout and ignore him for a few days. Now she wanted to end the relationship over being grounded?

"I think you need to chill a little, Lindz." She stood and put an arm around Lindsey's shoulders. "It will all work out. This is just a bump in the road. Plus, it's only been a couple weeks."

Lindsey tilted her head. "It's a pretty big bump, Em. I'm not allowed to see him…pretty much at *all.*"

"I know," Emily replied, letting her go and sitting back on the bed. "And that does suck, but you guys are the ones refusing to make a simple promise."

Lindsey rolled her eyes shook her head. She sat on a stool in front of the mirror. "Just get over here and do my hair."

***

It was after six when the guests started arriving. Tracey and Matt walked in first, with Brittany and Tony right behind. They'd all met for lunch and then watched a movie together to pass the afternoon. As they entered the Overton home, they were laughing their heads off. Lindsey and Emily stood in the kitchen nudging each other as they watched them come in.

"I guarantee you I like Brittany less than you like Tracey," Lindsey muttered.

Emily giggled. "Stop," she said. "We're going to love everyone tonight because they've all come to wish my bestie a happy fifteenth."

"I'm not your bestie."

"You are def my bestie." Emily put her arm around her shoulders and squeezed.

"*Do not* talk like that," Lindsey protested, shrugging Emily's arm off. "I swear; you're ruining my birthday right now."

Emily looped her arm through one of Lindsey's and put her head on her shoulder. "Now, now," she said. "It's time to go greet your guests, Birthday Girl…or should I say…Birthday *Bestie.*"

She barely dodged Lindsey's elbow. The scene caught Tony's eye as he came into the room with Brittany, who was toting a birthday present and card. He grinned as the girls scuffled back and forth in front of him.

"Cat fight?" he said, grinning and rubbing his hands together in anticipation.

Brittany whacked him in the arm. "Hey!"

"Ow!" he said, rubbing his arm. "What'd I say?"

Brittany shook her head. To Lindsey she said, "Happy Birthday, Lindsey." She came over for a hug, which Lindsey grudgingly reciprocated.

Tony was next and he lifted Lindsey off her feet in a giant bear hug, pinning her arms to her sides as she was held suspended in the air for several moments. She sighed and shook her head. He always had to lift her up and give her massive hugs. What an oaf.

When he put her down, he planted a big wet kiss on her cheek and wrapped his arm around her shoulders. "Love this girl!" he shouted. Turning to her, he pecked her on her other cheek and put his forehead to hers. "Happy Birthday, Lindz."

She looked at him with her patented dead stare. "Thanks for getting spit all over me, you big goon...*and* for breaking my ribs."

"Get your stinkin' lousy paws off my girlfriend!"

The shout came from the front door, and Lindsey's breath caught in her throat. Kevin walked in with a big grin on his face. Lindsey shook off Tony's arm and ran to him, intent on jumping into his arms. At the last moment, she remembered his shoulder and just threw her arms around him and buried her face against his neck.

"Mmmmmm," she moaned, smelling the faint scent of soap. It was her favorite scent. It made her want to kiss him...but she had to exercise control. "I miss you, baby."

***

Karen Timmons and Abby Overton exchanged grins as their kids embraced. Kevin squeezed Lindsey and ran his hands up and down her back and over her shoulders while everyone watched with smiles on their faces. At Abby's signal, Karen joined her in the kitchen.

"Let's at least let them have some time with their friends without us hanging all over them," she whispered to Karen. "They won't do anything tonight. We'll just make sure they don't disappear upstairs. I've already warned Lindsey."

"You too?" chuckled Karen. "I told Kevin that if we caught the two of them doing anything we didn't like, he'd be grounded until he turns eighteen."

Chapter 18

Scott Webber and his date, Renee, a petite girl with dark streaks running through her golden locks, came in soon after the others, creating a little confusion among some of the guys.

"Dude." Tony nudged Matt. "Renee Zimmerman? What happened to Hannah? She was pretty hot."

"Old news," Matt replied with a head shake. "I think he still hooks up with Hannah, but he's definitely playing the field."

"Man!" Tony hissed. "Dude's on fire."

Brittany shook her head. "Guys are such pigs. He's on fire because he hooks up with Brette Girls two at a time?"

Matt and Tony both looked at her.

"He hooked up with *two* Brettes at the same time?" Tony asked in breathless awe.

"Oh, man! You guys are disgusting!" Brittany got up. "I'm at least going to try to make Renee feel welcome and not like a piece of meat for you dirt bags to ogle."

The party moved quickly from the initial greetings, smack talk, and jokes, to the food, and finally to the best part of the evening for the kids. They found their way to the living room where they cranked up the tunes, got themselves snacks and drinks, and hung out, talking about everything under the sun. The guys talked about sports, working out, and girls, careful not to say anything too crass.

Who wanted to deal with a bunch of angry girlfriends at a birthday party? The girls gathered around Lindsey and talked about clothes, boys…and…well, pretty much just clothes and boys.

At one point, Tracey noticed someone was missing from the group. She excused herself from the conversation, leaned over, and put her chin on Matt's shoulder.

"Have you seen Emily?"

Matt looked around. "I thought I saw her walk out a while ago. I figured she went to the bathroom. She never came back?"

Tracey shook her head, feeling like she knew what had happened. "I'm gonna go see if she's okay."

Tracey didn't have to look far. She found Emily sitting alone on Lindsey's bed. The door was wide open, but Tracey tapped on the doorframe before she entered. Emily looked up in surprise as Tracey came in. Her eyes told Tracey she'd rather do anything than talk.

"Are you okay?" Tracey asked.

Emily let out and impatient sigh, and nodded. "Yeah, I'm fine. I just needed a little break. I have a lot of history in that group."

Tracey nodded in sympathy. "I understand."

Emily shrugged. "I really don't care if you understand, Tracey. I just wanted a few minutes alone."

"Fine." Tracey shook her head as she turned to leave the room. "Whatever, Emily." Then she hesitated and took a breath. "Actually…no," she said, turning back around.

"What do you mean, no?" Emily asked.

Tracey folded her arms across her chest. "I mean, no, I'm not settling for this kind of a relationship with my sister's best friend."

Emily stared daggers at her. "Is that right?" she asked, her eyebrows raised and forehead wrinkled. "Guess what? You don't have much choice."

Tracey shook her head. "You're wrong. I can't make you like me, but I can control how I treat *you*."

"I don't care how you treat me," Emily replied. "Actually, I prefer if you just left me alone."

"That sounds like a great plan, Emily. Every time we're together at a party we have to stay on opposite sides of the room?"

Tracey shook her head. "Are we that immature? We have a really nice group out there. Don't you want to be a part of it? Give me one reason why Lindsey's sister and best friend can't be friends."

Emily snorted in derision. "I think you know the reason, Tracey. You just feel guilty and want me to say it's all good between us, but it isn't. And it's not because Matt chose you. I can deal with getting dumped. What I can't deal with is a sleazy skank looking me in the eye and telling me she's not interested in my guy and then going behind my back and seeing him anyway. So forget about the two of us becoming *besties* and me joining your little group. In fact, Lindsey's the only reason I haven't skinned you alive, so don't push it."

Emily's wounds were still fresh. Tracey knew her side of the story wouldn't matter. Perception is reality…she'd heard Kevin say something like that. As far as Emily was concerned, Tracey went behind her back and took her boyfriend. It didn't matter that Matt was the one who pursued Tracey, or that Emily and Matt had never been an official couple. Even her time with Tony hadn't diminished Emily's resentment.

Tracey lowered her eyes. She never meant to hurt Emily. Matt was Tracey's first love. She had no idea what she had gotten herself into until she found herself trying to navigate the landmines of dating Matt Kildare. The Emily and Matt saga was legendary at Kendall High. Somehow, in a single evening, Tracey managed to land square in the middle of it all, and she aroused the ire of the girl who laid claim to Kendall Township's Golden Boy.

"Emily," Tracey said. Her eyes misted over. "Do you think you could ever believe that I never wanted to hurt you?"

"I never said you did."

"Then why…?"

"Because," Emily said through gritted teeth. "You could have walked away."

"I did," Tracey insisted. "Matt pursued *me!* He came after *me.* I *tried* to stay away. When he finally broke up with you, I was just as surprised as you were. He didn't ask me out until later."

"You think that makes it okay?"

Tracey could see the tears filling Emily's eyes. She really needed to get it off her chest. Tracey was prepared to take whatever words Emily chose to throw at her. She silently prayed for the strength not to strike back. She really wanted their feud to be over.

Emily continued. "You think the timing of your *official* relationship is the problem? You *kissed* him, Tracey. You kissed him right in front of the whole world just a little while before he climbed into *my* bed. Do you have any idea how that felt when I found out he had been with you earlier that night?"

Tracey nodded. "I imagine it felt a lot like the way *I* felt when I found out he slept with you when he and I were broken up. You know, when he was coming up to me every day telling me he loved me and wanted to be with me?"

That paused Emily's tirade. Something changed in her posture. It was miniscule, but Tracey noticed. A glimmer of understanding flickered in Emily's eyes. "Yeah," she mumbled. "I guess."

Tracey leaned against the wall. "It's humiliating and it royally sucks."

"Yes." Emily nodded, letting out a little chuckle. "It does."

Tracey sighed. "It all works out in the end. That's what I've learned this year."

"Yeah," Emily replied, a hint of sarcasm in her tone. "It worked out great for you. You got the guy. I had him and lost him. *Then* I got another great guy and guess what? He's also in love with someone else." She shook her head and sighed, tears filling her eyes. "And the reason is because I have so screwed up my reputation that I might as well be a Craigslist hooker, the way everyone looks at me now."

Tracey wanted to cry. Emily was just a lonely girl, no different from any other high school girl with a broken heart. She experienced her first love as a freshman and thought it would never end. She thought her looks would be enough, but they weren't. Tracey's heart broke for the girl. Here she was, unquestionably the prettiest girl Kendall Township ever produced, and her heart was in tatters over boys. She was no different than Tracey. Her heart was just as fragile. She didn't like who she was. Tracey could definitely relate.

Tracey took a tentative step forward, then sat next to Emily. She hesitated for another second, but then laid her hand on Emily's back. That little touch set Emily off in gentle sobs. Tracey knew she was holding back; Emily didn't want to cry in front of her enemy, but Tracey wanted her to know she wasn't alone. She put her arm around Emily's shoulders and pulled her close. At first, Emily resisted, but Tracey wouldn't let her go. Finally, Emily collapsed and let it all out. She cried for several minutes and wound up lying in Tracey's lap with Tracey's fingers combing through her hair.

When she calmed down, Tracey assumed she would jump up and compose herself, like nothing happened, but she didn't. Emily just lay there, her cheek on Tracey's thigh, her eyes staring absently at the open door.

"Do you think guys do this?" she finally asked.

Tracey frowned. "Do what?"

"Cry on their friend's lap while the other one strokes their hair."

They very thought of it caused both girls to burst out into laughter. Tracey didn't miss the use of the word "friend."

"Oh, my God," Tracey said. "I just had this disturbing visual of Matt crying in Anquan's lap."

That set off another round of hysterical laughing. Tracey felt like the two of them finally turned a corner. It felt good to laugh with Emily. She hoped it would be just the beginning of many fun times just hanging out and laughing together.

"So," Tracey said, afraid to get her hopes up . "We're good?"

Emily took a breath and sighed. "I guess so...yeah, we're good." She then leaned toward Tracey and hugged her.

"What did you do to my best friend?" Lindsey's voice interrupted their tender moment.

Tracey looked up at her and smiled. "Hey, Birthday Girl. I didn't do anything to her. I'm just sitting here talking to my new friend." She smiled brightly. Emily smiled too, though with considerably less cheer.

Lindsey shook her head. "You're not friends with Emily."

"Sorry." Tracey shrugged. "It's a done deal. We're buddies."

"No," Lindsey said, grabbing Emily's arm and pulling her away from Tracey. "You can't have her. She's mine."

Tracey shook her head in mock sadness. "Sorry, sis, you're gonna hafta learn to share."

"No way," Lindsey protested. "You get Church Girl and I get the Sex Goddess." She looked at Emily. "Or is it the Lust Goddess? What do they call you, anyway?"

"Rati," Tracey said as she departed the room. "The Hindu Goddess of passion and lust. Geez, Lindz! She's your best friend! Try getting to know her."

"Whatever!" Lindsey shouted at Tracey's fleeing back. "She's mine!"

She turned to Emily, who stood with a rueful smile. "Should I slap you now or later?"

Emily pointed to herself as if to say *Who? Me? What did I do?*

"You dumped me for my sister," Lindsey accused.

"I'm not dumping you, baby." Emily threw her arms around Lindsey's neck. "You're my one and only."

Lindsey pouted. "Do we have to hang out with Tracey and Brittany now?"

"They have boyfriends," Emily shrugged. "Maybe they'll forget about us."

"Ugh." Lindsey sighed and pulled her best friend through the door and back to the party. "Only if our luck changes."

*****

"Omigosh!" Tracey gushed. "This is sooo exciting!"

"I know. I couldn't sleep at all last night."

As they pulled out of the Overton driveway, neither Tracey nor Matt could keep the grins off their faces. It would be a landmark day in both their lives. They would remember the day as long as they lived. They were about to answer the biggest question on both their minds. Pink or blue?

"All right," Tracey said unable to control her excitement. She twisted in her seat to face Matt. "What's your gut telling you? Boy or girl?"

Matt looked over at her. He shook his head and smiled, turning his eyes back to the road.

"What?" Tracey said, slapping his arm. "Boy or girl? Pick one. We have to bet on it."

"You're so cute," he said, a playful smile creeping onto his face. *"Boy…or…girl?"*

He chuckled and looked at her as they pulled to a stop at a red light. The look in his eyes took her breath away. It never got old. Other guys looked at her, but it wasn't the same. She knew what was on *their* minds. It was new to her, but she was catching on. Matt's look was different. Soooo different. Tracey had seen that look before, on the faces of two guys, to be exact. Kevin and Tony both looked at their girlfriends like that. Now, the boy Tracey loved more than anyone in the world looked at her with those same soft eyes. Matt's eyes conveyed a message so pure, words could never contain it.

"What?" she said in a soft, timid voice.

Matt shook his head. "I'm so in love with you."

Whew! Is it getting hot in here?

"I love you too, Matt."

He smiled and continued driving. After a few seconds, his hand slid over and covered Tracey's. She took it and held it in both of hers. She rubbed her thumb over the back side of his hand as they drove together in silence.

"Oh yeah," Matt finally said, his eyes never leaving the road. "It's a boy."

Tracey shook her head. "Guys are all the same. Of course you think it's a boy. You just want someone to play with."

Matt raised his eyebrows several times. "And to teach how to pick up hot chicks."

"You're disgusting. You better not teach my son to be a player, Matthew."

Matt just whistled and drove.

"I'm serious, Matthew."

***

Inside the office, Matt and Tracey signed in and waited until her name was called. It took a million years, as far as Tracey could calculate. Matt just sat there as calm and collected as ever. It annoyed Tracey. He wasn't half as impatient as she was. Her foot tapped an anxious rhythm on the floor and he put his hand on her knee. She felt an instant sense of calm wash over her.

How does he do that?

"Tracey?"

The nurse's call broke through her thoughts and it was their turn. They rose in excited anticipation. Tracey's heart rate jumped a thousand percent. Of course, Matt looked the same as always. Maybe that's what years of playing football under the bright lights of the Cobras' Nest does to a guy. Maybe that kind of pressure makes him impervious to nerves even when he's about to discover the sex of his firstborn child.

Guys are such jerks!

After Tracey was weighed and her vitals taken, they had to endure another twenty-minute wait in the exam room, and then a trip to the ladies' room for a urine sample. Finally, Dr. Regina Mozer came into the exam room and Tracey, now dressed in a hospital gown, lay on her back with her feet in stirrups.

***

Matt had no idea what to do and he wasn't about to peek. Who knew what happened to a girl down there during pregnancy? He didn't want to have any nightmares, so he just sat as close to Tracey's head as possible and held her hand while Doctor Mozer examined her.

The moment of truth came when the doctor pulled the ultrasound equipment close to the bed and drizzled a bunch of gooey green stuff on Tracey's stomach. She then took the wand in her right hand and moved it over Tracey's belly until images appeared on the screen. At first, Matt couldn't figure out what it was he was looking at, but then Dr. Mozer smiled and pointed out the baby's features.

"See?" she asked, pointing at a little black spot that kept growing and shrinking. To Matt it just looked like a shadow. The doctor smiled. "That's the baby's heart." She let it sink in as the young couple stared in awe at the screen.

Tracey was the first to break the silence. "The heart…is it…"

The doctor smiled. "It's perfect. Everything looks perfect." She continued moving around Tracey's belly, taking several images and showing them the arms, hands, face, and feet.

"Awww!" Tracey squealed. "Look at those little feet!"

Matt was speechless. He was looking at images of a *living* human being! *His* baby! Tears flooded his eyes.

"So," Dr. Mozer asked. "The question is…do you want to know the sex of your baby?"

Tracey looked at Matt, and both of them nodded.

"Okay." The doctor moved the wand to the side of Tracey's belly and pressed a little harder to get a clearer image. She smiled at them. "See here? You're having a little boy."

That was it for Matt. He lost it. He pushed through the tears and the swelling of his heart and pulled Tracey's hand to his cheek, laying his head on her shoulder and whispering in her ear. "I love you so much, baby."

Chapter 19

"So, what's the good word, Matt?"

Pastor Morgan perched on the edge of his desk as Matt leaned back in his chair. The smile on Pastor Morgan's face was surpassed only by the one on Matt's as he thought about the pastor's question. He'd made sure Tracey and Brittany hadn't broken the news to the Morgan family yet. Matt wanted to be the one to tell the pastor.

"It's a boy," he revealed, beaming. His eyes even began to water. Almost a week later and Matt still couldn't keep his emotions under control.

"Ha!" The pastor slapped Matt's knee and jumped up from the desk. "That's outstanding, Matt. I'm really happy for you. A boy!" He looked at Matt closely. "The look on your face tells me you're thrilled, so I won't ask what you were hoping for."

Matt grinned and shook his head. "To be honest, I just want a healthy baby. I don't want my selfish desires taking over."

"Well," Morgan nodded, "you should always guard against those kinds of sinful behaviors and feelings, but you also are allowed to enjoy good things."

Matt contemplated the pastor's words. "I'd rather set those aside and enjoy God."

Pastor Morgan sat down heavily in the chair behind his desk and watched Matt's face. After a moment he nodded and smiled.

"You know who else felt the same way?"

"Paul," Matt shot back before the pastor could answer his own question.

Pastor Morgan was impressed. "You *have* been reading your Bible, haven't you?"

"Every day," Matt replied with a confident nod of the head. "To be honest, it takes me a long time to understand most of it. I was always a decent student but I usually hate reading. I don't know why but I just can't put the Bible down sometimes."

Pastor Morgan nodded. "Boy, I know *that* feeling." He leaned forward and pointed a finger at Matt. "You know, son, I have a feeling about you."

"What kind of feeling, sir?"

Morgan pursed his lips and leaned back. "Well, let's just wait and see. I don't want to steer you. Just keep doing what you're doing. Put God first, take care of your family, and keep your heart and mind open to whatever it is that God may have for you."

"I will, sir."

The pastor nodded. "I know everyone would answer that way, but somehow I believe you really mean it."

"I *do* mean it. I wake up every morning and pray God will lead me. I don't want to be in charge at all. I've already screwed up enough to last a lifetime. I figure if I'm not controlling things, it's got to get better."

The pastor laughed. "I couldn't say it any better, Matt. I don't think I've ever known anyone who regretted turning their life over to God. You can't go wrong letting Him take the reins." He thought for a moment. "Say, what are your college plans?"

Matt shrugged. "That's kind of up in the air. I have a few scholarship offers to play football, but that would mean leaving just a few weeks after the baby is born and basically not seeing him or Tracey all school year. I don't think I can handle that."

Pastor Morgan nodded in understanding. "That would be tough. I remember when Brittany was first born. I used to sneak home every chance I could to see her. It was amazing just to hold her tiny body and sit with her. I couldn't get enough of her. I doubt I could have lasted a single night away from her the first few months."

Matt grinned at the thought of Pastor Morgan sneaking out of the church offices to go see his newborn daughter. He tried to imagine Brittany as a baby.

"Actually," Matt said. "I was afraid I'd miss Tracey too much to be away. How could I take care of her from a football field on the other side of the country? Add the baby to that and I think I need to adjust my dreams a little."

"I see," the pastor replied. "That's a mature attitude, Matt. Again, it's very selfless."

"Not really," Matt said with a wry grin. "I'm thinking of myself. I can't be away from Tracey, not even for a little while. I just…*need* to be near her. I thought I was gonna die when we broke up."

"That's not such a bad thing," Pastor Morgan commented. "That's just love."

Matt chuckled. "Love? Not lust?"

The pastor shrugged. "Well, there's probably some of that in there too. You *are* a teen boy, and she is a beautiful young lady, but I don't think that's all you two have. I think you've been through a lot this year together and I think you've both gotten yourselves on the right path, meaning you've both made decisions for Christ. That's a heck of a good place to start, Matt. So, since you're both heading in the same direction spiritually, *and* you have a baby coming, I think it's a great thing that you don't want to be without her. She needs you."

Matt lowered his eyes. "I wonder if people will agree with you about that. When I'm eighteen and she's only sixteen, a lot of people are going to object to us, don't you think?"

The pastor pressed his lips together. "I think the only people to be concerned with as far as all that goes is you, Tracey, and her parents. If you're not involved sexually, there's no real issue, and I'd imagine they'd want the father of her baby in the picture. I wouldn't worry about anyone else's opinion."

***

"Maaaaannnn!" Earl exclaimed. "You a good cook, Professor! I ain't never had no beef like this!"

Almost a month following his near nose dive off the roof, Everett Overton was alive and feeling a little bit better than he'd felt in a long time. Some people might try to tell him the reason for that was friendship. Since the day they'd met, Earl hadn't given him much space. It was like the guy was going to single-handedly keep the professor alive.

At first, Everett tried to remain annoyed with his new "friend," but Earl proved impervious to the snide hints and even some of the more overt comments he'd made. Earl just came and found the professor wherever he was and engaged him in conversation, usually about some mundane topic until the professor turned it into a religious debate. He'd used that tactic to try to get Earl away from him and all it seemed to do was to draw the man closer. It was like he thrived on the abuse.

After a few weeks, Everett figured his new "friend" was here to stay and he no longer had the strength to fight it. In truth, he was starting to enjoy the company. The debates were interesting, mostly because Earl's debate strategy consisted mostly of nodding and saying things like "Hmmm" and "I think I get watchyou sayin'," all the while frowning and expressing concern and understanding with his eyes.

"This is Kobe beef," Everett said, slicing into the top of his baked potato. "Very top shelf. I know a restaurant owner that sells me a few cuts from time to time."

"Mmmm, *mmm*!" Earl chewed slowly, savoring every bite. "Know what? I think the Lord knew what He was doin' when He gave us taste buds."

Everett rolled his eyes. "Every single time."

Every conversation ended up the same. Earl had a way of saying something that sounded totally innocent, but it always conveyed his beliefs. Everett knew Earl had been working on him right from the beginning. It wasn't that big a deal. Everett could handle anything Earl tried to throw his way. Intellectually, Everett was light years beyond Earl, though he had a feeling Earl played the dumb groundskeeper role a little too well. There was a sharp mind behind all the Deep South twang and slang. What had begun to bother Everett of late had more to do with the fact that he found himself listening to Earl a little more closely than he otherwise would have.

"What? I open up a can of worms?" Earl sat back in mock surprise. "You don't think God wants us to enjoy our food?"

"If I believed in God, that question might make a little more sense."

A slight smile crept onto Earl's face. He nodded as he forked another small piece of meat. "You believe," he said, and chewed contentedly. "*Mmmm!*"

Everett's eyes widened. "I believe?" he asked. "Is that what you think? You think I all of a sudden believe in God?"

Earl looked at him and took a deep breath. "No," he replied. "Not all of a sudden. I think you done came to it over time. I think you found God in your work. I think *that's* what caused you to lose faith in…whatever it was you say you believed in before. You did your experiments and research and the answers you got pointed you to God." He looked Everett in the eye and shrugged. "Go on. Tell me I'm lyin'."

Everett sighed in frustration but he couldn't reject everything Earl said. He was a little stunned at how close Earl had come to the truth. "How do you know about my work?" he asked softly.

Earl shrugged like it was no big deal. "You told me."

"No…I didn't," Everett countered.

Earl shrugged again. "It ain' no big deal, Professor. It's kinda obvious you found something you ain' *wanna* find."

Everett shook his head. "But that doesn't mean I found God."

"No, it ain't," Earl allowed. "But I 'spect that's what happened. Somethin' shook up your world." He let out a loud guffaw. "Ah haaa! Yeah, Professor! Jus' like Moses an' the burnin' bush!"

"It wasn't God," Everett said. He leaned back in his chair and let out a breath. "It was just a gradual erosion of the things I believe in."

Earl nodded. "Like God don't exist an' all that?"

Everett sighed. "Would you knock the God crap off? I'm saying the things I have put my faith in are far more fragile and frail than I ever thought possible."

"You right about that, Professor."

Another frustrated sigh. "It's got nothing at all to do with God."

Earl pointed a finger at Everett and said, "Wrong, Professor. It has *everything* to do with God."

Before Everett could respond, Earl continued, "We friends, right, Professor?"

"I suppose."

"You suppose!" Earl laughed. "Tell you what, I'll take it. I'm thinking an' "I suppose" from you is like a "Damn right!" from anyone else." Earl continued to laugh. He finished his steak and pushed his plate to the side. "It's real simple, Professor. The problem ain't with what you found. It's what you *lookin'* for."

Everett chuckled. "Well, that's a wonderful forensic explanation of the scientific method."

Earl grinned. "The problem is that you wanted to disprove God, plain and simple. You can't disprove God by studying His creation. It don't make no sense."

Everett spread his arms. "Well, there's the fundamental disagreement."

Earl shrugged. "Agree. Disagree. None o' that matters. God *is*, Professor. Whether we all agree on it don't matter."

There was silence between them for a moment.

"Tell me you didn't see Him, Professor," Earl said gently. "Tell me you didn't see God."

"*See* God?" Everett scowled and shook his head. "Don't be ridiculous."

Earl shook his head and grinned. He said nothing. He just smiled in his maddening, yet knowing way.

"Fine." Everett shrugged. "You want me to say I think current scientific assumptions are wrong? I admit it. We don't know what we're talking about when it comes to origins, life, and how it all came to be. *Something* created it. Everything I've believed for my entire life is a lie. I've watched everything I've ever worked for, given my entire life to, and sacrificed everything, including my family for, crumble and fade into nothingness and now I want to follow it. Are you happy?"

Earl let out a long breath. "You soooo close, Professor." He looked up at Everett with pleading eyes. "Just let go a all that. Let go a all the things you depend on. Let it all go, Professor."

Everett sighed. "What if I don't *want* to let it all go?"

***

Tracey's eyes never left him. She just scanned his body as he drove. It was kind of steamy, knowing he was all hers. It was a warm night for March, and Matt wore a light sweater. Tracey had already swooned when she saw how it hugged his shoulders and biceps, draping over his chest, revealing the deep indent leading down to his stomach. When he picked her up, she ran her hands all over his chest, shoulders, and arms. Her mother warned him about Tracey's hormones. Just about six months in and she was almost out of control. He wasn't complaining.

She kissed his cheek at the first red light. "I love you, you know."

"I know," he replied with a smile. "But I love hearing you say it anyway."

She smiled. "Have I told you lately how happy I am?"

"Pretty much every day, but I love hearing that too." Matt reached over and touched her chin. "And I still can't get enough of this gorgeous face. The face of a Ging—"

"Don't say it." Tracey rolled her eyes. She hated her nickname. "I feel like a balloon…not a goddess."

The light changed from red to green. Matt had to look away and drive. He was a lot more careful with Tracey in the car. Brittany's mom said something about "precious cargo" and it resonated with him. Tracey had always been precious to him, but now, the breathtaking redhead carried his child, his son. He'd always scoffed at the sappy husbands who pretended their pregnant wives were the sexiest things they'd ever seen. Now he completely understood.

"I hope people don't stare at me in this dress," Tracey said, changing the subject and the mood in an instant. She wore a dark blue, ankle-length, silky dress that didn't hide her bump to her satisfaction. Lindsey, Brittany, and Emily picked it out for her and surprised her with it that morning. It was the first thing Emily participated in with their new "group" since Lindsey's party. How could she *not* wear it?

"People *will* stare at you," Matt said. "'Cause you're totally hot."

Tracey smiled at him. He was so sweet. How was it possible that this guy was all hers? He was so sexy, so sweet to her. They'd survived some rough patches, but now he was all hers. And she was happier than she had ever been. But she was fatter than ever as well.

When they pulled into the Kildare's long driveway, Tracey's smile grew in anticipation. "This is gonna be perfect," she said in blissful anticipation. "Just you and me, eating in peace and no one looking at my big giant belly."

***

Uh oh! Matt tried not to panic. The story he'd fed her was a quiet, candlelit dinner for two. He was supposed to cook for her—because a guy who could cook was apparently sexy. He may have laid the romantic dinner line on her a little too heavily. It was hard to throw Tracey off the scent. Between her and Lindsey, a guy didn't have a lot of room to maneuver. He made his plans in meticulous secrecy and managed to keep the secret right up until show time. He pulled into his normal parking spot and hurried around to open the door for Tracey. He knew she loved that kind of thing. When he bypassed the walkway to the front door, she scrunched her nose.

"Where are you going?" she asked.

"Oh," Matt said. "We have to go in through the back."

"Why? Did you forget your key?"

"Yeah," he said, feeling lamer by the second. "I know it was stupid, but we can still get in through the back door."

"This is weird, Matt," she said. "What's going on?"

It was going bad real fast. Matt shook his head. "Just come on." He grabbed her hand and led her around back. Somehow, the brute force approach worked. Tracey shrugged it off and followed him. Perfect. He just needed to hold it together for a few more seconds. Just until they came around the corner where everyone should be ready to...

"SURPRIIIIISE!"

***

The shout came as soon as Tracey cleared the corner. Her eyes widened in shock as the sound hit her and she took in the scene. It seemed like the whole world was there. Abby Overton came forward first.

"Happy Birthday, sweetheart," she said, beaming at her oldest daughter.

"Mom," Tracey said. "I can't believe this. You threw me a surprise party?"

"Oh no," Abby replied turning to Matt. "This is all your boyfriend's work. Have fun, just don't overdo it."

Moments later Tracey was swarmed by friends from school. The whole cheer squad was there, along with the Brette Girls and most of the football team. Matt invited everyone. Tracey was overwhelmed by the amount of attention. Finally, the partiers spread out into their typical groups. One group in particular had waited until the crowd cleared. Tracey grew misty-eyed as they approached.

"I tried to tell him surprise parties suck," Lindsey said as she hugged her sister.

Emily shook her head and elbowed her in the ribs. "Knock it off." To Tracey, she said, "Happy Birthday. You look beautiful."

"Thanks, Em." Tracey hugged her. "And thanks for coming. It means the world to me."

"You were totally surprised!" gushed Brittany, throwing her arms around Tracey's neck.

Tracey giggled. "No kidding. I don't know how he managed to keep something this big from me."

"And you look totally hot in that dress. We did good, right?"

Tracey felt the fabric in her fingers. "Yeah, I love it. Thank you for doing this for me. I love you." She looked around. "But where are your boys?"

Brittany scrunched her face. "Tony took Scott to try to see if they can break Kevin out of prison for the night."

Chapter 20

"Kevin, you're going to have to deal with this at some point!"

"I *am* dealing with it, Mom. *This* is how I'm dealing with it."

Kevin didn't understand what made his mother unable to grasp the fact that he didn't want anything to do with his father. He hated the guy. It seemed pretty simple to him. Why did he have to deal with it any further than that? But she wouldn't let it go.

"You think ignoring him and hanging up the phone whenever he calls is dealing with it?"

Kevin shrugged. "He's not even worth the breath we're spending on him right now. There's no way I'm gonna give him the satisfaction of a conversation. It's just not gonna happen. Everybody needs to deal with *that*."

"Ooooh," Karen Timmons said in exaggerated understanding. "We just need to deal with our fifteen-year-old son's refusal to speak to his father. Now I understand perfectly. Hear that everyone? Just deal with it."

"Mom," Kevin replied, trying to appeal to her logical side. "I appreciate what you're trying to do…not take sides against Dad, try to see to it that he has a relationship with me, be the peacemaker between your convict ex-husband and your arrogant jerk son, but it's hopeless. I won't ever speak to him. It wouldn't end well, Mom. It will just turn into an ugly, ugly mess of a scene. Why not just avoid it?"

"Why not tell him yourself?"

"Why not just let him get the picture and *you* stop encouraging him?"

"Because parents don't take their cues from their children, Kevin. You don't get to decide whether your father gets to see you. He has rights." She rolled her eyes, knowing what Kevin was about to say. "At least he will when he gets out."

"Really?" Kevin raised his eyebrows. "Then let's get this in front of a judge and see if *he'll* make me see him. Not that it matters to me, anyway. I *won't* see him, but I am curious about these "rights" you mentioned." Kevin was nearing the end of his patience. "You know, Mom, you can make me do a lot of things, but you can't *make* me have a relationship with someone any more than you can make me *not* have a relationship with someone."

The last line was a little jab at the whole Lindsey/Kevin grounding in which neither of them had given an inch. Seven weeks and counting was the longest Kevin had ever been punished. Of course, his mother continued to pretend it wasn't a punishment. She knew the battle had been lost. As far as Kevin was concerned, it was pure ego keeping her from admitting reality…just what she always accused *him* of.

"The two are not the same, Kevin."

"I never said they were," Kevin replied. "All I'm saying is that you can't control everything. What else can you do to me?"

"I'm not threatening to do anything to you, Kevin," Karen said with a sigh. "It's not about piling on punishments. You've made your decision about Lindsey and you seem to have accepted the consequences…"

"And nothing has changed," Kevin chuckled. "I see her every day at school."

"You're not sleeping with her anymore."

Kevin hid a smirk with a timely swipe of his hand. "Is that what you think? That we're not sleeping together because of this silly punishment?"

"Could there be another reason?"

"If we wanted to have sex, Lindsey and I can do it every day."

"Uh huh."

He could see his mother was skeptical, though Kevin was not the bragging type. Even she made a distinction between Kevin's arrogance and bragging. The look in her eyes told him she wasn't as sure of her opinion as her skeptical words sounded.

"The school has plenty of…*private* spaces…where a couple can be alone." He shrugged. "I haven't really done it myself, but if this punishment was the only thing keeping me from her, I wouldn't hesitate a minute. Really, all you've accomplished was to keep me from the rest of my friends. Tracey's surprise party is tonight. Matt's hosting at his place. Kinda sucks not being able to go to stuff like that, but I'll live."

"You're telling me that you and Lindsey are not going to sleep together anymore, and it has nothing to do with this punishment?"

He could tell his mother was having trouble wrapping her head around the whole notion of a fifteen-year-old kid taking a punishment for something he had no intention of doing. It must seem insane to her.

"Mom." Kevin winced. "I decided long before you punished me that I wasn't going to sleep with her again. I told you that."

"No, you didn't," Karen argued. "You wouldn't promise me…"

"Right," Kevin interrupted. "I wouldn't *promise* you…I still won't. But that doesn't mean I intended to sleep with her." He shrugged. "You don't understand. This wasn't about having sex for me. It was about a promise."

"Seriously? You're *that* stubborn?"

"I won't promise you not to have sex with any other girl, either."

"Oh, *that's* reassuring." Karen stared at him for several moments before her eyes got really wide and her mouth dropped open.

"You totally changed the subject!" she practically shouted. She pointed a finger at him. "We were talking about you and your father and you somehow got me on you and Lindsey, a subject you're much more comfortable discussing."

Kevin could barely restrain his laughter. It was a classic Lindsey move, changing the subject like that, though she was much better at it than Kevin. "I don't know what you're talking about."

She'd be so proud of me right now…

It was worth the effort, just to watch his mother's reaction to getting played, but he knew she was determined to finish their conversation. "Kevin, you have to talk to him. He's getting out soon and he'll be coming to see you."

"Getting out *soon*?" Kevin was incredulous. "When?"

"June," his mother said. "Mid-June, assuming his parole comes through, which it will. He's been involved in every early release program he could and hasn't had any incidents."

Kevin rolled his eyes and looked at the calendar on the refrigerator. "Three months." He shook his head. "This really sucks. Maybe I should take Princeton up on their offer and just get away from here."

"That's real mature, Kev," Karen said with a bland look on her face. "What about football?"

He shrugged. "I guess it's a question of what's more important."

A car pulled up outside the house and Kevin frowned as Tony and Scott Webber hopped out. They came to the back door and Tony opened it without knocking, as he always did.

"Sup, Yavs? Webbs." Kevin looked from one to the other for some indication of what was up.

"Hello, boys," Karen said. "How are you?"

"We're fine, Mrs. T," Tony said, the words tumbling out of his mouth faster than usual. It meant he was anxious. Kevin's frown deepened.

"Well," she said, standing up. "We'll talk later, Kevin."

Before she could leave the room, Tony said, "Wait, Mrs. T. We're actually here to talk to *you*."

She turned back. "Me?" She squinted in suspicion and glanced at Kevin, who shrugged. "Why?"

Tony took a breath. "Well," he began, "I was wondering…"

"*We*," Scott interrupted, nudging him in the arm.

Tony glanced at him. "Sorry, dude. *We...*" He paused and looked at Scott again.

"Thank you," Scott said with a confident wink.

"You're welcome," Tony replied. Turning back to Mrs. Timmons, he continued, "We were wondering, if it would be possible...I mean, if you would be willing, as a favor to me..."

"And me," Scott added.

"Yeah," Tony said. "And Websey too. Anyway, we were wondering if it would be possible for you to see your way clear to possibly considering the possibility of *maybe* thinking about..."

"Oh, my God!" Kevin finally had enough. "You guys are giving me a migraine! Mom, they want to know if I can go to Tracey's party with them."

Tony frowned. "Well, I was *gonna* say please."

Scott put his hands together like he was praying. "Yeah, Mrs. Timmons, pleeeassse! Can Kev come out with us just this once?"

Karen tried to maintain a stern expression, but she couldn't do it. Kevin kept a straight face. The two of them together were just too pathetic to turn down with their pleading eyes. She shook her head.

"Do all mothers fall for this act, or am I the only lousy parent around?"

Tony threw an arm around her shoulders, squeezing her and practically crushing her collar bone in the process. "Don't worry, Mrs. T. That's why you're our favorite. Bad parents are the most fun."

***

Tracey felt normal for the first time in months. She sat around the patio with her friends and fell into their natural topics of conversation, clothes and boys. Though she went to school every day and saw her friends all the time, her life was filled with doctor visits, childcare classes, childcare books, and baby planning. Not that she was complaining. Tracey loved her new life. She was back in church. She had Matt, her sister, Brittany, and now even Emily by her side. Her mother was a rock for her. She often thought about her father, and though she'd been angry at Lindsey for telling him about the pregnancy, she was now more stung than ever at his absence. Even with the knowledge that she was pregnant, he still was nowhere to be seen. What a shame.

Her thoughts were interrupted as Matt came up from behind and wrapped his arms around her, pulling her close and burying his face in her lush red hair. It was his favorite move. Tracey snuggled back into his embrace, tilting her head to the side, giving Matt access to her neck, which he gently kissed.

"You're in trouble," she said as he led her away from the crowds.

He kept his lips against her neck but froze in place. "Why? What'd I do?"

"You lied to me."

"What?" he protested. "It's a surprise party! What was I supposed to do?"

"I'll think of a way you can make it up to me." She giggled.

"You're crazy."

"You lied to your fiancée," Tracey replied. "But I will forgive you if you kiss my neck really softly right now."

Matt grinned against her neck. "Absolutely." He followed her wishes and was rewarded by her soft whimpers as he brushed his lips across her delicate neck. "Let's get back to the party."

They strolled, hand-in hand, and mingled with the guests. A pair of arms suddenly wrapped around her from behind in a bone crushing hug. Like there was any doubt as to who it was.

"Ugh! Tony!" she squealed. "There's a baby in there. Give the little guy a chance to grow, huh?"

"Oh yeah, sorry."

Tony let her go and she turned to see his sheepish grin. He always made Tracey smile. Talk about a rock. Tony had never failed to be there for Tracey. He was like her personal knight in shining armor, always there to rescue her, but without all the kissing and romance and happily-ever-after stuff. He reserved all that for Brittany.

Kevin was right behind him along with Scott Webber. "Hey, Trace. Happy Birthday." He handed her a large rectangle-shaped gift which Lindsey grabbed and took over to the gift table.

"Thank you for coming," Tracey said. "I hope you're not in trouble for sneaking out."

"No sneaking," Tony objected. "All it took was a little persuading from the Great Persuader."

Lindsey smirked. "Yeah? What'd you do, stupid her to death?"

Tony put a hurt look on his face and pointed a finger at her. "You just don't appreciate what a great convincer I am."

"Convincer?" Lindsey retorted. "Do you even speak English?"

"All right," Kevin broke in with an exasperated grin. "Let's not make the birthday girl's party about my prison sentence."

Lindsey shrugged and leaned into Kevin's chest. "Well, since you're here, can we at least have sex?" She put her hands up in surrender before Kevin could object. "I'm *kidding*." She gave him a playful push and leaned over to whisper in Emily's ear, "Not really, ya know?"

***

The girls all huddled together to talk about girly things, so the guys made their way to a less estrogen-rich environment, which at Matt's house meant the game room. It was in a downstairs room, accessed from the rear of the house through a set of sliding glass doors. It was the ultimate party room, complete with a pool table, foosball, air hockey, and various other games, along with a killer sound system. The guys lacked for nothing except food and drinks.

Kevin did his best to join in the games and joking but his mind was on everything lousy in his life. His relationship with Lindsey was in a downward spiral. His relationship with his mother was strained at best, due to his sexual awakening combined with his disdain for his father. For whatever reason, she felt like Kevin ought to give the jerk a chance. It didn't seem to matter what Kevin wanted, but he was also the sex-crazed fifteen-year-old, so what could he really expect from adults?

"So, are you gonna talk to me or do I have to drag you outside and beat it out of you?"

Tony stood behind him. He spoke in a soft voice, so no one else could hear it, but his tone was serious.

"What are you talking about?" Kevin asked, knowing it wasn't going to convince his best friend. The thing about having a really small, tight-knit group of friends was all it took was a single look, an altered posture, the slightest wrinkling of the brow to draw attention.

Tony played the big goon to perfection, but he was a natural people reader. He threw an arm around Kevin's shoulders and steered Kevin out the sliding doors. They continued away from the partiers and around to the front of the house where it was quiet. He released Kevin and leaned against a stone bench near a large garden of what would become bright-colored flowers in the spring. Kevin rubbed his now tender neck.

"You know, I'm still recovering."

Tony didn't even blink. "You're gonna be recovering from a whole lot more if you don't start telling your best friend what's going on with you."

Kevin shook his head and leaned on the bench next to him. "It looks like my dad's going to be getting out of prison pretty soon."

Tony frowned. "Okay? So what? I know you hate him, but you don't want him to get out of jail?"

"I don't want him bothering me," Kevin said. "Hanging up on him and never calling or visiting ought to send a pretty clear message, shouldn't it?"

Tony shook his head. "Come on, Kev. He's stuck up there and he can't get you to face him. No matter what you do, he's at least going to get you face to face so he can talk to you. Even if it's just the one time and you tell him off and never see him again, that conversation is going to happen."

"I don't see why I should even acknowledge his existence," Kevin said, feeling his blood start to warm.

Tony let out a breath. "I don't see how you can get out of seeing him at least once. He's going to want to talk to you and tell you he's sorry and all that face to face. Just get it over with, dude."

Kevin shook his head. "Screw that. He doesn't get to apologize to me. He doesn't get to have closure."

"So you just want to punish him."

It wasn't a question. Kevin had an unquenchable need to punish disloyalty. In his world, there was no greater sin. He demanded unconditional loyalty from his friends…probably why he had so few really close friends, but he offered that kind of loyalty as well. Once Kevin Sinclaire adopted a friend, he'd go to hell with him just to prove it.

"To put it nicely," Kevin replied. "Yeah. I'd like to do *more* than punish him."

Tony nodded. "Ahh. You're afraid to see him, aren't you? You think if you see him…" Kevin saw the lightbulb flicker on.

"If I see him, I'll probably kill him," Kevin finished.

Kevin almost never lost control of his temper. He was a shining example of self-control and discipline, but every now and then, under the right circumstances, he could be pushed over the edge. Matt Kildare came close the previous summer during football camp. An out of control parent succeeded right after the first game of the season. That guy spent seven weeks in the hospital with fractures to both the front and back of his skull after a single blow. If Kevin himself was afraid of what might happen, there was genuine cause for concern.

"What about you and Lindsey?" Tony asked, changing the subject. "You guys didn't even kiss when we got here. What's up?"

Kevin shook his head. "Nothing good."

"Really?" Tony looked him in the eye. "It's that bad?"

Kevin felt his eyes dim and lose focus. He lowered his head and fought the wave of emotions.

"We're…" Kevin began but his throat tightened and he had to swallow hard. "I don't think we're gonna make it, man."

"You don't?"

They both cringed at the sound of her voice. When Kevin forced his eyes up, he saw the wounded yet furious look in Lindsey's icy blue eyes.

Chapter 21

"So, we're not going to make it?"

They were alone. Tony scampered off like the scared puke he was, leaving his best friend to face Lindsey's wrath alone. Not that it mattered. Kevin was tired of the whole mess. He was tired of feeling down and helpless. He was at the end of what felt like a very long rope and if she wanted to have it out right then and there, so be it.

"I don't know," he said. "What do *you* think, Lindz?"

"I think if you don't want to be with me, maybe you could just tell me so I don't have to sit around the house punished every night because I'm standing by my boyfriend."

"You know that's not true."

"Then tell me what *is* true, Kevin!" Tears poured down her cheeks. "What do I have to do to get the love of my life back? Don't you see you're breaking my heart?"

Kevin's eyes burned as he held back tears. He did know. Lindsey wasn't the only one to blame for their problems. He hadn't given her much to work with lately. Everything could have been handled better by both of them, but it just felt too late. They had drifted so far from what was great about their relationship; Kevin could see no way back.

"I see," he whispered.

She stared at him. "But you won't do anything about it."

"I don't know what *to* do about it, Lindsey. I don't know how to fix us."

"Do you love me?"

"Of course I love you."

"Then why isn't that enough?"

Kevin shook his head and shrugged. "It was never enough for *you*."

He regretted it the instant the words passed his lips. He hadn't meant to throw it in her face again. He was just trying to show her that their problems were not new ones. They were repeating the problems they'd tried previously to fix with sex, but he just went and blamed *her*...again.

The hurt flooded her eyes and the tears followed. "You're never going to forgive me, are you?" She blinked away the tears. "Just like you won't forgive your father."

Kevin closed his eyes and breathed. He gritted his teeth and clenched his fists. Why did she always have to do that?

"I'm not getting into this, Lindsey. I told you I don't want to talk about my dad. Stop trying to make me out to be some lucky kid because my dad wants to talk to me."

"You *are*," she insisted. "At least *your* father wants you. That's why it's so easy to act like a childish idiot. You know whatever you do, he'll still want you."

"Yeah, Lindsey, I have it great," Kevin responded. "Tell you what...mind your own business."

"You *are* my business," she countered. "I *love* you. This was your big complaint. We never talk. I'm trying to change that."

"Good!" he shot back. "Then talk about something else."

"No," she said. "You need to deal with this. It infuriates me that you won't even see your father one time."

"Lindsey," Kevin said in a slow and even tone. "I'm going to tell you this for the last time. I'm not going to talk about it with you. I'm not going to see him. Give up. Don't push me. I'll say something I'll regret."

***

She knew what he meant. He was about to burst at the seams. She could practically see the blood boiling behind his eyes, but she couldn't help it. She just couldn't leave it alone. How could he hate his father so much? The pain in her heart from her own father's rejection was almost more than she could bear.

"You make me so sad, Kevin."

"Come on, Lindsey," he sighed. "Why do you have to make this about you?"

"It's not about me!" she cried. "I just don't understand how you can be such a callous jerk. I can't believe I'm in love with a boy who doesn't love his own father. I'd do anything…*anything*, to get my dad to love me."

"First of all," Kevin said in the same slow and even tone, though his voice was beginning to sound more and more ominous. "Our situations are not the same. They're not even similar, so stop comparing them. And second, you can walk away from me at any time."

And there it was. They had never before discussed breaking up. Maybe she'd pushed just a little too far. Lindsey's eyes filled with tears and she lost her breath. It took her ten full seconds to find her voice, and when she did it was little more than a whisper.

"Is that what you want, Kevin?" She was almost afraid to hear his answer.

He took a breath. "What I want," he said, a little calmer, yet maintaining his eerie monotone, "is for you to go back to your sister's party and to stop asking me about my father."

The look in his eyes told Lindsey not to argue. She looked at the ground. Tears dripped in a steady rhythm from her eyes, one at a time. She tried to get Kevin to look at her, but he stared off into the distance, his mind a million miles away. She struggled against her craving to put her arms around him, to kiss him, and have him hold her. She was torn between just walking away like he said, or going to him and embracing him as she had so many times before.

He must have read her mind, because just as she made the decision to go to him, he said, "Just go, Lindsey."

Her jaw dropped open but no words came. The witty girl who was never at a loss for words was overcome with sadness and had nothing to say. She didn't bother trying. Maybe they'd talk tomorrow after the anger subsided, but she doubted it would ever be the same. She lowered her head and walked away.

***

Tony stood with his arms around Brittany, talking to Tracey and a crowd of friends from school, when a pale-faced and tear-streaked Lindsey appeared at the corner of the house. She leaned against the building, trying to steady herself. Even from where he stood, Tony could see her red eyes and damp cheeks. His arms dropped to his sides in surprise and he stepped away from the group.

"Keep everyone away from her," he whispered to Brittany, whose eyes widened as she caught on.

Within seconds Tony wrapped his arms around Lindsey. She didn't resist, complain, or remark at all. Tony felt her collapse into his arms, wailing into his chest. Her body convulsed with every sob. He'd never even seen her sad, let alone cry.

"It's okay, baby," he whispered, his arms crushing her to his chest. As much as he and Lindsey traded barbs and insults over the years, he loved her every bit as much as he loved Kevin, and his heart shredded with every tear that fell from her eyes. He could only imagine what Kevin was going through.

"Let me take her," Emily put a hand on his shoulder, her eyes telling him it was okay to let Lindsey go. "Go find him." When he hesitated, she urged him with a little push. "*Go*. I got her."

***

Matt guided the girls into his house and upstairs to his room. After getting them a few bottles of water, he left them alone to care for an uncontrollably distraught Lindsey. Within a few minutes, Emily had her sobbing more gently in her lap while Tracey stroked her hair and Brittany held her hand.

Emily couldn't help but smile at the irony of it all. Lindsey hated to make a scene. If she were standing in the room watching, she'd probably roll her eyes. It wasn't that she was heartless. Lindsey was quite sweet, but she had a cynical and sometimes mean way of expressing it. She didn't like attention and would rather have people care for her by leaving her alone. In reality, she needed closeness just as much as anyone else. She'd held Emily countless times after her breakups with Matt and Tony.

***

Tony found Kevin right where Lindsey had left him, leaning on the bench and staring off into space. He slowed to a walk. Kevin felt his presence even before he saw Tony in his periphery. His best friend was pissed.

"What's your problem?" Tony shouted, shoving Kevin.

"Stay out of it, Yavs." Kevin didn't shove back, but he also didn't retreat.

"What did you do to her?"

His tone was threatening. The two of them were close to blows. Tony was out of his mind right now because he loved Lindsey and she was hurting. If things were reversed, he'd be in Lindsey's face, maybe not threatening to beat her up, but definitely in her face. Unless Kevin wanted to fight his best friend, he'd have to be the one to back down.

"I didn't do anything to her," Kevin said. "We had a fight." He sighed and leaned on the bench again. "It was bad."

Tony shook his head. He took a breath and leaned on the bench next to Kevin. "Wanna talk about it?"

Kevin shrugged. "Do I have a choice?"

"Nope." Tony grinned. "I think I've been pretty patient with you two, but you're tearing each other apart." He looked closely at Kevin. "Do you love her?"

"Absolutely."

Tony shook his head. "No, you don't. Not like you used to."

"What does that mean?"

Tony chuckled. "It's funny you can't even see it. There was a time when Lindsey Overton was the only girl in the world. Just mentioning her name would cause you to smile for an hour. And when she was in the room...it was like the sun rising in your eyes."

"So?" Kevin raised his eyebrows. "Come on with the romantic crap, Yavs. I love Lindsey just as much now as I ever have."

Tony chuckled without any hint of humor. "No. *I* love Lindsey just as much as I ever have. We still talk the same way. We still laugh at the same things. She still calls me names and beats me up. Nothing has changed between us. *You,* on the other hand, can barely stand to be in the same room with her anymore."

Kevin pushed himself off the bench. "Maybe you're right. I don't know." He turned and faced Tony. "Can you tell Tracey happy birthday, and apologize for me?"

"Where are you going?"

"I'm gonna head home. Tell Lindsey I'm sorry, and I'll talk to her later or she can call me if she wants." Kevin squeezed his eyes tight for several moments before opening them again. "And tell her I love her."

"I'll get someone to give you a ride," Tony protested.

Kevin shook his head. "Nah, I'd rather walk. I need to think." He looked at Tony again. "Just tell her, okay? Make sure she knows I'm not mad at her and that I love her."

***

"Hey, beautiful. How you feelin'?"

She had no idea why, but Lindsey welcomed his voice. She would never tell the big goof how much his voice soothed her. She'd never tell him how comforting it was just knowing he was there. She would never tell him how much she needed him. The previous night was the only time he ever had to comfort her, and she never planned on being that pathetic again.

"Go away," she replied. Might as well get things back to normal. She'd fallen asleep in Tracey's arms and hadn't moved from her bed since. If Tony was over on a Sunday, it had to be afternoon because church services at Grace Gospel ended at twelve. That also meant that she was about to be swarmed by a group of happy girls led by her sister. Ugh!

"Nope," he said. "I'm here to take care of you. I got rid of all the chicks so we have the whole house to ourselves."

"Can you shut up? I'm trying to sleep."

"It's time to get up, Princess." She half expected him to yank the covers off and make her stand up, but all he did was sit on the bed next to her and grab her hand. "How are you feeling?"

She closed her eyes. "Like crap. Get out of here and let me sleep."

"I want to be here for you, Lindz. You're my best friend, and I love you."

"Kevin's your best friend. Go get in *his* bed."

"You're my best friend too. Kevin's fine and you need me. Now slide over and let me lay down."

Lindsey looked up at him like he was crazy. "You have a girl-friend, idiot. And somehow I'm supposed to be friends with her." She put her head back down and closed her eyes. "Not really sure how *that* happened," she mumbled.

Tony chuckled. "Don't worry about Brit. She's not jealous. You're the last person she's worrying about. Now move over."

With an annoyed sigh, Lindsey shifted to the other side of the bed as Tony kicked his shoes off and took his spot, moving the pillows behind him for comfort.

"Thanks for taking all the pillows, dope," Lindsey moaned. "How is this going to make me feel better?"

Tony patted his chest. "Come on. This'll make you feel better."

"What? What are you trying to do, Tony?"

"I'm trying to hold you," he replied. "Come on." He patted his chest again. "Trust me, I'm a good holder. Ask Brit."

She didn't need to ask Brit. She knew how good he was at wrapping his arms around her. It wasn't a romantic offer and she wasn't looking for anything like that from him, but she felt safe with Tony, though she'd never admit it to him.

"My mom would so not approve of this scene," she said. She slid close to him and rested her head on his chest, closing her eyes and allowing his arms to surround her. She let out an involuntary blissful sigh and immediately felt her cheeks burn with embarrass-ment. She hoped he wasn't looking at her just then.

"Does this feel better?" Tony asked.

"Mmmm." Lindsey wasn't going to give him any reason to leave. "This is nice." She giggled. "You *are* a good holder."

"Told ya," he replied. "I know all about them females."

"Ugh," Lindsey said. "You know what? Don't talk. You're going to make me want to slap you."

Tony's response was to chuckle and squeeze her even tighter, but he didn't say anything else and Lindsey didn't complain, which was completely out of character for both of them. All she did was let out a soft moan as he squeezed the air out of her. When he loosened his grip, she snuggled against him like a child and closed her eyes. Within moments they were both asleep.

"I'm gonna have to thank Brittany," Lindsey muttered almost two hours later, as she awoke, feeling much more alive. Tony's arms had never moved and she slept better in the last two hours than she had all night.

"Thank her?" Tony asked with snort. "For letting me sleep with you?"

"Don't be disgusting," Lindsey said. "Ugh! You were doing so well. Why do you have to blow it by opening your mouth?"

"Sorry," he said. "But I'm happy to help." He kissed the top of her head and she sat up, pulling her legs underneath her. He looked at her with a sympathetic smile. "Feel like talking?"

She shrugged. "What's there to talk about? He's done with me and I don't feel like fighting for him anymore."

Tony pursed his lips. "He told me to tell you he's sorry. He said he loves you and hopes you'll call him."

Lindsey nodded and shrugged with a glum sigh. "I know you hate to see Kevin and I fall apart, but I don't know if we can be together. It's just getting too painful."

Tony's shoulders slumped. "You two are like...the perfect match. You were so totally in love last year. What happened, Lindz?"

She shook her head, tears filling her eyes, but she didn't let herself cry. The truth was, she had no idea why things were the way they were. She'd been thinking about little else for weeks, and concluded that even Kevin didn't know what was wrong. Sex was just an excuse as far as she was concerned. It wasn't like he'd ever turned her down or complained about it. Once they'd done it the first time, it was like floodgates opening.

Maybe they *had* lost some of the depth they'd once had. Did that have to be such a bad thing? It turned into a more normal relationship. It wasn't nearly as serious, the sex notwithstanding. It became pretty fun actually, at least for Lindsey. Kevin never complained until his injury and after they'd had some time apart.

Maybe he has brain damage, she thought with a wry grin. It would explain a lot, but she knew that wasn't the case. Kevin Sinclaire was as sharp as ever. He just didn't love her anymore, no matter *what* he told Tony.

Chapter 22

"Goo-goo, gagaaaa!"

"Seriously?" Lindsey said. "The kid's not even born yet and you're already talking baby talk to him?"

Tony glanced up at her and made a face. "Well, that's the language he's gonna be speaking when he pops out."

Lindsey shook her head. "You guys are idiots."

She'd been sitting in the living room recliner watching Matt and Tony make fools of themselves talking to Tracey's belly. Brittany and Emily were near hysterical on the floor, watching the whole embarrassing scene. Tracey did a wonderful job of putting up with the two morons. She sat with her feet up on a bunch of cushions piled on the ottoman. She had a look of contented amusement on her face. While everyone else in the room watched the imbeciles talking to the unborn baby, Lindsey watched Tracey. Seeing her sister so happy warmed Lindsey's heart.

But it also made her miserable. She was glad at least one of them was happy. A month had passed since she and Kevin fell apart at Matt's house. They'd patched things up…sort of…with an awkward conversation at school, but they hadn't corrected anything. Ever since, Kevin had grown more and more distant. For a while, Lindsey made every effort to pursue him, but he was sullen, withdrawn, and generally unhappy.

Before the tears could begin to fall, she rose and hurried upstairs to her room. She knew the biggest reason for Kevin's recent misery was largely to do with his father's upcoming parole. The whole thing set Kevin spinning off into a spiral of anger and depression. He seemed set on breaking things. That he'd apparently chosen their relationship was excruciating. Lindsey tried to get over it, but as March turned into April, she began to wonder if she would survive losing him forever.

"Hey." Emily's voice broke into her thoughts. "You okay?"

Lindsey shook her head. "Not really, no."

Brittany came in and kneeled on the floor in front of her. "Are you thinking about Kevin?"

Lindsey's eyes filled with tears and she nodded. She hated the way she was feeling but no longer had control. She went from being the girl who never let her emotions control her to the girl who turned into a basket case every time she thought about her…*boyfriend?* She didn't even know what to call him anymore. He certainly wasn't calling *her.*

"It's okay, sweetie," Emily said, sitting behind her and wrapping her arms around her.

"It's *not* okay!" Lindsey cried. "The guy I love doesn't love me back. How is *that* okay?"

Emily put her head on Lindsey's shoulder and closed her eyes. "Trust me, no one understands how that feels better than I do."

Even with her heart crumbling in her chest, Lindsey knew Emily was right. For someone so incredibly beautiful, Emily had the worst luck with guys. She could get any guy to go out with her, but it seemed like they always managed to fall in love with someone else. It was actually pretty impressive.

Brittany held Lindsey's hands. "We love you, Lindsey. And we're here for you."

Most of the time, Lindsey couldn't stand the perky blonde-haired, blue-eyed cheerleader, but Brittany really was a sweet girl who only wanted to help. Plus, she had a remarkable ability to comfort. It wasn't the first time she'd been there for Lindsey. She'd offered advice to Lindsey about having sex with Kevin months ago. She said that kids their age weren't prepared for all the emotional baggage sex brought into a relationship. Maybe she was right. Lindsey had plunged ahead with her intentions, disregarding Brittany and her Bible-thumping opinions and look where it had gotten her. Christians might not be the most interesting group of people, but Brittany sure seemed happy most of the time and she never appeared to be confused or pressured about sex.

"Thank you." Lindsey looked at Brittany with the most genuine expression of gratitude she could muster. She closed her eyes and let Emily pull her back and lay her down on a pillow. Emily lay behind her and propped herself on an elbow while she stroked Lindsey's arm. Brittany pulled the desk chair over and sat next to the bed as Lindsey sobbed off and on.

After a half hour, Lindsey decided enough was enough. She didn't want to be a crying mess anymore. She didn't want to spend the last couple months of her freshman year feeling dumped and forgotten. She wanted to get back to having fun. She got up, looked into the mirror, fluffed her hair a little, and turned to Emily.

"We're going to a party tonight," she announced.

Emily's lips pushed to one side of her mouth in skeptical frown. "Really? You sure you want to deal with that kind of attention right now?"

Lindsey looked back in the mirror. "Definitely. You and I shouldn't be sitting at home on the weekend. You're single. I…" She shrugged in hopeless frustration. "I might as well be."

"Lindsey," Brittany said in a suspicious tone. "What are you planning?"

"Having fun, Brittany," she replied, keeping her tone as matter-of-fact as she could. "That's what high school is all about. And I was having a lot of fun with my best friend before we let a couple of guys ruin it for us." She turned her icy gaze on Emily and said, "So? Are we going out tonight or what?"

Emily grinned and shrugged. "Why not?"

"Good," Lindsey said. "Now let's get back down there and make sure those imbeciles aren't filling my nephew's head with a bunch of caveman nonsense."

As they made their way down the stairs, they heard Tony and Matt still talking to Tracey's belly and giggling like a couple of first graders who just discovered they could make fart sounds with their armpits. Lindsey shook her head and rolled her eyes at Brittany and Emily.

"How could you two allow yourselves to be seen with these two schmucks?"

"Aww," Brittany said. "They're cute. Leave 'em alone."

"Everything okay?" Matt asked, eying the girls as they returned to the room.

"Everything is perfect," Lindsey said. "Where's the party tonight?"

"Party?" Matt asked. He shrugged. "There are a few. Who do you want to hang with?"

Lindsey smiled. "Tell me about all of them."

Tony grinned and looked at Tracey's belly. "Hear that, little man? This is what chicks do. Chicks like to plot out their night so they can be wherever the hot guys are…guys like your daddy and especially your Uncle Yavo. We'll teach you all about chicks. Plus, we're gonna show you how to throw a football and hit like a tank. You're gonna rule this school when you get big. The chicks are gonna be all over you."

He caught Lindsey's glare, which was nothing compared to the look he was getting from Brittany. He turned back to Tracey's belly. "But you gotta treat chicks with respect, bud. You can't take advantage of the fact that they're unstable creatures. Well," he said, glancing back at Brittany, who stood, hands on hips, with raised eyebrows. "Not *every* chick is unstable. I mean, your Aunt Brit's pretty cool, but your Aunt Lindsey? That chick's totally whacked in the head. You want to stay from chicks like that."

Lindsey wasn't amused. "If my nephew's first word is chick, I'm gonna beat you with my shoe."

***

"Can we talk about something, Trace?"

Uh oh.

Tracey hated it when people started conversations that way. Conversations like that never ended well. She cuddled in Matt's arms. Brittany and Emily had dragged Lindsey out to the mall for a little girl time. Tracey begged off because she was exhausted and just wanted to be alone with her boyfriend for a while. Now, her heart raced. It was too good a day.

"I guess," she said slowly, not really wanting the conversation to go any further.

She wanted to be at the mall. She wasn't sure why she was so anxious. Matt had been great ever since they'd gotten back together. His parents were wonderful. He and Tracey were back in church and doing well. She had her best friend back and was even developing a more personal relationship with her sister. Heck, she'd even made friends with her mortal enemy. Everything was peaceful in her life.

Please don't ruin it now, Matt…pleeeease.

Matt must have sensed her apprehension because he took her hand in his and rubbed his fingers over her knuckles.

"It's nothing bad, Tracey," he said with a knowing grin.

Oh, thank God!

He continued, "I just wanted to talk about us."

Tracey sat up and gave him her attention. They'd talked about having the baby together and raising him, but it was mostly abstract plans. Matt's family was wealthy. They loved Tracey as their own, so money wouldn't be a big concern, though Tracey didn't intend to be a leech. The Kildares refused to let her quit school. They insisted on providing whatever assistance Tracey and Matt wanted or needed while the two of them finished school, and that included college if that was what they both wanted. As for the *real* future, Tracey hoped part of Matt's plan was to one day be her husband. She was in no rush, but she was desperately in love with him and wanted to spend the rest of her life with him.

"Yeah," Matt said. "I've been thinking a lot about what we're going to do once the baby's born. I've been praying about it every day too. We haven't really made plans. We've kinda talked around it, but summer, and the baby, will be here in just a couple of months."

"Yeah," Tracey replied. "Are you nervous?"

"Oh yeah," Matt grinned. "I mean I'm excited too, but scared. I want to be a good dad…like mine is."

Tracey's eyes glistened. With her hypersensitive hormones, she was always on the verge.

Oh great! Yeah, go ahead and cry every time he says the right thing.

"You'll be a great daddy," she said, choking back the tears. *Unlike mine.*

She allowed a small taste of bitterness to creep into her mind and then pushed it aside. She had promised herself that she wouldn't allow her feelings toward her own father to cloud her beliefs that a guy really could step up and take care of his family. She imagined Matt being a father to his daughter just like Pastor Morgan was to Brittany. She was glad Matt had his own father and the pastor in his life as positive examples.

"Thanks." He smiled, touching her face. "I love that you believe in me. You're one of the few."

Tracey held his palm against her cheek. "You'd be surprised how many people believe in you these days, Matthew Kildare."

He smiled and rubbed his thumb back and forth over her full lips before pulling her close for a kiss. When he pulled back, he said, "How did I end up with the best girl in Kendall High?"

Tracey's face broke into a playful grin. She rubbed her belly, raised her eyebrows, and shrugged with a teasing look in her eyes.

He caught on and feigned offense. "Oh, that's real cute, you little brat. Just for that I'm not taking you for ice cream later."

"Nooo!" It was the ultimate punishment. It was worse than taking medicine from a dying patient. "You haaaave toooo."

"Nope," he replied, folding his arms. "You're mean."

"But you can't do that!" she pleaded. "Ice cream is a necessary part of a pregnant girl's diet. You're going to cause all sorts of problems. Who knows what'll happen to him if he doesn't get the proper amount of vanilla chocolate twist?"

Matt turned his head away and held his chin high in the air. "Say you're sorry."

"Ugh!" Tracey pouted. "This isn't fair!"

"Saaaay you're soooorrrrrryyyyy!" Matt sang in his best choir voice.

Definitely stick to football, buddy.

Tracey was already fighting for her ice cream fix on one front. He'd probably torture her for two days if she insulted his singing voice. Matt could be as vindictive as a high school girl.

"All right, fine," she said. "I apologize for offending you, my sweet love. You are the best boyfriend ever."

Matt squinted at her as if trying to decide if her apology was acceptable. "Tell me how handsome I am."

Easy peasy. Let me count the ways…

Tracey edged closer so she could put her arms around him. "You are the sweetest, sexiest, hottest, handsomest, *sexiest*, *hottest*…did I already say sexiest?"

"I think so," he said. "But I think it's worth hearing twice."

Tracey giggled. "I love you so much, Matthew. You make me so happy."

"Do I complete you?" he asked, throwing in a little *Jerry Maguire* reference as he pulled her close.

"Absolutely," Tracey said, leaning into his kiss and wrapping her arms tightly around his neck. She didn't wait for Matt to lead. Instead, she deepened the kiss and grasped the hair on the back of his head as she parted his lips and felt him lean back against the arm of the couch.

He had been pretty PG in his kissing of late, and Tracey assumed it had something to do with his newfound faith and walk with God. He wasn't quite sure how to set boundaries in the more intimate areas of their relationship. Tracey appreciated his concerns and wanted just as much as he did to do things the right way, but she needed a *little* more heat, at least PG-13.

She'd settle for PG-13, though what she really wanted was the R rated kissing. After all, it was only kissing, and Matt was a supremely talented kisser. Having felt his lips assault hers with ferocity in the past, it was hard to be satisfied with his recent restraint. Their relationship began with a high level of passion, and while they could not go all the way back to that state, Tracey was determined to have at least a little of it so they could keep the spark alive.

"So, what was it you wanted to talk about?" Tracey asked as she reluctantly pulled back, dragging her hand down his neck, shoulder, and squeezing his bicep. Her lips screamed in anguish. They felt betrayed and teased with such a little bitty taste. And the way his muscles felt beneath her fingers? The temperature in the room felt like it rose ten degrees in the past few seconds.

The look on Matt's face told her he hadn't been nearly ready for such a deep kiss. "Whew!" was all he could manage at first. Tracey loved when her kisses affected him the same way his affected her. She always felt like an amateur, but it didn't seem to matter. She saw tiny beads of sweat break out on his forehead.

Good. Let him think about that for a little while. And don't think I'm through with you, yet, Mr. Golden Boy.

"Uh," he stammered. "I wanted to talk to you about after the baby comes." He rubbed the back of his neck. "Good Lord, Tracey! Now I can't remember what I wanted to say!"

She laughed. "Sorry, but I'm glad I have that effect on you, even if I am a big fat tub right now."

Matt touched her belly. "You're not a big fat tub, baby. You're a beautiful angel, and I love you so much I can't stand the thought of being away from you."

Tracey's eyes teared up. "Well, we have a few months together before you have to report to summer camp. We'll work it out. I'll come visit with the baby after the season gets started and you can come home whenever you get the chance. It'll suck, but we'll manage."

Matt looked at her in admiration. "Are you really okay with that? Do you really want me to go off to UCLA and leave you here?"

"It's what you've worked all these years for, Matt. You're the love of my life. All I really want is to finish school and be your wife and this baby's mother."

His eyes widened at those last few words. Tracey couldn't believe she'd said them, not because they were untrue, but they'd never really talked about getting married, other than in the abstract, like everything else. She hoped it wasn't too much too soon.

The look frozen on his face was unreadable, but she'd already said it so there was no going back.

"Is that okay, Matt?" she asked tentatively. "I don't want to pressure you or scare you. I wasn't thinking about what I was say—"

"Shhh," he said softly, touching her cheek. "It's okay, Tracey. I—"

"I just don't want you to—"

"Shhh," he smiled. "It's totally fine. I'm trying to—"

"Matt," she said desperately. "I don't want you to feel rushed into *anything*—"

"Tracey, you're not rush—"

"Just take your time, Matt. Make sure you feel the same way before you say it. I'll always—"

"I'm not leaving."

Chapter 23

Tracey's mind raced to catch up. She stared at Matt in confusion.

"What are you talking about?" she said, shaking her head. "You accepted the scholarship."

Matt shook his head. "I accepted that scholarship before I really thought about it. Even though you and I were together and everything was okay, I was still living my old life, which meant going to college on a football scholarship."

Tracey touched his cheek. "You can still do that. Your dreams are *my* dreams now. Please, Matt, I don't want you to—"

"No," Matt replied. His voice was firm, and he shook his head for emphasis. "It's not about what I'm willing to give up. It's about what I'm *not* willing to give up."

"I don't understand." Tracey pulled her legs up under her and faced him. "What is it you're *not* willing to give up?"

The look in his face told her the story. "Oh," she whispered, looking down, her hand coming up to her mouth. When she lifted her eyes to meet his gaze again, all her thoughts were confirmed. Matt's smile caused her cheeks to flush. It still had that effect on her. She imagined it always would.

"I can't be without you," he whispered back. "And when that baby comes, I don't think I'll want to be on the other side of the country."

"Matt…"

"I'm staying *here*, Tracey. I'm not leaving you. Not ever. I've already spoken to UCLA. I'm staying here…with you."

"What about school?" Tracey asked. "What about football?"

Matt smiled. "Well, football is not important. It's not like I'm going to turn pro, right? I can join as many local sports teams as I want if I feel like playing sports. There are plenty of leagues. I'll keep in shape."

"And school?"

"I'll go to school locally. We'll see what happens after you graduate. At least then, if we want to go somewhere, we can do it together…*after* we get married."

He let it sink in for a moment as her eyes widened and her mouth opened and closed slowly. He slid off the couch and down onto the floor, pulling something from his pocket. He took her hand in his.

"Tracey," he began. "Everything I want in life is right here in this room. I need you to believe that I'm not really giving up anything. It's just that my dreams have changed, that *you* are my dream…you and him." He pointed to her belly. "I can't even express it in words. I love you so much, my entire body aches when you're not with me. I *hate* it when we're not together. I literally hate it. So, I'm staying."

He was about to lose it. Tracey could see the tears forming, starting to fill his eyes.

"I want to spend the rest of my life with you, Tracey Overton. When you graduate high school, I want to marry you and give our little boy a home and lots of little brothers and sisters."

Tracey beat him to it. Her tears spilled over onto her cheeks, which were already flushed red. She had to wipe them away in order to see the magnificent blue diamond in a platinum setting as he held the ring between them.

"Tracey Overton…will you marry me?"

Tracey didn't hesitate and didn't need time to think about it.

"Yes!" she shouted, collapsing into his arms, her tears pouring from her eyes.

He pulled her close, with one hand tangled in her thick red hair and the other around her ever-expanding waist. How could he love her when she was this huge? It didn't matter. He did. She unloaded a series of frantic kisses all over his face and neck, alternately squeezing him so tight he could barely breathe and smothering him with more kisses.

Matt's laughter was the only thing that slowed her down. "What?" she asked, putting her hands on both his cheeks and crushing her lips to his. "You don't like getting a thousand kisses after proposing to a girl?"

Matt grabbed both her wrists and held her back a little bit. By now she straddled him, trying to escape his grasp so she could return to her all-out kiss assault. He maintained his grip with ease, and smiled at her as she struggled.

"Actually," he said in a calm tone. "I love every one of your kisses."

Tracey shot him a wicked grin. "Good…'cause I love kissing you. So, let me go and I'll kiss you 'til my mouth gets tired."

Matt shook his head. "Can't do that."

"But whyyyyyy?" Tracey whined and pouted. "I want to make out with my fiancé."

"Because," Matt replied with a grim smile. "You're not *officially* my fiancée."

"Excuse me?" Tracey said, her eyebrows raised and a serious don't-mess-with-me look on her face. "You asked me to marry you and I said yes. So, you, Mr. Kendall Township Golden Boy, are mine…all mine…forever and ever."

"You're right," Matt replied. "Except you never took the ring. It doesn't count if you don't take the ring. Hence…" He shrugged. "No engagement."

She looked at her left hand. "But my fingers are fat. It won't fit."

Matt smiled. "I measured your finger when you were sleeping two weeks ago. It will fit perfectly." He took her hand and slid the ring onto her ring finger. It fit perfectly. "And *after* you have the baby, we can have it resized."

She held the hand with the ring in her other hand and stared at it. She'd never seen a blue diamond up close, only the typical clear ones. It was breathtaking. The round-cut blue diamond had to be at least two carats, set in a sleek platinum band with smaller diamonds set all the way around. The centerpiece was such a brilliant blue; Tracey couldn't take her eyes off it.

"Matt," she said, her voice shaking, her eyes riveted on the blue galaxies resting serenely on her left ring finger. "This…" She shook her head. "I…"

"Tracey," he said as he stroked her arm. "It looks amazing on you. Hold it up to your face."

She wrinkled her forehead but complied, holding her hand up to her cheek so the ring was facing out. Matt grinned.

"It's almost exactly the color of your eyes," he said, clearly pleased with himself. "I had to look at a million diamonds to get one that close."

She should have known. He didn't just go out and find a beautiful ring for her. She'd have appreciated anything he put on her finger. But the fact that Matt felt it so important that he had to get the exact shade of blue to match her eyes made it even more special. The love of her life actually saw *her* in this ring, so it was special to him just as it was special to her. Her heart swelled. He was constantly surprising her.

"It must have cost you a fortune," she said, staring again at it as she held her hand out in front of her.

Matt put his hands behind his head. "Actually, I settled for that one. It turns out they don't make a ring beautiful enough for the girl I love, so you're stuck with that one. Sorry."

Tracey smiled and looked down at him. "I love it. I absolutely love it." She bent down and rested her arms across his chest, staring as deeply into his eyes as she could. "And I love you. And I'm going to spend the rest of my life loving you. You're gonna be so sick of me by the time I'm through with you…"

He moved like lightning, somehow rising up and lifting her onto the couch so that he loomed over her. She let out a shriek and a giggle as he did so. Now, with their positions reversed, he leaned in and kissed her waiting mouth, their lips barely touching. He lightly brushed his lips back and forth across hers, basically driving her insane with desire.

"And that," he said, "will never happen."

***

Earl tapped a finger on Everett's kitchen table. "You know watchyou problem is, Professor?"

Everett sighed. "That I still have a pulse?"

Everett's frustration had only grown in the past couple months. Following his confession that science didn't have all the answers, he half-expected to receive some kind of revelation from the universe. Maybe this god everyone keeps talking about would show him whatever it was he showed people to make them believe.

Receiving no such answer didn't push Everett in God's direction. He wasn't the sort to just go with it. He needed something concrete on which to base a conclusion. Earl kept talking about a change of heart versus a change of mind, but Everett had no idea what that meant. It sounded like more religious doubletalk. Earl insisted it wasn't about religion at all. It was about a relationship with God, but that sounded even more like religious nonsense.

And round and round they went for weeks on end. Everett and Earl were inseparable in the evenings. The professor decreased his evening hours. When he wasn't teaching a class, he put in limited lab time and generally went home in time for dinner, a change that caught the attention of most of his colleagues, including Andrew Michaelson, who saw it as a positive sign. After refusing vacation time to go home and see his family, Michaelson thought Professor Overton would crash and burn in short order. The changes seemed proactive and healthy, so for the time being, he would accept the new status quo.

"You comin' to the truth." Earl was pulling a big pot of God-knows-what out of the refrigerator. He took it to the stove and turned on a single burner, placing the pot on top.

Everett chuckled. "The truth. I'm sure you're wrong.

Earl chuckled right back at him. "Yeah, well, I'm a glass-half-full kinda guy. I got ta take what I can git witchyou."

"Look," Everett said. "Just because I admitted the failures of science in certain areas doesn't mean I believe in God all of a sudden. I'm still a scientist and I still believe in science."

"Just not as the end-all-be-all source of knowledge." Earl stirred.

"It depends on what we're talking about," Everett said. "Science has given the world an awful lot. Even *you* have to admit that." It was so elementary Everett couldn't believe he was bothering to make the point.

"Oh I ain' denyin' what science done for the world," Earl said, still stirring in smooth, practiced strokes. "I think we jus' have a difference of opinion what science *is*."

"What science *is*?" Everett frowned. "We're back to that?"

Earl chuckled. "I never knew we talked about it."

Everett shrugged. "I don't remember. These conversations all run together and they always end up back at the same place."

"Oh really?" Earl queried. "What place is that?"

"With you trying to get me to believe in God."

"Now, Professor," Earl shook his head with a knowing grin. "We both know you already believed in God 'fore you ever met me."

Everett took in a deep, frustrated breath. Earl threw comments like that around ever since they'd met. Everett knew the technique well. Comments like "you and I both know" was a classic debate strategy to appeal to one's opponent's desire for peace and conciliation. Earl did it naturally in conversation, and had a way of condescending without offending, which meant he was a natural debater.

"First of all," Everett said. "You and I don't agree at all. I've never believed in God a day in my life. Just because I can't explain the origin of life doesn't lead me to God. You need to accept that I'm not interested in God, even if He *does* exist."

"Ahhhhh!" Earl stopped stirring and pointed at Everett. "See? You admit He *might* exist!"

Everett sighed and put a hand to his forehead. "I don't think He exists."

"But He *might*."

"I doubt it."

"But *maybe* He does."

"No," Everett said with too much emphasis. "He doesn't."

Earl chuckled, pulling out two bowls and spooning a hefty portion of his concoction into each. He placed one in front of the professor and sat down with the other one across the table. As was their custom, Earl said a prayer for the food while the professor sat respectfully and waited until he was done before eating.

"This is good," Everett said after a couple of mouthfuls. He took another bite. "This is *excellent*. Is that molasses?"

"Yeah," Earl replied. "They's some molasses in there."

Everett chewed with a contemplative expression on his face, like he was searching for something. "And mango?"

"Might be one or two." Earl grinned across the table. "This is one a dem everything-but-the-kitchen-sink kinda dishes."

Everett nodded. They ate in silence for another few minutes.

"You know," Everett said, wiping his face with a napkin. "This would go well with a nice glass of Cabernet."

"Mmm," Earl said. "'Spect it would."

"But you don't drink."

"That's true. I don't."

"Because you're a Christian?"

"Naw. That wouldn't make sense."

"No, it wouldn't," Everett said. "Jesus drank wine."

"Yes, He did," replied Earl. "If He existed, right?"

Everett smiled as he spooned another mouthful and chewed for a few seconds. "Actually, Jesus is an historical person, so I don't dispute *His* existence."

"Ahhh," Earl said. "So, what's the problem, Professor?"

"I said I don't dispute that *Jesus* existed. I definitely dispute who Christians claim He is."

"Is?" exclaimed Earl.

Everett rolled his eyes. "Was."

"No." Earl grinned. "You had it right the first time, Professor. I think you done had one a them…aww man, what they call it when you say something your brain means, but *you* ain't mean?"

"Freudian Slip?"

"That's it!" Earl pointed.

"It wasn't a Freudian slip," Everett said with a snort.

"Well," Earl replied. "It was *something*. And that something made you right."

Everett shook his head. "You really believe God became a person so he could die for you?"

"Yep."

"Don't you think that's a little arrogant on your part?" Everett wrinkled his forehead. "To think that God would need to die just to save your soul."

"Well," Earl replied, "not just mine."

"It's just silly, that's all."

Earl studied the professor's face. You tryin' to get me ta preach to you, Professor? I tend to know what it looks like when a man's searching."

"I might be searching," Everett allowed. "But I'm not searching for *God*."

Earl raised his eyebrows. "See? That's where you wrong, Professor. *Everyone* searchin' for God. Just don't everyone *know* they's searchin for God."

"That makes no sense whatsoever."

"Really? It ain' possible for people to spend their lives going from one experience to the next, never feelin' complete, never gettin' what they need…not for very long, at least? Ain' none o' that possible, Professor?"

"Of course, that's possible," Everett said dimly. "But to suggest that they're all searching for the same thing is patently ridiculous."

"Hmmm. So, it's ridiculous to think that even though dey doin' pretty much the same thing, and even though dey all turn out the same, least the ones that don't find God do…it's ridiculous to think that dey all *looking* for the same thing, but it's a'ight to think dey all lookin' for something different? How *dat* make sense, Professor?"

Everett was a little thrown by the logic. He'd been through similar debates in the past but had never been confronted with that argument. It was so simple, yet there was an elegance to the way the uneducated groundskeeper maneuvered the conversation. The man was an enigma.

"Okay, fine," Everett conceded. "Maybe they *are* looking for the same thing. But it doesn't have to be God. It could be something more rational, like…"

"Happiness?" Earl smirked.

"Very funny," Everett said. "But just because there is no such thing as happiness doesn't mean people don't want it."

"True," Earl replied. "But maybe when you talkin' bout happiness, what you really mean is God."

Chapter 24

"It sounds crazy to me." Mike wound up and fired a baseball down the middle of the plate.

Hisssss…POP!

"It's *not* crazy," Matt insisted. "It's different and maybe unexpected, considering my life, but it's definitely not crazy."

Hisssss…POP!

"Wow!" Matt said. "You're really throwing hard these days. I guess the foot's a hundred percent?"

Mike went through his full wind-up and let loose with another wicked fastball. Mike broke three bones in his foot at the beginning of football season. It was the end of his football season, but even worse was the possibility of missing baseball season. Mike had scholarships to virtually every college in the country with a baseball team. He was even scouted by professional teams and was expected to be drafted.

Hisssss…POP!

"Yep," he replied. "Thank God."

"Exactly," Matt nodded.

Mike shot him a quizzical look. "Are you serious about all this? I'm worried about you, dude."

Matt shrugged and wrinkled his forehead. "Why worried?"

Hisssss…POP!

"All these changes," Mike said. "I get the whole relationship thing. You're in love with her and she's having your kid. But the rest of it? You pretty much gave up the rest of your life. Was all that necessary? You couldn't play baseball for one more season? She wouldn't have understood?"

"Who? Tracey?" Matt shook his head. "She had nothing to do with me quitting baseball. She didn't even know about it 'til I told her I wasn't playing. Then she kinda whined a little about not getting to come watch me in my uniform." Matt chuckled and shrugged. "I don't know what was necessary and what wasn't, but I didn't want to play ball because I wanted to spend my time with her."

Mike nodded. He eyed Matt for a minute. "And the religious stuff? That all about Tracey too?"

Hisssss…POP!

Matt shook his head. "*I* was the one who got *her* back into church. She was in a bad place after we broke up."

"And so now you're throwing away your football scholarship and staying home."

"I'm about to be a father, Mike. Who leaves their newborn baby to go across the country for a game?"

Hisssss…POP!

"No," Mike said. "I'm not knocking it. You've just made some huge decisions in a short period of time, and now you're telling me you want to be a pastor?"

Matt shook his head. "I didn't say I *wanted* to be. I said I *might* be feeling a pull in that direction."

"What's the difference?"

"Hey, Mike!" the catcher, Gordy Dunn, shouted. "Let's see some curves and sliders. I want to see what kind of stuff you have."

Gordy was a tactician behind the plate, much like Scott Webber was at quarterback. He always wanted to know exactly what the pitcher had working for him before they took the field. Mike obliged him because Gordy was great at reading batters and knew how to set them up for disaster.

"The difference," Matt said, as Mike wound up and threw a nasty slider. "Is that I would never even have considered being a pastor on my own."

"No kidding," Mike said dryly. "Do you really expect people to take you seriously?"

Matt shrugged. "I would hope that if God pulls me into ministry, He'd handle the part about people taking me seriously. Plus, don't you think a pastor with my kind of history might have something worthwhile to say, especially to kids?"

Mike nodded. "I guess it makes sense in a way. And your fiancée's on board?"

"Well," Matt said, "I haven't told her everything yet. I'm still trying to wrap my head around the possibility and I'd like to talk to my pastor about it before I start picking out seminaries to apply to."

***

Matt lay in bed late, absently tossing a ball up until it almost touched the ceiling and came back down. He'd been doing that since he was six years old and had it down pat. He could do it all night and never even think about it.

After picking Tracey up and joining Vivian at the ball field, they watched Mike throw another complete game no-hitter and cheered as the Cobras won 7-0. After the game, they all went out for ice cream before heading home. Matt spent another hour or two kissing Tracey on her front step, enjoying the way her lips felt against his and how her hands felt against his cheek.

Matt felt like all his dreams were coming true. There was something about having the girl he loved in his arms that made everything else in the world okay. Then he realized he'd been feeling better about himself even before Tracey had reached out to him. It wasn't the girl who fulfilled him. It was his relationship with God. That was the change having the greatest effect on his life. It was the change leading to every other good decision he made. Perhaps that was the reason he felt so right. He knew it had to be from God. It couldn't have come from himself.

What he found remarkable was the knowledge was not limited to his head. Pastor Morgan had pointed out more than once that Matt was not simply regurgitating things he'd read, but living them out in his daily life. He was doing it, in many cases, without even realizing it. His heart had changed. His behaviors were changing as a result. It was an inside-out transformation, according to his pastor.

Over the weeks, Matt's desire to grow only increased. He asked scores of questions, joined the pastor's study group, and impressed every pastor on the Grace Gospel staff. He also impressed Brittany, who used to look at him like he was a monster, but now looked at him like he was some kind of hero. Tracey was tearful, overjoyed her best friend was so accepting of Matt's transformation because, in some way, it validated the changes within. She believed in him. And *that* made him believe in himself.

But he quickly realized believing in himself was a major mistake. Non-Christians spend all their time believing in people. Those who don't believe in people need to believe in something else, otherwise they usually end up depressed and suicidal. So, Matt made the decision to focus on believing in Christ and the changes *He* had made in him. And *that* led Matt to his more recent thoughts of becoming a minister.

Matt reasoned such drastic changes, so quickly in a person, must mean something, but Pastor Morgan talked him out of that speculation.

"You have to stop ascribing human reasons for God's actions. You can't just go with what seems logical to you and assume God thinks the way you do. Going into ministry might not make any sense at all. It might be the most ridiculous thing you've ever done in your life."

Matt gave up trying to figure out why he felt such a strong pull in the direction of ministry. The next thing he knew, the pull grew stronger and he realized he could not leave for college. He had to stay home, not just because Tracey was here and she was about to have a baby, as if that wasn't reason enough. The reality was, he had a strong sense he needed to remain in his home church. Whenever he thought of leaving, he got anxious, as if leaving

Grace Gospel would somehow result in disaster. Pastor Morgan told him to pray about it.

"If you're just scared, you're not letting the Spirit guide you," he said. "If these feelings are in your heart, it could be because God has something different for you than what you originally planned."

Matt argued if God wanted him to stay home for school, wouldn't He use his family or Tracey, or something like that to urge him to stay?

"He might," the pastor had responded with a small smile. "Then again, He might not."

***

"Dude, this is stupid."

Tony shook his head as he looked across the shop at Kevin, who offered no response. He probably couldn't hear. Kevin was making delicate finishing cuts on the piece of box elder mounted and spinning on his lathe. Kevin had crafted what was once just a four-inch-wide square by sixteen-inch-long block of wood into a beautiful, delicate, long stemmed goblet with two intertwined "captive" rings on the stem. These goblets were among Tony's favorite pieces in Kevin's repertoire. What made them so impressive to Tony was how thin Kevin was able to get both the stem and the walls of the goblet. By the time Kevin was finished, the goblet's walls would be less than one eighth of an inch in thickness. The final piece would be so light and delicate, Tony was always afraid to handle them lest he break one.

Tony came closer and admired Kevin's work. He was always impressed by his friend's talent and patience with those pieces. They were so beautifully crafted; Tony understood why Kevin had so many orders for them. They were perfect wedding gifts. As much as he loved to watch his friend work, Tony had other things on his mind.

"This is stupid, Kevo," he repeated. "Staying home every Friday night is not cool."

Kevin shrugged. "Being cool isn't something I really ever cared about, Yavs."

"No, I mean, not hanging out with your best friend is not cool."

Kevin grinned. "Getting tired of hanging out with Brit?"

Tony shook his head. "Not at all." He bit his lip. "Hey, I wasn't ever gonna ask you this, but I'm curious."

Kevin frowned and paused while the machine continued to spin the goblet. "Okay."

"How come you never hooked up with Brit?"

Kevin looked at him like he was nuts. "Why would you ask that?"

Tony returned his stare with a disbelieving look of his own. "Come on, dude. She already told me she's always had a serious crush on you." He grinned. "I think she felt bad about liking you…like there's a girl in Kendall Township that *doesn't* like you."

Kevin laughed and looked at Tony. He pointed to his face. "It's the eyes," he said, shaking his head. "They love the eyes."

Tony nodded. "Uh huh. Anyway, how come you never made a move on her?"

Kevin shrugged. "She couldn't be with me. I'm not a Christian."

"It didn't sound like *she* felt that way." Tony sat on a shop stool and folded his arms over his chest. "Brit made it sound like all you had to do was ask."

Kevin went back to sanding. "Well then, I'm glad I never asked. I hate to think of what would have happened to her if I had gotten with *her* instead of Lindsey."

Tony tilted his head. "You don't think she'd have been able to handle it?"

Kevin shrugged. "Some of it, yes. But if she was that into me, the whole sex thing might have ruined her. You see what it's done to Lindsey and me. Can you imagine if Brittany had all that *and* the shame of committing such an egregious sin? Saving herself for marriage is a huge deal for Brit."

"You think she'da actually done it?"

Kevin shrugged. "No idea. I'm just saying the pressure over sex was intense."

Tony considered for a minute. "So, you think I'm gonna have an issue come football season?"

Kevin shook his head. "I don't know." He straightened up and looked at Tony. "But I know you need to do better than I did for Lindsey."

Kevin sanded for a few more minutes in silence before straightening up and switching off the lathe. As the piece stopped spinning, Kevin took it off and inspected it, wiping it down with a cloth soaked in denatured alcohol to get all the dust off. When he was satisfied it was flawless, he set it on a cart, which contained eleven others, all waiting for a final finish to be applied. These would all be stored, awaiting the day Kevin received an order for one. He would then add whatever personalization the customer requested and apply a finish.

"Anyway," Tony said. "Let's get cleaned up and go out."

Kevin shrugged. "I don't think so."

"Are you serious?" Tony was incredulous. "Look, chief, I want to party with my best friend. You don't get to sit around while I'm out having all the fun. Now put that crap away, get some clothes together, take a shower, and come over to my place. There's a little pre-Memorial Day fiesta going on at Fontaine's."

Kevin sighed. Once he sank his teeth into persuading Kevin, Tony would never let up until he got his way. He was like a girl that way, but he got results.

"Fine," Kevin said. "Let's do it."

***

Kevin hadn't set foot in Les Fontaine's house since before the state championship game. As he followed Tony and Brittany up the steps to the front door, he rubbed his shoulder. He was well on his way to full strength, but he still had the scars from the four surgeries it took to repair all the damage. They were a constant reminder of what he had put himself through to win a championship.

As he crossed the threshold into the house, all eyes turned and rested on him. He gave a one-size-fits-all head-nod to those in the room and followed Tony and Brittany into the party.

"Hey, Mad Dawg's in the house!"

Kevin recognized Anquan's voice without seeing him. As he walked into the kitchen, he saw Anquan, Scott, and a bunch of other Cobras. They crowded around and greeted him with high-fives and fist bumps. Though he'd been back to school for weeks, he was greeted as though it was the first Kevin Sinclaire sighting in years. He supposed seeing a person in school every day didn't qualify as "out and about." He supposed he had to show up at a party to be considered fully healed. It actually made a strange sort of sense as he thought about it.

"There he is!" Les Fontaine rolled into view. "The star of the show!" He put his hand out. "How you doin', Champ?"

"Hangin' in," Kevin replied, shaking his hand.

"Shoulder's all healed? I heard about all the surgeries."

"So far, so good." Kevin shrugged and rotated his shoulder a little. "Feels good and I'm starting to work out again."

"Think you'll be full strength for next season?"

Kevin nodded. "Yeah. They thought so even before I had the last surgery, and I'm weeks ahead of schedule now."

"Awesome," Les said. "Well, I'll let you get to your lady."

Kevin frowned. "Lady?"

Les wrinkled his own forehead. "Lindsey? The knockout you've been with since I've met you? Ring any bells?"

Kevin glanced at Tony who shrugged it off. "Lindsey's here?"

Les jerked his thumb over his shoulder. "She was in one of the back rooms, playing pool with a few people last time I saw her."

Kevin nodded and raised his eyebrows at Tony, who followed him as he went deeper into the house looking for his girlfriend.

"What are you gonna say?" Tony asked as he caught up.

"I don't know," Kevin said. "But this has gone on long enough. I guess I'll just suck it up and tell her I'm sorry and I love her."

Brittany grinned. "That could work."

Chapter 25

As they approached Les' huge game room, the door burst open and an agitated Emily Vasquez slammed the door behind her as she muttered to herself. When she saw the group approaching the room, her eyes widened in shock and she stopped in her tracks.

"Hey, guys," she said, glancing back at the door to the game room. "What's up?"

"Hey, Em." Kevin smiled. "Is Lindsey in there? I need to talk to her."

"Uhh…" Emily glanced back at the room. "I think…I mean, she…I…"

"What's the matter?" Tony asked, scrunching his forehead.

Emily held her ground and kept herself between them and the door.

Kevin scowled. "What's going on, Emily?"

"Nothing, I swear."

"Uh huh." Kevin stepped around her, but she grabbed his arm.

"Kevin, don't," she said. "Just…don't."

He squinted into Emily's eyes for a second before shrugging her hand off and pushing the door open. What he saw wasn't a total surprise. The look on Emily's face a second before made him suspect far worse. The scene couldn't have been more innocent, but the look on Lindsey's face told him all he needed to know.

Lindsey hadn't been doing anything when he opened the door…at least not that Kevin saw. However, she had the guiltiest look on her face he'd ever seen and the guy who was there with his hands on her arms removed them instantly when he realized who was in the doorway. The guy's name was Tom, or Tim, or something like that. He was on the wrestling team and Kevin's only encounter with the guy had been when a bunch of wrestlers had squared off against him in the cafeteria.

Kevin wasn't interested in the wrestler, though he was mildly amused at the fear frozen on the guy's face. He was about Kevin's size and one of the better wrestlers on the team, but he wasn't crazy, and he clearly thought Kevin was. Kevin's eyes riveted on the girl he'd spent the last year loving…and sometimes, *not* loving.

Though she was busted and guilty as could be, Lindsey did manage to gain control over her emotions enough to lift her head. She steeled herself and met his eyes with as steady and confident a gaze as she possibly could. Kevin saw the look in her eyes change and all of a sudden, the guilty look turned into one of defiance. Lindsey may not have planned the scene, but Kevin could see she was prepared to take advantage. She clearly had a message to send that she was unwilling or unable to verbalize. He stood there for several seconds. He felt hands on his arms and back. He knew at least one of them belonged to Tony, who was no doubt waiting for the inevitable explosion.

But it never came. Instead, Kevin did his best to relax his muscles and control his breathing, all the while maintaining eye contact with Lindsey. He had to give her credit. She might be the only person he'd ever met, save his mother, who had the nerve to stare him down. Lindsey wasn't afraid of him, never had been. He could be ice cold and downright nasty when he wanted to be, but Lindsey was made of similar stuff.

It was a battle between his emerald-green eyes and her ice-blue ones. Lindsey held his gaze without wavering. Their relationship was irreparable. They would both lose, but for whatever reason, neither of them was willing break eye contact. Kevin knew it wasn't a battle of wills. It wasn't a contest. It was the end, the final act. It was the end that neither of them really wanted.

Shut it down.

Kevin tried to get through the moment by feeling everything he had always felt for Lindsey. He didn't want to hate her. He didn't want it to end this way, but the look in her eyes told him that ship had sailed. His heart fought his will.

Shut it down, before you do something you can't take back…

It took Kevin's brain a matter of seconds to shift into a mode he reserved only for times of intense rage or violence. He breathed in and pushed it down, letting it out in a long, slow breath. As much as he wanted to, he would not permit himself to explode in a rage. Instead, he allowed his entire body to go ice cold; then he felt nothing at all.

Kevin finally broke the stare. He took another deep breath and let it out, nodding as he did so. He strode into the room, taking in the entire scene as he did so. There were several members of the wrestling team standing and sitting around the room, every one of them looked ready to leap to the defense of their teammate. Most of them hated Kevin and would love the chance to get into it with him, though none of them had the nerve to start that war themselves.

Kevin picked up a ball from the pool table and tossed it back and forth between his two hands. Lindsey now stood in anxious silence. Kevin scanned the room with his lips pursed. He put the ball back, leaned on the table with both hands spread on the felt, and looked at Lindsey again. She shrank back just a bit, no longer so defiant and confident. Kevin pressed his lips together, his eyes dark and vacant. He looked down and nodded, as if finally agreeing with something he had been wrestling with.

Looking up at Lindsey, he continued to nod. There wasn't much to say, so he kept it simple. "Okay then."

And he walked out.

***

Kevin's expression never changed as he left the room and strode past his friends. Tony and Brittany followed behind him in silence as he stepped through the crowd of Cobras and Brette

Girls still bent on worshiping him. He had half a mind to take one of the pretty Brettes upstairs just to be spiteful, but he could never be so cruel. Even the girls throwing themselves at him deserved a little respect, even if Lindsey didn't. He accepted their hugs and kisses as he made his way through the room and pushed through the front door.

"Kevin," Brittany said, laying her hand on his shoulder. "Please talk to us. I know you're hurting. Don't walk away from us."

Kevin turned to her and sighed. "I'm not hurting right now, Brit. That may come later. Right now, I need to get as far away from her and those idiots following us as I can."

As he walked away, Brittany turned to see what Kevin saw. Most, if not all of the wrestlers that had been in the room come pouring out the front door. Her eyes widened. She turned to Tony, but he was right behind Kevin. The wrestlers hustled to close the distance.

"Hey, Sinclaire!" Tim shouted. "Where you headed?"

Kevin didn't turn around. He continued down Les Fontaine's long driveway. Kevin wasn't the type to back down from a fight. The truth was, he couldn't wait to unleash on the wrestlers. He glanced at Tony, who wrinkled his forehead and licked his lips. Brittany ran to catch up.

"Are you guys going to get into a fight with *all* those guys?" Brittany asked, her eyes wide as saucers.

"Looks like," Tony replied. "You need to stay back."

"Hey!" Tim shouted. "You don't have the balls to stick around and fight for your girl? What kind of a punk *are* you? Wanna know what we were doing before you came in?" He laughed. "Trust me, dude, it was no big deal. It was nothing compared to what we're gonna be doing later on."

Kevin's pace slowed, but he hadn't turned around yet. He was about three quarters of the way down the driveway. They were out of sight of the house and not quite within sight of the road. The wrestlers were almost upon them when Kevin whirled around.

***

That was when Tony realized what Kevin had planned. He hadn't been backing down from the fight. He *wanted* the fight. He just wanted to get it away from the house. Les didn't like fighting at his parties. That might have been part of it, but Kevin also didn't want to be interrupted. And that meant fighting him now would be very dangerous for these wrestling idiots.

***

Tim hadn't been prepared for Kevin's sudden one-eighty. He almost walked right into him as he uttered that last line. Kevin's hand shot up into Tim's throat without any warning at all. It was a blade strike, which he pulled at the last second. There wouldn't be any real damage. In the short term though, Tim's hands shot to his throat as he gasped for air. Kevin launched repeated blows to his midsection until the other wrestlers caught up.

As they closed in on him, Kevin tossed the doubled over Tim at their feet and launched himself at the nearest target, the butt of his hand slamming into his sternum. Kevin was rewarded with the sound of bone splintering. He even felt the kid's sternum give a half inch before he doubled over and fell to the ground in a whimpering heap.

Kevin flowed into his next technique, spinning, dipping, and landing a reverse blade strike on the inner thigh of the next guy to step into him. He didn't break the guy's bone, but there was a nerve bundle where Kevin's hand slammed into his leg. The guy was instantly in excruciating pain, which rendered him unprepared for Kevin to straighten up and drive his knee straight up into his face. He went down like a lead weight.

Group dynamics was an interesting thing to Kevin. It didn't take much to get a group of testosterone-laden boys amped up enough to pick a fight with someone, especially when the odds were so stacked in their favor they doubted there was any real chance of getting hurt themselves. Once their delusions were shattered, it was always fascinating to watch the groupthink evolve.

After seeing three of their friends dropped in a matter of seconds, the rest of them acted on the every-man-for-himself principle. They stopped in their tracks. That was their second tactical mistake, because Kevin didn't. He waded through two more before any of them could react. There were four left, and they all backed away, but Kevin continued right into his sixth opponent, who caught a series of vicious punches to his face and chest before Kevin let him fall to the ground. The other guys held up their hands in surrender and backed away.

***

Tony stood spellbound. Before he even realized what had happened, Kevin had taken out all but three of the wrestlers. Tony felt like an idiot for not helping, but it was pretty much all over. Tim struggled to his feet once he caught his breath. Kevin came over just as he straightened up.

"So what's up, Tim?" he said as he approached. "You still tough?"

Kevin's fist slammed into Tim's jaw, sending him stumbling backwards.

"What's the matter, Tim?"

From Tony's perspective, Kevin's eyes looked dead black in the dim lighting. He continued his advance on Tim. This was bad.

"You were so funny when you were telling me all about the things you wanted to do to my girlfriend…well…*ex*-girlfriend."

Kevin chuckled and then landed two more vicious strikes, this time to Tim's right arm, which caused him to grunt in pain. Tony knew the guy's arm was broken.

"Well, Tim?" Kevin shrugged, driving two more strikes, this time to the other arm, with similar results. He followed those up with a brutal onslaught into Tim's chest. Five or six punches landed in a matter of two seconds. The attack plastered Tim up against a car with Kevin still coming at him. "Come on, champ. Tell me more about what you're gonna do to her later."

Kevin then went absolutely crazy, sending punch after punch into his midsection, face, arms, and even legs. It took Tony a couple of seconds to react, but he charged over and almost tackled Kevin to the ground to get him off Tim. Tony thought the prick deserved every last bit of the pain Kevin inflicted on him, but he wasn't about to let his best friend go to jail for manslaughter.

Once Kevin was under control, Tony glanced back at Tim, who slid to the ground. He lay in a crumpled heap but he was breathing. His friends, who had run off and left him, were back, cautiously making their way to each of their downed teammates. Once Tony walked Kevin away from Tim, they rushed over to him and checked him out. Tony heard them scramble to a couple of cars. They pulled one up next to Tim, loaded him into the backseat, and drove off. The others all managed to pile into the other vehicle and follow, presumably to the hospital.

Tony vaguely wondered how much fallout there would be. Would those guys tell the police who did all that damage? He doubted it. They were the ones who chased Kevin down the driveway. Tony knew Kevin had been leading them to a secluded spot, but it would still look as though they chased him and he had no choice but to defend himself against a pack of boys. Tony shook his head in amazement. Kevin's actions were brilliantly executed. He was completely covered if the police were brought into it.

Tony sighed. What was Lindsey thinking? She hadn't known Kevin was planning on being at Les' party that night, so she didn't plan for Kevin to find her with another guy, but she sure played the part of a cheat. What was that all about? Was Kevin supposed to hear about it through the Kendall High grapevine? And how was Tony supposed to deal with Lindsey now? He wanted to strangle her, for starters. He also wanted to shake her and ask her what she'd hoped to accomplish.

Kevin walked down the driveway without saying a word. His eyes were still a freakish black from the shadows. He looked possessed. His breathing was controlled, but Tony could see, just by his body language, Kevin was anything but calm. He had that same wild animal stare when an angry father pushed his mother. Kevin nearly killed *that* guy too. Tony was glad he was around to stop his best friend from doing too much damage…he hoped.

***

Brittany walked to Kevin. She put her hand on his shoulder. "Kevin, talk to me."

"Nothing to talk about, Brittany." He kept walking.

Brittany was insistent. "Just stop for a second, okay?"

Kevin stopped and looked at her, his eyes as dead and vacant as before. "What do you want me to say? It's over. I want to go home. Is that okay?"

She had no idea what to say to him. She only knew she didn't want him running off by himself. She looked back at Tony, who shrugged.

"Let's get a cab, Kevo."

"Yeah," Brittany pleaded. "Don't be alone right now, Kevin. Let us be there for you."

"There's nothing to 'be there' for," Kevin insisted. "I'm fine."

"You're *not* fine," she argued. "You just caught your girlfriend, who you're in love with, cheating on you, and got into a fight with the wrestling team! That's *not* fine. Now—"

"Look!" Kevin shouted. "I don't want any attention right now, Brittany. What I want is to walk home…alone. Goodbye." He looked at Tony pointed stare. "See you tomorrow."

Tony nodded and lowered his eyes. "Okay, man. Call me later."

As Kevin walked away, Brittany looked at Tony like he was crazy. "Tony…"

"Just let him go."

***

He couldn't tell if he was really unmoved by the events of the past half hour or if he was going insane. Kevin knew he ought to be feeling a whole lot more than he was feeling at the moment. He knew most people would react by emotion, either by getting angry or sad. Kevin's response had been to accept the situation and walk away. Sure, the idiots chased him down the driveway and he had to deal with them, and sure, the lead idiot, Tim, had to make those disrespectful comments about Lindsey, sending Kevin into a dimension of pissed off he seldom reached, but none of that had anything to do with Lindsey's actions.

He hadn't gotten more than a mile away from Les Fontaine's driveway when a car pulled up beside him. He recognized it right away. It was a taxi, but not just any taxi. When the window rolled down, he looked in and waved.

"Hey, Phil."

Phil Younger owned and operated Black Cab Taxi Service. He was one of the biggest Kendall Cobra fans in the Township. The kids all called him "Five Dollar Phil." He drove Kendall High students anywhere in the Township for five dollars apiece. This was huge, especially on nights when there was a party. It was far wiser and safer to spend the five bucks and get a safe ride home rather than risk the consequences of driving under the influence.

"Kevin Sinclaire!"

His smile was apparent even in the darkness. Phil loved Kendall Cobra athletes, probably because they made up three quarters of his business. And considering Kevin's role in winning the State Championship, he was as excited to see Kevin on the street as any celebrity.

"What do you think you're doin' walking the streets of Kendall Township when I happen to have an empty back seat?"

Kevin nodded. "Sorry, Phil. I just needed to walk a little bit."

"Well, hop in and let me give you a ride. It's on the house tonight."

Kevin didn't want a ride, but he also didn't want to stand there and argue with a really nice guy who just wanted to help. He got in and let Phil give him a lift. At least he'd be home and could work out or spend some time in the shop.

Phil watched him in the rearview mirror. "You okay, son?"

Kevin nodded, pressing his lips together. "I'm fine."

Phil nodded. "Yeah, women'll do that to ya."

Kevin wrinkled his forehead. "Who said anything about a woman?"

Phil chuckled. "Son, I've lived long enough to know that the only thing on this planet that can put a look on a man's face like the one you got is a woman."

***

Fortunately, his mom and Jeff were out to dinner and probably a movie, so Kevin had the house to himself for a little while. He sat out on the back deck and lay back with his eyes closed. He did his best to breathe and control his emotions. He allowed them to flow through his veins that night, feeling them touch every bit of his psyche. He knew it was a dangerous thing for him to do. Kevin hated emotions. They always led to disappointment.

Controlling emotions was what he did better than anything else. He never held back with Lindsey. Instead, Kevin allowed his emotions to run free when it came to that one girl. It led to some amazing moments and he felt closer to her than he'd ever felt to another human being. In the end, giving up that control cost him months of misery and he lost her anyway.

He knew it the second her eyes met his. She wanted out but couldn't bring herself to end it; so, she punted. Disloyalty. It was the only thing he couldn't forgive. Lindsey knew it and took full advantage. It was a pretty lame plan and one that revealed an unexpected lack of respect, though he doubted she saw it that way. It was cowardly, but then again, he wasn't stepping up and doing anything about the sorry state of their relationship either.

Kevin still loved her. He probably always would, but maybe it would fade. Maybe he would find someone else. The truth was, Kevin didn't want anyone else…well, maybe there was one. It figured the only other interesting girl in the whole township would be best friends with the girl who just broke his heart.

Chapter 26

It was the closest thing to a "what-have-I-done" moment Lindsey had ever experienced. The look on Emily's face told her all she needed to know about what her best friend thought, but she'd already expressed her opinion in the moments before Kevin's arrival. Emily had been frustrated and even a little angry at her. But after torpedoing her relationship with Kevin, Lindsey saw something different in Emily's eyes. Disappointment.

To her credit, Emily didn't walk out on her. Lindsey often wondered if Emily had what it took to truly be a friend in the Kevin Sinclaire sense of the word. He'd always demanded complete loyalty even when a friend was wrong. Lindsey half-expected Emily to turn her head in disgust and leave her sitting on the couch. Instead, she came over as the room cleared out and sat on the sofa next to Lindsey. She didn't say anything. Really, what could she say?

"I can't believe I just did that," Lindsey mumbled.

Emily nodded. Lindsey stared straight ahead, her heart still racing, but gradually slowing as she took deep breaths. She'd acted on instinct, made what she thought was the right decision. Everything worked to perfection, only now she didn't really know how she felt about it.

"Tell me I did the right thing, Emily."

"You did the right thing."

Lindsey turned to her. "You really think so?"

"Absolutely not!" Emily cried. "You're insane! You think there was something to be gained by breaking up with him like *that?*"

Lindsey shrugged. "It got the job done. Neither one of us was willing to do the right thing. This way he gets to walk away and I don't have to look into his eyes and tell him I can't be with him anymore."

Emily rolled her eyes. "You keep telling yourself that."

"Don't be mean, Emily. I might be the bad guy here, but my heart is just as broken as his."

"Don't tell me how to act," Emily replied. "I'm not your lackey. I'm your best friend. I tell you when you screw up." She looked at Lindsey closely. "And you really screwed up tonight, sweetie. I love you, but right now I can't stand you."

Lindsey frowned. "Why do you take it so personally?"

"Because I've been giving you advice since the day I met you and you keep ignoring me! You ruined your relationship with a really great guy, a guy I stayed away from because I saw how much you two loved each other. To see you tear his heart out like you just did hurt *me*. I can't imagine what *he's* feeling right now."

Lindsey scowled at her. "Well, if you care so much about him, why don't you go find him and uhhh…you know…take care of him?"

Emily blinked a few times. "Excuse me?"

Lindsey shrugged. "You told me months ago if I ever blew it, you'd be there to take him. So don't act like you're not finally getting your shot at the Kendall High hero."

"Are you being serious right now?" Emily stared wide-eyed at her best friend. "You really think that something I said right after we first met still matters now? You're my best friend."

"So you don't like Kevin?"

"Of course I like Kevin!" she shouted. "I've liked him ever since I first talked to him. Geez, Lindz! Who doesn't like him? But in case you haven't noticed, I'm your *best friend*. I *love* you. When will you get it through that insanely thick, stupid head of yours that I would never hurt you? I would never *ever* go after your guy!"

Lindsey leaned into her. "I know. I'm sorry. I just needed to hear you say it."

***

Bang! Bang! Bang!
"Come on, Lindz. I want to hang out with my sister."
"Go away!" Lindsey shouted.
Tracey kept banging on her door. She had been trying to get Lindsey to cheer up for five days, ever since Lindsey shredded her relationship with Kevin. What was interesting…mildly interesting, anyway…was that Tracey hadn't shown even the slightest hint of judgment. They hadn't had a real conversation about it, but Emily, Tracey's newest BFF, unloaded every ugly detail, making Lindsey look like a total brat. Tracey just smiled in sympathy, took her sister in her arms, and held her for hours until they both fell asleep. She told Lindsey she'd give her a few days to mourn and sulk, but then she'd make her snap out of it. A few days was up.

Bang! Bang! Bang!
"Open the door, Lindsey!" Tracey yelled. "I'm not going away, so you might as well just come watch a movie with me."
"Not in the mood! Leave me alone!"
Bang! Bang! Bang!
"Please open up, Lindz. Don't go through this alone. Let me in. We don't have to watch anything. Just let me sit with you."
"Ugh!"
Tracey could hear the covers being thrown off and then the door opened. She slipped in and shut the door behind her. Lindsey was climbing back into bed, but she didn't lie down. Tracey carefully climbed into the bed behind her and propped the pillows up. When she was lying comfortably, Lindsey sank into the space next to her, letting Tracey wrap her arms around her.

"What are you doing out of bed?" Lindsey mumbled. "Your doctor told you to stay off your feet."

Tracey was put on bed rest three weeks ago when she began feeling worn down and tired all the time. She did her schoolwork from home and just wanted to survive the last month until her due date.

"I'm fine," Tracey said. "I need a *little* exercise, right? The walk from my room to yours seemed pretty harmless."

They lay in silence for several moments.

"How are you, Lindz?" Tracey stroked her hair and shoulder.

"Crappy," she replied. "I threw my boyfriend away and now…" she couldn't finish her sentence.

"Do you want him back?"

Lindsey shook her head. "I don't know what I want."

"Why not call him? Maybe you two need better closure than this."

Lindsey sighed. "I'm sure we do, but that's not the type of people we are. We deal with things alone and the traditional cures won't work."

Tracey knew what it was like to lose her first love. Sure, she got Matt back, but that took weeks. She still suffered what Lindsey was going through. She knew there wasn't much anyone could do. A broken heart isn't really curable. Time was the only thing that could help.

"I love you, you know."

"I know," Lindsey said, squeezing her sister's arm.

"That doesn't help though, does it?"

"Not really," Lindsey said. "But I'm glad you're my sister."

It was such a simple, honest comment. From anyone else, it would have been a throw away comment. Coming from Lindsey, the statement was so personal it almost brought tears to Tracey's eyes. Lindsey always wrapped her feelings in sarcasm and wit.

"I'm glad I'm your sister too," she said, squeezing tightly. "Ooh," she moaned, feeling a twinge in her abdomen.

"Are you okay?" Lindsey said, twisting to look at her.

Tracey shifted so she was lying on her back and took a couple breaths. "I think I'm okay," she said. "I probably just have to go to the bathroom."

"Let me help you up," Lindsey said, coming around to help Tracey to her feet.

Tracey made her way slowly to the bathroom, feeling a cramp in her belly. After several minutes in the bathroom, she wasn't feeling better. In fact, the pain was a little worse. Then she looked down…and saw her nightmare.

"Lindsey!" she cried. "Get Mom! I need her!"

"Are you okay? What's wrong?"

"Just get Mom, Lindsey! Please!"

By the time Abby burst into the room, Tracey was in tears. She took one look around the bathroom and turned to Lindsey.

"Go start the car."

Lindsey ran out of the room and was back in seconds. She took one of Tracey's arms while her mother took the other. Together they helped Tracey to her feet and walked her out of her room and down the staircase. She kept hunching over because of a sharp pain in her side. She knew it wasn't a cramp and was becoming more and more frightened with every step.

"Mom," she said, her voice shaking with fear as Lindsey helped her into the back seat.

"Just relax, Tracey," Abby said in a gentle voice. "Don't panic. Just try to breathe and stay as calm as you can. Everything will be fine."

"But the baby," Tracey said, her voice cracking with emotion. "Do you think—"

"Everything is going to be fine, sweetheart." Abby put the car into gear and did her best not to speed through town.

"Hello?" Lindsey was speaking into her cell. "Yes, this is Lindsey Overton. My sister, Tracey, is a patient. She's eight months pregnant and on her way to the hospital right now with very bad pains in her sides. Could you inform Dr. Kennedy?" She waited a second and then said, "Thank you."

When she hung up, both Tracey and Abby were looking at her. "What?" she asked. "Was that wrong?"

Abby shook her head. "No. That was exactly right. Good thinking."

Tracey smiled. "Thank you, Lindz. Hey, could you call Matt and tell him what's going on?"

Lindsey nodded and tapped Matt's name on her screen. "Matt? Listen, we're taking Tracey to the hospital right now…we're not sure. She's got a bad pain in her side. It might be nothing, but we're not taking any chances…okay…you probably don't need to…okay, fine. We'll see you there. And drive carefully. We don't need you in the room next to her with a broken neck."

When they pulled up to the emergency room entrance, they were shocked to see a group of nurses and orderlies rush to the car with a wheelchair. They helped get Tracey settled into it and carted her away with Lindsey hurrying along behind them.

***

Abby never left the car. She sat bewildered for several seconds before realizing she needed to go park. On her way back in, she saw Matt pull into a parking space and waited for him to catch up. She told him what had happened.

"Yeah," he said. "I called right after I got off the phone with Lindsey. She's getting VIP treatment."

"You can do that?" Abby asked.

"I guess so, especially if your parents paid for the new psychiatric wing." He grinned and gave her a sheepish shrug. "I usually don't drop names and all that, but it's Tracey."

Abby put her arm around his waist. "You know something, Mattie? I love you more and more each day."

"You know," he said, putting his own arm around her shoulders and giving her a squeeze. "You're the only one who's allowed to call me Mattie besides my mom."

"Well," Abby replied, "I'll be your mother-in-law one day, so it makes sense."

When they got inside, they were told Tracey was already being examined up in the maternity ward, so they got into an elevator and rode it up to the fourth floor, where they were shown to Tracey's room and someone would be back to talk to them shortly.

"She already has a room?" Abby asked no one in particular. She glanced at Matt, who was grinning sheepishly again. "You again?"

He shrugged. "I just told them who Tracey was and that she was to receive the royal treatment. I don't really know what that *is* at a hospital, but…" He shrugged.

Ten minutes later, a pretty nurse dressed in pastel pink scrubs came into the room and smiled at them. "Hi, I'm Jessica. Dr. Kennedy just got here and will be seeing Tracey in a few minutes. If you want to come with me, I'll take you to her."

Abby and Matt followed Nurse Jessica to an exam room at the other end of the corridor. Tracey was lying back with her feet in stirrups. Lindsey held her hand as she sat up by Tracey's head. The maternity team already had Tracey hooked up to a plethora of machines and were busy monitoring both Tracey's and the baby's vital signs.

"How are you feeling, baby?" Abby rushed over and grabbed her daughter's other hand, careful not to touch the IV line on the top of her hand.

"Still hurts a lot, Mom," Tracey said, grimacing. Her eyes immediately went to Matt and her whole body seemed to relax. "Hey," she said with a weak and miserable look. "Why are you all the way over there?"

***

Matt gulped. Seeing her so pale and scared unnerved him. He was always strong for her, but right now he was helpless. He couldn't take her pain away. What was he supposed to do? He just came to her side and kissed her forehead.

She held his hand and looked into his eyes. "Don't leave my side, okay? Whatever happens, just stay right next to me."

He could definitely do *that*.

Chapter 27

"Okay, people. What do we have?"

All eyes turned to the commanding voice of Dr. Alison Kennedy. When she entered the room, there was no question as to who was in charge. She breezed in, took Tracey's chart from the nurse, gave it quick once-over, and got an update from the nurse who examined her.

"She's ready to go now. She's ten centimeters. The head is in position and she's contracting, but irregularly. She's also got blood and pain…"

Dr. Kennedy took in all the information and sat in the stool at the foot of the bed.

"Tracey," she said with a smile. "You're in pain, hon?"

At Tracey's nod, she said, "Well, we're a little bit too far along for pain meds, but we'll do what we can. Let me take a look."

As soon as she began her examination, her expression darkened. "That's not the head," she said dryly to the nurse standing next to her. "Get us an O.R. STAT."

The nurse ran to the wall phone and began instructing whoever was on the other end to begin prepping for surgery. Dr. Kennedy stood up and smiled at Tracey. "Well, this day was coming anyway, I suppose," she said calmly.

"What?" Tracey said, her eyes wide with fear. "What's wrong with the baby? You said something's wrong with his head?"

Dr. Kennedy frowned. "Wrong with it?" She shook her head. "No. The problem is that you're fully dilated and the baby is breech, which means his butt is coming out first. We don't want that, but he's too far down in the canal to do anything about it. So we have to do a C-section. The nurses will get you an epidural and prep you for surgery."

"What do you mean, surgery?" Tracey said, tears beginning to flow from her eyes. "The baby's not due for three more weeks. Is this okay?"

Dr. Kennedy looked at Tracey with a bright smile. "Do I look worried? From now on, your job is to relax. My job is to worry about the baby. Trust me, honey. In about one hour, you'll be holding your son. I hope you have a name picked out, because he's coming *right now*."

As the doctor left the room, Tracey's nurses helped her up and administered the appropriate drugs. Then they wheeled her bed right out of the room. Another nurse asked who would be accompanying Tracey into the operating room. Lindsey and Abby exchanged a look.

Abby laid a hand on Matt's arm. "Go."

Matt's eyes widened. "Are you sure?"

Abby smiled. "She wants you with her. She just told you not to leave her side. If I show up in there without you, she'll kill both of us. Now go. This is *your* moment. Take care of my daughter, Matthew."

Matt followed the nurse into another room where he was given a set of blue scrubs to put on, including over his shoes. When he was ready, they took him into the operating room. Tracey was already there. She looked scared and weak, but no longer in pain. There was a tent-like contraption over her chest. Matt couldn't see anything the doctors were doing on the other side, which, he imagined, was a probably a good thing. If they were going to do what he thought they were going to do, there was no place he'd rather be than on *this* side of the barrier.

One of the nurses slid a pole into position right above Tracey's head. Matt gave her a quizzical frown. She pointed up. What he saw terrified him. There was a mirror at the top of the pole.

"Just in case you want to watch," she said, and walked around to her side of the barrier.

Seriously? Matt thought. *Do they really think I'd want to see this?*

But for some sick reason he couldn't figure out, Matt found he couldn't keep from peeking as the procedure was performed. It was a bizarre mix of horror and amazement in his head. He'd never seen anything so disgusting and awful. Tracey's C-section was a barbaric procedure. There was nothing elegant about it. Surgeries on TV look so cool and sleek. The only similar thing was the constant stream of chit-chat. Dr. Kennedy obviously worked with this team before because she went on and on about their families. She knew their kids' names and even seemed to know how old they all were, what was going on in school, and a host of other unimportant details. Matt was surprised they could get anything done with all the chatter.

Tracey was awake while the procedure went on. Matt couldn't decide if that was a good thing, but she didn't seem to be in pain. He stroked her forehead and talked to her the whole time. She smiled at him but didn't say much. Whatever they had her on must be the good stuff because Matt would have lost it a long time ago. Instead, she was still the most beautiful thing he'd ever seen. Exhausted and frightened out of her mind, with her hair a tangled, sweaty mess, she still took his breath away. They were about to be parents together. He hadn't had time to really process *that* bit of information.

Matt's thoughts were interrupted by a sound he thought he'd have to wait another three weeks to hear. Crying. It was his baby crying! He looked up, but his view was blocked by the barrier. He resisted the urge to run around to the other side. He just sat and looked at Tracey. She had tears in her eyes. She looked up at him and stared at him with a loving smile.

"Hey, Daddy," she croaked. "Go see our son. Make sure they're being nice to him."

Matt grinned and stood up. He turned to where they were cleaning the baby, weighing him, and wrapping him in a clean, soft blanket. He peered over the shoulders of the nurses as they did a bunch of tests and took his temperature and God knew what else. Matt couldn't contain his amazement. Finally, Nurse Jessica turned around and carried the little bundle over to him.

"You can hold him for a minute, but we really need to take him back for tests."

Matt took the baby in his arms and followed the nurse's instructions about supporting the head and cradling him in his arm. He couldn't believe how tiny his son was. His eyes were just little slits, but Matt couldn't miss the bright blue peeking out. His little hands were curled into fists and Matt had to wiggle his finger into one of them to get him to grab onto it. He couldn't wipe the smile off his face. After a few seconds, the nurse took him back and Matt watched her put him into a wheeled cradle and push him down the corridor for his tests and examinations. He missed his son right away.

After another fifteen minutes, they wheeled Tracey out of the operating room and took her to Recovery. Matt was told he could change out of his scrubs, but he wouldn't leave Tracey, so he just kept them on and held her hand all the way to the recovery room. After several moments, Lindsey and Abby came in.

"Omigod!" Lindsey said. "Do I really have a nephew right now?" She looked at Tracey and wrinkled her nose. "You look like crap. Are you stoned?"

"Lindsey!" Abby whacked her on the arm and giggled. She hugged her oldest daughter as best she could since Tracey was still pretty out of it. "The doctor told us everything is fine with the baby and you're doing great. All your friends are outside, but they can't visit until they take you back to your room."

Tracey just smiled and nodded.

"Shoot," Matt said, pulling out his phone. "I need to call my parents. I told them I was meeting you here, but at the time, I had no idea what was going on. I need to tell them they're grandparents."

Abby laughed. "Don't worry, Mattie. They're on their way. Lindsey called after you went into the operating room. She's been all over the details tonight."

Lindsey rolled her eyes. "It's just because you were all panicking. Someone had to focus."

Matt stepped toward her.

"Oh God." Lindsey backed away. "You're gonna hug me, aren't you?"

"Oh yeah," Matt replied, his arms outstretched.

Lindsey braced herself. "You don't have to do that, *Mattie*. A simple thank you would be just fine."

"Don't call me *Mattie*," he replied, wrapping his arms around her and hugging her. "Thank you."

***

"Dude, you just have to get back out there."

"Yeah, that sounds wonderful."

"Trust me, man, I'm having the time of my life. The girls in this school are friggin' psycho. And I mean that in a good way...like...a fun way."

Kevin shook his head. "I'm just not into it right now."

Scott Webber shrugged. "Kev, you're wasting a lot of time. These girls wanna party with you. You're like...the *king* of this school right now. You can have anyone you want. Heck, you can have *all* of 'em."

It had been almost three weeks since Kevin and Lindsey's break-up. The police hadn't been involved because Tim and the other eight wrestlers didn't want to admit to picking a fight with a lone freshman. They also didn't want it getting out that the lone freshman beat the crap out of them and hadn't taken a single punch. That part didn't matter because the story was all over the school by the following morning anyway.

It didn't make Kevin happy. The whole Township already thought he was crazy. His legend grew to even more ridiculous heights. He didn't want the extra attention, but he was going to get it. The girls swarmed him ever since the first day back to school.

By the morning after the break-up, he'd received nearly sixty texts and emails from Kendall High cheerleaders and Brette Girls, along with other assorted classmates. He didn't answer any of them.

"I don't want them," was Kevin's bland reply.

Scott looked at him with incredulity. "You've got to be kidding. These girls aren't just girls. We're talking upper classmen here. *Women*, not just girls."

"Women, huh?" Kevin couldn't help but laugh.

Scott shrugged and grinned. "Well…close enough."

"Look, dude," Kevin said, "I just don't care."

"But why? Have you *looked* at them lately, with their little sundresses and shorts? How can you ignore all those tan legs and skimpy skirts? Are you *crazy*? What's wrong with you?"

"They're just not interesting, that's all."

"Not interesting? What about that Alli chick? Tell me she's not interesting."

Kevin frowned at him. "Alli Sylvester?" He shrugged. "She's okay, I guess."

"*Okay*?" Scott pushed him into the lockers as they walked by. "She's totally hot, Kevo, *and* she's totally into you. She has been all year. I swear to God; you must be blind."

"Maybe I am."

The truth was he just couldn't imagine being with any girl other than Lindsey. Even after her betrayal, his heart ached for her. He still wanted to be near her, to hold her in his arms again. Maybe he *was* crazy. Everyone else certainly thought so. But some part of Kevin couldn't let her go. Tony said something to him earlier about first loves. Emily told him to figure out what he wanted and go for it. That was the only useful advice anyone had given him.

Maybe the best thing to do would be to start seeing other girls and see if just having a little fun might change his outlook. Maybe Scott was right. After all, *he* was having the time of his life, dating a different girl every other day. Maybe that was what high school was really all about. Being tied to one person might run counter to the whole experience of youth.

Figure out what you want and go for it.

Emily's words. It seemed like sound advice. It's the kind of simple advice a person ought to be able to hear and act upon. Kevin had always known what it was he wanted and had never been shy about going for it. So why was he finding it so difficult to answer one simple question? What did he want?

Did he really want Lindsey? Girls approached him every day at school, via phone, email, and text, trying to get him to go out, but he resisted their advances. Why? Was it out of some misplaced loyalty to his ex? Was he somehow holding out hope for her? Was he the only one who didn't realize it was really over?

Figure out what you want and go for it.

Scott shook his head. "You know what your problem is, Kevo? You don't know how to loosen up."

"Is that a fact?"

"It is." Scott spread his arms. "On the field, you're loose, ready for anything, so you can react to *everything*. But off the field, you're stiff, unapproachable…"

"Uh huh."

Figure out what you want and go for it.

They reached the top of the stairs and walked through the second floor stairwell doors into the main corridor. As they came around a corner, Kevin saw Emily Vasquez at her locker. His heart reacted instantly, racing, fluttering, and he felt like a swarm of butterflies invaded his stomach. He stopped in his tracks.

Scott stopped and looked back at him with a quizzical expression. Kevin's eyes were riveted.

Figure out what you want and go for it.

Kevin was transfixed. How had he missed her all this time? She was…*perfection*, absolutely breathtaking. He wanted to tear his eyes away from her, but couldn't. All of a sudden, Emily Vasquez had the same power over him that she had over just about every other guy in the school. Why now? Perhaps his love for Lindsey kept his impulses at bay. Now that Lindsey was no longer with him, they ran free inside him.

Scott shook his head with a rueful grin. "Dude…*Emily?*"

Kevin snapped out of his trance, but kept his eyes on Emily, who still had her back to them.

Kevin nodded. "I think so, yeah."

"Wow. That might be a problem." Scott chuckled. "Are you sure?"

Figure out what you want and go for it.

Kevin shrugged. "I don't know. I don't want to hurt Lindsey, but…"

"But it's Emily Vasquez," Scott finished. He glanced down the hall and shrugged. "You know, it's not like you owe Lindsey anything. After all, she was the one who cheated on you." He glanced at Emily. "On the other hand, this'll really stir it up, don't you think?"

Figure out what you want and go for it.

Kevin looked at Scott. "You said I need to get back out there."

"Yeah, but I meant—"

"You said I've been wasting time."

"I know, I said that, but—"

Kevin raised his eyebrows. "And you said I'm crazy for ignoring all these pretty girls."

"True," Scott replied. "But—"

"I think it's time I move on from Lindsey Overton."

"Yes." Scott nodded. "You should, but I think—"

"So." Kevin said. "Here's step one."

He approached Emily from behind. She was still unaware of his presence. When he was just a couple steps away, he called out to her.

"Hey, Emily. How are you?"

When she turned around, he was right in front of her. His eyes bored into hers and her surprise at his proximity kept her from reacting right away. Before she could say a word, Kevin cupped his hand gently on her cheek, stroking it softly, and then he tilted her face up to his and kissed her, and not in a friendly, hi-how-are-you-doing kind of way. He put everything he had into it.

***

The surprise of the kiss was surpassed only by its intensity. Emily was too stunned to react and she didn't immediately kiss him back. Her mind raced to formulate the correct response. She knew there was a clear right and wrong, but she couldn't, for the life of her, figure out what that was. This kiss was a full-on assault on her senses, a surprise attack.

In a matter of seconds, she kissed him back. She couldn't think, so she didn't bother trying. All she could do was grasp the front of his shirt and pull him into her. He had both of his hands on her face, and his lips owned hers. His right hand slid around to the back of her head, threading itself into her hair just as she felt herself crash back into the lockers behind her. That was the other part of the fantasy, Kevin slamming her up against her locker, locked in a ferocious kiss.

It was the most intoxicating moment of her life and it was only a kiss. Kevin didn't end the kiss quickly either. Instead, he intensified it just when she thought he would back off. His tongue slid between her lips, parting them and then attacking her tongue as his hands moved back to her face and he stroked her cheeks with his thumbs. She couldn't breathe, but she couldn't bring herself to break the kiss off. She felt his muscular body pressed against hers and her imagination took control.

Just as she was losing all control, he pulled his head back but not his body. He was still pressed up against her, pinning her to the locker. Their eyes were locked on one another's. Emily's head spun and her eyes glassed over. She couldn't focus her vision, like she was drunk. Kevin leaned into her a little more, with a seriously hot, almost cocky grin on his face. Emily felt her body temperature rise five degrees just looking into those gorgeous green eyes.

My God! Is this how Lindsey felt all the time? *Oh God*...Lindsey! *What am I gonna tell Lindsey?*

The thought hit her hard, but Emily still could not find the willpower to push Kevin away. Instead, she was frozen in place, staring lustfully into the most amazing sea of green she had ever seen. Part of her wanted to pull the cocky freshman into a secluded stairwell and teach him a serious lesson about taking a girl by surprise and getting her all worked up. She didn't get a chance to think about what the other part of her wanted to do because Kevin pulled himself away from her, still touching her cheek. He stroked it with the backs of his fingers and looked so deeply into her eyes, she wondered if he could read her mind. God, she hoped not.

He leaned in and whispered into her ear. "That was worth the wait. I'll see you later."

He left her leaning back against her locker, short of breath, knees too weak to move, and too stunned to speak. As she fought for control of her breathing, she shook her head and tried to gain some control over her brain function.

Who does that? Who strolls up, lays a life-altering kiss on a girl, and then just walks away like nothing even happened?

***

Kevin strolled past a stunned Scott Webber and continued on down the hall like he hadn't just practically had sex with the hottest girl in school against the sophomore lockers in front of everyone in the hall. Every person he passed stared like he'd just returned from a mission to Mars. You didn't just walk up and kiss Emily Vasquez like that and get away with it.

Scott caught up to Kevin and draped an arm around his neck. "Dude, you are totally my hero. I'm gonna just shut up and learn." He glanced back over his shoulder. "Man, she's still just standing there. How can you walk away from that?"

Kevin didn't even blink. "It's easy when you don't care."

Epilogue

"I can't believe he's really ours."

Tracey's eyes glistened with joy and contentment as she held her son, Brian Everett Kildare, named after both their fathers. It was Tracey's idea…sort of. She was the one who insisted upon naming the baby after Matt's father. She knew Matt wanted to honor his father that way but was too generous to suggest it. Even after Tracey made the suggestion, he insisted on naming him Everett Brian, giving Tracey's father top billing. Tracey refused, insisting her father didn't even deserve to *meet* the child, let alone be honored with a namesake. In the end, Matt would only bend as far as to allow his father's name to take the top spot. Tracey's father would still have his name on the birth certificate.

"Well, believe it, baby," Matt said, wrapping his arms around her and kissing her on the cheek. "And he's beautiful, just like his mother, with that red hair."

She stroked his soft head. Baby Brian had a full head of bright red hair. Over the past two weeks, as his head grew, his hairline receded and it seemed like he had less hair than he started with. Tracey had secretly hoped her son would have blond hair, like his daddy, but Lindsey shot that hope to pieces when she explained the whole recessive/dominant thing. Tracey didn't wish red hair on anyone, but she figured it would be far easier to be a red-headed boy than a red-headed girl.

"It looks so much better on *him*."

"Hmmm," Matt said. "I don't know about that. I mean he's obviously going to be a total heartbreaker, but his mother is absolutely beautiful. And I love her red hair. It's my favorite thing about her."

She turned in his arms, trying to see his face. "Really? My hair?"

He buried his face in her thick red locks and breathed in the scent of her shampoo. It was like a drug for him. He could never get enough of it. It never got old.

"I could do this all day," he said, his face still covered in a tangle of red.

"That wouldn't be so bad," Tracey purred. "Let me put this guy down for a nap and maybe we can lay down ourselves. You can wrap your arms around me and…sniff my hair…or whatever it is you do."

"Definitely."

Their moment was interrupted by the ringing of the doorbell. Matt let her out of his embrace and stepped away.

"I'll get that," he told her. "You put the heartbreaker down."

"Okay."

Matt went to the door and opened it. "Hello? Can I help you?"

The man standing at the door wrinkled his forehead and squinted at him. "Matt, right? You must be Matt."

"Yes, I'm Matt."

"It's nice to finally meet you, Matt," the man said, extending him hand. "I'm—"

"Daddy?" Tracey's voice came from behind Matt and sounded so stunned and almost childish that Matt had to turn around to confirm it was her.

"Yes, honey," the man replied, with a tentative smile. "It's me."

He hesitated before continuing. Tracey's expression was one of confusion and despair. She held the baby close to her, as if protecting him. Looking at Matt, the man introduced himself.

"Everett Overton." He shrugged. "I'm Tracey's father." He looked down. "Biologically, at least." He looked up at Tracey. "The truth is, I haven't really been a father to her or her sister in a long…well, ever."

He hung his head for a moment, but then straightened up and met her eyes once again. "But I…" He swallowed hard. "But if they'd be willing to give me one more chance, I'd like to try again."

Excerpt from Desire
Book 4 in the Quiver Saga

"Think Websey'll jump on board?"

No way he heard that. Tony shook his head.

The chatter of tool against wood spinning at 3000 rpm made it impossible to carry on a conversation. In Tony's mind, it was crazy to think about Christmas in eighty-degree June weather, but the demand dictated Kevin prepare for the holiday sales six months in advance. He needed all the help he could get, but Tony knew he only wanted to work with his friends. A few days prior, Kevin asked Scott Webber to join the Wood N Treasures team, and help in the shop over summer break.

"Think Websey'll jump on board?" Tony repeated a little louder as he shut off his machine and pulled the five-inch wood cylinder off. He breathed in the scent of the chocolate-colored wood. There was nothing like the smell of fresh-cut walnut. He set it atop the pile of similar pieces.

Kevin's eyes never left the wood spinning on his mini-lathe. He made smooth, delicate cuts with a slender tool. He turned the lathe off to inspect his work. He nodded as he peered down at his work. "Definitely. He needs to make money. Girls are expensive."

Tony grinned. "You're telling me. And Brit never even asks me for anything."

"Well, at least Brit's worth it." Kevin laughed as he started sanding along the grain of the walnut.

Tony nodded. "Very true." He was silent for a minute. "So, what about you?"

Kevin's eyes never left his work. He started the lathe again and continued his sanding. "What *about* me?"

"Any action with the ladies since…you know?"

Kevin shrugged. "They call, text. I just…I still can't believe it's over with Lindsey."

Tony nodded in understanding. "Yeah. That's tough. He raised his eyebrows and mounted a new piece to the lathe. "Of course, you did make out with her best friend in the school hall, so there's that."

"Yeah…*after* she hooked with some wrestling turd."

At that moment, Scott walked in. "Wassup, boys?" He took a deep breath. "Man, it smells good in here."

"Walnut," Tony said, holding up a piece of the brown wood and putting his fist out for Scott to bump. "Always smells awesome in here."

"How come there's no chicks around?" Scott asked, scanning the room. He walked over to a workbench and picked up a half-finished bowl. Turning it over in his hands, he said, "I can't work in a place full of dudes."

"The goal is to get things done," Kevin chucked a little piece of wood at him. "Not hook up with chicks."

Scott exchanged skeptical glances with Tony. He shrugged and Kevin showed him around the shop. He demonstrated some basic tasks Scott would be responsible for. It was all simple stuff. Tony added a few comments on how easy everything was, but let Kevin do most of the talking. He was, after all, the owner of the business.

"Most of it is tedious and repetitious," Kevin said. "But we just crank up the tunes or talk or whatever." He shrugged and gestured around the room. "So, what do you think?"

Scott nodded gave him a thumbs up. "Count me in. I can start tomorrow."

"Awesome," Kevin replied, bashing fists with him. "Welcome aboard."

Scott perched himself on a bench. "What are you guys doing now?"

Tony looked at his watch. "I gotta go home and get a shower. I'll be gone all month. It's a missions trip in some dirt-poor country in South America."

Scott cast a horrified look in his direction. "Seriously?" When Tony's expression remained impassive, he shook his head. "Not me." He turned to Kevin. "What about you, Kevo?"

"I was just gonna work out for an hour. After that…?" He shrugged.

Scott pointed a finger at him. "Come with me to the gym."

Kevin shook his head. Scott had been trying to get Kevin to join up with him for the summer. Flex Fitness had a summer special for Kendall High students.

He jerked his thumb over his shoulder. "I have my own gym right back there. Why don't you stay here? I'll whip you into shape."

"Are you kiddin me?" Scott smirked and flexed a toned bicep. "You ever see anything that pretty in your life? You come with me and *I'll* show *you*! Besides, your gym probably doesn't have twenty hot girls, in spandex, with their little ponytails bouncing up and down when they run."

"Ponytails, Websey?" Tony whooped. "That's what you're looking at when you go to the gym?"

Scott flashed a brilliant grin. "I didn't say that was *all* I looked at. I just love it when they run and their pony tails bounce up and down. It's cute." He gestured at Kevin. "Come on, Kev. Everyone'll be there. You'll love it. Plus, Rick, the owner, wants to meet you. He's a huge Cobra fan."

Kevin relented, and after he showered, put on a pair of loose basketball shorts and a tank top. He grabbed his black and silver Kendall Cobra gym bag, and he and Scott took off on bikes for the three-mile ride to Flex Fitness. When he stepped through the door, Kevin realized he knew half the people there. The gym was crawling with Kendall High students. The whole place stopped when he walked in. Shouts of greeting filled the air as he and Scott strode to the counter where the owner, Rick Grady, waited with a giddy grin on his face.

"Kevin Sinclaire!" he shouted. "Hero of Kendall High! Welcome to my humble establishment!"

Kevin nodded at Scott. "He said you had a lot of girls here."

"You better believe it." Rick nodded with an easy smirk. "Can I sign you up for the summer?"

"Why not?" Kevin said, pulling out his wallet.

Rick shook his head. "I don't accept money from my heroes. This summer is on me."

Though he knew it was futile, Kevin protested anyway. He hated free passes. Ever since he was named a starter on the Cobra football team, restaurant, and other business owners, gave him things for free. After he led the Cobras to the state championship, it got even worse. He couldn't step outside his house without someone offering him a free product or service. It felt funny to take freebies from people who worked hard, especially when he was capable of paying his own way. But, he found too much protest could backfire and insult some people, so he usually wound up choking his pride back and accepting their generosity.

Rick ignored Kevin's money and directed him to a touch screen monitor where Kevin entered his info. After that, Rick printed an ID card and Kevin was a complimentary summer member of Flex Fitness. He and Scott deposited their duffels in a locker.

"What's first?" Scott asked.

Kevin shrugged. "What do you normally do?"

"I like to run first."

"So, let's run."

Running was the most therapeutic activity for Kevin. Since his painful breakup with Lindsey, he ran five to ten miles every day. He used the time alone to think and work out his emotions. In a gym, with people all around him, he couldn't zone out like he could outdoors, on the open road, so he focused on the local scenery. Ten minutes in, he turned to Scott.

"You were right about the pony tails."

Scott laughed and almost fell off the treadmill. "I told you," he said when he recovered.

There were more than a dozen Kendall High girls in the gym. Some ran on treadmills, while others used elliptical machines. The rest worked out on various weight and resistance machines. They all wore spandex outfits in pinks, purples, yellows, and other girlie colors, and they all wore their hair in pony tails. All of them. It was mesmerizing to watch a room full of pony tails bouncing up and down in sync with their movements.

For the first time since his break up with Lindsey, Kevin noticed, really noticed, the girls all around him…and the attention they pretended not to be paying him. He wasn't blind, and he wasn't an idiot. He had always known the girls at school liked him, but he was so into Lindsey, he paid them scant attention. He wasn't interested and didn't want the distraction. Now, he felt as though a veil had been lifted.

Scott cast a knowing grin Kevin's way. "See anything you like?"

Kevin shook his head in mock awe. "I don't know where to begin."

"Well," Scott replied with a chuckle. "You could start right there." He nodded at four girls who had just entered the gym. At a glance, Kevin recognized them from school, one in particular. It was his own Brette Girl from the previous football season, Alli Sylvester. Kevin spent the better part of the season avoiding her subtle come-ons and trying to convince Lindsey nothing would happen between them. Alli always swore she was just flirting, and that it was all in fun, but Lindsey always remained unconvinced. Kevin raised his eyebrows as he looked at her with fresh eyes.

"Interesting," he said to Scott. He kept his eyes focused on the pretty brunette across the room. "You know, I never really thought about how hot Alli was."

Scott shook his head and bit his bottom lip. "Dude, she's *all the way* hot, and totally into you. Everybody knows it."

They averted their eyes when one of the girls glanced up in their direction. She nudged Alli, who stopped in her tracks when she saw Kevin. He watched as she grabbed the arm of another girl point their way as she whispered something, never taking her eyes off Kevin's.

Scott looked over at Kevin. "She's locked in. Dude, you hafta go for it. You just need to break the ice. Get with Alli and then maybe your brain will let you have some fun this summer."

Since the breakup with Lindsey, Kevin hadn't gone out on a single date. He launched a kind of all-out assault on Emily Vasquez in the final weeks of school, but it was a disaster, and a shocking one at that. He thought she would come around and go out with him, but she was terrified of hurting Lindsey. He didn't want to hurt Lindsey either, so he backed off, but he regretted it and withdrew once summer break began.

It didn't take Alli long. She wasn't the bashful type. With all the confidence of a proven winner, she strode up to them and leaned on the front of Kevin's treadmill. Her chestnut hair was pulled back in…surprise, surprise…a high pony tail. She wore black and silver Brette Girls Capri spandex and a stringy black tank top which read, **"Why be flabby and pasty, when you can be toned and tasty?"** in silver lettering. How appropriate. With her soft brown eyes focused on Kevin, she gave a quick nod to Scott. "Hey, Scotty."

"Yo." Scott pulled his ear buds into his ears and hit play on his MP3 player. He clicked the speed on his machine up a little bit and got really interested in his running. Traitor.

Alli smiled at Kevin. "Hi, Kev. How are you?"

"Okay, I guess. You?"

"Not bad," she replied. "I'd be doing better if you would return my calls and texts."

Kevin winced. *Oops*. "Sorry about that. I've just been…you know…taking a break since Lindsey and I…"

"Since you got screwed over?" Alli finished. She shook her head in sympathy. "Yeah, I get it, but you need to give some of us a break and pick up the phone when we call. We're your friends too, okay?"

Kevin sighed. "I just don't know what to say to anyone right now and I don't really need another shoulder to cry on."

Alli giggled. "That's a relief." She came around the side of the treadmill and touched his arm. "But maybe what you need is a little female companionship…maybe take your mind off her for a minute."

The look in her eyes told Kevin all he needed to know about what Alli had in mind. Now that he was untethered, Kevin took a good, guilt-free look at Alli Sylvester. He had no idea why she never made an impression on him before. Whatever the reason, Kevin was beginning to see the girls of Kendall High School in an entirely different light. Scott Webber's influence only fueled this phenomenon.

He gave Alli a confident nod and a smile. "Okay. Let's do it."

Her eyes widened and her smile brightened. "Really?" She bit her lip and flashed him a coy smile. "Cool." She turned back to her friends, clustered around a large piece of gym equipment where some football players were working out. After a moment's hesitation, she turned back. "We always get lunch after we work out. How bout I come by after that?"

Kevin blinked. "Today?"

Alli's shoulders lifted, as if to say, *why not?*

"Sure," she said, sticking her bottom lip out in a cute pout. "Unless you don't want me to."

Kevin looked over at Scott, who struggled to maintain his composure. He gave Kevin a look that said, *don't even* think *about turning her down, you idiot!* Kevin had to agree. It was time to get in the game. He'd sidelined himself for too long after the train wreck ending of his and Lindsey's relationship.

He looked down at Alli's beautiful smile.

"Text me when you're on your way."

Other Books by Christopher Merlino

A Quiver of Cobras Series
Follow a group of Kendall High School students as they navigate their high school social scene, experience new relationships, and test the bonds of friendship and love.

> **Beginnings**
> **HEAT**
> **Broken**
> **Desire**
> **Limbo – Coming Soon**

The Zak Fischer Chronicles
Zak Fischer is a teen age musical prodigy who is on the verge of fame and fortune. He is also a strong Christian kid with beliefs that are contrary to the pop culture world he wants so badly to be a part of. As he and his band rise to national prominence, Zak must deal with all the temptations that come with it.

> **Viral – Coming Soon**

Nico Scarlatti Novels
Follow Nico Scarlatti as he struggles to navigate a world few ever get to see. With enemies on all sides, and a darkness inside him he can barely control, Nico.

> **Essence – Coming Soon**
> **The Alphas – Coming Soon**
> **Mother of All – Coming Soon**

The Collide Series
The Story of Harper and Riley. She is the number one female artist in the world and he is a nobody who writes a little and plays music with his buddies. She hangs out with the most talented and recognizable people in the world. He has a close circle of friends, none

of which have ever graced the cover of Vanity Fair. A chance meeting brought them together. They both knew it could never work. But the attraction was too much for either of them to resist. The only question left is, what will happen when two vastly different worlds collide?

Worlds Collide – Coming Soon
We Collide – Coming Soon

About the Author

Christopher Merlino is married to Charmine Merlino, and the father of three beautiful girls, Alexis, Cecilia, and Isabella. He makes his living selling cars and insurance. He has a Master's degree in English and Creative Writing. In addition to writing, Chris spends his time in his woodshop, making things like pens, bowls, and other knick-knacks out of domestic and exotic woods.

Chris is a fan of most genres of books from non-fiction historical and theological to fiction drama, action, fantasy, and comedy. He enjoys music and golf...well...who really *enjoys* golf? He *plays* golf from time to time and generally refers to the game as "The Refiner's Oven." He was born and raised near Atlantic City, New Jersey, and currently makes his home in Egg Harbor Township, New Jersey.